I0594808

Worlds in Words

Anthology of Sci-Fi and Fantasy short stories

By

Aiki Flinthart

To all the authors out there – both published and aspiring – don't give up.

Worlds in Words by Aiki Flinthart

Cover artwork by Croco Designs
Cover design by Pamela Jeffs
Published 2020 by CAT Press
Copyright © 2020 Aiki Flinthart

All stories are original to this collection or acknowledged as reprints

A Cataloging-in-Publications entry for this title is available from the National Library of Australia.

ISBN-13: 978-0-6487736-7-2 (Trade Paperback)
ISBN-13: 978-0-6487736-6-5 (e-book)
CAT Press
PO Box 3388, Darra
QLD 4076, Australia

Heartfelt thanks goes to my wonderful, supportive, fun-loving husband and my loyal, huggable, strong son. Also to all the authors in the Springfield Writers Group, for their enthusiasm, support, and kindness; and to my many wonderful family and friends who are helping me through this difficult time.

This collection of stories has no theme to tie them together. They are simply a compilation of all the short stories I've written over the last 3-4 years. Many are published, some are not. Several have been shortlisted in respectable awards and competitions. I'm quite proud of them.

But mostly they are all here in one place as a memento – so my husband and son can find them without having to dig through my incomprehensible filing system.

Contents

Fantasy & Sci-Fantasy

About the Author

Urban Fantasy

She Walks on Frosted Fields

First Published "Aquarius" anthology Australian Speculative Fiction 2020

Top 8 Shortlisted in USA Writers of the Future Competition

Her bare feet leave no prints in the snow. Her pale body casts no bruised shadow on the field of broken diamonds. She smiles back at me, with teeth white and sharp, and eyes of green ice and darkness. The weak sun turns her white hair into a crown of glittering glass knives.

I must be delirious. There's no other explanation. Altitude sickness. Dehydration.

'You're not real,' I mutter, holding on to sanity. 'I'm Andrea Chen I live in Sydney. I just have to get off this glacier. Tell people that Michael's dead...' I grit my teeth against the lump in my throat. Tears will only steam up my goggles. Guilt is pointless. The best I can do is get to town and find people to retrieve his body.

She gestures with a slender hand and drifts across the glacier like a snowflake. Wafting downhill. Toward the valley, maybe? I've been on the ice so long I can't be sure which way leads to safety. The clouds have turned me in circles. Now they've parted maybe I can find my way out.

She waves again. Urging me on. Such a beautiful figment.

I follow, compelled. She's the first…person?…I've seen in two days.

Light glints off snow. Blue-shadowed, fae light; dimmed by my goggles to bearable levels. Clouds close overhead and dull the anaemic sun.

My chest aches and I press a hand to my side as I hurry to catch up. I shouldn't have come hiking with fractured ribs. But I'd spent months planning this trip. The injury had only made me more determined. I'd missed too much of life, already. No more.

I touch my belly. Is the flutter there just my imagination?

My breath mists the air, obscuring the figure gliding away. Panic swells in me.

'Wait!' I call. My voice is lost in the vast, broken whiteness; captured and returned distorted by the stony arms imprisoning the glacier.

But she pauses. Gestures. Her long grey skirt sparkles and floats about her ankles like snow. How can she possibly be warm enough? Even in the sun it's barely above freezing.

I squint at the sky and check my watch. Maybe an hour until sundown. The sun abandons the world for longer each night. And half the day it cowers, like a frightened child, behind the black stone ridges that slice the sky on three sides.

I need to pitch my tent soon and get some rest. Eat the last of my rations. I've miscalculated. Michael carried more of the food. His pack is at the bottom of a crevasse.

Clouds thicken and tumble lower in the valley; a tide, surging over the foot of the glacier, swelling up toward me, drowning the world. They smother me and she's gone. I yell a hoarse cooo-eee. Roiling clouds suck the sound from my lips. I'm alone again.

I shove the goggles onto my forehead. Bitter cold stings my eyeballs and tears form. I rub them away and hiss as my clumsy, gloved fingers press against the bruise on my left eye. The week-old cut on my cheek is closed, at least. No stitches needed this time.

I stumble onward, peering at treacherous ground obscured by shifting mists. Ice crunches underfoot with the unsteady rhythm of my steps. In a cocoon of swirling grey, that's the only sound: crunch, crunch, crunch. Steps eating distance, carrying me closer to...to where?

Which way to safety? Is there such a thing, anywhere? At any moment I could misstep and plummet to my death. Then the glacier would have two more victims. Three, instead of one. Guilt and despair close my throat and curl around a knot in my stomach.

My thighs burn. My lungs ache in the thin air. My icebound heart drags at heavy feet and a boot catches in a crevasse. I stumble, collapsing into the snows. The backpack lurches forward, pressing my face into the ground. The weight holds me down. I fist handfuls of snow and crush it into hard lumps. The snow stifles my scream. Cold soaks through my pants, through my jacket, eating into bone and flesh hardened by guilt and grief.

I shatter again. I cannot go on. But I must.

A thousand regrets pin me to the ice. Things I should have said to him. Things I should have done for him. To him. But he's gone.

The glacier speaks in deep groans and creaks. It sang to Michael. He swore he heard voices in the clouds; followed them. Fell. I couldn't stop him. Didn't.

I don't care anymore. The glacier can take me if it wants. Suck me into one of its thousand, groaning mouths—as it did Michael. Chew me up, swallow me into its dark bowels—as it did Michael.

The ice growls at me, echoing my despair, my hope. The fluttering sickness, low in my body, pushes me to rise; to carry on; to start a life after Michael. I roll stiffly and scramble to my knees. Half-healed ribs grind painfully together.

The pale woman...creature re-emerges from the swirling cloud, her head cocked to one side, white brows raised. A faint, uncertain smile curls the corners of her pale mouth. She waves me on, urgent, frowning now.

'Who are you?' I call.

She drifts away. I stagger after her. Is this wise? Should I find somewhere sheltered to pitch the tent? But another endless, solitary night huddled around the tiny burner, listening for Michael's voice in the creaking ice holds no appeal. My rations are almost gone. My butane tank almost empty. Without food, I can maybe last another couple of days. Without water, less. My mouth is parched. Surrounded by endless frozen water. Unable to drink. The irony doesn't escape me but I fail to appreciate it.

On I trudge, tripping over shattered ice, following a broken dream and a fantasy. Is that the faintest sound of laughter? Or true delirium setting in? She glides ahead of me, one with the mist; her outline a blur of wet grey paint on a white canvas.

I follow the snow-sprite. What other choice is there? This is insanity, but so is the entire trip. The madness of the desperate. The desperation of the fearful. The fear of the wounded.

At this point, I have little to lose by following a delusion. But if she saves me, will I be truly saved? Guilt gnaws at my stomach, eating me from the inside out. I miss him. Not what I expected when I started planning this journey three months before. Anticipation, excitement, relief—yes. Not pain and guilt.

The light fades. I stumble on. The air is slightly warmer now. Thicker. With a faint tang of salt. Or that could be my imagination.

Decisions are too hard. They involve thinking, which triggers memories. Walking is easier. No thought required. The adrenalin has long since worn off. The nausea in my stomach after Michael fell is a dull, distant uneasiness. Bearable if I ignore it.

A chasm looms at my feet and I gasp, teetering on the edge, flailing at air not thick enough to grab. Her white head appears from within the gaping crevasse. She points to my right. In the last glimmer of daylight, I make out what seems to be a rough set of stairs, carved in ice. She smiles and nods.

I fumble in my pack and pull out a torch. The stairs are little more than tumbled blocks of ice, arranged and chipped into risers. The brilliant white of my torch illuminates blue walls, smooth and carved into gleaming sculptural curves. The crevasse descends into the body of the glacier. When I look up, the sky is indistinguishable from ice and I'm entombed.

Snowflakes drift down and wind wails an eerie chorus across the opening high above. Too late to go back up. I can't set up the tent in a blizzard. I continue down. The ground levels out and I stamp my crampons so I don't slip on the smooth floor. Chipping away at blue diamond-hardness with teeth of steel.

The walls widen and curve into a hall that appears almost man-made in its perfection. Ice underfoot gives way to grey, tumbled rocks. I unclip the crampons and stuff them into my pack, then tug off my ski-mask. The flutter of a pale skirt ahead draws me on.

A rushing sound overwhelms the glacier's groans and crackles.

The roar grows louder. I emerge through an arch, into an enormous cavern of ice. The torchlight plays across a cathedral ceiling carved of glistening concave gouges. Water drips occasionally, but it's lost in the gurgling wash of water tumbling over the stones at my feet. A river, deep under the glacier. Milky blue-green; the colour of blindness.

I fill my water bottle, keeping my gloves out of the icy chill. The water makes my teeth ache, but I gulp it down anyway. And shiver as it hits my stomach.

The tunnel extends beyond my torchlight in both directions. Downriver should lead me out, into the valley and the little town at the foot of the glacier. To questions about Michael's death.

I hesitate and flash the light upstream again. She flinches, raising a hand to shield her eyes from the glare. She seems more substantial down here. Her skin gleaming with moisture. Her dress heavy with damp.

'Sorry,' I say, but the word is lost in the waterfall of noise.

She dances lightly from rock to rock, heading upstream. I follow.

Another graceful arch leads to a smaller tunnel that twists into the glacier's belly and emerges into a new cavern. The river is now a muted rumble in the background. The blood of the glacier pumping through its artery. Around me, the ice-bones creak and crackle, complaining of age and unwelcome warmth.

The floor of the cavern is level and reasonably smooth. Warmer and less terrifying than the blizzard raging above. She nods and smiles as I pitch my tent and unroll my sleeping bag. My legs give out and I sit on a rock, head hanging. The relief of being off the glacier after three days sets my body trembling. I hold back a sob with my gloved hand.

I'm dimly aware that I need to eat to help stave off hypothermia.

Rummaging in my pack results in two muesli bars and a silverfoil pack of food. I tear open a bar and movement catches my eye. She's still here. Standing just outside the beam of my torch, watching me. I offer her the muesli bar.

She creeps closer and sniffs it. A small nibble and she screws up her nose. Up close her skin is a bluish hue and she has four slits in the skin under her jaw, low behind her ears on each side.

'What's your name?' I ask. I point to myself. 'I'm Andrea.' I can't believe I'm having a conversation with my hallucination.

Her mouth opens and closes. Squeaks emerge. I shake my head.

'I can't understand.' I wave a hand at her, and myself, and at the cavern. 'Thank you for this, though. For saving me.'

She smiles gently. I hope she understood, but I doubt it. She touches the cut on my cheek. Her fingers are cold and webbed up to the second knuckle. Her green eyes widen. A milky lens, the same colour as the river, sweeps briefly across them. She touches the bruising again. Harder. I pull away with an indrawn hiss.

She cocks her head, frowning.

'Yes,' I say wryly, pointing to my yellowing black eye. 'Let's just say you have the right idea—living down here alone.' I press at my ribs, testing them. The pain isn't any worse than ten days ago when it happened. I'll survive. I lay a hand on my belly and smile for the first time in months.

I open my pack and pull out a small cooking pot. She watches in apparent fascination, following my every movement. I set up the butane stove and empty my last packet of dehydrated unlabelled something into the pot. Stir water in. She screws up her nose again. I sniff the pot. Curry. Again. But I haven't eaten all day and I'll need strength to make it out of here in the morning.

I light the stove. The flame hisses blue-yellow in the arctic darkness. She squeals. So high-pitched it drives through my skull like a hot wire. She vanishes down the hall. I wait but she doesn't come back.

Left alone in the splintering darkness, I eat and try not to think about him. Every time I do, guilt twists at my stomach and I want to beg for his return. But I can't. He's gone. I ache for his guidance. Why wasn't I better? Was it my fault? Did I do the right thing?

I methodically pack away my cooking gear and curl up in my sleeping bag. There, nestled in the womb of the old woman glacier, I rest well. Fear, my bedfellow for over twelve months, has fallen from me.

#

When I wake my watch says it's six am. Down here the darkness is absolute. I flick the torch on and strike camp. I eat my last muesli bar and drink again. I need to pee but I don't want to pollute her home. I'll hold it until I reach the river.

I want to say goodbye but she's nowhere to be seen. Not surprising, given she was all in my head. Michael would have known that. He would have set me straight.

I stand at the exit from my shelter and stare into a future with no Michael. A future full of interrogation and tears and endless guilt...and hope. A future that cannot be avoided. I need closure and the world will need answers. Demand answers.

Answers to the wrong questions. Questions asked of the wrong person.

Lifting my chin, I shoulder my pack and follow the tunnel back to the river. But I choose the wrong path and step into another chamber. A thin fall of sunlit water cascades through a hole in the ceiling. Diamond drops of light coruscate and dance through the air. A fragile squeal echoes over the noise of water. I swing the torch around and the light bends into a deep, clear pool beneath the waterfall.

Five of my hallucinations float in the water, their white hair swaying like seaweed. They climb from the pool and gather around me. I swallow and hold still as they touch my clothes, my face, my hair. They are smaller than the one who led me to safety. Children of varying heights. Female. Unclothed. All with the same green eyes and webbed fingers.

They don't seem to mean me harm but I back out the door, my heart racing. Not hallucinations. Real. These are real beings. But how?

I can't deal with this. My mind is too full of Michael. He would know what to do. He would tell me what to think about this. I run back down the tunnel. And take another wrong turn. Overhead a narrow crevasse lets watery blue light fall into the tunnel. A huge boulder blocks my path. I swear and turn around.

She's standing silently behind me. I squeak and she flinches, eyes wide.

'Sorry,' I say. 'I have to go. Can you show me the river?'

She smiles and touches my face, gently. I recoil. I can't help it. She steps past me and leans her shoulder against the stone. Why? It's too big to move. The rock grinds against the granite underfoot. I edge backward, gaping. The boulder rolls aside, revealing a dark opening. She waves me in.

Hesitant, I flash the torch. Dark piles of what looks like fur lie mounded against the walls. The scent of animal and death wafts out. I'm reluctant to go any further. But she's in there, waving me on. I step in, half-expecting the door to rumble closed. It stays open.

I pan the torch around. The light wavers in my hand. Curled against a rock, a man lifts his head and blinks. Hopeful fear lights his face and he holds up a hand, squinting.

'Who's there?' His voice is thin and quavery, made old-mannish in his fear. His blond hair lank and oily. Blue eyes shadowed with sleeplessness and pain.

She urges me in. I resist, trembling. The torch falls from my hand, tumbling and dancing over the rocky floor. It's unbreakable, unlike me. It comes to rest with the light shining in my face.

'Andrea! Thank God! Get me out of here.' Michael's voice takes on the command tones I'm used to and my feet move of their own accord. Two steps toward him.

I stop, torn. Ripped asunder. I want him. But he's gone. I was almost used to the idea.

'Andrea.' He sounds confident. Certain of me.

I collect the torch and shine it on him again. She stands before him, one hand pressed against his chest. She's looking at me. There's an unmistakable question in those green eyes.

'Andy? C'mon, sweetheart.' That wheedling tone gets under my defences. 'You have no idea how glad I am to see you! I told you this trip was a bad idea. Dunno why you were so dead set on it. But I came, right? Now let's go home. I promise I won't be mad at you.'

He loves me. I know he does. I take another step toward him. He nods, eager.

'When I fell into that crevasse, I thought this...this...'

'Woman,' I say.

'Whatever.' He dismisses her with a flick of a hand. 'I thought it was rescuing me. But it dragged me down here. I thought I was a goner.'

She cocks her head and utters a sharp, lilting creel. She's still looking at me, still pinning Michael to the wall. Michael shoves at the arm holding him in place.

She doesn't move. Isn't affected. He's taller and broader in the shoulder but she holds him like he's half her size. His brow clouds and I cringe back.

'Let me go, you bitch!' He swings at her, fist balled, aiming for the cheek.

She blocks his arm with casual ease. Slaps him so hard his knees sag and he half-slips down the boulder face. His eyes roll back and he groans. She straightens and dusts her hands.

Looking in my direction, she points at Michael. Then at herself. Her hands outline a lump over her belly. Then she mimes rocking a baby in her arms and smiles, crooning.

Michael groans. His hands flex and curl into fists again.

'Andy.' My name emerges thick from his bloodied mouth. He scowls. 'Don't piss me off. No more games. Just call it off and get me out of here.'

My ribs twinge. The cut under my eye throbs. I stay where I am.

He regains some of his power and straightens. Wiping at his mouth, he sees the blood and grimaces. 'See what it did to me?' He touches a fingertip to the cut on his cheek again, anger gathering in his eyes. And just a hint of fear.

I shiver. I recognise that look.

Her lips draw back in a knowing smile and she leans closer to him. Michael recoils. She casts a knowing, glittering grin over her shoulder at me. She touches the cut on his face, then the same spot on her own cheek, leaving a dab of scarlet on her pale skin. Then she points at me, and at the door.

'Andrea!' Disbelief tinges his cry.

I hesitate. All the early days of our time together flood into me, filling me with the memory of warmth and laughter. Then the torchlight catches the crimson spot on her face, and on his. My fractured cheekbone aches.

The child in me is a little storm; a sickness in my stomach at the promise in Michael's eyes.

I swing the torch around the chamber. Michael's not the only inhabitant; just the only living one. The piles of fur are eight mummified bodies. They lie against the walls, curled into foetal positions. I light up Michael again. His eyes are wide, stark.

'Michael,' I say, rolling his name on my tongue, tasting it again. 'Did you know that eight men have gone missing on this glacier in the last twenty years?'

'What the hell are you talking about? Get her off me, damn you.' He shoves at her arm again.

I back away. The chamber opening is right behind me. The river's breeze tosses hair into my eyes. Cool, fresh, clean. Water rushing toward the ocean.

'Do you know what the locals call this glacier, Michael?' I ask.

'What the hell? Stop blathering. Get back here! Andy!'

I'm outside the chamber, standing free of darkness, bathed in light.

'The Widowmaker,' I say. 'They call this glacier the Widowmaker.'

The Image is the Thing

Once we were beautiful. Grotesque, powerful protectors. Deadly grace incarnate. Winged, fanged, silk-smooth stone.

The time nears when humans must make us so, again. They need us, though they know it not. For I feel the wall between worlds fading. The old gods will return.

Soon.

But we are unprepared, imprisoned, unheeded.

Six hundred years ago the masons chiselled me clear from rock. My freedom in exchange for human safety. They placed me high upon Notre Dame's graceful arches, amidst my fresh-hewn brethren, to watch over the city. To guard the world from ancient dangers—which will come again, despite humanity's discontented disbelief

So I waited, huddled with my brothers amongst Our Lady's elaborate carved-stone spires, and watched in endless silence over the dirtied peaks and crowded streets of Paris. Watched as time crawled across the Earth and turned my granite siblings into faceless, formless memories of strength. So long we waited that they abandoned hope, accepting their crumbling fate.

Until I, alone, remain, watchful, grateful for even a small life.

Until I wasn't.

For the human masons have omitted part of their contract. They no longer complete the ritual.

Yes, they released us from goddess Gaia's flinty womb, but the words of dissolution are left unspoken; the umbilical cord to Gaia's heavy body remains uncut, tying us in place as no mortar can. Yes, they admired us, but then forgot to worship us. Yes, they remembered dread, but then feared us instead of the old gods from whom we shield the churlish world.

I am the last who knows, recalls, watches. And they have tied me for all time to Our Lady.

Half-alive. Undying. Unfulfilled. Unfed.

Pacing the boundaries of our allotted home, I move only at night, or in thunderstorms. Times when human eyes cannot pin me in place with their expectations. Times when darkness and water veils my stiff, jerky movements from eyes designed to catch motion at the edge of focus.

I crouch on high, listening to the sonorous clang of bells and staring down on the humans' hurrying, shuffling littleness. Breathing in the bitter fumes of their impatience and listening to the grumbling roars of their desire to be elsewhere.

They are oblivious.

Soon their enemies will again slip through. Humanity cannot survive the coming war.

Yet, they do not release us.

They have forgotten the time when, with their spells and sorrow, they struck us free of stone and worshipped us instead of the old gods.

We, in turn, destroyed their foes. One by one, until none remained. Our teeth tore the throats from gryphons and wyverns. Our claws rent the hides of manticore and chimera. Our granite eyes gazed back at basilisk and gorgon, unaffected. And, with their monsters vanquished, the old gods slipped between worlds to bide their time in twisted anticipation of return.

The masons, thinking themselves safe, thinking they needed us no longer, took their secret spells and hid them deep. They turned from us to the One God. But they could not resist the inborn urge to carve our hidden forms free from rock, and we became a mockery of our purpose.

So, I am condemned to this half-life of watching and waiting and wanting.

Watching them scurry past, oblivious, content in their path to self-destruction.

Waiting for them to remember the old stories.

Wanting to tear them to pieces for their ignorance; for our atrophied joints, and our eyes clouded by smoke and lichen, our claws and teeth blunted by millennia of rain and wind.

Yet always hindered by our geas to protect and guard our makers; our once-worshippers.

Long have I listened to their petty problems. Watching through wars waged over resources and ritual, famine and feast, ignorance and indigence. Willing them to feel again their bond to us and to the earth-mother.

Now, at last, desperate folly rises as faith loses ground to arrogance and greed. They experiment with the old ways, but lack humility or fear. The humans don't listen to Gaia's groans as she tries to warn them. They play at pentacles and power, laughing and drinking beneath the stars, between the standing stones; disdaining their One God and pretending to embrace again the old ones. Awakening those we vanquished. Those who will slip through the thinning walls and once more infest the planet.

The old gods and their monsters are poised; waiting to sup their fill on the soft, abundant flesh of mankind. So many millions, now. So few of us. Such a feast they will find.

The signs are there. The time is close. There must be one amongst the humans who can read the portents.

#

When, at last, one comes, it is not the giggling girls I expected, with their black nails, lips, and lace; their whispered incantations, their faces flushed with wine and desperation. Instead, he is a mason—one who has been here before.

He came with others and erected great metal spider-web frames around us. I hid as they took away my still, time-battered brethren. When they returned, my new brothers were mere copies of the originals. Beautifully carved, but cold and solid; not yet awoken to their living state. Not even aware they were trapped. And I, lonely in my exile, grieved for my lost kin, my heart cracking.

I never thought to see the masons again.

But he has returned and hope leaps in my breast.

I smell his fear on the cool wind curling up from the river beneath. The breeze brings the stink of pollution and the smells of humanity. But his nervous sweat overpowers all of those. The smell of deceit and fearful intent. With it, the musty scent of bindings broken, pasts half-remembered, and secrets unearthed from their tombs.

He waits until the great timber doors below have closed, their hollow thud shutting out the secrets of night and imprisoning the impatient darkness. With the sun set I crawl stiffly across lead and stone to peer in through warped-glass windows.

His soft steps creep up the stairs, spiralling toward Heaven. His breath is laboured; his eyes glitter feverishly in the glow of moonlight made bloody by the great rose windows. His hands tremble and clutch a black-wrapped parcel close to a thin chest.

I try to rouse my sleeping brothers; to stir them from their stoicism, so we may all witness our release. But they have not yet shaken off the torpor of millions of years trapped in stone and merely stare at me with black, tourmaline eyes.

Alone, I slip into shadows and watch my jailer, my liberator, my servant, my master.

A small access door creaks open and he slips through with a grunt, leaving skin scraped on sharp metal and blood dripping black on the pale ground. The first sacrifice.

My solid flesh quickens at the scent.

He clambers to the heights and peers out across the city, blinking as the cold wind sharpens with the tang of metal and a distant scream. He shrinks back, swallowing, and lays his bundle in a sheltered place. From within its sable swaddling he draws forth a tome of thick, crackling paper, bound in skin darkened with smoke and age. The cover is blazoned with the ancient masonic symbols.

He lights a stick of incense. Three drops of blood tremble on his fingertip and drip, sizzling, onto the glowing coal. Smoke spirals up, rich with the hot smell of blood and sandalwood ash.

I quiver and breathe it deep.

With shaking fingers, he finds a page and traces faded letters. Pale lips form whispered words that are swallowed by the wind before I can hear them. I edge closer. He pauses, glancing around. His eyes skip over me and return to the book.

I catch a phrase or two. They are mangled. Old words of power formed by a new mouth unused to the thin vowels and knife-edge consonants. But it's close enough. Energy thickens the air. Slows the sick, grey-orange clouds scudding across the sky. Shadows the stars and bloodies the moon where she cups the night in her crescent hand.

The power spills over the parapet and oozes like lava across the busy streets; hot and glutinous. But to the eye it seems nothing more than a shimmer, distorting the world and worming into the fossil bones of my brethren. Preparing to free us.

I revel in the warmth seeping into my flesh. I stretch a clawed hand and marvel at the strength and cunning of each digit. My wings shift into brittle flexibility. Around me, others of my kind begin to crackle and stir on their plinths. Mortar breaks. Limbs stretch. Fanged mouths gape.

He continues to speak and I silently urge him on. His voice gains confidence and I hear more of the words. Yes. He speaks them more clearly now, as though they guide his tongue to their correct form.

A surge of power washes through me like sun after winter. Heady honeyed warmth explodes across the world and unbinds us all.

It is done.

I stretch my wings, ready to take to the forever-sky.

But he continues to speak.

What madness is this? Has this, too been forgotten? Surely, he will stop.

Too late, I catch the next words. Too late I leap from my place. Too late I tear the fateful sounds from his throat in a spray of moon-silvered blood.

The final phrases escape in a bubbling whisper from his scarlet lips. Released. Fatal. With a smile, he fixes his gaze on the star-swept sky and his soul flies to freedom. But he has entombed us. Doomed us. Buried my kind and his own.

I crouch over him, mute with sorrow and the weight of what is to come. My brothers join me, keening their grief and fear to the darkness.

Or is there yet time?

If so, we have none to waste on regret. We must act if we are to save humanity from their own arrogance. For we are bound. Children, both, of the earth-mother. Our fates tied. We cannot live without them. They cannot survive without us.

At my urging, my brothers leave the softly-dead human where he lies and clamber down narrow stairs to the echoing, empty cathedral below. With a scrape of stone claw on steel candelabra, I strike a spark and set the walls ablaze. When the great spire falls, our absence will be hidden in the tumble of crumbled stone.

And I emerge into the misted light of dawn with my new-awakened sibling to face the consequence of my hesitation.

For the human has spoken beyond the words that free my kind from Gaia's loving embrace. He, like all of them, had forgotten that the image is the thing, not merely a symbol. Forgotten that not all our kind are content with little ceremonies of fire and blood and incense. With the taste of monster flesh, rather than human.

For four thousand years the king of our kind has drowsed, bedded beneath golden sands on the banks of the Nile. His sleek form—half-man, half-lion— was chipped from stone by worshipful, ignorant hands, but left sleeping by their wisdom.

Now, beneath the soft sands, his claws curl.

I gaze toward the brightening southeast horizon. I must gather my comrades. Find them in their buried, long-dead cities; their dusty, crated storage places; their mortar-fixed mansions. Find them and rouse them into action.

For soon we must fight a war on two fronts.

Conditions of Sale

Every once in a while, someone came along with the next step to Vandra's future casually tucked into their wallet. Vandra tapped scarlet fingertips on her folded arms and watched that bulging wallet as her client paid the cafe bill. A glossy black crow, hopping across the baking tarmac nearby, eyed Vandra's half-eaten muffin with equal hunger and screamed 'Faaark! Faaark!', echoing her impatience.

Wolf Lebkuchen tipped the waitress a twenty and complimented her service. The girl blushed, protested and thanked him twice when he refused to take it back. He flashed a charming, distant smile.

Vandra eyed the note as the girl tucked it away. A twenty? For delivering a mediocre cup of lukewarm coffee and a stale muffin along with a boring recitation of her life?

Wolf's phone rang and he answered it with calm goodwill.

Honestly. Vandra glanced at her watch. At this rate she wouldn't even get to *see* this precious house of his before it was too dark. Lebkuchen had engaged her to sell the property quickly; said he wanted to get it on the market today and under contract fast, before he left the country in two weeks. So why was he wasting time?

He continued his phone call; unhurried, solid, glancing occasionally toward the glittering ocean.

As Vandra waited, sweltering in the late afternoon heat, a skinny kid of about ten or twelve sidled up to her. He held out a white plastic bucket, half-full of gold coins and labelled with a sticker about saving some pointless historic building.

'I have better things to do with my money, kid.' Vandra jerked her chin. 'If it's that important to you, go get a job and donate your salary.'

The boy hesitated and wandered away toward the café. He passed Lebkuchen and held out the bucket in a mute plea. Lebkuchen nodded and stuffed in a twenty without missing a word in his conversation. Then he actually ruffled the kid's hair. Vandra rolled her eyes. He was a sucker for a sob-story, obviously.

He was too *nice*. That's what was wrong. So damned nice it was almost sugary. Nobody was that bloody good. At least, nobody who succeeded in this world. So how had he succeeded, then? The perfect hair, white teeth, tailored clothing and handmade shoes all reeked of money; enough to make her palms sweat. And he was eye-candy, with short, dark hair and glass-clear pale blue eyes. Built like a brick shithouse: tall, broad-shouldered and muscular in a way that spoke of more than just time in the gym. A pro footballer maybe? She wasn't a fan so, who knew?

A couple of head knocks could explain why he was a few sheep short in the top paddock, as they said. Vandra allowed herself a tiny grin. With that syrupy smile and a mind like an untenanted rental he should be a pushover. If she couldn't negotiate an extra couple of percent commission out of this sale there was something wrong with her. Everything about Wolf Lebkuchen said she should be able to eat him for lunch.

He even *smelled* nice, for heaven's sake. Homey. Like…her mother's kitchen. Comforting.

For chrissake. Where had that come from? This guy was her ticket to freedom. Nothing more. Her mother had been an idiot. Tied to an oven and a job, pushing out kid after kid, barely able to feed them and too caught up playing happy families to see how she'd wasted her potential. She'd settled for life in the burbs, just one paycheque away from poverty, pretending it was bliss. Really, death must have been a release for the poor woman.

Vandra lifted her chin. No way was she going to burn out like that. This was her year. One more decent sale was all she needed.

Lebkuchen thumbed his phone and pocketed it, giving her that sweet, toothy smile. A flash of something like hunger in his pale eyes made her take an involuntary step backward. She crossed her arms. Definitely something off about this guy. Those white, white teeth gave her the willies.

'I do apologise for the delay, Miss Ivithia.' He laid a hand on her arm, his fingers rough and warm. His mellow voice held just a hint of some sexy European accent with back-of-the-throat consonants.

'Oh, don't be silly Mr Lebkuchen, I have *heaps* of time!' Vandra patted her neatly-pinned blonde hair, regrouping. Running a hand down her slim curves to draw attention to the best rack a trip to Thailand could buy, she picked up her tablet and swept a finger across it. 'Now, where were we?'

'I believe,' Lebkuchen said, 'we were about to drive out to see my house.' He glanced at the dust-burnt setting sun, then back over his shoulder at the purpling ocean horizon. 'We've timed it perfectly. When we get out there the full moon will be just rising and you'll see how wonderful the view is. Shall we?' He waved a hand toward his car.

Vandra kept a businesslike front and found her own keys in her shiny, candy-red handbag.

'I'll follow you.' She dangled the carkeys. 'You said it was a ways out of town and I have to zip off at about half-past six to…get to the hospital.'

His dark brows rose, his expression oozing empathy. 'Nothing serious, I hope?'

'Oh…' She turned her face away and touched a fingertip to the corner of her left eye, careful not to disturb the makeup. 'Just visiting my mother. She's not well.' She walked beside him to the cars and put on a brave smile. 'But that's not why we're here, Mr Lebkuchen.' She stopped just short of batting her eyelashes. He wasn't *that* dumb.

'No, indeed.' His smile widened, teeth reddened by the afternoon glare. 'It's not why we're here, Miss Ivithia.'

Vandra slipped into her serviceable little Camry and followed the money-glutted roar of his Porsche out of the carpark. He even *drove* nicely. In a car that ached to scream down the highway at full throttle, he footled along at sixty, doing exactly the speed limit, obeying all traffic signals. He didn't deserve that kind of money.

As they left the outskirts of town and the road climbed into bushland, the houses got bigger and further apart. She'd lived in this area for ten years now, selling and re-selling the same houses over and over, including some of these. Surely she'd seen every high-end house by now. How had she missed his?

Meh. She shrugged. It didn't matter. The sale was hers now. If she could land a buyer for this one, she'd be able to move down the coast, to where the really *big* dollars were. She'd done her time in the 'burbs. Learned the skills. Time to move up.

Ahead, Lebkuchen stopped in front of a massive, sandstone-and-iron gate that shouted expensive security. The house hid from sight of the road, surrounded by pale, cicada-sung eucalypts. Views back toward the ocean encompassed a great sweep of dust-green forest, softened by sunset's burnished light. Beyond that, a golden shimmer on the dark ocean horizon hinted at moonrise.

Vandra's heart thudded. If the house lived up to the promise of the gate and the position, this could be better than she imagined.

Lebkuchen unfolded himself from the Porsche and sauntered across. He looked over the Camry, back east toward town, then leaned down. His broad shoulders were a wall, blocking the last flares of sunlight.

'Give me a minute. I need to get…changed and prepare a few things, turn on lights and that sort of stuff,' he said. 'Then I have to go back out, so I'll leave you to look around all you want. I'll call you in the morning about next steps. In five minutes the moon will be up, I'll open the gate and you'll see the house at its best.'

Vandra nodded. What else could she do? He slid back into the car and rolled up the curving driveway. She drummed her fingernails on the steering wheel. Dusk slipped soft pinks and greys across the across the landscape as the gate swung silently closed behind him.

A few minutes later, it opened again and her tyres crunched up the long, rising driveway. On either side, ancient trees crowded close, creating an atmospheric, olde-worlde approach to the house bound to appeal to new-age ditzes and wannabe landed gentry.

Vandra rounded the corner, saw the house façade and choked on a giggle. It was a good thing Lebkuchen wasn't around. Hiding her reaction would've been impossible.

She preferred clean lines, acres of glass and sharp, cubical shapes: modern, sleek, minimalist. This was the antithesis. The peaked roof, dormer windows and black-and-white timbered exterior could have been transplanted straight from snow-bound, medieval Germany. The house sat uncomfortably, discordant with the hot, dry Australian landscape.

A weathered, carved sign over the door identified it as *Lebkuchen House,* presumably in case the family forgot their name. To make things even more tasteless, someone had gone berserk with a fretsaw. Every eave and window frame dripped with ornately-carved, white-painted, curling timber decorations. It was so ridiculous, Vandra half-expected someone in lederhosen to dance out and perform a schuhplattler, complete with bells and a sloshing tankard of beer.

Her client list scrolled through her head. Who combined money with poor taste?

Oh, wait! The Bakers. She'd just sold their house and they were looking for something bigger. Yes, Hannah and Greg Baker might just be the perfect couple for this place: naïve, romantic idiots. They were grateful to her for the sale of their little first-love cottage and nouveau riche enough with a recent inheritance that they'd probably pay whatever she suggested for this place.

She tapped her phone, scrolling through the recent calls list. There.

'Hannah?' Vandra tried to keep the gushing to a minimum but it was tough with her heart racing in anticipation. 'Darling, I know it's a bit late but I'm just viewing a property that you and Greg just *have* to see! I insist. It's just what you're looking for. Come now. The owner wants a quick sale so you'll get a great price and you'll *adore* it!'

The enthusiasm was genuine. Hannah wrote stories about magic and elves. This house had to be her dream home. Vandra gave Hannah the address and hung up. She climbed out of the car and eyed the house speculatively.

Rust-orange light gleamed off the second story windows as the full moon cleared the trees behind her. A clean ocean breeze sighed through the treetops to swirl around the hulking structure, stirring leaves into a whisper of imaginary voices. The house creaked, groaning like an arthritic old man, settling as the temperature dropped. The blank windows were blind eyes in its huge, white face.

There were no other houses nearby. Town was just a haze of light pollution in the distance. Isolation ate at Vandra's certainty and she shivered.

Shaking off the ridiculous notion that the house watched her, she turned her mind to a price. She knew what Lebkuchen was asking. It wasn't enough. These kids would pay more. Her heart stuttered at the thought of all those zeroes. She allowed herself to dream, just a little.

She hurried inside, anxious to see if the internals lived up to the promise of the exterior. Pausing just inside the front door, she swept a quick look around and smiled. Perfect. Even welcoming. How bizarre. Past clients had sometimes commented that houses had 'personality' and she'd always nodded, while disagreeing completely. Now…

She pushed the fanciful thought aside and focussed on her purpose—valuing. As she moved from room to room, a half-hysterical laugh caught in her throat. It couldn't be better. Stuffed with what romantics like Hannah called 'character', it boasted exposed beams, low ceilings, uneven flagstone floors, hideously warped walls and inconvenient, huge stone fireplaces.

Vandra paused in the entrance to the kitchen. Had Lebkuchen already left? She held her breath, listening hard, but only heard the slow thud-thud of her own heart in her ears. Slow? She frowned, touching her chest where her heart pounded rapidly against her ribs. She shook her head and the low-level throbbing subsided. Must have been her imagination.

She strode into the kitchen and smiled. Again, perfect. Enough modern amenities to make it workable, but also a massive, cast-iron oven as a feature. Its heavy, black warmth dominated the room. A fire crackled in it, which was crazy on this humid evening, but somehow added to the hominess of the place and made the kitchen comfortable.

Vandra moved closer, admiring the solid workmanship of the piece. The door was big enough to stuff in a whole pig and the oven took up a stupid amount of space, but it was the heart to the house. A hint of sweet-baking wafted in the air. Lebkuchen must have put a batch of cookies in before he left. Nice touch. She reached out to open the door and check.

A car door slammed outside. Blinking, she stepped back from the oven.

'Halloo!' Greg's cheerful greeting floated in from the dusk.

How had they got here so fast? Vandra hurried to the door and waved them in. Greg bounded up the stairs, greeting her with an enthusiastic kiss on the cheek and an expression of genuine delight at seeing her again. She brushed it off, more interested in Hannah. For all her quiet dreaminess, Hannah was the decision-maker. By the sparkle in her big, dark eyes, it wouldn't be a difficult sale.

Hannah wandered up the garden path, her long skirt drifting in the soft evening breeze as she touched plants with light fingers and gazed up at the black-and-white façade in wide-mouthed awe. She climbed the shallow front steps and gave Vandra a sighing air-kiss.

'You were quick.' Vandra paused to let her take in the view.

Hannah's eyelids flickered. She glanced toward Greg, then away again, her lips briefly pressed into a hard line. 'We were in the area.'

Vandra frowned and opened here mouth to ask where, since there was nothing nearby, then thought better of it. No point in starting out with an interrogation. She was here to sell a house.

Hanna smiled and laid a hand on Vandra's arm, easy and gentle once again. 'You were *so* right! I love this place. I can't wait to see the inside.' With a wistful sigh she turned her face eastward. 'And did you see that glorious moonrise? I *adore* the full moon. So...'

'Romantic?' Vandra prompted, anxious to get her into the house.

Hannah shook her head, eyes glimmering. 'Fey. Mysterious. Dark. Can't you feel it? Strange things happen on the full moon.'

'Please don't tell me you believe in were-wolves?' Vandra couldn't quite censor the sarcastic tone.

Surprisingly, Hannah didn't take offence. She just gave a light laugh and linked her arm with Vandra's as they entered the front room. 'Were-wolves? No. That's silly. Oooh! I *love* these exposed beams!'

And so it continued. By the time they finished the tour and reached the kitchen, Vandra's fingers were already wrapped around the blank property sale contract she kept permanently in her bag. This was a done deal. The money was practically in the bank.

She sat the pair down at the massive oak kitchen table and smoothed the contract out on the timber, hardly able to keep an unprofessional smile of triumph off her face.

'Can't you just see yourself here? Baking with this oven. Having guests for dinner at this table.' She gave a laugh that came out more breathy than she meant it to. She itched to shove the pen into Hannah's hand. A couple signatures, that's all she needed.

Vandra took Lebkuchen's price and added a hundred grand to it for good measure. Since he was in a hurry, and the Bakers were smitten, neither was likely to argue much. If Lebkuchen wanted his cash he'd agree to the extra commission when he saw she already had a signed contract. She had them all right where she wanted them. Her cheeks warmed. Hopefully Hannah would attribute the flush of colour to the heat from the oven. Vandra pushed the pen across the table and held her breath.

Hannah reached for it. She touched it delicately, with the tip of one finger, then hesitated. She exchanged a quick look with Greg. He gave her a cryptic little smile and a shrug. Vandra clenched her hands together beneath the tabletop to prevent them betraying her excitement. Hannah picked up the pen. It hovered over the signature line. The ball left a tiny dot of black ink on the paper.

Vandra snapped her teeth shut on hasty words. She smiled reassuringly, hoping it didn't look too forced. Hannah bit her lip and looked at Greg again. He nodded, then grimaced.

Vandra sat back, inspecting the couple. Maybe she'd underestimated their finances. Maybe they couldn't actually afford it? No, they would have tried to negotiate if they didn't have the money. They were naïve and young, but not stupid. Come to think of it, they hadn't even blinked at the cost, so why the hesitation now? She frowned, wiping it when Hannah glanced up.

Hannah paused again, watching Vandra as though waiting for her to speak. Vandra suppressed a tiny flicker of guilt and switched her gaze to the pen, leaving expectancy to speak for her.

A slow, creaking, blood-thudding silence gripped the room.

Greg sniffed loudly and frowned around the vast kitchen. 'Does anyone else smell cookies?'

Startled, Vandra glared at him, but he was right. It hadn't been as strong before, but now there was a distinct odour of baking in the air—sugary and chocolatey; mouthwatering, but on the edge of burning.

She turned to look at the enormous oven. It squatted in the middle of the room, glowing, smoke gently curling from hell-fire red cracks around the massive door.

'Maybe we should take them out before they go too crispy,' Greg suggested, raising a brow at her.

Vandra cast an irritated look at the unsigned paper. With a quick, artificial smile she shoved back from the table. Snatching up a teatowel, she grabbed the heavy iron handle, yanked the oven door wide and bent to look inside.

Heat blasted her face.

There were no cookies.

Something shoved at her backside.

#

'Wolf, darling,' Hannah said, petting a wall of the great house, 'we'll meet you in town tomorrow morning, shall we? Take your time Changing back to human form. That little witch looked a little tough and I do hate having to clean your oven, especially if her boob implants give you indigestion.'

She picked up her beaded bag and Vandra's shiny red purse and wandered toward the front door. She gave the doorframe a kiss and stroked the timeworn, silky timber lovingly as she passed through the opening.

Greg secured the oven door and jogged out after her. He hooked an arm around Hannah's waist as she dug in Vandra's bag for the keys to the Camry. Together they turned back to admire the house, gleaming in the moonlight. Hannah leaned her head on Greg's shoulder.

He grinned down at her. 'I quite like Australia. Their real estate agents are so predictably greedy, although I did think she was having second thoughts at the end there.'

'Not enough to stop ripping us off, obviously,' Hannah retorted.

'Nevermind.' Greg squeezed her waist and planted a kiss on her head.

Hannah shrugged. 'Well, I'm just glad Wolf's using his Change-time Hunger to do something positive for the world. I feel like we're really making a difference. He said we're going to target lawyers in Germany for next month's full moon. You know how he detests them.

He's always in such a good mood after he eats one.' She gazed off at the moon, tapping a finger to her lips. 'Maybe he should look into politicians as well.'

'Why not? No one more deserving.' Greg chuckled. 'I just hope he changes his name before he gets to Germany.' He raised his voice, addressing the house directly. 'I mean, really? Lebkuchen? "Gingerbread" will be a bit of a giveaway there, don't you think, Wolf?'

A hollow laugh ghosted from the open door and shook the house's frame. Greasy black smoke burped from the oven's chimney.

A Broken World Awaits in Darkness

First published Aphelion Magazine 2019

Fire flickered in grey stillness and I paused. The dim-lit art supply shop was just another tourist trap in Venice's mind-bending streets, but I stopped anyway. Grocery bag handles cut into my fingers. Mike, Shoniqa, and Peyton would be waiting.

Still, I stared at the feather-pen on display behind the plate glass window. Was it the reflections of passers-by that gave the illusion of movement, or my imagination?

In the doll's-village street, people jostled each other and apologised—or not—in various languages; laughed, chattered, hurried with collars raised against the coffee-scented cold and umbrellas clutched in gloved hands. Bright red jackets, or black with blue silk scarves. Stylish.

I felt drab and invisible by comparison. My short blonde hair hidden under a utilitarian beanie. My nose reddened by the cold.

Someone bumped my shoulder and muttered, 'Scusi.'

I stretched my lips into a thin smile. 'My fault.' But he was already too far away to hear; dragging suitcases. The clackity-clack of plastic wheels bounced off stone walls too weighed down by the centuries to stand straight.

Underfoot, pigeons cooed and strutted—possibly trapped and unable to fly away in the narrow street, more likely content to stay and eat scraps forever. Flashes of iridescent purple amongst grey feathers hinted at ambitions for beauty and transformation. But perhaps that was just whimsy.

I sighed. I'd saved for four years to get to Venice, only to find that the city wore a gilded mask of foreign expectations painted over the dull reality of crumbling mortar and waterlogged basements. I ached to tear off the facade and find the passion beneath; to meet the real people—the ones with family here, roots deep into the mud, and hopes higher than the church-spires.

But that could take a lifetime and I had only a week left. Disappointment welled like disturbed, murky canal sediment.

I closed my eyes and blocked out the chatter and footsteps, concentrating on the wind fluting across chimneys, the slosh of water in a nearby canal, the first bells chiming the hour. Imagining myself living here, part of the vibrancy beneath tourism's superficiality.

What I would give to stay, to just immerse myself, to write and write and never go back.

No. That was silly. I had family, a secure teaching job, a boyfriend who loved me.

I'd just have make do with the time I had. At least, with Peyton and Shoniqa along, I could afford this extra weeks' accommodation. Mike had been thoughtful to invite my two best friends. Now that my conference and research was over, I could spend time with them and absorb the history and atmosphere at leisure.

My phone buzzed in the pocket of my baggy jeans. That would be

Mike, checking on my whereabouts; making sure I hadn't forgotten anything on his list. As if I would, after all these years of meticulous reminders.

It buzzed again so I lowered the grocery bags and pulled it out to send an acknowledgement. He wouldn't quit, otherwise.

I had everything, except the wine he wanted. That was my last stop. Then home. How quickly an apartment became 'home' in a foreign place—complete with cooking and cleaning.

Still, after I made dinner, I could write the last scene of the romance book that paid the bills then make a start on the fantasy novel. Up on the cold rooftop deck, overlooking the red-tiled roofs, and a thousand years of history. Alone. Unburdened by a To Do list for once.

Maybe.

The shop door behind me opened with a brassy little tinkle of the bell dangling above. A small man emerged, his face obscured by a low cap. He stuffed a silk-wrapped parcel into a pocket, drew thin gloves over green-stained fingers and brushed past without speaking. I snatched up my bags and apologised, surprised. The darkened shop was open?

A woman, who held the door ajar, smiled and gestured. I found myself inside without quite knowing how. The woman swept back a lock of waist-length grey hair and wiped her hands on a patchwork apron. Beneath it she wore a loose red blouse and dark purple skirt, reminiscent of a Renaissance peasant outfit. From a doorway behind a beaded curtain, faint strains of gypsy music drifted into the room, along with a hint of camphor.

I smiled politely. This place had tourist written all over it. But some of the watercolours on the walls weren't half-bad, even if they were all the standard images of Venice: the Rialto, the Piazza, the

Cathedral. The shop was warm and smelled of paper and paints, reminding me so sharply of my mother's studio that I had to put down the bags and wipe at my eyes.

'Can I help you?' The shopkeeper's English was broken and heavily-accented.

Inadvertently, I glanced at the window display. I couldn't afford it, but would it hurt to look? I pointed at the scarlet feather.

The woman hesitated and scrubbed her palms down her skirt again. Then she shrugged, reached over the top of the display and gathered up the item in gentle hands.

I stroked the feather reverently. Nestled in its white-velvet-lined box, together with a set of coloured-ink cartridges that would fit inside the thick quill, the pen cried out to be used in the crafting of a masterpiece. The feather shimmered. Purples, oranges, and peacock-blues slipped like fire and oil over the blood-coloured vanes.

'It's beautiful,' I murmured. But utterly impractical.

Everything I wasn't.

The shopkeeper tilted her head inquiringly.

'Bellissimo,' I translated. The woman nodded, but her dark brows pulled together.

I pointed at the feather. 'What kind of bird?' I searched my high school Italian vocabulary, determined not to use Google Translate. 'Uccello? Bird? Che tipo di uccello?'

The woman's brow cleared. 'Fenice.' She flapped her arms, pointing to her elbow. 'Fenice piuma.' She wagged a finger and smiled mischievously. 'Badare. Stregato. Scrive ciò che il tuo cuore detiene.'

I chewed my lip and stroked the feather once more. *Piuma* was feather and *fenice* must be the name of a bird. Something red and big. Maybe a macaw. Most of the rest was unfamiliar, but *cuore* was heart and *scrive* must be write.

'Write from the heart'?' I hazarded.

'Si,' the woman said, nodding. She tapped her own chest. 'Cuore.'

I stared at the box. 'I shouldn't. I'd have to buy cheaper wine and Mike will be annoyed.'

#

I emerged from the shop elated and guilty, at once. I really shouldn't have. Funds were so tight with Mike still at university. But I worked hard. I deserved a little indulgence.

Across the street, the dark-wood-and-grapevines interior of a café called. Mike could wait just a few minutes for his wine. With a sigh of relief, I sank into a corner table and ordered an espresso.

I smoothed a sheet of the thick, crackling paper the shopkeeper had added to the purchase, and plucked the feather from its nest-box. In the warm café lights, crimson and gold played along its length. I swept the soft tip across my cheek and neck, closing my eyes in sensual delight. A frisson of warmth tingled up my arm, into my chest, and I shivered. The faintest scent of woodsmoke teased my nose.

Yes. This was the way to write a fantasy story: sitting in a Venetian café, using a quill. Excitement knotted, low in my chest. I touched nib to paper.

As the ink flowed, so did the opening scene between Alderion, time-thief, and Rhenna, swordsmith; perfect and easy. Not a word needed to be changed. At the end of the scene, I re-read it, blew gently on the ink then hugged the paper to my chest, where it fluttered with the staccato of my heart.

This was going to be the best trip ever. Tucking the paper and feather carefully into my bag, I rose, ready to handle anything.

#

A few minutes later, I struggled up the four flights of worn marble steps to the Airbnb loft apartment. My fingers ached with cold and the weight of the bags. My thighs burned. I really needed to exercise more. Maybe if Mike would do a little more around the house… I laughed shortly and shoved the antique key into the lock.

'I'm back,' I called, closing the thick oak door behind. Laughter and chatter came from the living room. 'Hey guys, I'm back.' I turned sideways, shuffling down the narrow, polished-timber hall.

Emerging into the living room, with its vaulted ceiling of blackened beams and stark, white walls, I dropped the bags and flexed my fingers.

Mike twisted on the couch and lifted a glass of red wine. 'Hey, Kath. Just in time. We're about out of supplies. Can you pass me the cheese?'

'I haven't even unpacked, yet,' I said.

He sipped. 'As soon as you find it, then. No rush.'

Shoniqa nibbled on a cracker and put her bare brown feet up on Mike's lap, her head on Peyton's shoulder. Her frizzy dark hair tangled with Peyton's sleekly-straightened blonde locks. Mike stroked her foot and she hummed a noise of pleasure.

'That's so nice. My feet are killing me after traipsing around the palace this morning.'

'Is it still cold out, Kathy?' Peyton asked, looking up from her phone.

I hefted the bags onto the kitchen counter. 'Freezing and stuffed with people. Must be another cruise ship in dock. Crazy out there.'

'Did you get the wine?' Mike held his half-empty glass up. A sunbeam speared through the red liquid. Blood-light fluttered and trembled on the white wall.

'They didn't have the one you wanted.' I placed a bottle and a wheel of the blue-vein he liked on the coffee table. 'Sorry.' I suppressed a tremor of guilt and smiled apologetically.

'You should have tried another shop,' he said, studying the fresh bottle critically. 'This looks a bit cheap.'

'I know.' I returned to the small kitchen. 'But like I said—crazy-full of people today. I…I guess I can go back out, if you like.'

Mike opened his mouth, but Peyton cut in with a dismissive wave of one hand. 'You'll survive, Mike, and the change will do you good. You're too anal. Do you need a hand with dinner, Kath?'

I cast her a grateful look and shook my head.

'Sorry, babe,' Mike said. 'It'll be fine. We can get the other one tomorrow.' He opened the bottle, poured some for himself and Shon then held it out to Peyton. She waved it away. Mike made a laughing comment that she needed to keep up. He sniffed the wine, screwed up his nose, then chugged half his glass.

'It'll do,' he said. 'What's for dinner?'

'Pasta,' I said. 'We're in Italy.'

Mike laughed. 'Well, the wine'll definitely do for your pasta.'

Shoniqa giggled. Peyton pressed her lips together but said nothing. I stoically finished putting away the groceries and let the joking banter wash by, my thoughts on the box in my bag.

When Mike opened a third bottle of wine after dinner, I pleaded work and retreated with my bag and laptop to the bedroom. The roof deck would have been quieter, but a light drizzle made that impossible. So I sat, crosslegged under the quilt, with my back against the bedhead, a pile of cushions on my lap and a tray on top of that.

I extracted the quill pen and admired its shimmer in the bedlamp's buttery glow. my current, paid, work in progress was due to the editor in two days and I was stuck on the climactic lovemaking scene that would finally bring the lovers together. Sex scenes were always the most difficult to get right.

Perhaps the pen would add spice. After all, it was a historical romance. Only fitting that it be finished with a quill pen.

Now…to throw Jane into Lord Haverley's manly arms. The nib scraped a black line onto the thick paper.

Shoniqa's sultry voice drifted down the hall, echoed by Mike's shout of laughter.

Absorbed in the elegance of the Regency era, I let the words flow without re-reading for a good ten minutes. The scratch of the nib and the rustle of paper under my fingers sated some long-unrecognised itch in my soul. Light danced along the feather vanes like flames licking a burning log.

Finally, I carefully wiped the nib clean before laying it aside. This scene felt good, too. It felt right. Now, to see if it read well.

Jane dropped the grocery bags to the floor and glared at Lord Haverley. 'I am not *your slave. You want different wine, go get it yourself.'*

'Aw, c'mon, babe,' Haverley whined in that childish, manipulative tone that always got on her nerves. 'You could have gone to another shop.'

'Fuck you,' Jane said. 'I'm done.' She snatched up her bag and strode from the room.

I gasped and dropped the paper. What the *hell?* That was not what I'd written. Where was the sizzling love scene? I frowned and read the words again. The scene continued, with Jane packing her bags and leaving on a ferry to the mainland. *So* not what I'd written.

I glanced at the feather, glimmering in the light. No. That made no sense. It was just a feather.

Flipping open my laptop, I called up a translation app and typed in *Write from the heart.* The Italian phrase contained the right words, but had the shopkeeper said that? She'd said other things. What were they? Bernice, Darnice? Nope.

I closed the lid, cursing my unreliable memory. No. It must just be some…suppressed emotion. This whole trip had been more stressful than I'd expected, with Shon and Pey along, and Mike fussing over every arrangement I made.

Still…I studied the feather dubiously. Maybe best to finish the love scene on the laptop. my editor would be annoyed if the submission was late.

A shriek from the lounge area startled me. Shoniqa. Mike's voice joined in. It sounded like they were singing and Mike shouted 'Wahooo!' What the heck?

I put the laptop aside and clambered out of bed. I wrapped a robe over my pyjamas and pattered into the living area.

Mike and Shoniqa were dancing an energetic polka around the small space, while Peyton looked on with a thoughtful smile. Peyton spotted me and gestured me over.

'Mike just got a text from the uni.'

I sucked a quick breath. 'He got accepted into the PhD program?'

Peyton nodded. 'Seems pretty happy about it.'

'Yes,' I said, watching them cavort. Shoniqa laughed up at Mike, eyes sparkling and teeth white against rich teak skin.

Mike broke away and grabbed my hands. Excitement and wine flushed his pale face bright pink. Red veins threaded his blue eyes and his blond hair stood out in all directions, as though he'd been dragging his fingers through it—as he was wont to do when he was worked up.

'I got it, Kath! I got in and my topic has been approved.'

I smiled and squeezed his hands. 'I'm so glad, Mike. You've worked hard and you deserve it. In three years, you'll be Doctor Michael Hobson and there will be companies falling over themselves to hire you.'

He grinned, then his face fell. 'Oh, but it does mean we'll have to cut the holiday short. My prof wants me back by Monday to plan a schedule. He's right. I've seen too many PhD candidates fail because of lack of planning. Not gonna be me.' He kissed my forehead then peered blearily at me. 'I'm really sorry, babe. That's ok, isn't it?'

I gripped my hands together and swallowed a surge of bitterness. Then acceptance, familiar and comfortable, doused the unaccustomed burn of resentment. Of course it was ok. We were a team and this was big for him. My conference was over and I'd done all the research for my next book—which were the official reasons I'd come.

The next week was just a holiday, after all. It didn't matter. Really.

'Sure,' I said. 'It's just a holiday and this is your career. I'm proud of you.'

He grinned and kissed me, tasting of wine and the revolting mustiness of blue cheese. 'You're the best, babe.'

Shoniqa handed him a drink and he turned away, toasting his success with a clink of glasses and a glittering splash of red wine on the rug.

Then he stopped in mid sip, eyes widening. 'Hey, Kath? I just realised—the return flights. You'll take care of them? I've got so much else to organise. You can handle that, can't you? You don't mind?'

I nodded, not trusting my voice. I caught Peyton looking gravely at me and managed a bright little smile. Then I returned quietly to bed. I'd rebook flights in the morning. Maybe I could get a partial refund on the accommodation.

But I'd need to finish that love scene tonight, otherwise days of travel would mean a missed deadline and I couldn't afford to lose the publisher's good will. There were a million women trying to make it as romance authors these days. I needed the money. Even with twenty books out, I still had to work full time to make ends meet and support Mike while he slogged through uni.

I brightened. But once he had his doctorate and a good job, he'd promised I could quit work and just write. Then Alderion and Rhenna's story would come into its own.

Half an hour's work on the laptop produced a love scene for Jane and Haverley, though it was so dry and stilted I almost wished it was on paper so I could tear it up. But, as the saying went, a crap scene could be edited, a non-existent one couldn't.

Sighing, I sent the manuscript off, put the computer away, and switched out the light. I fell asleep to laughter not mine and barely noticed when Mike finally stumbled into bed.

#

I woke early, to the delicious chime of bells across the city and fingers of rosy light curling around the blockout blinds. Beside me, Mike lay sprawled, still dressed, snoring. No point in trying to wake him.

I rose, dressed, and gathered what I needed for the day. I would go out and make the most of what time I had left. Maybe today the Rialto —which I'd been avoiding because of the mad crowds—would be worth a visit.

On impulse, I tucked the paper and quill into my bag. Rather than lug my laptop around, I could write in a café and add to that first scene.

The living room was flooded with pink light from two windows that overlooked the canal and neighbouring roofs. It was also a mess of half-eaten cheese, unwashed plates and glasses, and broken crackers, crushed into the rug.

I set about cleaning up as quietly as possible. Mike was a bear when he had a hangover. Best not to wake him.

When the place was clean, I hesitated, unsure what to do next. I ought to stay. Wait and see if they needed anything. They would be feeling awful and wouldn't want to go out. I could get some writing done and rebook flights, here in the quiet living room.

Jane's words, scrawled in black ink on yellowed paper, popped into my head. *Fuck you.* I smiled faintly. I wrote a note on the fridge whiteboard and left. There was still enough food in the fridge. They could cope for a few hours, surely.

#

It was still early enough that only hardy tourists, and a few savvy shopkeepers opening for the breakfast trade, were about. The air was sharp, the sky clean and blue for the first time in a week. I strode out, enjoying the relative emptiness of the backways, comfortable in the little section of Venice I now knew well.

When I reached the Rialto, I dutifully admired and photographed the canal view: glittering water, elaborate marble architecture, ferries and gondolas. A pretty face the Venice of three hundred years before had presented to the world. Just a different kind of façade. I wanted something more interesting, so I continued over the bridge and chose a street at random.

Lilting strains of Vivaldi drifted over the rattle of storefronts opening and I stopped, trying to pinpoint the source. It came from a nearby cathedral; desanctified, by the lack of crosses and insignia. Old, by its simple design and worn stonework. Signs out front were for a music concert.

I peeked around the iron-studded oak door and slid into the dim, lofty interior. The music grew louder, but there were no musicians in sight. Just a reception desk and a series of cabinets containing exquisite antique instruments. I studied a viol, envious. I'd played violin for years, only giving up when we needed money for Mike's university and had to sell everything of value. Maybe I could take it up again one day, soon.

Summer wrapped seductively around me and I picked up a brochure advertising a concert that evening. Impulsively, I bought two tickets. It would be nice to have an evening out, just with Mike, before we left. We could do dinner near the venue. Have some time without Peyton and Shoniqa. Rekindle a little romance.

Smiling, I tucked the tickets away and wandered out in search of hot chocolate.

#

At a quiet outdoor café, I stirred a chocolate so thick my spoon stood up.

My phone buzzed. A text from my father, in Australia, checking in. I sent back a selfie with the hot chocolate. Another text popped up. From Mike. Written late last night. I hadn't heard it. Or the patchy reception meant it hadn't come through until now.

Hve u rebked the flights yet?

Seriously? He'd been ten steps away in the living room but he'd texted? I hesitated, my fingers poised over the letters N and O. But he would still be asleep. I switched the phone off and shoved it deep into my bag. This was my last morning. *My* time.

My fingers brushed the quill and I pulled it out, determined to write the next fantasy novel scene. But Mike's face lingered in my thoughts and the hot chocolate only masked the taste of resentment on the back of my tongue. My fingers tingled with warmth as I wrote, even though cold bit through my clothing.

Done, I re-read the scene, pen poised to cross out and correct, expecting imperfection this time.

Rhenna gripped Alderion's hands and stared at his flushed face. He grinned stupidly, his head bobbling like one of those irritating dashboard figures. His breath reeked of wine.

'Let me get this straight,' she said, her voice low and hard. 'You want me to cancel my holiday. The first holiday I've had for six years. The holiday I paid for with my teaching wages. So you can have another three years at university, living off my hard work, telling me what to do, and leaving your shit lying around my house like a badly-trained five-year-old?'

'You don't mind, do you, babe?' he said fatuously. 'It's really important.'

Rhenna dragged her sword free of its scabbard and plunged the iron deep into his body. 'Actually, Ald, I do mind. I do fucking mind.'

I choked on a sip of chocolate, spattering muddy sweetness across the page of bitter dialogue. I grabbed a napkin, dabbing at the spray, smearing it. The words remained sharp and clear. my hand slowed as I read the passage again.

The image gave a deep, visceral satisfaction; horrifying and fascinating in equal measures. The bloodied sword protruding from Alderion's body. His lifeless form crumpled, oozing at my feet—at Rhenna's feet. Spatters of scarlet dripping on the cobbles.

'Oh, my God.' I stared at the glistening red feather, pinching it between two fingertips. 'What the hell *is* this thing?' I shoved it back into my bag, with the paper, and half-ran from the café. The woman at that art shop. There must be some logical explanation she could provide.

#

I retraced my steps from the apartment to the grocery store, peering into every shop along the way. So many looked the same. Electronic gadgets, masks, restaurants, cafes, multi-coloured glassware, stationery. But none were the shop I was looking for. I stopped, hands on hips, glaring down the narrow street.

This was ridiculous. There were no such things as magic shops that disappeared after selling a cursed item.

I turned back, thinking my way through yesterday's return journey. Oh! Yes, I'd turned right here instead of left. There it was: the window now full of feather-pens and hand-made paper, watercolours and art supplies. A twist of fear dissolved into relief and I pushed confidently through the tinkling door.

A man emerged through the beaded curtain. He smiled and I temporarily forgot why I'd come. His face was angular, with deep-set chocolate eyes and a thin nose, and his smile could light fires.

'Buongiorno,' he said.

'Um…' I shook myself and dug out the feather. He frowned and glanced sharply at me.

'Where did you get that?' His English boarding-school accent took me by surprise.

I waved the feather vaguely. 'There was an older woman here yesterday. In a red shirt. Long grey hair. She sold it to me. But it's…' How on earth did I explain without sounding insane? I tugged the papers from my bag and brandished them. 'Look. Read.'

He frowned over the three scenes, reading each one carefully. 'And?' He handed them back.

'This one…' I pointed at the first fantasy scene. 'It's perfect. Not a mistake in it.'

'This is good, si?' He shrugged.

'But these ones.' I waved the other two. 'The women…they're…me. At least. They're what I…No. That sounds wrong. They're doing what I…' I sighed and dropped my arms heavily to my sides. 'What am I doing here? You have no idea what I'm talking about.'

The bead curtain swayed and clacked. The older woman appeared, hair loose, her clothing a patchwork of gaudy, mismatched colours and cloths. She smiled serenely.

'Mama,' the man said. Then he launched into rapidfire Italian, gesturing at me and the feather. The woman lifted her brows and her chin. At last he wound down and she threw her arms wide, replying with some heat, ending with a scornful sniff.

The man turned back and gave a shallow bow. He held out a hand. 'My mother apologises. She should not have sold that to you. I'll give you a full refund—or you can choose another. Please.' He waved a hand around to indicate the shop.

I clutched the feather and papers to my breast. 'No! I don't want a refund or a replacement. I just want to know how it works. Yesterday I thought she said I had to write from the heart. Is that what she said?'

He scratched at the back of his head, grimacing. Then he stepped past me, locked the door and pulled the shade down. I gasped and retreated a few steps.

'Scusami,' he said. 'I don't mean to frighten you. I'm Matteo. This is my mother, Lucia. I just don't want interruptions.'

'You're not going to take it away?' I eyed them suspiciously.

He shook his head. Lucia spoke few quick sentences.

'She says it cannot be taken, only given or sold. If it's taken, it will find its way back to you,' he added. 'And she asks what your name is.'

'Katherine.'

'Caterina,' he said to his mother, who smiled beatifically and nodded, speaking again.

'She says,' Matteo continued, 'that you needed the feather. That you're a good writer, but you've locked the best of yourself away and this will bring it out.'

I gaped. 'How…I never said I was a writer.'

He gave a lopsided smile. 'It's an easy guess. Only writers buy our quill pens. She's not magic.' He glanced at the quill.

I followed his gaze. 'But this is?'

Lucia patted her breast. 'Fenice piuma. Stregato. Scrive ciò che il tuo cuore detiene.'

'She said that yesterday,' I said. 'What does it mean?'

Matteo sighed and ran his fingers through his dark hair. 'She thinks it's enchanted. The feather of a phoenix. She says it writes what you hold in your heart. Nothing more, nothing less.'

'A phoenix feather?' I scoffed, laughing. 'There's no such thing.'

Lucia drew herself up, looking down her nose. She gestured and led the way through the curtain, into the back room. Matteo smiled wryly.

'She must like you. She never shows anyone who's not a customer the back room.'

I frowned at him. 'But I—'

He held up a hand. 'Not a…regular customer I should have said. Come. It's ok. She's a little eccentric, but not dangerous, I promise.' He flashed that charming smile and I found myself smiling back.

In the dim-lit back room, the overpowering scent of mint and camphor made me cough and blink.

'Sorry,' Matteo said. 'Helps to keep the vermin from the herbs.' He nodded at the shelves. Floor to ceiling, the room was lined with hundreds of small, meticulously-labelled wooden drawers of all sizes. Bunches of dried plant hung in neat rows from the rafters. A bench along one wall held three mortars and pestles plus a stash of brown envelopes and lengths of plain silk, hessian, cotton and linen.

I turned in a circle, awed. 'It's like an old apothecary store.'

'Si!' Lucia grinned. 'Ammaliatrice. Erbe aromatiche.'

Matteo shrugged. 'She says she's a herb-witch. This shop has been in the family for five hundred years. Passed down mother to daughter. The skills for curing all manner of diseases with it. She's the last, though. No daughters.' He gave a sheepish grin. 'Or even daughters-in-law.'

I chose to ignore that and peered closer at a drawer label. *Menta, Aconito, Lavanda.* They were obvious—mint, aconite, and lavender. Then there was *Artiglio di manticora.* Something of the manticore. Another drawer read *capelli di driade.* Capelli was hair. Hair of a dryad?

Seriously?

I looked at the feather in my fingers. Even in this dark room tongues of orange and purple flickered from nib to tip. In fact, the feather seemed to glow faintly, lighting my hand an eerie orange-yellow.

Phoenix feather? No. That was plain crazy. Just some LED lighting trick, for sure.

I hesitated. Perhaps I should return it. The words that came from it were…wrong. Unthinkable.

But the fantasy scene…that was so good; just as I'd imagined. If the rest came out as perfectly, the book would be a best-seller. How could I give that up?

But I loved Mike. I didn't wish any harm on him. What would he say if he ever read such words? He would be devastated.

I held the feather out to Lucia. The older woman smiled sadly and shook her head. She curled my fingers around the quill and pressed warm palms over my hand. Lucia spoke a short sentence, her gaze unwavering.

Matteo cleared his throat. 'She says you're not ready to return it, yet. If you still want to return it tomorrow, then bring it back.'

Lucia patted my hand and moved to the bench where she began

grinding something sweetly-pungent. Matteo led me through the shop and opened the front door.

'Why tomorrow?' I asked. 'I'll be leaving Venice. Going back to Australia. I might not have time tomorrow.'

'Then you will keep it,' he said, simply. 'It's just a feather. You will remember Venice and it will inspire your work.'

I gazed at him shrewdly. 'Do you honestly think it's just a feather?'

He gave a twisted smile. 'I've seen my mother work minor miracles with her medicines, but I've never seen her do magic. I think, perhaps, it may work as…what is it called? A placebo. Her words about the quill are just an excuse to release your true feelings.'

I shivered. My true feelings. What sort of monster was I to think such things about the man I'd lived with for nine years? The man I was going to marry. He loved me and I was imagining stabbing him?

Matteo ushered me out the door and shook my hand. 'Ciao. I hope we meet again, soon.'

Lucia's voice called from behind and he smiled.

'She says she hopes you enjoy the concert tonight. Addio.' He lifted a hand and closed the door. The lock snicked and the blind dropped down while I was still gaping at the place where he'd stood.

Blindly, I headed home.

#

'Where have you been?' Mike grabbed me by the arms and pulled me into a hard hug. 'I've been so worried. You've been gone all day. You didn't answer your phone.'

I frowned. 'I wasn't gone that long. You were sound asleep, anyway. What time is it?' His eyes were still bleary and his breath rank, so he couldn't have been awake long.

He led the way into the lounge room, where Peyton stood, staring out the window and Shoniqa lay, sprawled on the couch, heavy-eyed and yawning. Peyton hurried over.

'You're back. You had us worried. Are you ok?' She inspected my face and hugged me. 'It's three o'clock. Where have you been?'

'Really?' I looked at the wall clock. Three o'clock. Surely it had only been around eleven when I walked into the art shop. Come to think of it, I was awfully hungry.

'I was just…wandering. I did some writing. Must have lost track of time. My phone battery went flat.' I stopped myself from blathering any more and smiled. 'Totally fine. Sorry to worry you.'

Mike flung himself down on a couch and groaned. 'My head's killing me. I've been so stressed I didn't even think about rebooking flights or dinner or anything. Kath, did you sort the flights?'

'No,' I said, rummaging in the fridge. I hesitated, then added, 'There aren't any free seats until Thursday.' It was an outright lie and I wondered at my own daring. My cheeks burned so I pressed a cold drink to my skin.

'Thursday!' He sat up. 'I have to be on campus on Monday. That's not going to give me enough time. I knew I should have done it myself.'

'Well,' I replied, 'I'm sure something will come up. I'll check again tomorrow.'

Mike frowned. 'What's up with you? You're usually the one getting all bent out of shape if our plans go pear-shaped.'

I plucked out an apple and closed the fridge door. 'Actually, that's you, not me. Anyway, while we're here, I got two tickets to a Vivaldi concert tonight. Played on early instruments at a cathedral over the other side of the Piazza.' I checked my watch. 'Starts in two hours so we have time to go to dinner.'

'Dinner and a concert?' He struggled to his feet and made a moue of disappointment. 'I'm not really feeling up to it, babe. I have a headache and we need to book the flights. This is pretty important. My whole future depends on getting back in time.'

He gave me a winsome smile—the kind that always squirrelled its way past my defences—and slid his arms around my waist. 'C'mon, babe. I need your help. You don't want me to screw up my first day with the prof, do you?'

I wavered. He did need me. He wasn't capable of sorting out the petty day-to-day stuff. His mind was on bigger things; more important things. My time would come in just a few short years.

Rhenna dragged her sword free of its scabbard and plunged the iron deep into his body. 'Actually, Ald, I do mind. I do fucking mind.'

I studied the soft familiarity of his pale face for a long moment then kissed his cheek. 'You're right. If you're not feeling well, you should go back to bed. I'll go out and get some dinner and paracetamol, then sort out the flights when I get back.' I turned to Peyton, who was watching us, her brows lifted. 'Want to come for a walk?'

Peyton sent Shoniqa a quick, questioning look. Shoniqa sighed and closed her eyes.

'Don't look at me. I'm going back to bed, too.'

'Er…you sure, Kath?' Peyton asked.

'Please.'

Peyton hesitated, then nodded and dragged on her boots and coat.

'I've just got to grab something from my room,' I said. 'Give me a sec.'

I ducked into the bedroom and rummaged through my suitcase. I shoved a couple of essential items into my bag, then pulled out the crimson feather and a piece of paper. I smoothed the paper and held the pen, poised. A tingling warmth snaked its way from my fingertips to my groin. I savoured the taste of woodsmoke, smiled, and wrote a short sentence.

Once the feather was safely back in my bag, I joined Peyton and waved goodbye to Mike and Shoniqa.

We walked in silence down the stairs, boots clattering on the marble. Outside, in the narrow alley, I paused and drew a deep breath. The sun barely skimmed the horizon but my breath already frosted in the chill early evening air.

I tucked my hand into Peyton's arm and grinned. 'Where shall we go to dinner?'

'Wait, what?' Peyton blinked at me and stumbled as I turned right at the end of the alley. 'Dinner? I thought we were going to the pharmacy.'

'Oh, yes,' I said, 'there's an apothecary I must show you. First, I want dinner. I'm starving. Somewhere with free wifi, though. I have to do some stuff on the laptop. Then I want to go to that Vivaldi concert. You still play cello, don't you?'

'Well, yes, but—'

'You'll love it. You should see some of the old instruments in their museum. Just gorgeous.' I sighed. 'I miss my violin.'

We stepped off an arched bridge and Peyton stopped abruptly. 'What the hell is going on, Kath? I've known you since we were eighteen—what's that, eight years?—and you're acting super-weird right now.'

I laughed and shook my head. 'Nothing.' I dragged her into the Piazza.

'No, I mean it, Kath.' Peyton wrenched free. 'You do know what's going on at the apartment right now, don't you?'

I stopped, my heart lodging in my throat. 'Don't, Pey.'

She grabbed my arms. 'You must have seen the way they look at each other. I came along hoping I could play chaperone and stop anything happening, but I think it was too late before this trip.'

With a sigh, I sank onto a stone bench. 'I know. Well, I suspected. I didn't want to know, really.'

Peyton dropped onto the bench with a thud, mouth open. 'You knew? How long?'

I shrugged. 'About six months. It wasn't until I saw them together, here, that I was really sure.'

'And you didn't say anything? To him? To me, even?'

'What was to say? Every time I thought about confronting him, all I could see was the complications, our history, and the way he could always wheedle his way out of anything. Convince me he was right and I was wrong.' I laughed bitterly and tucked a loose strand of hair behind my ear.

I stared across the Piazza at the colonnaded walkways and the warmly lit, expensive shops. 'I guess I was hoping it was a phase and he'd grow out of it. That he really did love me, not her. Stupid, huh?'

Peyton gripped my hand. 'No. We're all guilty of being wilfully blind and dumb sometimes. Of wanting things to be different. But what are you going to do? You can't keep going like this. I can see what it's doing to you. You're miserable.'

I tightened my hold on Peyton's fingers and gave her a determined smile. 'You're right. I can't. So right now, we're going to dinner. Then, while we're at dinner, I'm going to change Mike's flights to tomorrow. But I'll also transfer all my money out of the joint accounts, cancel the apartment lease, and get Dad to clear the place out. Then I'm going to stay here for another couple of weeks.' I glanced over my shoulder in the direction of the apothecary's store.

Peyton covered her mouth, eyes wide. 'You're not! But what will you tell him when you get back tonight?'

'Oh, I'm not going back,' I said. 'I left him a note. He'll get it when he finally goes into our bedroom.'

'What did you write?'

'Just something simple, from the heart. It says *While you were fucking her, I was fucking you.*'

Peyton's laugh rang out across the piazza, startling a dozen pigeons. The birds flew free from the shadows and, in the last rays of the dying sun, their feathers turned to fire.

Science Fiction

All the Right Things in
All the Right Places

First published "Rogues' Gallery" CAT Press 2020

I'd never been arrested, but today it seemed inevitable. While the exact nature of her crime wasn't clear, Carol's obsessive excitement over the computer and enormous vat of burbling goo in the middle of my toolshed's stained concrete floor worried me. That, combined with the tangle of cables and wire framework dangling into the vat, made me think a permanent vacation might be due.

Carol might not care if she blew out the power grid. But outside, baking in the white-hot haze that passed for early summer in Sydney, were people who did. Right now, there were only two noises: greengrocer cicadas shrilling as they pissed tree-sap on the parched earth, and the distant rattling thrum of airconditioners. But if this went wrong, a torch-bearing posse would bash on the door, screaming for their cold air.

She grinned, handed me a circuit board and a screwdriver, and pointed to an empty slot on the side of the vat. I eyed her dubiously. I had a crappy job to keep and a deep desire to retain the house I'd wrested from my ex-husband's lawyers. To spite him, more than anything. Not because I really gave a shit.

'Carol…' I tried for reason but found only heat-wearied resignation. 'I realise you're a certified genius, but you've flipped into mad scientist mode. What have you got me into? You've been crashing on my couch, using my shed for secret-squirrel stuff, and making me write code for two months. What the hell's going on?'

Her ginger, wire-brush head reappeared from behind the vat, topaz blue eyes sunken and shadowed, gleaming above a knife-edge grin. Her collarbones and cheekbones protruded. She wasn't eating properly; too nauseated to eat most of the time. Or too focussed on this madness, whatever it was.

'You're not well. It's hot. You should be resting.' Flapping my t-shirt did nothing to cool me, only wafted the scent of sweat into my nose.

'No time to rest, Lisa-lu. You know that.' She held an orange male-end power cord in one huge hand and the matching dirty-cream female extension lead in the other. Her prominent Adam's apple bobbed. 'What's something you've always wanted?'

'To be shot of everything. This whole world is fucked.' There was no point in telling her what I really wanted. Our friendship was worth more than a futile declaration.

She pursed her lips and sent me a level look.

I shrugged. 'Failing that, to be filthy, stinking rich?'

'So, if you had the chance to be, would you?'

'No catches?'

She shrugged. 'Not that you know of.'

'Sounds a bit soul-selling-sign-in-blood-ish.' I pointed at the vat. 'What's the connection? Where'd you get the money for all this? Is this some get-rich thing?'

'Maybe, if it works.' Another nervous swallow. 'Sold everything but my bike. Sold my mother's house.' Pain flickered through her eyes. 'About the only good thing she ever did for me was die at the right time.'

I said nothing. Her mother had been a class A bitch.

'So,' Carol said, brightly, 'it seemed appropriate to use her money to get what I always wanted. What she'd never let me have. What millions of people want.'

'A really good latte first thing in the morning?'

Carol accorded that no more than a brief eye-roll.

'Fine,' I replied, humouring her and reciting her favourite quote, 'All the right things in all the right places.'

Her grin turned cheeky. 'You got it!' Her excitement challenged my doubts. Challenged but didn't defeat. She clung to a belief that a righted wrong would make her happy. In my experience, it just made you feel superior for a fleeting moment, before all the other insecurities came crashing in. But my worldview had never been exactly rose-coloured.

'Just hang on a mo.' I held up a hand and peered at the goopy beige mess inside the vat. 'For days you've had me writing software for running servos and hydraulics, while you tinkered in here. Now you've called me out to see…what?' Beige liquid like snotty pancake batter dripped off the end of my finger. I sniffed at it and screwed up my nose. 'This stuff smells like fresh meat. What the hell…?'

'Just wait and see,' Carol trilled in her falsetto range. Her eyes sparkled with a manic glee that stirred ripples in my shallow well of inner calm.

'This'd better not be anything like last time,' I said.

The electrical cables twitched in Carol's hands. Her voice

dropped back to its normal, masculine, gravelly depths. 'That did get a little out of hand. Still, no-one died. Well, ok, one cat died, but that was an accident. I made the owner a new one.'

The smile returned, accompanied by a tilt of the head and a coy-innocent look that would have been more convincing on someone ten years younger and a foot shorter. She hitched up the strap of her daisy-printed singlet top over a broad, hairy shoulder and waggled the cables at me.

'This time I know exactly what I'm doing.'

'And what is that, exactly?' I repeated.

'Saving my life and the lives of a crapload of other people.' Carol chortled, low in her throat, and jammed the cables together.

'Wait!' I re-ran our conversation. 'What do you mean you made her a new cat?'

I stared in horror at the vat.

The liquid crackled and stirred as electricity arced through it and played delicately across the visible fragments of wire frame, skipping and dancing. Ozone left a metallic tang in the air. The centre of the liquid bulged. Ripples spread. How far? Beyond my shed and my backyard if my fear was realised.

An amorphous, rounded blob of goo thrust upward. A black hole gaped in it. Slime poured off and vague lumps resolved into vague features. A face. A head. A slender neck. Slim shoulders emerged, followed by a torso, dripping beige goop.

'What the hell have you *done?*' I whispered. An inkling of her intent made my stomach lurch. 'Is this some sort of 3D printer?'

Carol nodded, watching the emerging figure with stark longing in her angular face. 'Sort of. Bit more complicated than that. Called in every favour to get hold of bunch of prototypes.' She leaned over the edge and gripped the figure under the armpits. With a schlorping noise, she hauled the…whatever it was…out. Carol stood the…female, definitely female…on the floor and gave a soft laugh of triumph.

The urge to run from the future pushed me a step back. I tripped over the power cable and collapsed ingloriously to the concrete, smacking my head hard enough to turn the world sepia for a few seconds.

#

'You can't call her Francine,' Carol said, choking on a laugh as she swigged a cold beer.

We stood in my dingy melamine-and-pine kitchen, discussing the immediate future. At least, I was attempting to discuss, while holding a gel ice pack to my head. Carol was mostly grinning at me in a fond way that made my heart jitter. The robot-woman sat on my worn-shiny blue couch, her expression blank as she stared at the tv.

'She needs a name,' I protested. 'I can't keep calling her 'it'.'

Carol's smile shifted, rueful. 'For starters, the monster was named Adam, not Frankenstein. And for finishers, tomorrow her name'll be Carol.'

'How?' I flung out my hands, splashing beer onto the cracked linoleum floor. 'How the hell are you going to transfer your consciousness into another body—an artificial body? I know the chemo means you can't have the gender reassignment op, but it'll be over soon and you can have the surgery next year. This is a pretty extreme alternative. There's got to be another way.'

For a moment her diamond façade slipped, revealing a subterranean flash of stark, fear-filled desperation.

'Don't, Lisa.' Her voice cracked. 'I don't have anyone else to help me. I've tried everything. The latest tests came back. The chemo finished months ago and it hasn't worked. Why do you think my hair's back? I've got maybe three months, max. This is my last shot. And if it works it won't help just me. Think how many other people need new bodies. The *right* body. I watched Dad die this way. I can't…' She turned aside, jaw clenching and fingers white on the bottle.

Sinking horror knotted my stomach. I knew that look. I'd seen it in my reflection the first few weeks after my husband left and a warm bath with a cold razor started to seem attractive. Still did, some days. If Carol hadn't breezed into my house at the right moment, and provided a sounding board for my angry, alcohol-fuelled ravings, I might have acted on my impulse.

Every day I wished she hadn't, even while I was grateful she had. As much as I resented the interference, I owed her. The world owed her. She'd had it far worse, for far longer. Thirty years in the wrong body; a body that was now failing her.

'You know if I could change places with you, I would.' The words came out in a rush.

'I know, Lisa-lu.'

Before I could speak, the glittering smile returned and she lifted her chin.

'As to the mind transfer, leave that up to me,' she added. 'I have a plan. I just need some proprietary coding and a specific cable that I've got to get from—'

'No!' I held up a hand. 'Don't tell me. The less I know the less I can say when they call me into court.'

Carol snorted. 'My favourite pessimist. So what *do* you want to know?' She glanced at her watch. 'Make it quick. I've got to be in Sydney before the rush hour so I can… Ah, best you don't know that bit.'

'What's she made of?' The robot's skin looked human even down to the tiny pale hairs, pores and creases. The afternoon light gleamed off her autumnal hair and slanted eerily through amber eyes. But she wasn't perfect. Her nose was a little crooked; her eyebrows uneven; her skin lightly freckled. My faded t-shirt and cargo shorts hung limp on her slender form. Her very human-ness unnerved me.

Carol followed my gaze toward the living room. 'A heat-sensitive type of silicone-graphene-polypeptide. Basically, a new type of organic plastic that stays pliable but cohesive between minus-twenty-five and plus sixty-five degrees Celsius.'

All sorts of questions about maintenance and every-day reality danced on my tongue, but I was reluctant to play Devil's advocate and possibly destroy her hope. Carol's achievement staggered…and terrified me. The potential was so vast my head threatened to explode. I glanced at the robot and a frisson slipped down my neck. Yes, it was a good thing we'd destroyed all the evidence in the shed. All that remained was the consciousness-transfer software on her laptop— which sat innocently on my stained melamine dining table.

The world wasn't ready for this. I pressed the cold beer bottle against my hot cheek. I wasn't ready. Part of me wanted to stop her, afraid to lose her. But if she didn't do this, I would definitely lose her.

'Righty-ho.' Carol balanced her bottle on top of the pile overflowing the recycling bin and brushed at her mouth. 'I'll be off. See you tomorrow morning early if all goes well.' She now wore a dark t-shirt and dark long pants. I didn't want to know why.

'What do I do with her in the meantime?' I jerked my head toward the motionless figure on the couch.

'She doesn't need anything but sunlight occasionally to recharge. Super-efficient photovoltaic fibres. Her hair. One of those prototypes,' she added when I lifted my brows in question. 'She'll power down at ten pm.'

'And between now and then?'

Carol tapped her own temple. 'Nothing up here yet, so don't feel obliged to make conversation. Maybe run her through some of the basic range of motion exercises you programmed. Just to make sure everything's working.'

She kissed my cheek and strode out. The screen door slammed behind her. Seconds later the growl of her Harley rumbled down my long, dirt driveway and dopplered into the distance. I stood for a long time, watching the dust of her passage dissipate in the heavy air.

Shit.

#

Brilliant midday heat melted into afternoon dust-gold outside the kitchen window. Kookaburras warmed up for their dusk chorus of chortling at my shortcomings. The robot's head jerked up. Her eyes flicked to the window before returning to the tv. I frowned. She didn't move again. No. I must have imagined that. Anthropomorphising a blank-minded automaton. Bad idea. The whole thing was a bad idea. I shuddered and turned my back on the living room.

I stomped into my office, closed the door and switched on the airconditioner. It hummed and rattled, comforting background noise as my fingers clickety-clicked over the keyboard for an hour. But my concentration sucked and the net was slow. Treacle and peanut-butter slow. Drumming my fingers on the tabletop did nothing to speed it up. It was only four-thirty pm. Download speeds didn't usually lemming off a cliff until about six.

I snapped a pen by accident and scrubbed at the writers-blood ink staining my fingers black. Fuck. Burying my head in my arms, I clenched my teeth. Who was I kidding? I should have said something. Should have told Carol how important she was to me. If this whole ridiculous charade went wrong, she would die and I'd be left with regrets. But I knew she didn't see me that way. Hell, she didn't see anyone that way

Tears pricked my eyelids and I sucked a deep breath, getting fear under control.

The computer slowed to a worm's racing speed and I swore at it, but felt no better. There were no obvious bottlenecks in my software. The old favourite standby of rebooting didn't even help. In desperation, I reached for the power button on the router. I had actual paid jobs to finish, even if they were just distractions while I waited.

'Please don't.'

I screamed and jumped. My foot caught under the chair and I fell to the cool wood floor in a tangle of plastic wheels and sweaty cushions.

'I'm sorry,' the soft voice said. 'I didn't mean to frighten you. Let me help.' A warm hand grasped my upper arm and hauled me upright.

I gargled as pain lanced up my arm and shoulder bones ground together at a dislocation-prone angle.

'Let go!' The pain reduced to dull throbs. I rubbed at my arm. Five red finger-marks encircled it.

Before me, Caroltoo…robo-girl…whatever…waited with a patient expression on her ordinary face.

I gaped in moronic disbelief. Talking. She was talking. She wasn't supposed to do that. Or anything.

'Did I injure you?' Her arched brows twitched together in a perfect frown. 'I apologise.' She inspected her hand, opening and closing the fingers. Did I imagine the faint whir of servos?

'Why…' My voice cracked like a boy soprano hitting puberty. I tried again. 'Why did you stop me turning off the rout…oh.' The router's net-connection light flickered so fast it was basically solid. 'Are you connected to the net? Did Carol put wifi in you?'

'Carol?' The robot blinked. 'Is that not a female-gender human name? But the person who created me was male gender. Explain?'

I waved a feeble hand. 'Complicated. Er…just go with it. I'm Lisa, by the way.'

'I have no name.' She gazed at me with such simple honesty and guileless innocence I had to look away.

In the long silence that followed my brain produced a dozen scenarios for the next twenty minutes; the next twenty days—none of them good. Carol was going to kill me.

'Francine,' I muttered. 'Your name is Francine.'

'Thank you. Yes,' she said, 'I'm connected to the internet.'

I cringed. 'Well, don't believe everything you see. Most of it's rubbish.'

Francine tilted her head, soft waves of auburn hair sliding over her shoulder. 'Explain?'

'I don't think I can.' I chuckled. 'Tell you what. Go research critical thinking. Then take a fresh look at things.'

Her amber eyes unfocussed for a moment then she nodded. 'I understand. Thankyou. That's useful.'

She stood too close to me and I inched backwards. She followed. I repressed the urge to run. Memories of every sci-fi movie, Asimov story, and horrible nightmare battled with logic. Logic won, eventually, but sweat stained my shirt and my heart raced. Francine watched me, still with that open curiosity, like I was the experiment and she the researcher.

The lounge room seemed safer. Bigger, anyway. I led the way, collapsed on one of the armchairs and gestured toward the other. She sat with enviable grace. At least my software worked.

Silence squirmed uncomfortably between us. No small-talk needed, huh? Liar, Carol.

'So,' I said, 'what else have you learned? Where did you start on the net? There's a lot to digest.'

'I began with your browser history,' she said evenly, 'and links you had followed from your social media.'

Oh, Christ. The last few things I'd procrasti-read. Feminist blogs, cat videos, the latest climate change forecasts, some Star Trek trivia to settle an online argument, more bloody cat videos. What a first impression of our world. Best not to ask what she thought of us. I probably wouldn't like the answer. Definitely.

'How…' I waved a hand vaguely at her. 'How did this happen? Carol said you were…blank.'

Francine tilted her head. 'There was a code. One of the codes running my servos contains a command sequence to learn from mistakes. That merged with another code in my operating software.' She held out her hands, palm up, in perfect imitation of a very human gesture. And then she smiled. 'And here I am.'

Her smile undid me. This wasn't just a well-programmed robot. This was a sentient being. I swore and swiped both hands over my face. It had been a long time since my last decent sleep. I'd done the self-correction servo coding last; copied in haste from a previous job. This was my fault. I should have been more careful.

'My code, dammit,' I muttered. 'Bloody Carol and her bloody secrecy. If I'd seen her OS I might have anticipated this.' I swiped a palm over my face and glanced at the clock. Five-ten. If Carol's estimate was right then I had until maybe ten hours to undo this.

I shifted and pain spasmed in my arm again. The finger-mark bruises were purpling nicely now.

Francine rose and vanished into the kitchen. She returned and offered a gel ice-pack, wrapped neatly in a tea towel. After a moment's hesitation, I accepted and pressed it against my arm.

'How did you know to do that?' I gritted my teeth against the cold-ache.

She sat and shrugged in an exquisitely-smooth motion, distracting me with my own genius for a second. 'I've read a lot of human anatomy and first aid. I wanted to understand how I'm different to you. What it means to be human…or not.'

'What, just in the last few minutes?'

Francine nodded, wide-eyed. 'As you said, there is much to understand and much that conflicts.' She paused and a frown flickered across her face. 'Humans are…contraditory. Both peaceful and violent, wise and blind, selfish and selfless.' Her fists clenched and opened a few times as she studied her hands. Thin slivers of metal extended and retracted from beneath her fingernails. Carol's nod to Wolverine, or maybe the Borg. Typical.

'And…er…' Mathematical formulae of power-to-weight ratios and pressure computations danced in my head. She was far stronger than any human, even with the limitations I'd built into her program.

'Which of those am I?' she finished for me when my throat tightened on the words. She glanced at the tv, its silent screen now a dark mirror. 'I'm not sure. Which is better?'

'For me, or for you?' I laughed weakly.

Her return look was both contemplative and innocent. 'An interesting question. What would you suggest I study to formulate my answer? I've been created to appear human. How do I learn what it means to *be* human?'

'Er…we've been asking the same question for thousands of years so tell me if you find out.' Philosophy wasn't my strong point. In fact, I knew little, which I now regretted. 'Buddhism, Daoism maybe?' If I could steer her away from extremism of any religions maybe I could…crap! What the hell was I thinking? She wasn't my student or child. This robot was meant to be an empty vessel into which my best friend could pour herself and live the life she'd hungered after for years.

I had no right to take away Carol's chance at happiness—and life—because of a dumb coding error or some misplaced Pygmalion complex.

'Look…you,' I said, rising. 'I have…work to do. Power down now and we can talk more when Carol gets back.'

The robot rose as well. 'You are lying,' it said, matter-of-factly. 'I heard you state that Carol intends to transfer his consciousness into this body on his return. What will happen to my consciousness?'

'I…' I sank back to the chair, my legs crumpling under the burden of guilt. 'I don't know. This has never been done! Crazy enough when it was just one mind.' I flailed helplessly. 'Ah, crap!'

'Why does Carol wish to do this? Will it not entail great risk?'

'She's spent her whole life in the wrong body,' I said. 'Hating herself. She can't have the surgery to correct the problem, because she's sick. So this is her only shot, I guess.' I rubbed at my forehead. 'And now I've screwed it up. What the hell am I going to do?'

'And this…artificial body will make her feel more human?' The robot flexed her fingers again and touched her cheek, her eyes mimicking puzzlement. Or perhaps she was puzzled. Who was I to say her feelings were just imitations of ours? Did she even have feelings?

'I think it's about identity, rather than humanity. Carol's always been human—just the wrong gender.'

Francine's eyes blanked again. 'Why cannot she undergo the gender reassignment surgery? The procedure seems straightforward.'

'Did you just research that, too? Well,' I said when she nodded, 'you'd better check out metastasised lung cancer, then, because that's what she's got. Only a few months to live. She's weaker every day and there's no more money. This…' I pointed at her. 'You were her only chance.'

'Ah,' Francine said. 'I see.' She stood and strode to the window, her gaze absent.

I joined her. There was nothing through the grimy glass to warrant her attention. In the eucalypts, the flock of kookaburras imitated an audience at a comedy fest; and I was the lead act. Darkness swept over the dusk-silvered land and Venus glittered above the eastern horizon.

'Tell me about you. And about Carol,' Francine murmured. 'Who is she?'

I shivered as evening chill crept through uninsulated walls. 'Complicated. Driven. Brilliant. Badly hurt. Confused. Human, basically. But one of the good ones.' I smiled bleakly. 'She's worth two of me. If I could swap places with her, I would. She saved my life once, even when I didn't want her to. And look what she's capable of.' I jerked my chin at the robot. 'She can fix the world with this technology. Or she could have. I'm just a coder.'

Francine tilted her head and turned that curious, amber gaze on me. 'But would she be the same person, in this body? And what of me? Is she more worthy of life, simply because she was born human?'

I threw up my hands and moved restlessly away. 'I don't know, ok? I don't know! What do you want me to do? The rest of the world is forty years or more away from this sort of breakthrough. This could change humanity.'

'For better or for worse?'

'I don't know that, either,' I admitted. 'I just know we need people like her to have any hope of surviving as a species. If Carol dies, her knowledge goes as well.'

'No,' Francine replied, cool. 'I would still be here.'

'But Carol's notes are gone. She didn't want anyone to find them if the transfer didn't work. Didn't want them to fall into the wrong hands. All that's left is the transfer software on her laptop.' I sent Francine a bleak look. 'So the only way to duplicate you is to tear you apart and find what makes you tick.'

'Why would they want to do that?'

I shrugged and studied my hands, twisting the hem of my shirt. 'Curiosity?'

'No,' Francine replied. Was that wistfulness in her even voice or was I imagining it? 'Fear. They would fear me. I look human, but I'm not.'

I cleared my throat, unable to deny the truth. 'You're just a little too early, I think. Maybe in fifty years. Oh!' I gripped her wrist. Her skin felt subtly wrong. I released her and wiped my hand on my shorts. Her eyes followed my gesture.

'I can back you up,' I continued hurriedly, picking up Carol's laptop from the table. 'When Carol returns with that cable she needs to connect you, I'll use it to back up your mind. Then Carol can build you a new body.'

Francine stared out the window again. 'You'll have to tell her about me, then.'

'No!' I grabbed her wrist and held it this time, searching her face. 'No. Because I know her. She wouldn't go through with the transfer.'

Francine's brows lifted. 'Explain.'

'It doesn't need explanation,' I said. 'She'd let herself die to save you. It's just who she is. If you were human, you'd understand.'

There followed a long silence. I held my breath, trying to gauge her reactions without seeming to watch. A frown drew her brows close and she sent me a quick, assessing look.

'I have another idea,' she said quietly. She turned to me and gently pulled the laptop from my hand. Laying it on the table, she opened it and plugged in a cable that extruded from a port in her hip.

I opened my mouth to ask what she was doing. She smiled. Her hands shot out and grasped my head.

I jerked back but that implacable grip held firm. Francine leaned in. Her warm lips pressed to my forehead and her fingernails dug into my skull. Agony skewered my brain and flared down my spine. Darkness obliterated thought.

#

I opened heavy eyelids as the grey fingers of dawn crept over my bedroom windowsill. A bone-deep ache weighed down my arms and legs. My body felt too big, too heavy, too full of pain. Pain which pinned me to the bed. Every shallow breath drew fire into my lungs. What the hell was wrong with me? Why couldn't I move? And there was some sort of helmet strapped to my head. A laptop screen glowed, just at the edges of my vision, on the bed next to me. Carol's laptop. With a new, twisted-silver cable leading from it to the helmet on my head.

Carol must be back from Sydney. She would help.

'Lisa-lu? You ready?' that was Francine's voice, but it sounded strange: happy, not calm or curious. And only Carol called me Lisa-lu 'My break-in at the lab's all over the TV. Police'll be here soon.'

Her break-in? Oh. The transfer must have been successful. She was in the right body. She must be so happy. I tried to reply but lethargy and pain held even my tongue still. I rolled my eyes toward the door, willing her to come in.

A female figure pushed the bedroom door open and hurried to the bedside, saying, 'Just have to get your laptop, Carol.'

I managed an incoherent gargle.

My face leaned over me. My grey eyes examined me with distant curiosity. My fingers…whose fingers?… flew over the laptop keyboard. My voice murmured in Francine's flat inflexions, 'I had to transfer you to Carol's old body, as she left it, to free space for her consciousness in the laptop.' She tilted her head…my head. 'Shall I put you back into the laptop? Convince Carol to make you a new body, too?'

The robot appeared at the door and glanced in. 'Don't waste your time on that old shell, Lisa-lu,' it said. 'It's burnt out; dying.' Carol swept a hand over her new hips and flashed a knife-edge smile. 'I have all the right things in all the right places now. C'mon. Leave the laptop. And the headgear and cable. Cops'll be here any minute. That was the plan. They can take that body away, charge the old me for theft, and it won't matter. We'll take your car, go to your mum's and pretend we were never here.' The sheer delight in her voice made my heart ache. She hurried away.

I gazed up at my own face and saw a strange kind of future for myself, there. One of boundless curiosity and vast intelligence. One unfettered by unreturned love or embittered memories. One better than any I could hope for.

I whispered, 'Go. Take care of her. When the police come, I'll confess to the theft. Like Carol said: all the right things are in all the right places, now.'

A Little Faith

Shortlisted for best Science Fiction Short Story, Australian Aurealis Awards

First published "Like a Woman" anthology Mirren Hogan 2017

'Ah, dammit! She's gone again.' Mark's voice floated down the hall. 'This is ridiculous, Lyn. Why we don't just...' his words died away to resigned grumbling.

I groaned and continued buttering bread for Cathy's lunch. I really didn't need this today. Not after four days straight of kicking badguy-ass. Tired didn't begin to describe how I felt.

I put the knife aside and picked up the remote. 'Tell me when you're ready.'

He grunted and I heard shuffling footsteps as he slid his way carefully down the hall toward our bedroom. We really needed to keep a spare set of glasses in every room. If only they weren't so expensive.

'Fine! Go.'

I thumbed the remote and slipped on my infrared goggles.

Blockout blinds snapped shut across the windows. The TV and every light went out simultaneously, plunging the house into darkness. Cathy hollered a protest from behind her closed door. Something thumped against the wall as she vented her pre-teen frustration. Hopefully Faith wasn't in there. She shouldn't be. Cathy knew to keep her door locked at all times. She'd learned that lesson the hard way. We all had.

The kitchen and lounge room took on an eerie, greenish hue as the goggles picked up heat signatures. A quick scan showed nothing unusual. One electrical socket was a little brighter than normal. I should call an electrician to check for a possible short or foreign object. We went through a lot of power points due to Faith's penchant for sticking things into them, usually butter knives. No protective cover stopped her, so it was a good thing she seemed to be immune to electrocution.

'Found her!' Mark's triumphant shout carried clearly. 'Ow! Don't *bite*! I know your molars are coming in, but it's not funny, Faith.' High-pitched giggles followed as he collected our daughter and brought her out to me. His green-grey figure appeared, Faith a squirming blob in his arms. 'She was hiding next to the radiator. Getting trickier, the little fiend.'

I accepted his wriggling burden and turned her upright. 'C'mon, don't call your daughter a fiend. She's two. She can understand you. She's invisible, not stupid.' I studied her ghost-green face wishing, not for the first time, I could see what colour her eyes were.

'She's taken her clothes off again.' Mark held a bundle of dark cloth by two fingertips.

'Well…' I sniffed the air significantly. 'Your turn. I found the last one. Put those in the laundry. I'll do them when I get back from the school run.'

'Ah, crap!' He swung around and stomped back down the hall.

'Exactly,' I muttered. 'Mark! Just wait a few minutes for it to cool down. Then we can switch the lights on and see it.'

'I know! I *know!*' His reply bounced off the high ceiling and devolved again into resentful muttering I was probably better off not hearing. I did catch the words 'late', 'meeting', 'promotion' and 'not what I frigging bargained for', and had to bite my tongue. This wasn't exactly my dream life either.

I carried Faith into the bathroom and cleaned her up. 'What am I going to do with you, little rodent?' She didn't reply. She rarely did. She'd learned early that if she stayed quiet she could hide longer. But she listened and she understood. Oh yes, she was definitely not stupid.

'You can't keep doing that,' I said, tugging a new pair of underwear over her chubby little toes. 'You're a big girl. I think you just like making mischief. I've heard you giggle when someone treads in it.' I tried to scowl at her, but wearing goggles and being in the dark made it pointless.

Sure enough, a smothered, snickering snort of a laugh escaped her lips.

I pulled a frilly dress over her head and carried her back to the kitchen. It would be nice if there was some type of clothing I could keep on her; something she couldn't shed at the drop of a hat. It was our only way of finding her. We'd tried everything, even onesies with a zip up the back she couldn't reach. She always managed to find a way out.

We'd painted her face once, but anything on her that warmed up to body temperature became invisible as well. Her clothing tended to be very fluffy and loose, so some part of it would stay visible. She had a wardrobe full of tulle fairy-dresses that revolted me and delighted her.

Maybe it was time I took her to see Mr Tailor. If anyone could design something, it was him. He was, after all, costumer to Australia's super heroes. He had material suited to every super-power.

Maybe designing something for a baby would get him out of the habit of creating those stupid plunging-neckline-and-butt-creeping numbers he insisted were the correct uniform for female supers. They were *so* last century, but he just couldn't get his head around the concept of comfort and practicality. He'd been disheartened when I'd showed up, with my A-cup breasts and big ass. Even more so when I'd asked for Kevlar and pockets. Poor guy. He still cringed every time he saw me.

Well, I had to take my costume in for repairs anyway, so it was a good excuse. My last encounter with Hadron had left me with one shredded sleeve and a number of dents in the body armour. Kevlar wasn't very flexible either, and I wasn't quite as fast as I'd been fifteen years ago when I'd started this gig. I needed something lighter and stronger if I was going to avoid being shot.

'Mother!' Cathy's door flew open, and she stormed into the kitchen, her tantrum slightly spoiled by the fact that she wore goggles and pyjamas. She folded her arms and, from the angle of her head, was probably glaring at Faith.

'You have to *do* something about her.' She flung her arms wide. 'This is *ridiculous.* I can't get ready for school because I can't *see* anything.' She began to pace, warming to her oft-repeated theme. 'She's a pain in the ass. I have no *life!* I'm *twelve,* and I can't have friends over because someone might trip over her or step in something revolting, or find out your secret identity. I can't *do* anything or *go* anywhere because you're always fussing over her, or running off to fight some stupid supervillain so I have to babysit. And Dad's *always* at work.'

I clenched my teeth and settled Faith on my hip, reluctant to set her down until Mark finished cleaning and Cathy closed her door.

'Where did you want to go, Cath?' I said, struggling to keep my tone mild and non-confrontational. It wasn't easy. Resentment bubbled. I drew a long breath. This was something they never taught me at super-training: how, after two sleepless nights and four exhausting days, to deal with a daughter heading into puberty and brimming with hostility.

I did feel sorry for her. Not only did she lack a super-power, but her younger, accidental sister had one and drew all the attention. I tried hard to stay patient, but sometimes she made it…difficult. Today was not the best timing.

'I want parties,' she snapped, tossing her head. 'Sleepovers, the mall, friends' houses. Anywhere but here! I want—'

'So, what do you want me to do?' Exhaustion broke through my tenuous calm and I raised my voice, overwhelming hers. 'This?'

Switching on my speed I raced down the hall into Faith's room. I laid her in the cot and flipped the lid closed. Then I locked it and pocketed the key. It was a thing we rarely did. It was wrong and we knew it, but sometimes…just sometimes…at least she was safe and we could relax for a few seconds.

My stomach twisted as Faith sat up and a puzzled frown crossed her plump little face. Her mouth opened and a wail soared out, small and frightened at first, then winding up in to full-blown anger and frustration such as only a toddler can master. Her fingers wrapped around the bars and rattled them. The lock shook. She reached through and yanked at it, the wail turning to screaming sobs when it didn't break or open.

Turning my back resolutely, I sped to the kitchen again. The whole thing had only taken maybe thirty seconds. Cathy still stood there waiting, defiant. I pulled off the goggles and thumbed the remote, returning her glare for glare as the blinds vanished, the TV sprang to life, and the lights all flashed on.

Faith's voice, calling 'Mummy, Mummy!' penetrated her closed door and wafted soul-tearingly down the hall.

I pointed, managing to keep my voice even and reasonable, though my throat tightened. 'There. Is that what you want? Now we're free. Let's go the mall, shall we? I never get to go, either, not with an invisible baby.'

'That's not fair, and you know it!' Cathy yanked her goggles off and threw them aside, not even flinching when they shattered on the tiles and sprayed glass across the floor.

I raised a sardonic brow at her and folded my arms, weary and disheartened. 'What do you know about fair, Cathy? Is it fair that a stupid lab-accident that turned me into a speed-freak? Is it fair that I had to give up my job when Faith came along?' I flung my arms wide in imitation of her earlier action. 'Is it fair that I have to do all the housework at normal speed because we can't afford the food bill if I do it at super-speed? Remember that I don't get paid to risk my life saving people from the likes of Hadron and Blackstar.'

Cathy pressed her lips together and glowered. She backed away, her eyes narrow, matching my annoyance with resentment.

'Life's not fair, Cathy,' I said. 'So, I'd like you to get your backside into your room and get ready for school. I've got to clean up your mess and settle your sister, so I can't drive you. You can walk.'

'Fine!' she shouted. Tears glistened and spilled onto her flushed cheeks. She strode to her door and slammed it shut, only to open it immediately and yell, 'But don't be surprised if I don't come back. *You* don't want me here! I *hate* you and I wish Faith'd never been born! And I hope Hadron takes you *both* away next time! *I* wouldn't stop him.' She slammed it again and the lock clicked. There was a screaming torrent of incomprehensible words. Things thumped against the wall.

I sank into a hard kitchen chair and dropped my face into my hands. My heart rattled against my ribs and bile stung my throat as the argument replayed in my head. Oh my God. How could I have said that? How could she? Did she really hate me that much?

'Hey.' Mark's gentle voice startled me. He laid warm hands on my shoulders and massaged the tension there.

I sighed and leaned my cheek on his wrist. 'I'm sorry. I don't know what's wrong with me. How do women *do* all of this? I'm a bad mother, aren't I? And a bad wife, too.' I stood up and faced him, hoping for denial.

He brushed a loose red curl from my eye and twisted his mouth into a half-smile. 'You're doing your best. We all are.'

That stung. Looking down, I folded my arms across my stomach and clamped down on the rush of tears that turned the neat floor tiles into wobbly lines. 'So I am, then. You think so, too.'

'What?' He frowned at me. 'How the hell did you get that from what I said? No, you're not a bad mother. This is just a tough time for all of us.'

'Oh, really?' I pursed my lips, too hurt to mind my words. 'I don't see it being all that tough for you. You've got a job. You get to go out and talk to people—normal people!' Pushing past him, I paced around the other side of the table, needing space.

'I get to stay at home with a baby I can't even see.' I pointed out the window. 'Or get shot at while exchanging witty banter with megalomaniacs who always seem to want to rule the stupid world. I'm so *tired,* and no one ever says 'thanks' anymore—not you, not Cathy, not Faith and not even the people I save, over and over again. I would *love* to be an ordinary woman, with an ordinary family, and an ordinary job, like you, with no responsibility and people who appreciate you.'

'No respons—!' Mark snorted a disbelieving half-laugh and turned away, picking up his keys. 'Well, I'd love to have an ordinary family too, but it looks like neither of us get what we want, do we? I have a meeting after work. I'll be late. Don't wait up.' He spun on his heel and strode out the door without looking back.

Shit! Appalled at myself and at him, I ran to the door and opened it, yelling his name. Too late. His car was already down the driveway and about to take off up the street. I could catch him, of course, but not without my fascinated, sixty-year-old neighbour, who stood watering his garden, seeing plainly what we'd hidden for the last fifteen years.

I closed the door, sank onto the couch and held my head, trying to work out where I'd gone wrong. I'd never totally lost it like that before. Cathy's words had cut me to the core—to the spot where my deepest guilt and fear lay. I was neglecting her and Mark in my desperate attempt to be everything to everyone; to meet the demands of being a full-time mother and superhero. I must be mad. No-one could do this, could they?

Oh, but of course they could. A flicker of movement caught my eye and I glowered at the muted newsfeed on the TV. There, in full, confident colour, wearing her ridiculous, fitted armour and skin-tight, cleavage-exposing, green-and-gold spangled costume, was Ms Majestic, widely-sung hero of Australia. And standing next to her, with arms akimbo and legs spread in the approved super-hero stance, were her two teenage children: Prince Majestic and Princess Majestic. And those really were their hero-names. Talk about delusions of grandeur.

Ms Majestic was a fourth-generation hero and seemed to know exactly how it all worked. Never made a mis-step with the press, always looked glamorous with perfect lipstick, cape billowing and glossy black hair streaming in a non-existent wind. No-one ever talked about her husband, if he existed.

The scene on TV changed to one of smoking destruction, and I frowned and reached for the remote. I normally kept it muted so I could hear Faith's movements. The last two years had made my hearing exceptional. But she was still in her crib, yelling, and this story called for sound. Something wasn't right. I hit the button.

'And this news just in,' the smoothly-coiffured talking head said. 'The Majestics seem to have disappeared. Sources close to them say they were last seen fighting Hadron and his minions in downtown Sydney. But they all, including Hadron, vanished in a flash of light yesterday afternoon, leaving behind an estimated twenty million dollars-worth of damage but no assurances that Hadron is contained. Supporters and detractors of Ms Majestic have taken to social media in a storm of arguments about the event, some claiming the heroic mother of two has been kidnapped by Hadron. More from our reporter on the scene...'

There was no more, really, just padding. I muted it again, thinking hard. That was a first. Undoubtedly the 'flash of light' would prove to be some new gadget of Hadron's, but Majestic would have prevailed. Of course she would. She always did. It was unusual, though, for her not to hang around and lap up the publicity after defeating a villain.

Maybe I should check in with Headquarters? No. If there was trouble, even I couldn't get to Sydney and back to Brisbane before three o'clock. I'd missed a lot of school pickups over the years, what with villains having a complete lack of care about these things. Today was probably a bad day to miss another one.

Majestic would be fine. She'd never needed my help before. I had enough problems here to deal with.

Down the hall, Faith's yelling subsided into distant, sniffling sobs that were no less heartbreaking for being quieter. Cathy's room was suspiciously silent. I rummaged through a drawer for the spare key and unlocked it.

She was gone. The window stood wide. A breeze shifted the faded blue-flowered curtains and fluttered papers left strewn on her bed. A quick check showed her school bag and uniform missing. Her pyjamas lay discarded on the floor of her bathroom. Nothing else seemed to be gone, but it was hard to tell in the mess.

Damn. I was guilt-sick that she'd left without resolving our argument. I'd call the school later to confirm she made it okay, and I'd move heaven and earth to be there to pick her up. I'd make it up to her. Everything would be alright.

Hopefully.

At least I could redeem myself with one of my daughters right now. I headed for Faith's room and unlocked the cot. She lay curled up, hugging one her stuffed toys, crying softly into it. I gathered her into my arms. She stiffened then, when I murmured humble apologies into her ear, softened and threw her arms around my neck. We blubbered together for a while and eventually felt better. Well, I did, anyway. It was hard to tell with Faith.

I let her lead me to the kitchen in search of food, and smiled at the space above the neck of her green net dress, while I cut up cheese and ham sandwiches into eight tiny squares, as instructed.

'So,' I said, mustering cheerfulness, 'when it's time to go get Cathy from school, shall we get icecream on the way back?' It was blatant bribery, but I needed her to co-operate. It'd been a long few days, and I was just a tiny bit worried Cathy may not be there. She was good at holding grudges.

Faith made a pleased little noise, which I took to mean 'yes'.

I left the knife and bread-crusts on the table, too lethargic to bother cleaning up. We wandered into the lounge, and I read her a story while she ate. It was her favourite: Jack and the Beanstalk. She loved it when tiny little Jack trashed the big scary giants.

I was in the middle of fe-fi-fo-fumming and watching her sandwiches vanish into thin air, when the doorbell rang. I blinked in surprise. No one who knew us rang the bell. They called first so I could contain Faith and make sure she didn't slip out an open door. She was tricky that way.

'Sweetie?' I wagged a finger at her. 'You stay right here, okay? Don't wander off. I'll be right back, and then we'll finish the story.' I touched her head and felt a nod. She scooted back in the seat. The red pompoms on her socks rose and fell as she kicked her legs in restless patience.

The lounge wasn't visible from the entrance, so it was safe enough to open the door, at least a little way. I peered out through the peephole first. Groaning, I leaned my forehead on the wooden panel. Two police officers stood at my door, with Cathy's stiff-necked, glowering face visible between them. Now what? I sucked a fortifying breath, plastered on a grin and opened the door.

'Good morning, officers,' I said brightly. 'What can I do for you? Is Cathy alright?' I gave her a quick, sharp glare. She lifted her chin and narrowed her eyes right back at me. Clearly not at all repentant, then.

One of the officers, a young man, said politely, 'Sorry ma'am, but is this your daughter?' I assented, and he continued. 'I regret to say, ma'am, she was caught shoplifting.'

'I was *not!*' Cathy snapped. 'It's a *lie.* They just showed up out of nowhere and grabbed me!'

I closed my eyes briefly, trying to get a grip on my first reaction, which was to give her the 'how could you do this to me' speech right then and there. That wasn't going to help.

'I'm so sorry, officer.' My voice emerged a little tighter than normal. 'She's never done anything like this before, and I guarantee it won't happen again.'

Cathy gave a growl of sheer frustration and folded her arms, looking away. Tears spilled onto her cheeks. 'It's not *true.*' She sniffed.

The female officer smiled and laid a friendly hand on Cathy's shoulder. 'We know ma'am, and the storekeeper was nice enough not to press charges. So, since it's her first time, we're letting her off with a warning. There's a little paperwork to do though, so if we can come in for a moment?'

'Uh…' I glanced over my shoulder. 'Sure, just give me a sec.' Shutting the door, I dashed back to the lounge.

Crap. Faith's green dress and red socks were limp and empty on the couch. This was *so* not the time. I did a quick race around, hissing her name and waving my arms at knee height. But she was well-hidden. I couldn't really slam down blackout blinds while the police were on the doorstep.

I shoved her clothing into her room and tidied way all evidence of her presence from the lounge room. Then I zipped back to the door and opened it.

'Sorry, just a bit cluttered. Please, come in. Would you like something to drink?' I waved them toward the lounge.

The kitchen was still a mess. It wasn't in full view of the lounge, but it was still too big a risk to clean it fast. I loaded the water glasses onto a tray and grimaced at myself. What did it matter? They weren't here to judge my housekeeping.

The front door opened and closed. I frowned. Who had come in? Or left? Maybe one of the police officers had returned to the car for something. Hopefully Faith hadn't slipped out. I hurried back into the lounge, anxious to get rid of them and find her.

On entering the room, I almost dropped the tray. It rattled in my hands.

There, larger than life in my drab lounge room, stood Hadron. Dressed in shades of black and grey armour, with his grey-winged helmet tucked under one arm and his grey silk cape swirling, he dominated the room. Even more insanely, he was flanked by the glittering Ms Majestic and her perfect children, all looking down their noses at me. Behind them, Cathy sat rigid on the sofa between the police officers, her eyes wide and frightened. Two pistol muzzles pressed indents into her temples.

I gaped, made mindless by the incongruence of it all. 'What the fuck…?'

'My dear Velox,' Hadron said suavely. 'Such language in front of the children.'

'Velox?' I managed to gather my brains and stuff them back where they belonged. 'You've made a mistake. I'm not Velox. I'm no superhero. I'm just a housewife.' I set the tray carefully on the coffee table.

'Aha ha ha ha.' He actually said the sounds in a parody of a laugh, and waved a languid hand. 'Don't bother, Velox. Ms Majestic here told me all about you.' Ms Majestic lifted one shoulder in an apologetic shrug when I glared at her.

'You know,' he said, cocking his head at me, 'Mr Tailor is right: you really do look much better in ordinary clothing.'

I growled at him and switched into speed-mode. In less than a second I would have both guns in my hands, and he would be toast.

Nothing happened.

I gaped down at my uncooperative feet. I'd taken two steps forward—at normal speed.

Hadron smiled condescendingly and jiggled a small, blinking, electric gadgetty-thing at me. 'Oh, don't bother trying to use your speed. I've neutralised your abilities thanks to this handy little device. With a little persuasion, Mr Tailor was most helpful with giving me details on all of his clients' powers so my techs could make this. Although he seemed quite keen to give me yours, Velox. I don't think he likes you.'

He turned the gadget over and frowned vaguely at it. 'No idea how it works, but evidently my techie guys attuned it just to you. I have them for the Majestics, too. Very handy. Please, sit.'

I raised my brows, trying to play it cool while my stomach knotted. My knees gave way and I sank onto the couch opposite. 'Your name is 'Hadron' and you don't understand the physics of your own tech? Seriously?'

He raised haughty brows at me and gave Cathy a significant look, so I resisted the urge to annoy him again. Witty banter was for the battlefield, not my house.

'Fine. What do you want?'

'Why, nothing more than your loyalty.' He bowed elaborately. 'As Ms Majestic has given hers.'

'And what do I get in return?' I held up a hand. 'Wait, let me guess—you leave my family alone, right?'

'Exactly!' He beamed as though pleased I was so quick to understand. 'Your husband and daughter will live a blameless and peaceful life, if you assist me.'

'My husband and daughter…' I caught Cathy's eye and looked

quickly away. 'I see.'

'Mum?' Cathy's quavering question held more than a plea for reassurance. It held undercurrents of apology, approval and determination. Pride surged. There she was, with guns to her head, but the mulish set of her mouth said she was on my side, prepared to support whatever I did next to save us.

The problem was: I couldn't think of a damned thing that would.

'Mum,' she repeated, lifting her chin and rolling her eyes as far as they would go to the left, toward the hallway. 'It's okay. You know I have faith.'

Ah, so Faith was still in the house. Thank God.

'No, sweetheart.' I sighed and shook my head. 'I can't risk you. I'm sure things will work out.' I looked Hadron in the eye and raised my voice, 'But you're right: I just need a little *faith*.'

'Well.' He smiled serenely. 'You may look to me for that. In fact, you may worship me as a god, and so shall all of your kind. With you as my enforcers I shall rule the world!'

'Oh yes,' I agreed earnestly. 'For with faith we can triumph over anything.'

The faint slap of bare feet on tile reached my keen ears.

'Of course,' I mused aloud, 'you haven't converted me yet and, well, you are what I call a "bad man". I don't really want you in my house.' I shrugged. 'If you don't leave, bad things will happen.'

Hadron's smile slid toward condescending. 'You're in my power. I have your daughter.' He patted the gadget in his hand. 'And I have this. Without your speed, you have nothing.'

'Oh yes, you've taken my power, but I have faith. In fact, I think my faith might be stronger than your tech.'

'Er…' Hadron lifted his brows at me, just the faintest hint of doubt behind his steel-grey eyes. 'Really? I'm not religious myself. I don't really put much stock in the power of belief, so I don't think—'

'Yes,' I said firmly. 'My faith is strong enough do *everything* I've ever said was the wrong thing to do. To you. Now. Please.'

An almost-inaudible scrape of metal on timber came from the kitchen.

Hadron blinked at me and exchanged puzzled looks with his minions. He laughed hesitantly, clearly not sure what the joke was.

'You are a very strange woman, Velox.'

A whispered 'fe-fi-fo-fum' seemed to reach only me, for no-one else reacted. Then Ms Majestic tilted her head, a slow, secret smile twitching at the corner of her mouth.

A stifled giggle broke the silence.

There was a long, confused pause in which Hadron frowned at Cathy, then me, then Majestic and her two children. They shrugged their lack of responsibility. His head swiveled, eyes narrowed as he inspected every corner of the room.

He eyed me. 'Is there someone else in this...' He sniffed the air. 'What is that *smell?*'

Ms Majestic grinned and pulled her children out of harm's way.

The policewoman shrieked, clutching at a neat double-row of teethmarks in her ankle. The other officer echoed her, letting his gun fall and grabbing at his leg. Cathy elbowed them both in the nose and ran.

The box in Hadron's hand sparked and crackled. He dropped it with an oath, sucking on his fingers. A knife materialised, apparently from nothing, sticking drunkenly out of the black plastic. Smoke spiralled, thin and acrid.

Hadron frowned and took a step forward. Something squidged, audibly, under his foot. He made a noise of disgust, moved to take another step...and fell over something that wasn't there.

He screamed and cracked his nose on the corner of our wooden coffee table.

Then my speed returned.

Less than two minutes later, it was all over bar the cleaning up.

#

Cathy and I made up over the trussed body of my arch enemy. Hadron glared up at us from the floor, his threats muffled by a wad of glittery silver tulle. Faith, dressed now in a purple fairy costume, complete with wings, sat on him and bounced, giggling. His minions were tied up with anything handy—teatowels, curtain tiebacks.

Ms Majestic thanked us profusely, apologising for her mistake in underestimating Hadron. Cathy and Princess struck up an enthusiastic conversation about the difficulty of having a super-mum. They exchanged phone numbers.

Prince Majestic offered to tweak one of Hadron's gadgets to a wavelength that would neutralise invisibility. We accepted. Marvellous though she was, for the sake of our sanity, there needed to be limits to what a little Faith could do.

Mark, alerted by Headquarters that something was going on, rushed home and swept me and both his daughters into a crushing hug, murmuring reassurances of love into our ears. My heart swelled and I smiled beatifically through tears of relief. I held my family close, treasuring each one.

Maybe I could do this. After all, I wasn't just a woman, I was a super-woman.

And When We Return

First Published in "RETURN" CAT Press 2017

800BCE

Incinerating in the belly of a star a hundred light-years from home was not the end I'd anticipated. I'd hoped to choose my method of death. At home, surrounded by people I loved. Perhaps on a new colony-world I'd discovered.

But the choice might not be mine.

Dren, if you don't lock down that regulator, we'll lose the starboard engine! Vanin's thought reached me as I hurtled through the tiny sleeping section and slapped a breather over my face.

I thumbed the control for the iris separating the front of the ship from the back and leapt into the airlock.

On it now. Just keep us out of the star's gravity well.

I will, if you get me control of that engine, Vanin snapped. *I told you we took damage in the debris cloud outside this system. We should have checked.*

I did check, I shot back. *All the diagnostics came back clean.*

Vanin didn't reply and I had to concentrate on repairing the damaged regulator. The ship juddered and flung me against the curved wall. I staggered to my feet.

Hurry up, Dren! We're heading right for the star.

My shoulder ached where it'd taken the brunt of my fall. I hooked both thumbs of my left hand around a handhold and braced myself. The regulator panel ripped easily off the wall and clattered to the metal walkway. The ship shook and spiralled toward flaming death. The floor tilted. My chin cracked on the wall, but I clung doggedly to the handhold.

Turn off grav back here. I can't work when I'm being hurled around the place like a jonball.

The artificial gravity nullified and I drifted, peaceful. Purple blood from my chin formed a sphere and floated away. I yanked out the faulty regulator control circuit and jimmied a temporary bypass. The ship steadied its headlong pace through the solar system and levelled out.

I sighed. My skin's stress-grey subsided and returned to resting-green.

Grav, please. I hauled my feet back to the floor and took the renewed weight with flexed knees, then leaned against the wall. Blood splatted onto the walkway by my boot.

It's a temporary fix, Van, I warned. *I'll need to get the replacement out of stores before we try using the skip-drive. But we're out of danger. A few minutes more and the fault would have fed back into the engine and blown us to cosmic dust.*

A claxon blared beside my ear. I jumped and swore. A swift diagnostic through the biocom neural interface told an unpleasant story: I'd fixed the regulator, but revealed a deeper issue. I checked three times, swore again and retreated to the sleeping quarters, sealing the airlock irises.

I pressed a med seal onto my chin and arrived back in the cockpit just as Vanin finished inputting new navigational directions. Vanin looked up and the holo-nav display vanished.

'Good news and bad,' I said brightly, checking the engine performance one more time through my neural link to the biocom.

Vanin grimaced and ran a hand over sleek scales on a bare head. 'Dren, last time you gave me bad news we had to bypass a perfectly good planet and eat recycled waste for a month.'

'That planet was inhabited by sentients,' I said. 'We're supposed to find colony sites, not commit genocide.'

Vanin curled a lip. 'We've been searching for over a year. We have to return to Haos soon and report. I don't want to go back empty-handed. Our people are depending on us.'

'I know, Van,' I said quietly. 'But we're not the only search team. I won't be responsible for destroying sentient races because we wrecked our own planet out of stupid shortsightedness.'

'I don't understand why you took this mission if you're not prepared to do whatever it takes to save our people.' Vanin sent me a glare.

I grinned wryly. 'I know you don't.'

'So, what's your good and bad news, then?'

'Two lots of good news. Starboard engine's functioning fine now. We're in no danger of fiery oblivion in the heart of the star.'

'I know that!'

'And,' I said, pretending the interruption hadn't occurred, 'just before the regulator alarm went, the biocom showed the third planet in this system supports life. Gravity's a little higher than we're used to, but not much. Year's a little longer and days are shorter, but well within tolerances.'

'That's excellent. I'll take us in for a look.' The holonav appeared again as Vanin's thoughts altered our course.

'The bad news,' I finished, 'is that we have a small fuel problem.'

Vanin turned wide black eyes on me, the gold vertical pupils their only colour.

'Well, maybe not so small,' I admitted. 'We have plenty of water-fuel in the tow-tank behind the ship, but we're leaking crion particles. The damaged regulator was feeding false readings to the biocom.'

'Can we repair the damage and stop the leak?'

I shook my head. 'Looks like a meteor's punctured the crion reactor tank in two places. To repair it outside, I'd be exposed to more radiation than the exosuit can handle.'

'Can we get home?' Vanin's hands twisted together. All twelve digits and Vanin's smooth-scaled arms flushed from resting-green to ash-grey.

'No,' I said. 'We're alright at sublight speeds. But if we switch on the skip drive, the crion emissions will ignite and blow the starboard engine. We're safe in here and we have time to work out a solution. But, until we do, we can't go home.'

'So, what now?' Vanin's facial skin colours and textures fluxed, changing to match the grey biocom console then shifting back to a sick shade of resting-green.

I ignored the bad manners of shifting in front of me. Vanin was new to recon missions and under stress. This was my twentieth. The Council of Colours supposedly matched recon partners for compatibility, but they'd messed up with our pairing. Van coloured me the wrong way, as much as I tried to hide it.

'Now the engine's stable,' I said, 'the easiest solution is to land. Then we can shut down the reactor and do the repairs.' I pulled up the solar system specs on the holo and enlarged the third rocky planet. The biocom ran a closer analysis and downloaded details into our minds through the neural link.

Breathable atmo, seasonal weather changes due to axial tilt. Nothing too extreme that our bodies couldn't cope with—especially if we stayed closer to the equator, in habitats more like Haos used to be. High water to land ratios and massive carbon readings, which usually meant abundant life.

'But we can't take this ship into atmo,' Vanin said, frowning. 'The crion leak would contaminate the whole world and it's the first suitable planet we've seen for months. What about the fourth planet? It's the only other potential. Can we land there for the repairs?'

I ran a few calculations in my head and re-checked as the computations appeared on the holo. 'No, the fourth planet's out. If we can't restart the reactor we'd be stuck there and there's no breathable atmo. We'll have to take the escape pod to the third planet and set the ship into long orbit around this star. On the planet we can gather what we need to contain the crion leak, and return later to repair the ship in orbit.'

'For how long?'

'The orbit?' I did the math. 'Maybe seventy-five of that planet's years. That way it won't dump too many crions in the immediate area.'

'No, crad you, Dren!' Vanin snapped. 'Not the orbit. How long until we can fix the ship and get home?'

I stared at the holo-image of the blue-green third planet. 'Hard to say. We're not close enough to tell if there are any sentients or any civilisations. The biocom hasn't picked up any transmissions or evidence of space flight, though. If there's no advanced civ then repairing the ship might be impossible.'

'Gred it!' Vanin wrenched off the piloting visor and threw it aside.

'I need to get home! This was only meant to be a one year mission. Two, at the most.'

'So? What's the problem?' I stood and faced my mission partner. Vanin was never the calmest, but this seemed excessive. Van paced a few steps to the back of the cockpit, then returned.

'You might think we have time to sort this out, but I don't. I'm transitioning. Early,' Vanin said, shoulders sagging. The grey flush now covered every visible inch of skin. 'I was meant to be home before it happened. I'm supposed to start a family.'

'Ah,' I said. 'Sorry. This is your first time in the female phase?'

'Yes,' she whispered.

'Don't give up hope yet. We might get home in time. How long will you be female? What's your family history?'

Vanin shrugged. 'Hard to say. My birth parent stayed in phase for over three centuries the first time. Five, the second time. Could be affected by the planetary conditions, though. But that's not the real issue.'

'So what is?' I thought I knew her pretty well after a year in this cramped ship, but the rapid shifts of skin colour and texture flashing across her body spoke of deep inner stress. What was she hiding?

'I…' She lifted her chin and straightened. 'I'll be First Female amongst my family. The responsibility of producing the Heir will be mine.'

'Congratulations.' I smiled wryly. 'Well, I can't guarantee we'll get back in time for you to fulfil that, but we'll certainly try.'

'No!' She gripped my wrist so tightly the thin bones ground together. 'You don't understand. I'll be First Female—and my family is Primary Blue. I *have* to get back to Haos.'

I gaped at her. 'Are you *serious*? What the crad were your family thinking, letting you come offworld? You should be sitting safely in

Council of Colour, with your parents, running the gredding world, not endangering your life out here. You should've told me who you were.'

'I wasn't allowed to tell anyone. I'm not even supposed to be First.' She glared. 'I have two older sibs who were meant to transition before me. One of them was to produce the Heir.' She stared out into the star-speckled darkness. 'The Prime Blue—my male-parent—insisted I join Exploration. I didn't understand why. But if I'm in trans, it means…something's happened to my sibs.'

Brilliant cobalt suffused her skin. The urge to shift my colour to complementary orange and kneel in subservience almost seduced me. I fought to keep my usual resting-green.

'My Colour is in danger and I'm the next Heir-Mother. You *must* help me get home, Dren. I order it!' Her righteous certainty battered on my thoughts.

I closed her out. Not an easy thing to achieve against a Blue, but I'd had many years of experience. I'd left Haos to escape the politics and do something active to save our people. Mindlessly obeying our planet's hereditary Primaries is what got Haos into trouble in the first place.

I laid a hand on her shoulder. 'Van, I know this is tough for you, but we have to prioritise. We can't get home yet. We'll send the distress call. First, we need to set the orbit and get down to the planet. Then we can work out how to handle your transition. I'll be with you every step, I promise. I've been through it twice.'

The hormonal changes transitioning from neutral to female could be pretty brutal. If the Prime Blue had sent her off planet so close to her time then things were worse at home than I'd suspected.

She glared at me, her skin flushing the indigo of rage, then she seemed to regain control. Her skin subsided to resting-green and the gold pupils in her black eyes narrowed to slits. 'Did you have offspring?'

I shook my head. 'Too busy trying to save the planet.' I said lightly.

The ache in my chest never got easier, even after four hundred and twenty years. Perhaps it never would. But I'd made my choice; missed my chance. Our world didn't need more inhabitants, it needed fewer. And that was my job. We needed somewhere new to live, or we'd die.

'You're neutral now. When will you trans back to male?' she asked abruptly.

I sent her weary look. 'Probably not soon enough and I doubt your Prime would be thrilled if you produced an heir from an orange, rather than another Primary.'

She cleared her throat in the awkward silence that followed and scrubbed a hand over her sharp cheekbones. 'Well, I guess we'd better get organised. We'll need to use all the heavy-water-fuel to create an ice coating on the ship. That orbit you've calculated'll bring it close to the star and the ice will keep it cool.'

'Good thinking.' I squeezed her shoulder. 'The ship's already dragged a tail of ice and rock from the debris cloud. And each orbit will add to it. So the ice'll thicken and protect the ship from damage, too.'

'There won't be time,' Van snapped. 'We'll have it repaired and be on our way home before the ship circles through the cloud again.'

I said nothing. We took our places again, sinking into the bodyform seats and activating the neural link. It was the work of minutes to instruct the biocom to sluice our fuel over the hull, keeping only the escape pod hatch and engine nozzles clear. The water froze into a thick shell.

What about the crion emissions? Vanin asked as she nudged the ship into the correct orbital path and cut the engines. *The planet will pass right through our debris trail in this orbit.*

But the concentration should only be at dangerous levels for a few days each orbit, when the ship's right in the planet's path. So the planet will only be exposed once every seventy-some years. Hopefully the dose won't have any effect on the native life forms.

That's a big hope, she said. *Crions cause mutations in our species. What happened to not destroying sentients?*

We don't even know if the planet has any, yet.

I switched off the integrated biosystems, one at a time, powering down the ship piece by piece until only life support, comms, and the escape pod were fully operational. Then I sent a distress call, switched off the life support and locked down the biocom with a final order to maintain orbit and eject the pod once we were in.

As I ushered Van toward the escape pod, a purple light flashed on the blank comms console.

'Crad!' I hesitated, then stepped out of the cockpit and thumbed the iris control closed.

'What happened?' Van opened the emergency pod iris and climbed in.

'Emergency beacon didn't work. We're too close to the star. Solar interference. Ship needs to be outside the system's debris cloud to tap into the skip-space relays.'

Her eyes widened. 'But that means…'

'Yeah,' I said, sealing the pod iris behind us. 'The biocom'll try again when the ship orbits far enough out—in thirty or so years. But the Council won't get our call for a while.' I grimaced and squeezed her hand. 'Sorry, Van.'

Her jaw hardened. 'No, it's not over. I'm not giving up that easily—not while my family's in danger. They'll hear it. They'll get us. I'll get home. It's my duty to my family and my people. My child will be Prime Blue. I'll make sure of it.' Her dark eyes glittered.

I kept silent.

The pod biocom enveloped us in gel-tanks to cushion against atmo descent, and launched into space. In the past, the ancient urge to produce offspring had resulted in borderline insane behaviour in our Primary Colour females.

I was in for a rough ride, no matter what we found on the planet.

#

'Atmospheric oxygen content a little higher than home.' I took off the breather and sniffed, then coughed and closed my nasal slits against the onslaught of unfamiliar scents. 'Whew. I can definitely smell animal life of some sort.'

'How can you tell?' Van stared, wide-eyed, at the vast grasslands surrounding the escape pod.

I'd instructed the biocom to search for evidence of habitations and set us down close enough to observe a settlement, but far enough away to be discreet. I didn't want to terrify the sentients.

I grinned at Van. 'Been to a hundred and fifty planets now. You get to know the smell of animal crap in all its forms. Carbon-based life is similar everywhere, from what I can tell. Bio's your speciality, not mine, but you pick things up in this job.'

The escape pod biocom pinged me and I downloaded the report through the neurals. 'You getting this, Van? Wow, this place has some serious diversity of single-celled and low-level multi-celled organisms.'

'I'm seeing a lot of potential disease-carriers,' she responded. She hadn't taken off her breather.

I grinned. Typical new reconner—never trusting the full spectrum anti-bios the medics gave us before we left home. We had boosters in the med kit and we'd need them if we stayed any longer than a year or two. After that, we'd adapt or die.

Luckily, we were a resilient species; long-lived and tough. Our DNA was different enough that local diseases shouldn't be able to get a foothold. If I could get Van safely through her first neutral-to-female transition she should be fine.

Right now, the priority had to be blending in with the natives. The escape pod had its own camo shielding. Once we decided our next action, it would bury itself and run on low power until we called it. The neural link would operate and send updates no matter where we were on the planet.

'Settlement was about an hour that way,' I said, pointing in the direction of the afternoon sun. 'We should get there and check out the locals before we decide where to go.'

Van nodded and shivered, wrapping her arms around herself. I felt it too: a cooler temperature than we were used to shipboard.

'Let's get our biosuits on,' I suggested. 'The adaptive fabric will make it easier to shift and match local physiques and colours. And they'll keep us warmer. Maybe we should have come down closer to the equator.'

Van shook her head. 'No, you were right. Too hard to travel through the vegetation and way more settlements. We'll check out the inhabitants here. Shift to blend in. Then travel south if it gets too cold.' Her gaze became abstracted. 'Biocom says we've got half a year at least until the coldest weather sets in.' She removed her breather and promptly fell into a coughing fit.

We changed into the biosuits and hiked for an hour—long enough for my muscles to tell me I'd been lazy in my onboard exercise routine. The geo-scientist in me was tempted to stop and study every rock, every landform, and every pile of dirt. And Van kept getting distracted by the variety of life to be found in even this bleak-seeming landscape.

Between us and the distant horizon rolled broad, sweeping hills covered in grey-green grasses. In the distance, a cloud of dust and shifting dark forms suggested some sort of herdbeast. I laid a hand on the met-gun holstered at my hip. Predators followed herdbeasts.

Overhead, the yellow sun yielded little warmth in a sky blue enough to rival Van's family colour. I smiled wryly. The Prime would love this place. Anything that reinforced the Blue family's dominance over the other colours.

We topped a rise and I grabbed Van's shoulder. We dropped to our stomachs on the stiff grass and stared in fascination at the little group of bipeds in the valley. I activated the neural-visuals link and zoomed in for a closer look at the circle of skin tents. Some sort of animal roasted on a spit over a central fire. Several bipeds rode on the backs of quadrupeds and shot a basic wooden projectile into a target. They were excellent shots.

'It's a small settlement,' Van said, doubtfully. 'We can't mimic any of them and be unnoticed.'

'No,' I said. 'But we can take them as a template and go to another settlement. We just need to learn the language. They're obviously speaking to each other. Can you link with one of them and download? You're better at it than I am.'

She smiled for the first time in hours and her dark eyes glazed as she merged thoughts with theirs. She frowned, shook her head, then her expression cleared.

'Got it. Fairly primitive culture but there's potential. It's possible we've just found a backwards tribe and there are more advanced civilisations in other areas.'

I picked the language out of the biocom and considered it.

'Linguistically complex. Tonal inflexions. Suggests a long evolutionary period. You could be right. Likely to be more advanced cultures in areas with more resources.' I glanced at her. 'Not sure now is the best time to be traipsing across huge distances, though.'

She glared. 'We have to get the ship repaired. I can't stay here. I must get back to my family. They're in danger and Haos needs me. Needs a Blue Heir.'

'I know, Van, it needs both of us. But have you checked your bioreadings in the last hour?' She'd already changed. Her face was rounder, her skin colour more vivid. Under the closefitting biosuit, her body had lost the sharp muscularity of a neutral gender and taken on the sleekness of a breeding female.

'Crad!' She looked at her hands and felt her face. Her eyes widened. 'I thought the transition would take longer.'

'Me too,' I said. 'Planetary effect, maybe. We should get back to the pod. The worst is yet to come. You're going to do some screaming and we don't want to scare the natives.' My wry grin and attempt at humour fell flat and Vanin turned away.

We returned to the pod in silence, with the shadows of afternoon lengthening before us in purple and grey streaks across the grasslands.

The screaming started before we'd made it all the way. I carried her the rest.

#

Her transition, which would normally take a month or more, lasted thirty-six hours. We stayed, cocooned and protected, in the escape pod. I plugged Van into the on-board medic in the hopes it would slow down the process and make it more bearable for her. But the pod biocom wasn't designed to cope with extreme medical situations.

After twelve hours the sedatives ran out and Van woke screaming again. I had to snap on restraints after her new claws sliced gouges in my arm. My blood spattered the inside of the pod and soaked my biosuit.

#

Shortly before the dawn of our second full day on the planet, Van calmed down. Her inner eyelids retracted, revealing eyes now brilliant green; the vertical gold pupils luminescent. Her transition looked to be complete.

I crouched before her and brushed back the shoulder-length crop of blue hair that hid her face.

'How're you feeling?'

'Like utter crad,' she said. 'But better than I was. Is it over?'

I grinned. 'Yep, you look to be fully transitioned.' I unlocked the restraints and she groaned, stretching muscles until tendons crackled.

'Everything hurts.'

'Well, a lot's changed. The question is, how long will you stay in female form?'

She sent me a dark look. 'If this transition is any indication, not long. Greddit!'

'Here.' I handed her a nutrition pack. 'Eat. You need it.'

She sucked it and a second pack dry. I mentally counted how many days rations we had left. Not many. I'd need to hunt in a day or so and hope our bodies could digest the native wildlife.

Van drank a full sack of water and sighed. 'Better. Thanks.'

She stood and opened the pod iris. We stepped outside into the cold pre-dawn and looked up at the glittering sky. To the north, shimmering, sweeping lights in green, yellow, and white arced and slipped along the horizon, creating a mesmerising display.

'I can't stay here, Dren,' Van said quietly, staring at the eastern horizon.

I followed her gaze. A handspan above a low range of mountains in the east, a fuzzy star shone brighter than the rest. A long tail glowed behind it.

'That has to be the ship,' Van said, pointing.

'Yep,' I said. 'Pod biocom confirms. Right on track in its orbit. Should be visible for sixty days or so.'

Van's claws extended then retracted. Her skin flushed sparkling sapphire and she drew herself up, regal and beautiful in her new appearance; every inch the Prime Blue's First Female.

Again, I fought an ages-old conditioning to kneel before her and offer colour-shift obeisance. Instead, I lifted my chin and met her gaze straight on.

'We will travel south. Now,' she stated. 'I have no time to waste on these primitives. We must find a civilisation that has the technology to repair our ship. I *will* get home before I transition back. If my other sibs are dead...' Her hands clenched into fists and she lifted her head. 'Then I'm the last Blue young enough to produce an Heir.'

'So, what do we do if none of the civilisations are advanced enough?' I laid a hand on her arm but she shook me off. 'Van, I know your position—your family's position—on Haos is important. But my mission is vital. My job is to find planets ready for colonisation. Our people can't survive much longer on Haos. But this planet already has sentient life. We can't interfere. We have to wait for our message to get through. They'll send someone for us.'

'And if they don't?' She turned on me, claws out and new incisors bared. 'I refuse to be stuck on this mudhole while my younger sib becomes next Prime Blue, or my whole family is wiped out by rebels. My rightful place is at the forefront of my family; my people. And if I have to drag these animals into a technological state that can get me home, then that's what I'll do. Whether you help me or not.'

Van's shape shimmered and changed. I recoiled. She stood before me in shifted form and it was all I could do to suppress a spurt of revulsion. Her skin was now smooth and gold-brown; her eyes narrow in a broad face. Her hands had only five digits, with just one opposable thumb. Her glorious blue hair now hung lank, straight and black. She'd instructed the biosuit to copy the clothing of the natives we'd seen: furs and rough cloth, beads, laced animal skin shoes, and all.

Only her green eyes, with their gold vertical pupils, belonged to our people.

'I'm going to get home, Dren. No matter how long it takes, or what I have to do. Don't get in my way.'

She strode away, lit by the first rays of the rising sun.

I had no choice but to follow.

#

Greece 467BCE

Van, these people are just not ready. They haven't even mastered the use of iron for anything beyond basic weapons and pots. They don't even know enough to call our ship a comet, not a sign from the gods.

You think I don't know that, Dren? But they have potential. Their short lifespans mean they're hungry for change. I've given these Greeks the basic mathematics to set them on the road to decent science.

But at what cost to their natural evolution; their culture?

What does it matter, Dren? We must keep the end in mind. Our people are more important. You must see that? I must get home.

I know…I just—

Enough. We've done what we can, here. We'll keep moving. There's sure to be more advanced cultures elsewhere.

#

Babylon 164BCE

Vanin, I can't countenance this. By backing that Parthian king's takeover of Babylon you caused the wholesale slaughter of thousands of innocents.

You're soft, Dren. He saw the return of our ship in its orbit as a sign. He had the drive and ambition we need to foster in these people if we're going to drag them into a technological age.

When are you going to stop this? We've been on this planet for half a millennia and—

And I'm still in the female phase. There's time. I can save our people and my heir will rule them on a colony. As long as I'm female, none of my younger sibs will change sex. Don't you see, Dren? If I don't get home, the Prime Blue family will die out completely. There will be no Heir!

And is it worth sacrificing the people of this world for that?

Yes, gred you! You're blinded by emotion, Dren. I've seen you with that…human woman.

Leave her out of this, Van. This is about you.

Yes. It's about me and our people. You're forgetting you're not human.

No, unfortunately I'm not.

#

Ireland 451CE

Dren, will you stop interfering? I know what I'm doing.

Like you did by encouraging the spread of this new Christ-religion? I get the feeling that's backfiring on you. Those villagers didn't exactly welcome you with open arms. If I hadn't been watching your back, you'd be sizzling nicely at the stake for witchcraft about now.

Shut up and stop following me. They were just frightened by our ship appearing in the sky again. Superstitious fools. Besides, fostering that faith seemed like a quick path to stability. The original messiah figure was a reasonable man. It's only his later followers who've been hard to—

Manipulate? Vanin, you've got to see reason. We can't—

We can. I can. Just stay out of my way, Dren, and I'll get these people where I need them to be. But only if you stop interfering.

#

England 1066CE

Vanin, please? Can't you see what you're doing? The endless wars…you're killing these people.

War drives invention and economies, Dren. You know that. War is the fastest way to bring about new technology.

No! These people deserve better than what we did to our world.

These people are nothing, Dren. It's our people who matter. Back off. There's an ambitious bastard son of a duke in Normandy who will serve my purposes excellently. He's already decided our ship is a sign of his success.

Him! No, Vanin. I'm working with someone in England. He's close to inventing flight.

Another lover? You disgust me.

Just give me time. An invasion now will disrupt everything.

You've had ample time, Dren.

#

Italy 1531CE

Vanin, where are you?

Does it matter?

Did you hear the message from the biocom?

Of course I did, you fool, Dren. It doesn't matter.

But they got our beacon. They'll send help. Our ship's back in the sky. If they come now we can leave.

The message said they're evacuating Haos. It could be another millennium before they reach us. My goal hasn't changed. I just need to get to the new colony, instead.

But you're driving these people at a rate this world can't sustain. How can you have lived amongst them for so long and not care about their welfare? They're not so different from us. C'mon. You're better than this.

...I can't, Dren.

Why?

If I let myself get involved I'll never get home. My people are more important. They have to be.

#

North America 1835CE

They've given our ship a name: Halleys Comet. Don't you think that's funny, Dren? Like they own it, or discovered it, these primitives.

No, it's not funny. Nor is what you're doing.

But we're so close now, Dren. I can taste it.

What, the death? The slavery and poverty? I'm done, Vanin. I've tried for two thousand years to bring you to your senses. You're a fool.

And you're a fool if you think the opinion of an Orange would sway me. That sort of weak thinking is what got our people into trouble in the first place. It's up to me and my family to save us. I'm the only one who can.

No, Van. You and the other Primary families were the problem on our home planet, exactly as you are here. You think you have the right to destroy a whole world to satisfy your personal ambition.

The ambition to guide our people to safety and prosperity can hardly be called 'personal'.

You're beyond redemption, Van. It's clear I can't stop you. You've put this world on an irreversible path. You've taught these people to place no value on their biosphere and no value on life…I only hope you can sleep at night.

#

England 1910CE

I've found them, Dren.

What are you talking about?

Scientists with the kind of minds I need. I'm so close to getting the ship repaired and getting us home!

Home to what, Vanin? Do you really think that, after two thousand years, our people will be the same? Don't you think they'll have changed, even if you haven't?

Why would they? They will always need a Prime to lead them, Dren. You've lived here too long, amongst these ephemeral creatures. They change quickly because they die quickly. They break your heart time and again and you keep championing them. Our people are more resilient.

You mean more resistant. In two thousand years these people have reached a level of technology it took ours twenty thousand to achieve.

Because of me.

You flatter yourself, Vanin. They're smarter than you give them credit for. But you've corrupted them and I fear for their future.

You have no vision, Dren. You ran from our homeworld when things got difficult, just as you ran from me when things got challenging, here.

Maybe you're right, Van. But I certainly can't see a happy result for your vision.

I'm your Prime, Dren. I know what's best for us.

I know you think you do, Van.

You're a fool.

So you've said.

#

Australia 2061

So, are you ready, Vanin?

Almost. The 1986 orbit of the ship excited too much attention, but this time the world's watching the new Mars colony. My little project is barely registering on the newsfeeds.

And you have what's needed to repair the ship?

Easily, Dren. Do you still doubt me?

…

You'll be returning with me, Dren.

I'm…not certain. There's someone here…

There's always someone here you care about, Dren. What about our people? Don't you care about them anymore?

…

Well, you know where I'll be, when the time comes. We're launching from the Australian site. Be there, or stay here. I don't care.

I know, Van.

#

Australia, 2061

'Dren,' Vanin said, neutrally. She nodded as I joined her in the observation lounge.

'Vanin.' I leaned on the railing and stared through tinted glass at the launchpad. The rocket was a sleek, white needle pointing skyward. Beneath it lay bare concrete, grey and cracked. Beyond the launch site, the vast, red-dust Australian landscape shimmered and baked under the white mid-winter sun. Heat hazed the blocky outlines of Roma city on the eastern horizon.

'Everything ready?' I asked. The sharp silence between us made me uncomfortable. We hadn't spoken in months and before that, decades. There was little left to say. I hadn't seen Vanin for over two hundred years. Earth was a big planet, even with the advent of atmo-skimming low-orbit transports.

I looked sideways. She hadn't changed much. She'd let slip the illusion of human-ness and stood at the picture window in her true form; still female though her resting-green skin was tinged brown with age. Her hair was now pale, mist-blue, rather than the cobalt of youth, but her back was straight and her chin lifted as she stared at the culmination of two thousand years of effort.

No regrets. No pity for humankind. Still that unquenchable drive.

'Was it worth it, Van?' I gestured at the arid, salt-crusted plains around the launch site. 'You've brought this world to the level of technology we need to get back. But have you stopped to look at what's happened to the planet to get to this point?'

She turned cool green eyes on me and her mouth lifted in a distant smile. 'So? We don't need this planet as a colony. Our people have found one. What does it matter? Besides, as you said—humans are resourceful. They'll recover the world.'

'Maybe,' I said.

'You've worked yourself into a position of trust…Prime Minister of Australia.' Van turned the title into a sneer. 'Taught them the right steps. The seedbanks, the cryo-freeze DNA banks.' She pointed northeast, to where a geodesic dome glittered in the sunlight. 'And the Habitats are protecting key ecosystems until the solar shield's completed and global warming's reduced. The Mars colony is successful, too.' Her smile turned bitter. 'They certainly won't die out in a hurry.'

I sighed and scrubbed a hand over my head. My human-form shift was still in place. Reflected in the window, my hand touched the greying hair on a human businessman.

Vanin's fingers gripped mine on the rail and I flinched. Her eyes glittered.

'Can't you see, Dren? I've done it.' She flung an arm toward the rocket. 'By this time tomorrow we'll be back in our ship. We can repair the drive and be on our way home!' A beatific dream of homecoming slid over her face.

I pulled free of her touch. 'We haven't heard from our people on the colony world, Van. We don't even know—'

'We do know.' She cut me off with a sharp gesture of denial. 'We got the signal from the colony when they started the homing beacon for us, remember?'

'But that was four hundred years ago,' I said gently.

She paced a few steps away, her eyes fixed on the rocket. 'They'd have a lot to do. Rescuing us wouldn't be a priority. Setting up the colony would.'

'Rescuing the Prime Blue not a priority?' I managed to suppress a laugh but not the sarcasm. 'Could it be you're not as vital as you thought?'

Her claws extended and she rounded on me with green eyes ablaze and skin flushed to match the dirty-blue sky. 'Sneer if you like, Dren, but when I get back my people will celebrate for a year. *They* want Prime rule. I'm still female and can bear a child.'

I straightened and cocked my head. 'Have you considered what you'll do if you get there and find the colony has failed? If they're all dead? Or they don't want Primes to rule any more. Or a dozen other possibilities that might make your obsession pointless.'

'Yes.' She turned back to the launch site.

'And?'

Her smile held genuine puzzlement. She waved a hand toward the distant city, hazed by pollution and glinting in the remorseless sun.

'I'll return, of course! The humans have come far, but these people still need me.'

'Ah.' I slid my hands into my pockets and looked away.

'You're coming with me, Dren.' It was an order from my Prime and, even after all these years apart, the tone was difficult to resist.

I gazed at her with pity. 'No. I'm not. Strangely enough, I care for these people.'

Disgust flickered across her face. 'Yes, you've grown attached to a few over the years, haven't you?' She shuddered. 'I don't see how you could. Or how you can stand losing them when they die. They lead such short lives.'

'Death is part of life. It hurts, but they're worth loving.' I glanced at the digital display on the window. 'But don't let me keep you. Almost launch time. Your chariot awaits, Prime.' I raised my voice. 'SAM, order the transport to the ground floor door. Captain Vanin is ready to depart.'

'Yes, Prime Minister Drencovic,' responded the building's automatic control system.

Van returned my steady regard with scorn. 'You always were soft, Dren. I'll tell them you died on this forsaken planet. No one will come for you.'

I bowed. 'I expect nothing less. Goodbye, Van.'

She spun on her heel and shifted into her latest human form: a young, female astronaut in an Australian Space Administration dusty green uniform.

The elevator opened and dignitaries from the city hurried in to watch the liftoff. I moved aside and took a less central position at the window. Vanin disappeared into the elevator without looking back.

Moments later, a support vehicle raced toward the rocket.

The rocket's ion-drive thrummed to life. Subsonic. Nothing more than a faint tremor through my feet and chest. An ache in my back teeth.

And a different sort of ache tightened my throat. There were times I wished our species could cry.

For me. For her. For the Earth and for Haos.

I withdrew a hand from my pocket and looked at the small, black plastic object resting in my palm. The blue-lit button in the centre glowed, tempting me. I hesitated.

On the window-display, the count began: a discreet ticking of numbers down from ten. The chatter around me settled into whispers and murmurs. Champagne glasses clinked elegantly. Coffee, that rarity from the highlands of Nepal, was passed around and sipped with reverence.

A rumble through the ground signalled liftoff.

I stroked the glowing button with a thumb and sighed as the rocket rose majestically into the sky.

I waited. It continued to spear toward the stratosphere. I'd been deluding myself to think she would change her mind.

When the rocket was the merest dot against the vast blue, I pressed the button.

A silent spark on high. A shower, spraying bright fireworks against the ceiling of the world. Gouts of billowing smoke and fire; cosmic dust. Gasps of horror from my fellow onlookers. Fingers pointed at trails of white smoke spiralling back to Earth. Returning to the surface, forever.

If they found enough debris to study, investigations would show a faulty regulator caused the ion engine to explode.

I tucked the remote back into my pocket and turned away, heart-heavy.

Then I went home, to one day choose my manner of death amongst people I loved, on a colony world I'd discovered—and might yet be able to save.

Infinite Monkeys

First published: Antipodean Magazine, April 2019

Something plucks at the edges of omniscience: an idea that won't be banished, burrowing through space-time. The Being considers it. Hypothetically, it ought to work.

The Being snaps omnipotent fingers.

The Void fills with an infinite number of monkeys. They are capuchins. Because capuchins are cute and even supreme beings have their weaknesses. Each animal has a banana-yellow Olympic typewriter and white paper.

Driven by their reason for existence, an infinite number of spindly fingers peck away at an infinite number of black plastic alphabets. Courier-font letters appear, as meaningless as their typists' existence. What little space remains in the Void fills with the clickety-clack of metal hitting rollers, and the deafening *ding* of the return lever.

Or it would, if there was any air. But the Being brought the monkeys into the airless Void. So only soundless fury accompanies the threshing of arms and the jiggling of bony elbows.

Within a very short time, as far as it is possible to measure time in this timeless place, the capuchins notice the lack of oxygen. Their toothy mouths stretch into silent grimaces. Their doe eyes blink, roll and widen. Their skinny chests collapse.

They die, still valiantly poking at the keys.

Their last, sporadic movements—in keeping with new laws of physics—push some of the limp little forms closer together. Tiny gravity-wells form, dragging other bony bodies and yellow typewriters near. Spaces appear in the mass of fur and metal. Groups form. Gravity increases. The deepest figures are crushed. More are drawn in. Local clusters grow into giant balls of pulverised monkey. The process accelerates, sucking gobbets together, ever-faster; spinning, smashing.

The largest reaches a gravity-threshold.

And implodes.

Monkeys, typewriters and paper vanish soundlessly into a vortex, which gathers speed and power, engulfing everything. Crushing and tearing limbs and keys into unrecognisable pieces, the Hole sucks infinity into its maw.

The Being looks on, intrigued.

All matter disappears. The last little clump of fur and the last, fluttering piece of paper vanishes into roiling blackness. All that remains of infinite monkeys, is their dark absence in the mouth of nothing.

Then, in an indescribable explosion of incalculable energy and light, the Hole spews forth all it consumed. Everything that was, is chewed and spat out into what is and will be.

Now the Void fills, not with monkeys, but with monkey-matter. In its tiniest forms it spins into emptiness. It scatters with all the energy of its source, but with less purpose and less need for air. Spreads, clumps, spirals, and condenses into nascent stars.

The Being raises metaphoric brows and sits back to watch what will happen. It is patient. This is far more amusing than monkeys typing nothings in the hope of something profound.

Some fourteen billion years later, the Being looks down upon one, insignificant, monkey-matter planet on the outer spiral arm of an ordinary galaxy.

And laughs.

The Bard lives.

The infinite monkeys achieve their purpose.

Revolutionaries of the Great Data Centre for All Knowledge and Wisdom

'Right,' I muttered, 'here goes.' I glanced over my shoulder for the tenth time to check the security bot wasn't watching my little corner of the room. But my fellow conspirators knew their jobs and the bot was off investigating a noise in the History of All Things Atmospheric section.

Under my hand, the palm-reader glowed scarlet. The great circular doorway, standing proud between the neat datashelves and flush against the stark white wall, pulsed with power. The runes, etched into its gleaming golden surface and written in a thousand alien languages, lit up in tasteful purple. A deep thrumming vibrated through my chest, growing louder and stronger until surely it must trip the building's Unusual Activity sensors.

Greenish-yellow light seared a bipedal shape onto my retinas then vanished. A few crackling flickers of lightning skipped from the door to earth themselves onto the surrounding datashelves. Something buzzed in the air like an angry insect. The scent of electrical smoke wafted through the room and curled into my slitted nostrils.

I sneezed.

'Bless you,' a cheerful voice said. 'So. What's all this, then? Cool décor. Very futuristic. Minimalist with overtones of extremely boring.'

I blinked away the fading purple after-image and hurried from behind the podium. I stretched out a hand, then hesitated. Who knew what gestures meant to this being? I could make some horrible flaw of cultural etiquette and unleash an inter-system war that wiped out my entire world.

Not that that would be so bad, given the current state of things with our tyrannical leader. But this venture was our last hope. After dozens of failed attempts, *now,* at last, we had the One.

I was sure of it. I'd risked my life and the lives of my fellow conspirators on it. I had to get it right.

I brushed at my pink-striped Polit-issue tunic, and pointed towards a padded seat nearby.

'Please, sit. You are exhausted after your journey through the Portal.' I bowed and straightened, going for regal and confident.

'Huh,' the other-world creature said, glancing around. 'I could actually hear the capital letter in that. Got a beer? I could kill for one. Which is weird, because I don't drink these days.'

The male cocked his head. I assumed he was male. He looked very much like our own people, barring a few small differences, like pale skin instead of fine pinkish scales. A lock of dark head-growth fell across his brown eyes and his mouth stretched wide in what I hoped was an expression of cheer, not an indication he was about to rip my throat out. I swallowed and edged backward.

'Please,' I said. 'Sit. Your need for a…beer…is probably just your electrolyte imbalance after the journey. I shall try to explain in simple terms you might understand.'

Instead, he turned around and eyed the Portal's gleaming golden frame. 'I take it the library book was some sort of transport lock device? Thought it looked a bit strange. The font on the cover—I mean *no-one* uses comic sans these days. And the title? *Dave Saves the World*?' His mouth stretched again, this time revealing the mixed teeth of an omnivore.

I shivered.

'Er…' I managed, trying—and failing—to get the script back on track.

'Well, I'm here, now. Let's get this party started.' He stuck out a hand. In the other he held a flat object made of multiple leaves of paper. 'Dave. Martinez. Programmer. You are?'

'Um.' I stared at his empty hand. He had only five digits. No claws, at least. Tentatively I grasped it in my own seven and we shared the bond of friendship greeting. Though how he knew to pump exactly three times and squeeze once, I had no idea.

He released me, tucked the flat object under his arm and rubbed his hands together. 'Right. What's the deal, then?'

'Um…' I blinked my nictitating membrane twice and tried to think. 'You…er…are disoriented; confused. You've been dragged from your primitive Terran world by our Culturally-Adaptive Portal Key, into a much more advanced culture. It's all overwhelming.'

His mouth opened, showing a pink tongue, and he made a strange, repeated huffing sound. But he seemed pleased, not angry. As far as I could tell.

He tucked both hands into the front of his dark blue leg coverings. No, not into the leg coverings, into some sort of hidden fold in the cloth. I gaped and the potential for such a thing exploded a dozen ideas into my mind. Why, I could…*keep* things in such a place. Little things. Useful things. Like… I couldn't think of anything at the moment but it would come to me.

'Nah, mate.' Dave scratched at the wiry dark growth on his chin. 'I know how this works. I read. You sucked me in from another world-slash-dimension, right?'

I nodded. 'World. Across the other side of the galaxy.'

He lifted and lowered his shoulder in a gesture I didn't understand. 'Which means you need me for something.'

I nodded again.

'Right,' he said. 'Don't tell me, let me guess. Umm…there's an alien spacecraft threatening to blow up your world, and you need someone who can destroy it by programming a virus into their systems?'

I blinked. 'Alien spacecraft? Why would they want to do that? I don't think we know any people who have the power to blow up a whole world.'

'Really?' He seemed disappointed. 'OK. Umm. Then you've got an evil wizard or a despotic king who's holding the city in thrall and you need someone to go up against him, spell for spell, sword on sword.'

He shuffled a few steps forward, waving one closed fist about. 'Ten years with the Society for Creative Anachronism. Just get me a blade.' He looked around the data shelves with their endless racks of neat black infocubes. 'And this place looks like a library to me, which means you're my mentor and I need to learn all these spells quick-smart before we go.'

'Go? Go where? I don't—'

He narrowed his gaze at me. 'Yeah, you're right. That's so overdone these days. And the décor is all wrong.' He waggled his fingers. 'No dribbly candles or dungeons. Although the light-up walls could be magic, I suppose. But I'm gonna go for some sort of electrically-activated glowy-paint. And the shelves look like they're full of very dull records. Black. Square. Perfectly lined up. No imagination, I'm guessing.'

My mouth seemed to be permanently open so I shut it with a snap.

'Besides,' he added, 'no way could I read all of this fast enough to get up to speed against an arch-wizard. Unless you've got some sort of info-dump software you can link me to? That'd be awesome. Hey, by the way, how is it you speak English? Universal translator?'

'What?'

His lips stretched wide again. 'Irony. Nice.' He tilted his head, then slapped at the side of it three times and jumped up and down. 'You…didn't…put…some…sort of parasite into my ear, did you?'

'What?' I repeated, floundering. 'Why would I—'

He straightened and waved a lazy hand. 'Just jokes, mate. Never mind. It's probably that black band around your throat, right? Gadget that takes your vocal output and processes it to my brain wavelengths? Some sort of voice-to-telepathy conversion thing?'

I slumped. 'You could say that. The throat-band is our Identity Collar. That which both lets us be Free of the Shackles of Ignorance and Misunderstanding and yet also holds us bound to servitude from the moment it's welded to our skin at birth.'

My hands clenched into fists and I glared towards the ceiling. High above me, on the top floor of the Building of All Knowledge and Administration for the World, our leader controlled every aspect of our lives with—

'Ahhhh…' Dave rubbed his hands together again. 'Now we're getting somewhere. Bound to servitude sounds very much like you're after a saviour. A super-hero to stand for Truth, Justice and the…' He broke off and frowned. 'Where am I, exactly? And what colour's your sun?'

'Er…kind of reddish-orange, I guess you'd say. You're in

Glodonosivskitadronia, capital city of the Pronstonkekninartidapulian Empire. We're in the basement of the Great Data Centre for All Knowledge and the Repository for the Sum of All Wisdom and Truths of the Farnendackitrunfellkinian People. Here we hold every fact that is known to our society.' I spread my arms wide. 'I…um…work here. Shelf maintenance.'

He snorted. 'Bloody hell, mate. Servitude isn't your only problem. I'm almost scared to ask, but what's your name, then?'

'Bill.'

Now he convulsed into some sort of coughing fit and covered his mouth, his dark eyes dancing. 'You serious?' He straightened. 'You are serious. Well, Bill of Glod of the Pron Empire. Nice ta meet ya. What can I do for ya?'

'What?' Why was this conversation not going to plan? All the previous times had gone perfectly. The import arrived, disoriented and frightened. I soothed their fears and told them what was needed.

They either helped or I shot them with the faz gun currently resting beneath the podium. We couldn't let them out to mingle with the populace or our attempts would be discovered. Their recycled bodies provided protein for the Population, so they weren't a complete loss.

We certainly weren't going to waste power and risk discovery by sending them home, so if they were of no use that was the simplest solution.

Yet somehow, with this Dave person, it was not simple. Where was he from again?

I surreptitiously checked the control board. Oh yes, Terra, a most primitive planet, still learning to control nuclaeic power. So how did he know so much about our technology? And what were these things he spoke of—wizards, spells, super-heroes? None of those words held any meaning.

'Right, Bill, what's next? Hurry it up.' He checked some sort of band strapped to his wrist. Did he have an identity collar as well? 'I don't have long. It's almost two at home and I need to be back by three to pick up the kids from school.'

'Never fear,' I said magnanimously. 'Should you succeed, the Portal to Access All Places will return you at the same time you departed.'

Dave's mouth twisted strangely. 'You guys *really* need to work on your naming. Have you *no* imagination?' He flung out a hand towards the Portal. 'That there, my friend, just has to be the Shadowgate, or…or… the Galaxy Lychgate, or…or…Eternity's Egress.' He screwed up his nose. 'Nah, that sucks. Shadowgate, I reckon.'

I opened my mouth but nothing came out.

'Anyway,' he said, laying the object he'd been carrying all this time on the seat next to him. 'Beside the point. You still haven't told me why I'm here?'

I shuffled sideways, trying to get a glimpse of the item. Runes covered the front. And an image that looked quite similar to the golden Portal to Access All Places. Could it be that his world had information about the Portal? Was that how he knew so much?

'Bill?' Dave waved a hand in front of my oculars and I blinked.

'Oh, yes. You're here because we—my friends and I—are working towards deposing the High Ruler. He has held the world in a tyrant's grip for fifty of our cycles. We are suffocating!'

'Riiiight,' Dave said, eyeing me. 'Well-entrenched, then. I'm betting he's got an army that guns down anyone who disagrees?'

'Yes!'

'Hmmm. Nasty.' He tapped his lips with a finger. 'And electronic surveillance that covers every inch?'

'Yes,' I moaned. 'We can't make a move without being watched. This room is only safe because five of my companions are tirelessly working in the security room for the Great Data Repository. We have only a few moments longer before they must let the bots return or it will become suspicious.'

'Uh-huh. And how many others have attempted this great coup of yours?'

I thought. 'Two hundred and thirty-seven and a half. Including an Iscean and a Kronck, two of the most warlike races in the galaxy.'

'A half?'

'A creature that was made of two merged together. They died gloriously on the fiftieth floor, just seven floors from the Ruler's office. Faz cannons. Very messy. But so close to the final goal.' I held out both hands at shoulder's width apart.

'Don't let that discourage you. Clearly, with your knowledge of our technology, you will be the One to succeed. All our hopes are with you. You're our last chance.'

Dave made the huff-coughing noise again. He did a lot of that. This time he kept going until his eyes leaked. Then he stopped and wiped at them.

'Sorry. But you've really got to stop talking like someone from a seventies sci fi movie.' He rose and collected his paper object. 'Well, it's been fun, but I've got to get back and pick up the kids. I'm not your Chosen One. Sorry.'

'But your knowledge! Your wisdom,' I protested. 'It's like you know us already.'

'I just read a lot. Doesn't mean I actually want to throw myself in front of faz guns. You're so keen, you do it.'

'I?' I touched my collar. 'I could not. He would know I was

coming the minute I went above my designated floor. You don't have a collar. It must be you. We cannot.'

'Wow.' Dave shook his head. 'You really are struggling with this whole revolution thing, aren't you? Mate, this isn't something one person can do. You have to get the whole population behind you. You've got five friends, find some more.'

'But we'll be killed.'

'And I suppose it's okay for me to be shot down?'

I pulled the faz gun from beneath the podium and aimed it at his chest. 'Yes. If you will not co-operate, you will die.'

'Oh, nice. Way to convince me. Look.' He held up his hands, the paper object still in one. 'How about if I give you the tools to do it yourselves without getting killed. Will that work?'

I lowered the gun slowly. 'It's not possible.'

'Well, okay,' he said, 'without *all* of you getting killed.' His teeth showed again. 'You guys just have too many facts and not enough stories. Come with me to where you picked me up. *My* Great Data whatever thingy, my "library", is way more interesting than yours, I'll bet. Here, start with this.' He threw the paper object to me. '*Lord of the Rings*. Big Quest to overthrow Evil Despotic ruler. Should be right up your alley.'

He pointed to the Portal. 'And if that thing really can take me to a specific point in time and space, then I have a television series—*Dr Who*—you absolutely have to watch.'

Four Hours of Instability

First published "Aries" anthology Australian Speculative Fiction
2020

'What the *fuck* do you mean, "it's not there"?' I leaned over, deliberately using my bulk to intimidate. It was a useful tactic. I was a big guy. It saved a lot of boring arguments. Arguments I had no time for right now.

This woman just raised her chin and glared at me. 'I mean,' she said in the slow, deliberate tones of someone speaking to an idiot, 'that particular line is gone. Successfully folded in. Done. No longer an option for hopping. Anything about that not make sense...' she flicked a look at the pips on my shoulder that denoted five hundred hops, fifty-two folds and fifty-eight saves. '...*Major* Joshua Singh?'

I tugged the jacket of my severe black uniform down. She was right, of course, I just didn't want to hear it.

The chronoliser on my wrist bleeped softly and flashed a yellow warning light. I swore again and sank onto a damnably-hard grey bench nearby.

Snatching off my black cap, I ran a hand over the soft bristles of my crewcut black hair and the harder bristles on my chin. I must look like crap. Six months of back-to-back hops and the shadows under my eyes were almost darker than my irises.

But we were so damned close now.

We were all working toward the same end: the hoppers, the line controllers, and the syncers.

We all wanted the same thing: a single, unfractured, peaceful timeline. Then to live linear for a while.

At least until some other arrogant moron came along and screwed it up again.

So, who'd authorised this fold of my line? And how had they fucked it up so thoroughly?

'This is bad,' I muttered, checking my chronoliser. Four hours.

The woman's eyes widened. She glanced back at the holo display, the hub of the control room—a spider's tangle of thin, glowing lines that grew and divided like tree branches from a thick central core. Their glowing tips inched ever upward and outward, second by second, microscopically.

When I'd started work here, it had been a giant ball, with more lines than any human could count. Now the end was in sight—but maybe not for me.

She crouched before me, violet eyes searching my face. She flicked back a ponytail of straight chestnut hair. Only then did I see the pips on her jacket. Seven hundred hops, sixty-six folds, and sixty-nine saves. I straightened.

'Sorry, Major...' I read her nametag: *Amanda Greenway* '...Greenway. Didn't see your rankings. Spoke out of turn. It's just that...' I swallowed, my gaze drifting back to the mesmerising holo display. One of the branches darkened and faded, vanishing to nothing, right back to its lowest branch. I groaned.

'Was it your line? The one you asked me about?' She sat beside me.

Around us the ops room continued in its hushed busyness. Grey sound-absorbent floors and walls. Silver, grey and black chrondatabanks, operated by syncers, like Greenway, in their dark grey uniforms.

Line controllers spoke to hoppers through the subvocal coms embedded into the skin of their throats—a dozen or more intense youngsters standing around the massive holo image, checking, scanning, referring back to the submolecular notes in their glove linesyncs.

Always alert for fuckups.

So, how had they missed this one?

Greenway was still waiting for an answer.

I nodded. '89beta was mine. A shitty, wardump of a line, but 89 is still my birthline and beta's the only one I survived to recruitment age in. Is it really folded?'

She frowned and stared at the miniature holo image hovering above her linesync glove. It responded to the thought patterns converted by the nanotech in her temple and fed information back to her.

I shuddered. Why had she given up hopping to take a sync job? Syncers and line controllers were bonded so tightly to the holo they stayed until death. And they usually started as teenagers and died young. What gave someone that kind of martyr complex? Greenway was by far the oldest in the group. Closer to my linear age of forty.

'Definitely folded, Singh,' she said briskly. 'No mistake. Looks like we found the crucial kill just before the Secondary Event. Once he was dead, that folded 89beta back in to 89alpha perfectly, along with 89gamma right through to sigma so far. The effects are still cascading. It'll take a few hours to be sure of the extent. Neat job, actually. Alpha's primed to fold into mainline, now. Captain Weller gets the fold credit. Still, they should have made sure...'

The images flashed across her holo too fast for me to interpret. Subliminal visions of people's faces, facts, data, names, consequences.

Then the holo vanished and her face blanked.

She rose. 'Sorry, Major. Nothing to be done. I suggest you keep that well-charged until they can reinstate you.' She nodded to the chronoliser on my wrist.

I stood. 'What the fuck was that about, Greenway? Weller folded my line without saving me? What did you see? Why was it folded without notice? No one warned me. No one stabilised me.'

I thrust my arm out and the chronoliser blinked orangish. 'And now all you can say is keep this charged?' I grabbed her wrist. 'Without this, I'm gone. You know that. Like I never existed.'

She stared coldly back. 'Take your hand off me, Major. I outrank you by fourteen folds and eleven saves. I'll have no hesitation in reporting you.' Her mouth twisted. 'But if you don't go charge your chronoliser now, that won't be necessary, will it?'

She jerked her chin at the door. 'Now, go. I'll come check on you when my shift's done. Half an hour.' Her violet eyes held some sort of message my hop-thickened brain was too sluggish to interpret. Numb, I spun away and left the room.

I stalked blindly through grey, low-lit corridors, following the subtle tug of my chronoliser toward my allocated room. Coming back from a hop, one never knew what had changed. A room allocation, wall colour, the name of the station cat. Never anything important. Minor things that were easy to assimilate or ignore. Just part of hopper life. A small price to pay for folding it all back into the single, peaceful line.

Minor, until now. Being eliminated from history was a pretty fucking big change.

I reached my room and the door slid open to my chronosignature. At least it still recognised me. Something, anyway. The room contained nothing but a slab bed, two chairs, a small table and a holo of my parents. There was no point in collecting possessions that might vanish after the next fold.

I slugged back a shot of restorative fifty-eight. Tasted like a cross between pure alcohol and cut grass. Revolting, but it woke me up and I sank onto a chair, staring blankly at the holo of my parents. Their sombre brown faces still stared back at me. Which meant their lives at the point that image was taken weren't affected by the folding.

Hardly surprising. The holo still had been captured six years before Event One divided the world into a hundred plus wartorn lines, and sixteen years before the secondary Event that fractured 89alpha into ten sub-lines.

I'd been born just a few days before Event One. In early April. I shook my head. Like that mattered. My father always said it made me stubborn and determined. I figured the shit that had happened to us had more to do with it.

My doctor-mother and younger sister had been killed when I was four. My engineer father was crippled in the same bomb blast. I'd grown up a street-rat, living hand-to-mouth, a thief at five, a killer at nine, recruited by the hoppers at seventeen.

I'd spent the last twenty-three linear years gladly hunting down Event radixes. Eliminating them in the hopes of eliminating the wars that killed my mother and sister.

That was the goal, after all. Undo all the minor fractures, one by one, until we were able to finally narrow down the one Event that had begun the whole damned mess.

Then we could fold back into the only line that had a peaceful outcome. The one line Admin had decided was the best result for mankind.

Mainline.

I laughed bitterly. Most of mankind. Not me, apparently.

Now, someone had found the secondary Event for my line and undone it—folded my line back into 89alpha.

I'd seen what folding did; what happened to families, towns, governments, whole countries, sometimes—gone. I knew it was for the greater good.

But I'd never expected it to happen to me.

My head ached just trying to imagine how my death might have happened. I'd been in a lot of pretty damned dire situations in the years between 89's secondary Event and being recruited by Chrono Admin. Any one of which could have ended me.

Had ended me.

Dammit.

My chronoliser blinked reddish. Three and a half hours left. Greenway was right. I should charge it. I only existed because it kept a record of me; constantly refreshing the central databank and reminding this limbo-world-between-lines 'reality' of my existence.

There were supposed to be safeguards against this shit happening. They told us when we were recruited: no matter what happens, you're guaranteed a life in the Mainline. Every time we stop an Event, they said, we ensure any hoppers in that line will still exist. *You work for us and we promise you'll live a full life in the Mainline.*

They held out the promise of peace and plenty to those, like me, tempered, trained, and embittered by a childhood of fear and death. A lure too great to resist. Even if it meant a life away from loved ones.

I tore off the badge denoting fifty-two saves and threw it across the room. Fifty-two other hoppers would live because of me. Because I'd taken the time to ensure their survival even as their Event ceased to happen and their line folded back in. But some asshole hadn't bothered to check my lifeline when he folded 89beta.

The door light flashed.

'Fuck off,' I muttered.

'It's Greenway.'

'Shit. Fine. Open.' I dialled another two restoratives, this time with double alcohol, and set them on the small metal table.

The door slid open and Greenway slipped in. She thumbed the lock code on the door and peered down the corridor outside, just before the door shut.

I rose, frowning. 'What the fu—'

Her warm lips on mine shut me up effectively. I froze for an instant, then relaxed into the kiss. Unexpected, but not unpleasant. She melted into my arms and pressed her lean body against me, deepening the kiss with an urgency that spoke of desperation, until I had to break free and hold her off to catch my breath and slow things down a little.

I frowned down at her and she gazed back, panting. Then her eyes widened and she stepped away.

'Shit.' She leaned heavily on the wall and pressed her lips together. 'You don't remember me, do you, Josh?'

I twisted a half-smile. 'You'd be pretty damned hard to forget, so no, I don't. Should I? As far as I'm aware, we met today in the control room.'

She paced twice across the small room, two fingers pressed to her forehead. 'It's starting sooner than I expected.'

'What?'

'It's Captain Weller,' she said, her movements abrupt, impatient.

'He's the one doing this.'

'Look, Greenway...Amanda.' I changed the name at her stricken look. 'Robert Weller is one of the best hoppers we have. What is it you think he's doing?'

She paced a couple more times then collapsed into the other chair as though her reserves had drained. She downed the restorative and made a face. 'That's foul. Now I know for sure you don't remember me. I hate that one.'

I sat opposite and gripped her restive hands. 'Tell me. Are we talking memory purge? Do you think Weller's purged my mind? I thought that was a myth.'

'I thought so, too, but it's the only explanation for you forgetting me.' She nodded. 'And for why Weller was sent to your line to do the fold. He must have found out. *They* must have found us out.'

'Found what out? Start back a little further. Assume I don't know what the fuck you're talking about, because you'd be right.'

Amanda gave a weak chuckle. 'You and I, and about six other hoppers. For six months now we've been working against the Chrono Admin. Trying to stop them from folding us all into one line.'

'Why the hell would we do that?' I'd seen the Mainline. Even stayed there on holidays a few times. Not a goddamned bomber in sight. No hunger, no poverty, no blood spattering the walls like sick gothic modern artwork. Idyllic.

'Some of us don't want our lines to be folded,' she said quietly. 'They weren't so bad. Not as bad as the Chrono makes out, at least. Not perfect, of course.'

'Then you were lucky,' I said harshly. 'Because mine was a hellhole of the worst kind. There is no fucking way I would be helping your little subversion. We need Mainline. We need peace. I want my family to live in that world, not one where a nine-year-old has to kill to survive.'

I rose and strode to the door. 'Now get out before I report you.'

'You don't understand,' she said, staying where she was though her face was pale. 'You found out what was happening before you left on your last hop. You were determined to stop it. Blindly, utterly determined. You wouldn't listen to me when I said we couldn't.' Her mouth twisted. 'But you never listen to me, anyway.'

'Stop what?' I hesitated. She wasn't wrong about my habit of cheerfully ignoring advice I didn't want to hear.

'Chrono isn't saving us any more.'

'Who?' I said, 'You or the whole of humanity?'

'Us. Hoppers.' She pointed to me and herself. 'At least, not all of us. Just a chosen few. That was why I quit hopping. So I could see for myself after two of my friends just...disappeared. I found out Chrono isn't keeping us like they promised. They're letting us die off, one by one. Captain Weller's leading the team that's doing it. They're just preventing Events and letting hoppers from certain lines die. And they always die. Somehow. Even the ones living peaceful lives in their folded lines.'

I frowned. 'Why the hell would Weller do that? Doesn't it cause loop paradoxes up and down the lines?'

She shook her head. 'We were told it would, when we were recruited. Told that if you kill the hoppers who've folded various lines, then the lines unfold again. That sort of thing. But it's not true. I don't know how they're doing it, but the lines are staying folded. Which means—'

'They're getting close to Event One,' I breathed. 'That's the only explanation.'

'But why kills us off? It makes no sense,' she said. 'After all we've done. Why would they renege?'

'Because,' I said slowly, drawing a long breath, 'we're a loose end.' I whirled and stared intently at her. 'If they fold everything back into the Mainline, then what's the worst threat to everlasting peace?'

She frowned, then her face cleared and her jaw dropped. 'Another cataclysmic Event. And the only thing that could create one would be a hopper with intimate knowledge of all the key world events up and down the Mainline. And the installed nanotech to hop back and cause the Event. But who would do that? Why?'

I snorted. 'Have you been to Mainline?'

'Sure. Holidays. Training runs. The usual.' Her soft lips quirked into a half-smile. 'I was born two hundred linears ago, so I've visited a few descendants to make sure they turn out alright.'

'We all do that,' I said absently. 'But there's one thing we never really notice—because Admin don't let us stay long in the Mainline.'

'Which is?'

I stretched my lips into a savage smile. 'How fucking boring it is. Everyone's *nice*. Everyone obeys rules. Everyone's conscientious and hardworking and so fucking happy it makes your teeth ache after a few months. We hoppers don't quite...fit in. Most of us carry too many years of death in our heads. We don't think the same as the natives.'

Her violet eyes widened. 'How do you know what it's like after a few months?'

I threw back another restorative and coughed. 'Because I've been with Weller on a deep cover Event One recon. We stayed a year. Almost drove me insane. Who else has been folded without being saved?'

She paused, thought, then said, 'Wu, Otaga, Hassan, M'temba and Blake.'

'Wu as well? Dammit.' An aching hole opened in my chest and pain fisted around my larynx. I stared at my hands, brooding. Wu and

I had been lovers for that year. The excitement of sneaking around and hiding our relationship a temporary relief from the mind-numbing dullness of conformity.

I cleared my throat. 'That's the whole team who went to Mainline with Weller and I for that year. I'm the last, then. Barring Weller, himself.' My knees gave way and I sat hard on the unforgiving seat. 'I thought we'd failed.'

Amanda cocked her head. 'At what?'

'Finding the crucial kill to stop Event One. But Weller must have found it and not told us. And he's killing us off, just in case anyone *does* work out the cause and tries to prevent the kill.' I frowned. 'Or maybe tries to steal whatever tech caused Event One in the first place. We never worked that out, either.'

Amanda dropped to her knees on the soft grey floor before me and grabbed my wrists. 'Maybe you know it, too! Or Weller thinks you know. Maybe you have the information in your head, somewhere. That's why they've started the memory purge. We must get you to a mindmapping station. Quickly. Once we know for sure, we can restore your line as well.'

She rose, hauling on my arm.

'Restore line 89beta?' I rose, frowning. 'Seriously?'

She nodded vigorously. 'Like I said. Some of us don't want to Mainline. We want our homes. Once we know who Weller's kill target is to prevent Event One, we can stop him. Then we can undo the fold on your line, at least. It's only fair. But we need to get to the mindmapper.'

'Do you know how to work one?' I asked. 'I'd rather not be wiped if you get it wrong.'

She hesitated, biting her lip and eyeing me uncertainly. I moved in closer and slid my arms around her waist.

'I might have been memory-purged of some things, but I'm damned sure I want to remember you this time,' I murmured.

Now it was my turn to kiss her and I took the time to enjoy it. Her lips softened and parted. I pulled her close, running a hand down her back to her ass. With the other I dragged the tie from her hair and slid my fingertips across her scalp. I deepened the kiss, tongues tangling, lips warm and sensual. She groaned and her fingernails scraped down my back.

We broke apart, panting. She glanced at the bed and flushed. I smiled faintly.

'If we're going to check what's in my brain and stop Weller,' I murmured, stroking her throat with a fingertip, 'we'll have to do it soon.' I held up my wrist and showed her the flashing red light. 'Three hours.'

Her eyes opened wide and she pulled back. 'Why didn't you charge it? A mindmap can take hours.'

I shrugged. 'I was about to when you turned up.' I grinned wickedly. 'We could find a way to pass half an hour while it charges, I'm sure.'

She shook her head and retied her ponytail with quick, sharp movements. 'No time. We'll rig a charger next to the mindmapper. Let's go.'

'Wait,' I said. 'If I'm going to help you, I want to know who the others are you're working with. And I want assurance I'll have somewhere to live that can keep charging my chronoliser once we leave here. In case you can't restore 89beta. Not all of the lines have this sort of tech.'

Amanda wiped her palms down her thighs and eyed me narrowly. 'Fine. Yokota, Helms, Fingaardson, and Espana. Wu and Blake were with us, too.' She gripped my hand and looked deep into my eyes.

'We'll restore 89beta, I promise. We'll find a way to be together.'

'Thankyou.' I straightened and flicked my cap back onto my head. 'Weller? Did you get all that?'

My door slid open and Robert Weller entered, flanked by four burly guards carrying stun weapons.

Greenway gaped and backed away. She cast me a pleading look. 'What are you doing, Josh? We're not your enemy, he is. He's the one who killed you. He's the one who killed all your team, remember? Purged your memory of us. We just want to live in our own lines. What's wrong with that? Help us!'

I shook my head. 'Too late. I've seen the other lines. Yours might have been alright two hundred linears ago, when you were born, but now every fucking one is a hellhole of human misery.'

Cocking my head, I shrugged. 'And there's no such thing as a memory purge. We never met until today. You just wanted to get me into the mindmapper so you could find Event One. Nice try, though. Get her out, Weller.'

The four guards manhandled her, protesting, from the room. I sighed and sank back onto the chair.

Robert sat in the chair Amanda had vacated and dialled up two drinks. He slid one to me and lifted his in salute. He downed it and coughed, his grey eyes tearing up.

He ran a hand through his short, blond hair and waited for me to speak. Letting people fill uncomfortable silences with stupid words was one of his strengths. Lean and intense, he was a linear decade younger than me, but so sharp several people had cut themselves on him.

I held up my wrist with the chronoliser and studied it pensively. 'When I was nine, I broke into a house looking for something to steal. Instead I killed a man. It was an accident. He surprised me. I shot him.'

'I know,' Weller said, his deep voice quiet.

I sent him a shrewd look. 'When?'

Weller shrugged. 'The year we were undercover in Mainline. I did some research. Hopped over to 89alpha and beta on the sly. Realised that you'd killed the one man who could prevent Event Three in that line. And in several other lines as well.'

'How?' I asked, turning the full glass on the table, back and forth, until the scrape annoyed me and I threw the drink down my throat in one burning gulp.

He leaned back, threading his fingers across his stomach. 'The man you killed now goes on, instead, to imprison the man responsible for the 89alpha Event Two—before it happens when you're ten. Event Two was caused by an engineer who created a temporal distortion weapon of unthinkable destructive power. He called it The Ram.' He shrugged again. 'But, in his defence, the engineer was actually trying to do something that he thought would be very simple.'

'Which was?' I held the glass so tight my knuckles whitened.

Weller's lean hand pried the glass loose and gripped my fingers. His gaze was sympathetic.

'Prevent a bombing before it happened. To save a woman who died in that bombing.'

I twisted a wry smile. 'There were a lot of bombings in 89alpha. And a lot of women died.'

Weller's lips turned up in an empty copy of my expression. 'But that wasn't the engineer's first attempt. His previous was more successful. The woman had originally died—of childbirth complications—in the year of Event One. The engineer invented The Ram, went back, and caused Event One. The woman and her child survive the childbirth trauma in every line he created—'

'Except Mainline.' I gave a bitter laugh and fiddled with the chronoliser on my wrist.

'Right. In Mainline the engineer kills himself when he finds out about her death, and the child's death. So, he never invents The Ram.'

I closed my eyes, trying to remember the future. Then I stripped off the chronoliser with a sharp movement and held it out to him. 'Do me a favour?'

He raised his brows. 'Anything, Josh, you know that. We've been friends a long time. Anything in my power.' The lines around his mouth deepened and his grey eyes were stormclouds in a stoic expression.

'When you kill the engineer before he marries my mother, make sure she lives a better life this time?'

I dropped the chronoliser into his open hand.

Historical Fantasy

Seeds of Discontent

If trees could walk, my mother would. If humans could grow roots, my father's feet would be buried deep into his land.

He named me Felicity—as though the name was the thing. She added Hope. Yet he is burdened by sorrow born of regret and fear, and she by despair grown from unbreakable bonds.

And I…I carry the weight of both their ties and their desires. The pain of my brother's death at war stabs sharper than his sword—hidden beneath the floorboards of my room. Yet we do not speak of why he left, only of why I must stay.

But, like my brother, a seed of human restlessness in me pushes against the safety of my father's firm embrace. Wanting more. Yet my dryad half is tied to home; bound by more than just tendrils of guilt and comfort. And the warm scents of baking bread and brewing ale vie with a wish to taste the salted ocean and hear the roar of lions.

Not yet, Father says each time he catches me looking with longing and fear out the window, toward hazy mountains. Not yet, when I snatch up my petticoats and run to the door at the sound of an eagle's haunting shriek. Not yet, when I trace a finger over the faded picture of my brother in his sharp uniform, glittering sword by his side.

Go, go, whispers the rustling voice of my mother from her place in the great oak outside. Go before it's too late. You're half-mortal. Your time will be less than an oak's life. And, unlike me, you're unbound, unfettered. Don't wait. Go.

Yet I hesitate, standing in the open door of the house my father built, gazing into sun and sky. I wait, cocooned in four sturdy walls of oak; the sliced up bodies of my aunts, butchered before my father knew of their existence. They embrace me. They murmur of security and protection, of fear and the pain of sharp blades cutting into flesh and timber. Stay, they sigh. Stay and be safe.

At night, when my father drowns in the heavy sleep of ale and guilt and axework, I slip out, carrying a book, and a candle to ward off the temptations of moon and stars. I sit cradled in my mother's oak and read to her. But my words of far-off treasures stir both of us. I douse the candle and we shed our skins and dance, wildlings beneath the platinum light of distant suns.

Always, after, I am afire with the urge to wander, to tread the path of heroes, brothers, and goddesses, to hunt with Artemis, feel Zephyrus' breath in my hair, and kiss Gaia's body with my bare feet.

And yet, I return. For in the window my father sets a golden lantern, a beacon and a question; a wish. He knows I'm out there. He understands, but he fears losing me as he lost my mother and my brother—to grief and the desire for more than this. Whatever this is.

So, drenched in dew and sweat, torn by the hopes of one and the happiness of the other, I go back to the prison of his contentment each night to sleep and dream. And each day I wake and press my cheek to my mother's rough skin and listen to her whisper and coax; wishing.

The years pass, but the yearning doesn't. My mother spreads her branches further, seeking something she can never reach. My father's arms weaken, the axe too heavy, the mill-work too hard. He lays the blade down but cannot easily shed the burden of remorse and loss. He carves delicate, dancing women from the broken limbs of my aunts and cousins, and uses mill offcuts to make furniture. Tables from their legs, benchtops from their bodies.

I taste their tears each time I spoon soup from a wooden bowl, feel their silken skin when I caress a chair, hear their lamentations in the scrape of the saw. Their golden hair lies in wooden curls on the workshop floor. The rich, earthy smell of their timber and sap, their flesh and blood, is the perfume of my childhood.

When I'm younger, I cry for them, with them. Father pats my shoulder awkwardly and speaks of rent and buying new clothes. Soon I stop telling, for I can't bear to hurt him more. But I never stop crying, in secret, while dancing with my mother to the silver sound of moonlight. We lament together and do not speak of her future, only mine.

I grow, as young plants do; blossom, as young humans do. I lengthen my skirts and put up my hair, master the needle, the stove, the curtsey. As I knead soft dough and breathe the tangy warmth of yeast, I gaze out the window, following the soaring flight cranes. I catch my father studying me, worry etching deeper shadows about his eyes and pressing his lips into bitterness. My maps and books of far-away cities pain him, so I hide them, damp with tears of loss, beneath the floorboards. Beside my brother's oiled, wrapped sword.

My father begins to point out young men in the village, judging them as though love is like apples or pigs and can be bartered for with tables and chairs. Something in me knows that to lay my hand within another's—to lay my body alongside another's—will kill the longing in me as surely as taking an axe to a tree. For with the hand and the body come the house and the children; the white-plaster-walled contentment of family and home.

My father's dream.

Not mine.

But yes, mine as well. For who doesn't wish to be loved, to be content, to be protected; to hold small, warm bodies in loving arms; to smell the sweetness of innocence?

Only one for whom those things are not enough.

And what if they're not? my mother whispers when I tell her. What if you have all that—are bound by the arms of a lover and a child—but want more? As I did.

Yet, I say, if those are not fulfilling, what will be? How am I to know what might be enough, unless I try what might not?

I leave her weeping beneath the stars and tryst instead with a young man. He loves me, he murmurs. His voice almost drowns out my mother's crying. The sight of my father's joy on my wedding day almost distracts from the caress of dry winds carrying the smell of desert sands from beyond the forest.

And the years pass. We live with my aging father and I learn to block out the tears of the trees with the cries of my child. Timber becomes merely wood. Night is bed time and no longer for dancing. Lions and sea salt are now in amusing stories I read to the little one.

Bread bakes. Ale brews.

I no longer taste the salt of anyone's tears, except my own.

The comfortable walls of my father's happiness now encompass me and my husband as well. My daughter laughs and plays beneath the great oak, tucking up her petticoats to climb its branches, shedding her blood on its bark. She does not hear the whispers. I barely hear them, myself.

But sometimes, her golden curls flying in an unseen breeze, she stops and smiles at the oak. And sometimes she kisses the bark and laughs at nothing. I catch her staring at the pale spring sky and my heart aches with fear and an echo of old longing. And, hardly knowing why, I hide coins beneath the floorboards, with my old maps and books.

Then comes a day when men arrive at our door. They wear coats of blood, carry axes, coins, and a paper. A war, they say. Ships are needed. Oak will be the bellies, the masts, the figureheads. We will be handsomely paid. My father is dead and cannot protest my mother's violation. My husband owns my house, my land, my mother. He doesn't know. Won't hear my despairing cry. It's just a tree, he says.

The axes rise and fall, hacking into her. The saws chew through her flesh. The soldiers cannot hear screams in her creaking boughs. Cannot smell blood in her sap. Cannot see fear in her trembling leaves.

But I can. And my daughter's wails tear away the rotting fruit of my contentment and lay bare the long-buried seed within. It splits asunder in my breast and I am almost strangled by the twining tendrils of regret and pain.

While the soldiers chop, I pack. I gather the maps and coins from beneath the floor. I belt my brother's sword around my hips and see his image in my reflection. My daughter slips her small hand into mine, my determination echoed in her summer-green eyes. She carries her favourite doll—one of my father's carvings of my mother.

We dress in too-large pants and coats and close the wooden door on my aunts' whispered pleas to stay. We leave in search of lions and sea salt, of deserts and distant mountains. Our bare feet caress Gaia's body and Zephyrus tosses our hair with breezes tasting of sky and snow.

And perhaps we will, one day, hear my mother's laughter in a ship's creaking, her sigh of delight in the wind whispering through her masts. Then, together under starlight, we three will dance across the waves to other lands.

A Maiden's Fate

First Published "RETURN" CAT Press 2017
NOTE: This story connects to "And When We Return" in the
appearance of Dren and the reference to Halleys Comet.

837AD

Near Rouen, Neustria

It irked me that I hadn't yet killed Remi. Seax raised, I glared at my twin—the pale mirror to my black rage—and slashed at him. Remi flinched and barely raised his shield in time to catch my blow. His return attack slapped on my kite shield but had no power. I sneered.

'Remi! Lift your arm and strike harder,' Hagen shouted across the courtyard. 'You fight like a maiden, not a man of sixteen summers! Put your whole body into it!'

I froze.

Remi blanched and his arm sagged. 'Astrion!' he hissed. 'What do I do?' His sky-blue eyes widened into terror beneath the peaked metal helm.

'Keep your arm up,' I snapped, 'or Father'll come over and see it's me training with you. Then we'll both be beaten.' Sweat trickled down my back. I resisted the urge to sneeze as dust, kicked up from the dry, packed earth, clogged my nose.

'But I just can't,' Remi whispered. 'My arm hurts. You hit me too hard. Why are you so *angry?*'

'Because it's not fair that I'm a girl and I can only train when Father's not around.' I smacked his shield and he cowered behind it.

Hagen growled. His heavy steps clomped toward us.

'Remi!' I growled. 'If you don't swing like you mean it, I swear I'll hit you so hard you'll be bruised for a month. Then Father will be the angry one…'

Remi whimpered and brushed a stray lock of blond hair from his face. His eyes flicked over my shoulder and back to me. His narrow jaw firmed. He lifted his arm and swung the wooden seax as hard as he could.

I raised my shield and blocked easily, but staggered to make the blow look more forceful. I kept my back to our father. I wore Remi's tunic and trews, and tied my long, blonde hair back with a leather thong so, unless Hagen saw my face, he should mistake me for one of Remi's usual training partners.

We exchanged a few more blows beneath Hagen's keen gaze before he grunted.

'Better, boy. But you'll never be as good as your older brothers unless you train more.' He continued muttering and strode into the servants quarters.

Remi and I scurried away, behind the main longhouse, gusting huge sighs of pent-up breath as we ran. We collapsed in the shade of our favourite oak and exchanged horrified looks.

'That was close. Why is he back so soon?' Remi said, staring at the wood-and-thatch longhouse. 'He was supposed to be away negotiating for your marriage to Theodulf.' His eyes narrowed and he ripped at a piece of grass, tearing it to shreds between long, blue-veined fingers; a bard's hands, not a warrior's.

'Don't remind me,' I said, tossing my seax and shield aside. 'Maybe the negotiations went badly and Theo's father refused an unwilling bride.'

Remi sent me a cynical look. 'Neither of them care about that. Be as unwilling as you like. As long as there's a bride-price and our father gets Count Berno's promise of men and arms next time the Danes or Emperor Louis's men come, you're marrying Theo.' He uttered a sound of frustration and jammed the tip of his wooden seax into the earth.

'And next time there's war, you'll go with Father to fight.' I leaned my head on the oak's rough bark and stared through brilliant green spring leaves at the turquoise sky.

Remi groaned. He twisted and lay down, pillowing his fair head on my thigh and crooking an elbow over his eyes.

'What are we going to do?' he whispered. 'It's not fair. I mean…you and Theo!' His slim shoulders shook and he bit his soft lips.

I sighed and stroked his long hair, so like my own in colour, but finer and softer. At sixteen summers neither of us were as tall and robust as our older brothers had been. We took after our mother: petite and slender; slow to develop. My breasts were barely fist-sized and Remi's shoulders were narrower than mine.

'I know,' I said. 'Not what I want, either. But what choice to we have? It's a daughter's lot to be sold off like cattle, and a third son's lot to be sent off to war.'

Remi sat up abruptly, his eyes made bluer by the reddening of tears. 'There *has* to be something we can do.' He stared in disgust at our wooden weapons. 'Father thinks I'm defective because I don't like to fight.' He clenched his fists and swallowed. 'Fighting just makes me…sick.'

'I know,' I repeated helplessly, drawing him into a hug. 'Don't work yourself up. We'll think of something.'

'What?' He shoved away, glaring. 'Father's been away a week and we still haven't thought of anything. Now he's back, which means you'll be married to Theo in a few weeks and I'll have to watch…'

'I don't know yet.' I stood and brushed off my trews and tunic. To the west, the sun hung low over the beech and oak forests behind our family estate. 'But we need to get cleaned up. Mother will call us in to supper and I can't go in looking like a boy.'

Remi rose, slapping at his buttocks. Dust floated, sparkling in a late ray of sunlight. 'They wouldn't even notice if you did—or if neither of us came in. We're just…just…things to dispose of. I'm going to die in a war I don't care about!'

'And I'll probably die in childbirth! Believe me, I'm happy to hear an alternative.' I glared at him and stalked away. Tears mingled with the dried sweat on my cheeks but I dashed the salt away.

#

'Astrion!' Gisela, my mother, hurried toward me. She flicked her blonde plait back and wiped her hands on a grubby overtunic that protected her favourite, green linen tunic-dress. 'Where have you been?' She didn't wait for an answer but frowned at me. 'You should have worn your blue gown, but there's no time now. The grey will have to do.' She checked my face, straightened the cream linen cloth I'd hastily thrown over my hair, then inspected my hands. 'What on earth do you do, child, to get such callouses on your hands?'

I yanked free, whipping the offending members behind my back. That Remi and I trained in swordfighting together was known only to

Einhard, my father's thane. To begin with, I'd only done it because Remi was afraid of the men in Einhard's command; all big, rough louts who had no patience for a skinny, timid boy. But now I trained because I enjoyed the rush, the soaring, breathless joy that came with slipping past a shield and planting a well-placed blow on an unprotected body.

'Nevermind,' Gisela said, huffing. 'Go to the strongroom and get out the silver bowls and cups. We have guests.'

I gaped at her. 'Who?'

My mother simpered and squeezed my cheek. 'Your soon to be husband, daughter. Theodulf and his father, Count Berno, are here for your handfasting. The wedding will be next month, when we've had time to make up the rest of your dowry and bride-chest.'

'Handfasting!' My knees sagged. 'Already! But I thought father was just negotiating.'

'Don't be so ungrateful!' Gisela fluttered thin hands to her pale cheeks, her eyes sparkling. 'It's such a good match! You'll be the next Countess of Rouen and everyone knows Count Berno and Theodulf have King Pepin of Aquitaine's ear.'

'But…' I couldn't think of anything that would change the state of affairs. Nothing I said, or even my mother said, would carry any weight with Hagen or Count Berno. I glanced toward the door. Poor Remi. He would be devastated.

'I don't want to hear any complaints. At least you're marrying someone you've known since you were a child. He's a good man.' Gisela passed over her keys and flipped a hand at me. 'Now go get the silver. And tell Rosamund to broach a new mead cask. I understand Count Berno has brought someone from the King's court with him!'

She bustled away, instructing one of the servants to lay fresh straw in the hall, fill the rushlights, and stoke the central hearth.

I slipped across the courtyard as the sun sank behind the oak forest, my heart heavier than the silver I collected. My mother was right, Theo was a good man; and a good friend. He was everything a maid ought to admire: handsome, a skilled warrior, the heir to a powerful man. But what my mother didn't know, was that Theo's heart belonged to another. He couldn't love me, nor I, him.

I emerged from the store room, silver bowls and cups slipping from my arms as I tried to relock the door.

'Allow me,' a light, cheerful voice startled me and I almost dropped everything. Someone relieved me of two bowls but I clutched the rest to my breast and backed away.

Shadowed in early evening gloom, a tall, slender figure loomed before me. I scurried toward the main hall, toward light and family. The figure paced silently beside me. I paused as we came into a flickering pool of light cast by a wall-torch.

'Who are you?' I studied the man's face. He was taller than any man I'd ever seen, but slender and with long fingers and high, sharp cheekbones, his jaw bare of beard and as smooth as a woman's. But it was his eyes that mesmerised and terrified me. They were a blue so dark as to almost be black, but the pupils were gold, and vertical like a cat's.

I gasped and retreated. My fearful breaths clouded the cold night air; an insubstantial wall.

'My lady,' he said. 'Don't be afraid. I'm a guest of your father's. I'm here with the Count.'

'Oh.' The reply was barely adequate. I should have curtseyed but I couldn't look away from his eyes. 'What's wrong with your eyes,' I blurted. Heat burned in my cheeks and I muttered an apology, bobbing a belated curtsey.

He smiled. 'No apology necessary. I'm perfectly safe, I assure you. I was born this way.'

I plucked up courage and peered closer. 'And you can see? You're not blind?'

'Not at all.' He inclined his head. 'In fact my night vision is better than most.' He plucked precariously-teetering cup from my slack fingers. 'But we haven't been formally introduced. I'm Dren. And you must be Astrion, daughter of the house?'

I curtseyed again. 'Yes, my lord.' The heat in my face blazed. 'I hope I haven't offended you. My mother complains that I can't control my tongue.'

'Not at all,' he repeated. 'I find it refreshing to speak with a woman as an equal in this day and age.'

I frowned. An odd turn of phrase. Women as equals? How was that possible. Men were stronger. It was natural for them to tend to warfare and heavy labour and the protection of the family. And only women could bear children, so how could there ever be equality?

A door slammed across the courtyard and I started, glancing over Dren's shoulder.

'What is *that?*' I pointed a shaking finger at the sky over the oak forest. A bowl slid to the dirt with a metallic thud. A handsbreadth above the trees, a fuzzy ball of light hovered in the lavender-dark sky. Two soft, glowing tails streaked across the sky behind it, pointing north. 'A sign from the gods!'

'You still believe in Woden and the old gods…?' Dren turned. He said nothing for a long time, but his lips pressed tightly together and his shoulders slumped. Then he straightened.

'What does it mean?' I whispered, shivering with more than cold as the spring dusk cooled into night.

'Astrion? Where are…' Remi appeared by my side, gaping at the star. He clutched at my arm. 'Is it an omen? About us? It has two tails.'

His voice rose toward hysteria. 'It must be about us.'

'Hardly.' Dren's amused comment broke the spiralling tension. 'It's just a piece of star-stuff, floating in the sky. It can be seen all over the…known world. You're not the only twins in the world, you know.'

I blinked at him. 'Floating in the sky? How can that be?'

He smiled thinly. 'Nevermind. Just believe me, it's not an omen. Not for you, at least.' He inspected Remi. 'And you must be young Remi, then? Theodulf has spoken much of you. He's fond of you both.'

Remi flushed, much as I had. I shoved a bowl into his hands to distract him.

'And we're fond of him, my lord,' I said. 'We should be getting inside.' With one more worried glance at the star, I retrieved the silver I'd dropped and towed Remi inside the hall.

'There you are!' Gisela hurried over and snatched the bowls and cups from my hands. She passed them to a servant with instructions to set the table. She fussed about with my hair again, then frowned at the amber and cowrie shell amulet I wore around my neck. She fingered it and chewed on her lip. 'Perhaps you shouldn't wear this, tonight.'

'Why?' I studied it. 'You gave it to me on my tenth birthday.'

'I know, but your father and the Count…they don't believe in the old gods as my family did. They're likely to…misinterpret this as a pagan sign. Best take it off. Wear the cross your father gave you, instead.'

I glared. 'There's no time to change it now.'

'Stubborn girl!' Gisela wrung her hands and glanced around the room. 'Very well. But take it off and tuck it into your purse.'

I was tempted to leave it on, in the hopes it would discourage the match, but there was no point. It would merely earn me a beating and achieve nothing. I removed it.

Belatedly remembering my manners, I turned to introduce Dren to my mother, but he had vanished. Remi was gone, too. Neither of them were anywhere in the hall. Gisela made a noise of frustration and vanished toward the head table, berating the servant laying the silver.

Theo entered and lifted a hand in greeting. I hurried over and dragged him back outside, into the cold-dark night.

'Why did you agree to this, Theo?' I gripped his wrist and glared up into his dark eyes.

He grimaced and shrugged one shoulder. 'You say that like I had a choice. Believe me, I tried. It was like arguing with a tree. You know my father.' Theo scraped thick fingers through his long, dark hair. 'Once he gets an idea in his head nothing short of a sign from God will shift it.'

I shivered and glanced over his shoulder at the bright, fuzzy star. 'Would he take that as a sign, do you think? Could we convince him it means we aren't supposed to marry?'

Theo raised a cynical brow. 'Nice thought, but he's already decided it means King Pepin will die and we'll go to war against Emperor Louis soon.' His mouth softened into a twisted smile. 'Besides, if I have to marry anyone, I'd rather it was you. At least you know me…who I am, I mean.' His face flushed and he lowered his eyes.

I relaxed my grip on his arm and sighed. 'Nevermind. We'll just have to make the best of it, I suppose. I'm just not sure how.'

He cocked his head at me and grinned. 'You'll think of something, Astri. You always do.'

Count Berno's rough voice, lifted in querulous irritation, called out Theo's name and we both jumped. Berno emerged from the hall and spotted us. His annoyance segued into tolerant amusement. He wrapped his fur collared cloak tighter against the cool spring evening and strolled over. His massive, dark shape blotted out the stars as he towered over me. I resisted the urge to shrink away and, instead, lifted my chin and straightened my back.

'Ah,' he said genially, 'there you two are.' He laid huge hands on our shoulders and my knees almost buckled. 'Come inside. Time we made this formal.' He winked at Theo. 'Then you two lovebirds can sneak away all you like. A handfasting might be a little old-fashioned, but it's as good as a wedding to me.'

Now it was my turn to blush. I followed, with dragging steps, into the feasting hall. I'd never thought of Theo as a husband or lover. The very idea made me cringe.

#

The handfasting passed in a blur. We said vows, bride-gifts were given to my parents. Theo gave me a heavy silver necklace with a circular pendant of sapphires. I gave him a seax, as was tradition. Afterward, I sat in miserable silence at the head table, picking at my food and avoiding Remi's mournful blue eyes. Theo smiled and laughed at the ribald jokes tossed around at our expense, but the smile slid away when no-one else watched. Under the table, his hand squeezed mine and I returned the pressure, grateful.

Before too long, the interminable feasting was over, and all that remained was for my father, his guests, and our thanes to drink themselves under the long tables until they snored with the dogs. Gisela rose gracefully and signalled to me. I stood with alacrity, longing for the peace of my bed in the women's house.

Count Berno glanced up and winked at me. He elbowed Theo and gave him a shove.

'Go on, boy. She'll make a man of you, I warrant. Get her with child so I can have a grandson before this damned war starts. Then you can fight at my side.'

Gisela pressed her lips together and shook her head at my father, but Hagen turned his back and grinned at Berno. Beyond Berno, Dren, who'd sat quietly throughout the boisterous festivities, caught my eye and sent me a sympathetic look. To his right, Remi hunched his shoulders and stared into his mead cup. He threw back his head and drained the liquid. It was his fourth or fifth cup, which worried me. He became a very lachrymose drunk with a tendency to tell his woes to anyone who'd listen. Hopefully Dren could handle him and keep him from annoying Berno and Hagen.

Theo's smile turned forced and no longer reached his eyes. He rose from the table and extended a hand toward me. The thanes erupted into loud cheers and beat their knife-hilts on the wooden tables in a deafening cacophony. The dogs roaming loose in the room howled. Theo's jaw worked and his grip on my hand slackened.

I tightened mine and lifted my head.

'Don't you dare leave me here, Theo!' I hissed. 'You'll shame both of us and our families. Move. Now!'

He sent me a startled look and nodded. We walked, with heads high, toward the guest quarters where he was housed. Gisela led the way.

She paused outside the hut and stood before the door. She folded her arms and glared at Theo.

'If you hurt her, boy...' She wagged a finger and scowled up at him.

I fought the urge to giggle at the incongruous picture they made: the hulking warrior backing away in horror from my petite, unarmed mother.

'Mother, it's fine,' I said. 'Can you find other quarters for Berno and Dren? They were to sleep here tonight but I'd rather we weren't disturbed.'

Gisela huffed. 'The amount they were drinking, I doubt they'll make it off the benches in the hall.' She sent one last glare at Theo before hugging me and hurrying away to her quarters.

Theo stood, shuffling his feet in the dirt. I rolled my eyes and thrust open the door, dragging him inside. I lit a rushlight with a taper from the fire, lowered the bar across the door and heaved a sigh of relief.

'Right.' I turned to face him and folded my arms. 'Now what?'

Theo goggled at me. 'Er…We're supposed to…' He made vague gestures with his hands and laughed uneasily. 'I mean…you know.'

'I know *that,* you fool,' I snapped. 'I mean what are we going to do about us…about this? You don't want to marry me and I don't want to be your wife. So what are we going to do?'

'But…' He frowned at me and sank onto a stool. 'We're handfasted. The wedding's set for next month. What *can* we do?'

'I know. You're right. They've made up their minds, haven't they?' I groaned and sat, dropping my head into my hands. We sat in despondent silence a while, distant laughter and song reminding us of our new state.

'Er…' Theo cleared his throat and looked significantly at the bed. 'What do we do about…?'

I shot to my feet and brushed down my skirt. 'Nothing. But we can at least make it *look* like we did something.' I stalked to the bed and flung back the heavy, quilted covers. My mother's best linen sheets covered the straw mattress. She wasn't going to be happy. I pulled my dagger from its sheath at my hip, pricked the tip of my thumb and squeezed out a large drop of blood.

'What are you doing?' Theo appeared at my side.

I gave him a measuring look and smeared blood on the bottom sheet. 'Now they'll think I made a man of you, like Berno said.' I pressed my lips together. 'At least the Count will stop pestering you.'

Theo glanced away, rubbing at the back of his neck. 'And when you…er…don't get with child?'

'It doesn't always happen straight away,' I said. He was an only child, his mother long dead. Clearly he had no idea about women and I certainly wasn't going to educate him.

I frowned and glanced at the door. 'My only worry is how Remi is going to take the news tomorrow. Our parents will check the bed and everyone will know ten minutes after sunrise.'

Theo paled and studied his hands as they twisted the dagger at his hip. 'I'll talk to him. He'll understand.' He sent me an anxious, doubting look.

I laid a hand on his arm. 'I'm sorry, Theo. This isn't fair on any of us. I promise I'll try to think of a way out of this.'

His dark eyes met mine with a kind of hopeless despair that wrenched at my heart. 'There is no way, Astri. We all know it.' He shrugged and sat on the end of the bed. 'I intended to go to war with Remi. He won't last a day without me there.' He laughed bitterly. 'But even that won't happen. Not while I'm my father's only son and heir, and you're not with child. Ironic, huh? I'm stuck here, and…'

'And Remi will go to war without us,' I finished. 'And he'll die.' I glanced at the unmade, bloodied bed and swallowed. 'We could…try, I suppose?'

Theo gave a half-smile and shook his head. 'No use. I don't think of you that way. You're my sister. Remi's sister. I can't…' He waved a hand at the bed.

He flung an arm around my shoulders. I leaned into his warmth, my body cold and heart weighted by worry. The sapphire necklace hung heavy around my throat; a beautiful slave-collar, tying me to my fate.

#

We awoke with the first grey light of dawn creeping under the door and someone thudding on the timber. I started. Theo's heavy arm lay around my waist. His body curled against mine. We were both still clothed. I shook him.

'Wake up, Theo. Someone's at the door.' I listened to the babble of voices. A horse whinnied in the courtyard. Who had a horse out of the stable at this hour of the morning?

Theo groaned and sat up, running a hand over his face. 'What's happening?'

I rose, straightened my dress and re-tied the cloth over my hair. 'It sounds like a messenger. To reach us at this hour he must have ridden through the night.'

Theo shot to his feet and we exchanged appalled looks. 'The Danes?'

I nodded. 'Or the Emperor's army.'

#

'Silence!' Berno thudded the hilt of his dagger on the table top in the great hall. Every seat was occupied and dozens more thanes stood along the walls. Every man was kitted for war, with sword, shield, dagger and lamellar armour.

I huddled along the wall behind the head table, with my mother, my eldest brother's wife and babe, and some of the thane's wives who'd come to hear the news. Gisela and I clung to each other. She hadn't even asked me about Theo, so great was her worry for her sons. Both of my older brothers stood by Hagen's side; tall, strong, raven-haired and bearing arms.

At the end of the table, Remi stood slightly apart, trembling, small and forlorn in his oversized armour. He hadn't acknowledged my greeting when we met in the hall and wouldn't even speak to Theo.

'Silence,' Berno repeated. The arguments died away and the Count raised his cup. 'It is war, men. The messenger brought news from court. King Pepin is dead. The Emperor has announced he's giving the crown of Aquitaine to his own younger son, Charles, instead of to King Pepin's eldest boy. So our boy-king needs every man that can be spared to march against Charles and Emperor Louis's armies.'

Hagen rose and nodded gravely to his men. 'I expect every man and boy over fifteen summers to join us. But if you're an only child with no heir or kin to work your land, you have leave to stay.' He gestured to his right. 'All of my sons will join me in the battle.'

'No!' 'No!' Theo and I spoke together.

Gisela grabbed at my arm and hushed me urgently. Hagen glared.

Count Berno raised supercilious brows at me and laid a hand on Theo's shoulder. 'Don't fear, girl, your promised husband stays. There's no other…yet…to succeed him.'

My cheeks burned and I glanced at Remi.

'Father…' Theo sent first Remi, then me, an agonised look.

Berno ignored him. 'Men, we leave tomorrow. Today, though…' His mouth twitched into a knowing smile. He nodded to Hagen. 'Today we celebrate!'

My mother gasped and squeezed my arm, her eyes glittering.

The Count continued. 'We've decided to hasten the wedding of our beloved children to unite our houses in this time of need. They'll be married today. This union will strengthen both houses and we will march with the king as one force! To Theodulf and Astrion!' He raised his cup high and drained it. The thanes, my brothers and father did the same.

I gasped, my knees weakening. Gisela held me up, beaming, her fingers gripping my arm so tightly my hand turned white.

Theo hastened to Remi's side and spoke urgently to him in an undertone. Remi hunched a shoulder, his face pallid and eyes huge. He shoved Theo aside. Tears coursed down Remi's thin cheeks. Theo called his name. Remi held up a hand, palm out and ran from the room, leaving Theo staring after him. I edged away from my mother and snuck out of the hall. Hagen spoke my name in angry tones. I ignored him. He could beat me all he liked, later.

'Remi!' I ran after my brother as he bolted between the buildings and headed for our oak. I caught him there, breathless, both of us crying. I grabbed his arm. He broke free and pushed me away with a cry of anger.

'Get away from me! Leave me alone.' He sank to the ground and buried his head in his arms, knees pulled up to his chest.

I dropped down beside him, bereft of words and ideas for once in my life. I wanted to reassure him; to tell him he wouldn't have to go, but I couldn't. He would leave tomorrow and I'd never see him again.

My twin. My best friend. My other half. I would stay and be wife to a man who couldn't love me but as a sister. There was nothing I could do about any of it. My chest ached and my throat closed.

Clouds closed in and soft rain pattered on the leaves overhead, dripping through onto my head. We sat, unmoving, unspeaking, until the sobs wracking Remi's thin body faded to shivers and the weight around my heart crushed hope.

A footfall scuffed on the bare earth beneath the broad tree. I laid a hand on my dagger and sprang to my feet, ready to defend Remi, to fight anyone who tried to drag him from my side.

Dren raised empty hands. 'Relax, child. I'm here to help.'

I sagged against the tree trunk and laid a hand on Remi's bent head. 'How? There's no way out. I'm to marry Theodulf. Remi will go to war. That's been the fate of women and men forever. We can't change that.'

Dren shook his head. 'Where I come from, people get to choose their destiny. It's not forced upon them because of their sex.'

Remi lifted his head, staring intently at the stranger. 'You said something like that last night, when we spoke before the feast. What do you mean?'

Dren stretched out a hand and drew Remi to his feet. He stood the two of us, shoulder to shoulder and stepped back two paces. He looked us up and down, then nodded.

'What would you do to save your brother and get out of this marriage?' He peered into my face.

I studied Remi's drawn, miserable expression and swallowed. 'Anything, my lord.'

Approaching again, Dren took my hands and inspected them.

'You train with the sword and bow, I understand?' He quirked a grin when I hesitated. 'Remi told me last night—after several cups of good mead. Who's the better warrior?'

Remi shrugged one shoulder. 'Astri, by a long way. She could probably beat our brothers if she got the chance.'

Dren nodded. 'And do you love Theodulf?'

'He's like a brother—'

'I didn't mean you, my dear girl,' Dren interrupted me. 'Remi? Do you love Theodulf?'

The blood drained from Remi's face. He shrank behind me, his eyes darting toward the great house. I laid a hand on my dagger again and interposed myself between my brother and this gold-eyed stranger who saw too much.

With a gentle smile, Dren shook his head again. 'Don't fear me, boy. As I said: my people don't segregate the sexes as yours do. All our people are equal; able to choose their own destiny; choose who they love.'

'I don't understand, my lord,' I said. 'How does loving Theo help us? Remi would be stoned if our father found out. Better he goes to war. At least that would be an honourable death,' I said bitterly.

'There's no such thing as an honourable death, child,' Dren said, his expression unutterably weary. 'There's just death.' His lips stretched in a thin smile. 'And there may come a time when you welcome it. But not right now. You both have much to live for.'

'I—'

He held up a hand. 'Just think hard about what you really want. Who you really are. Both of you. When you work that out, you'll know what to do next.' He waved toward the longhouse. 'There's no need to sacrifice anyone's happiness.'

There was a long silence. Remi and I exchanged bemused looks. Dren's mouth quirked in a lopsided smile. He bowed, turned away and disappeared into the great house.

'I don't understand,' Remi said. 'What did he mean?'

I stared after Dren and a smile pulled at my mouth for the first time in two days. I studied my hands, calloused and strong, then Remi's delicate face, so like my own. I stroked the sapphire pendant at my throat and looked again at the house. I'd expected to spend my whole life there, or somewhere just like it, raising children I didn't want to a man I didn't care for.

'I think I know what to do,' I whispered, hardly daring to voice the words, so preposterous were they.

'What?' Remi said.

'You do love, Theo, don't you?' I rounded on Remi.

'Of course!'

'And do you trust me?' I gripped my brother's shoulders and forced him to look me in the eye.

He nodded, but reluctance shadowed his gaze.

'Then believe me, brother, nothing happened between Theo and I last night.' I showed him my pricked thumb.

Remi's face lit up. 'You didn't…?'

I shook my head. 'I'm a maid, still. That star was an omen for us after all. Our fates are tied, but mine's not to be some man's chattel.' I tugged the necklace over my head.

'But the wedding!'

'Theo loves you, Remi. And we're about to fix this unholy mess so we both get what we want. Give me your shirt, trews and armour.'

I clasped the sapphire bride-gift around Remi's white throat.

Flight

First Published: "RETURN" CAT Press 2017

1066CE

Malmsbury, England

'I flew once, Brother Wulfsine. Like a bird. Did I tell you?'

'Yes, Brother Eilmer,' I replied. 'You did tell me. Yesterday, and the day before, and the day before that.' I knew little else about Eilmer save that he spent most of his days in this gloomy space, a converted storeroom in the west range's ground floor. I tucked the rough blanket around the old man's useless legs, then dragged his chair toward the door so he could watch the garden.

Eilmer scratched at his tonsured hair and ignored me, as he always did. 'I'll never forget. Tried to fly from the Danes when they invaded the village. Year of our Lord, 1010. Built myself wings from wood and vellum. Climbed up in the scriptorium tower and flew off, into the sky.' He raised a parchment hand and soared it through the dank air of his cell. 'Like Daedalus. No.' His shoulders slumped. 'More like

Icarus.'

'Yes, Brother,' I said again. 'Your wings failed. You fell and broke both your legs. I know.'

The straw in his bed reeked of mould and urine so I yanked the old mattress off and hurled it out the door, into the cloister walkway. I gagged and coughed at the stench. Hopefully Brother Kenway's illness would pass and he could return to care for the old invalid soon.

'No!' Eilmer's bushy white brows twitched together. His hand curled into a fist and smacked his chest. Dust rose from his black robe. 'My wings didn't fail. *I* failed.' Tears shimmered on his lower lids as he glared up at the heavy timber ceiling. 'I fell because I forgot to make a tail. Abbot Aelfric wouldn't let me try again.'

His gaze slid to the open door, where a sliver of spring-clear blue sky was visible past the cloister's arches and columns. One tear slipped down his creased cheek.

'No,' he whispered, 'that's not true. I fell because I lost faith in myself. I was free again and, as much as I wanted it, that frightened me. So I hid here.'

I paused. 'What do you mean, Brother? Didn't you choose to come to the abbey, either? Weren't you Called to God's service?'

'Called?' Eilmer turned sky-pale, red-rimmed eyes my way, scorn curling his thin lips. 'I was no more than six when I came here. What about you? A boy of fourteen summers knows little more than lust. Don't tell me you felt the Call?'

'No. I'd give anything to go home.' I clenched my jaw and snatched up the broom, turning my back. Blurting out my desire to go home was stupid and pointless. If he betrayed me to the Abbot I risked punishment again. I busied myself sweeping straw dust off the bed frame and cast about for a way to distract him from asking questions.

'So why did you join the Order? And why stay?' I dragged in the new mattress and wrestled it onto the wooden pallet, rearranging blanket and pillow.

'My parents were dead. My village destroyed by the northmen. I…had nowhere else to go,' Eilmer said, his words fading into a sigh. 'Now…it's too late. I wasted my one chance at freedom and it won't come again. And when the Danes return—which they will—I'll have no way…' His jaw clenched and he covered his eyes briefly.

'It's been over fifty years, brother. I'm sure the northmen won't be back.' I punched his pillow into place. 'I'm here because my oh-so-noble parents had no lands to give to a third son and my mother couldn't bear the disgrace of letting me do what I wanted.' Even I was shocked at the depth of bitterness in my tone. I'd prayed for humility, as the Abbott instructed, for months. Yet anger still burned a sullen torch in my stomach.

I turned my back to the old man to hide the hot shame in my cheeks. My foot kicked something that clattered across the rush-strewn floor. I picked it up.

'What've you got there, boy? Give it here!'

Golden afternoon light drifted through the door on dust motes and illuminated the tiny object nestled in my palm. An exquisite carving of an eagle in full flight. No, a man with the body and wings of an eagle. Carved of a piece of oak, each feather was picked out in perfect detail, even the flight pinions, ruffled by wind; each fluttering strand of hair on the head visible; each knotted muscle smooth. The man's face was alight with the ecstasy of one communing with God, his feathered arms outstretched like Jesus on the Cross. The oak's grain mimicked an eagle's natural colouring. I half-expected the creature to flip back its wings and dig claws into my finger.

'It's beautiful,' I breathed.

'Give it here, I said!' Eilmer held out an imperious hand, grabbing at air.

I blinked at him. 'But it's against the Rule to have personal possessions. I should give it to the Abbot.'

Eilmer flung the blanket aside and shoved up from his chair. He took two hasty, limping steps toward me and snatched the figurine from my lax hand as I gaped at him.

'It's a miracle!' I whispered and crossed myself. 'You can walk again. Praise be!'

Eilmer's lean fingers caressed the grotesque. He grimaced. 'Don't be ridiculous, boy. I've always been able to walk. I just got tired of all the praying and kneeling, so I pretended I couldn't.'

I gasped. 'You've been missing out on the masses, the charter readings, prayers…everything! How long?'

With an impatient shrug he tucked the little carving into his belt-pouch and peeked out the door.

'Twenty years or so.' He glared at me. 'I forbid you to tell anyone.'

'But, the Abbot! You must obey the Abbot.' I struggled to find the words and fell back on rote. 'The Book says: *"Have confidence in your leaders and submit to their authority—"'*

'Oh, don't quote *Hebrews* at me, boy,' Eilmer snapped, sitting back down and flipping the blanket over his legs. 'I've been reading the Bible for seventy years. For every quote you have, I can find a contradictory one. How about Romans 12:2: *"And do not be conformed to this world, but be transformed by the renewing of your mind."'* He tapped his temple with one gnarled finger. 'If God didn't wish us to think for ourselves, why did He give us a brain?'

I glanced out the door and wrung my fingers together. If someone came past and heard him talking like this…My stomach growled at the thought of being put again on bread and water for two days.

A footfall scuffed outside and Brother Cuthbert loomed in the doorway. 'You done in there, Brother Wulfsine?' His dark eyes darted around the room, his lip curling.

I flinched and bowed my head to cover my cowardice, hating myself.

'Almost, Brother Cuthbert,' I whispered, glancing at Eilmer. His head lolled to one side, white hair mussed, eyes half-closed, a string of drool sliding from one corner of his mouth. 'Brother Eilmer jus—'

'Brother Eilmer,' Cuthbert sneered, 'is a dribbling old fool who dreams of nothing but his birds and his regrets. Wipe his ass and move yours. You're to clean out the reredorter after Vespers.'

Bile rose in my throat. I'd cleaned the toilets yesterday. Today was rostered to someone else. Cuthbert's sly smile challenged me to argue. I held my tongue and hunched a shoulder.

He laughed, showing broken, blackened teeth. 'I can always come and…motivate you again.' He rubbed a hand down his inner thigh and his grin turned to a leer.

I said nothing, my face flaming. Cuthbert left with a chuckle.

He paused and turned back. 'I forgot.' He withdrew from his robe a folded parchment, sealed with a lump of red wax. My heart leapt. I knew my father's seal. Cuthbert's grin widened. 'You know the Rule. No letters from family or friends. Your parents didn't want you. Be grateful God does.' He tore my letter into tiny pieces and crushed them in his hand.

I clenched my fists, shaking in an effort not to fly at him. He was twice my age, a full head taller and with fists of lead. He laughed again and strolled away. Tiny bits of parchment fluttered to the ground like plucked feathers.

I let out a wordless cry and stalked twice about the room, tears tracking my cheeks.

Eilmer's chair creaked and I spun, glaring, waiting for some wise, monkish advice to spill from his mouth so I could throw it back in his face.

'So you can read, can you?' He wiped off the drool and patted his hair into place.

'Yes,' I said, taken aback. 'Latin and Greek. Brother Godric, our tutor at…home…' The word gathered my grief and anger into a ball that lodged in my throat. 'Brother Godric taught me.'

Eilmer's mouth twisted into a wry smile. 'Read any books from the library's restricted section?'

'Er…no?'

Eilmer was silent for a moment, staring at the door, then said gruffly, 'Well, meet me up in the library tonight after you've sung Compline and the dormitory roll-call is done. I have something to show you.'

'You want me to sneak out of the dormitory to see a book?' My heart pounded.

'You look pale, boy. Afraid?' Eilmer's eyes narrowed.

I hunched my shoulders. 'Five months ago I snuck out and tried to run home. Brother Cuthbert caught me. The Abbot ordered me to silence for a week and bread-and-water for two days. Cuthbert locked me in the cells beneath the east range for three days. He…' I shuddered. I couldn't bring myself to tell. 'Now he watches me like a hawk and reports every mistake to the Abbot.'

'I wondered why Cuthbert made you his latest chew-toy. And he gave you that black eye you're sporting?'

I nodded, touching the bruise. 'I was late for Matins.'

'Don't worry.' Eilmer broke into a yellow-toothed grin. 'We won't get caught. And it'll give you something apart from home and Cuthbert to think about.'

I hesitated, the lure of reading something other than the Bible, or the chapters, warring with fear of incurring the Abbot's displeasure again.

Eilmer grasped my hand and squeezed it. 'Don't fret, boy. I won't let them hurt you, I promise.'

The bell rang for Vespers, its deep tones reverberating through the cold stone walls. I gritted my teeth, hating the noise for the first time since I'd resigned myself to this life, five months before. The soft, obedient shuffle of feet rustled in the cloister walk outside.

'Go,' Eilmer said. 'Meet me in the library if you've still got any life burning in your belly. Wait.' His call stopped me as I reached the door. 'What did you want to be, boy? What was your mother so ashamed of?'

I kicked at the patterned brick floor, cheeks burning again. 'A falconer,' I muttered. 'I like birds.'

'Get along, boy.' Eilmer uttered a crack of laughter. 'You'll do.'

#

I fled to the chapel to take my place in the choir. But my thoughts were on the evening ahead and my concentration faltered. With my voice yet unbroken, every mistake lilted Heavenward in the cathedral's vaulted space. Cuthbert smirked at me and Father Beorhtric, our Abbot, scowled at me twice in the psalms before I forced myself to focus.

The few hours between Vespers and Compline passed in a blur and I hurried through my duties in the reredorter and gardens. After Compline was sung, and my own meal eaten, I lay in my bed and stared into darkness, listening to the snores and rustlings of my dormitory mates. My eyelids drooped and the soft warmth of my bed appealed more than the library's cold stone floor, or the ache in my stomach and body should I be caught and left again to Cuthbert's mercy.

But curiosity won and I slipped from under the covers. Shivering in the cool spring evening, I tiptoed between the beds and eased out of the dormitory. Stars bathed the cloister and garden in fey silvery light, brighter than usual. The abbey lay dark and silent, save for one lantern, burning in the Abbot's study. I froze as his silhouette passed twice before the leaded-glass window. The golden glow snuffed out and only the night's frosted glimmers lit my path.

I stole up the night stairs, trailing my hand along the stone wall as a guide in the darkness. At the top of the stairs, the door to the scriptorium and library stood ajar. I held my breath. The room was locked each night. Only Brother Halig, the librarian, and Father Beorhtric had keys.

Poised to flee, my heart thumping in my ears, I pressed two fingertips to the wood and pushed. The door swung silently open but the library was quiet. I crept in.

'Ah. You've come, have you?' Eilmer's voice whispered.'You source of tears to many mothers, you evil. I hate you! It's long since I saw you; but now you are more terrible, for you brandish the downfall of my country. But what more can you take from me?'

I gasped and backed away. Eilmer stepped into the misshapen rectangle of white light pouring through the open west window. His gaze was fixed on something outside. I glanced out the window and froze, gaping.

'What is it?' I whispered. Low above the western horizon, hung a ball of light four times the size of any star. Not the moon, yet to rise in the east. Three hazy streaks of light harnessed the star, tethering it to the sky like the reins of a celestial chariot. I crossed myself and muttered a prayer.

'An ill-omen,' Eilmer said, his voice low and harsh. 'One I'd hoped never to see again. Prayer won't help you, boy. Nothing will.'

'When did you see it before?' I couldn't look away, fascinated by the way the light balanced in the night sky, motionless. Where had it come from?

'Many years ago. Nine-eighty-nine, when I was a boy of six. It boded ill then and it does, now.'

'But what does it portend, Brother? What happened last time?'

Eilmer turned a bleak look on me, his face ghost-lit by the star. 'The Danes raided Malmesbury. My father died, trying to save me. They took my mother as a slave and left me to die. One of the brothers found me, half-dead, in the stream below the abbey. That's how I came to be in this place.' He limped toward the library's far end.

I followed. After hearing Elmer's tale, the ache to see my father grew again in my heart and I frowned to hold back tears.

'So what do you think this visitation means, Brother Eilmer?' I persisted. 'Is it a sign from God?'

'It means the Danes will come again,' Eilmer said. 'We need to be prepared. They sacked the Abbey in December 1010 and half our brothers died. I tried to fly away, but almost died. This time I won't be caught. The Abbot won't stop me. Look here.'

He unshielded two tallow candles on the study-table. Laid out on the oaken tabletop, was a book I'd never seen before. Eilmer turned a crackling page and a superb drawing of a man with outstretched arms and gilded wings shimmered in the candlelight. The man's face bore the same expression of ecstasy I'd seen on Eilmer's carved figurine. Behind him, a second winged figure soared, silhouetted against the sun's brilliant yellow disc.

Eilmer pointed at the writing. 'Read. It's the story of Daedalus and Icarus.' He leaned close and peered at me. 'Then, once you understand, you can help me. I can't do this alone and I'm running out of time. I know that, now.' He glanced over his shoulder at the window.

Obedient, I read the story. Immersed in the trials of Daedalus and his son, I barely noticed Eilmer moving about the library, muttering to himself. As Icarus plunged into the sea and Daedalus bewailed the loss of his son, a tear dropped from my cheek to the page and blistered the parchment. I wiped it away. The old man leaned over the desk and smiled at me.

'Will you help me, boy? When the Danes come, we'll be free. You can return to your father.'

I traced the gleaming figure of Daedalus, curled around his grief, mourning his son. My father hadn't wanted me to leave. What had he written in that letter—a plea for my return?

'Yes,' I whispered.

'Excellent!' Eilmer rubbed his hands together. 'I'll make you a list of what we need. You can move about more freely than I. Timber, vellum, feathers, glue, twine.'

'Where will we store everything, Brother?' The Abbot subjected the dormitory to regular bed inspections to root out any hidden personal items.

Eilmer's grin widened. 'Beorhtric gave up inspecting my room when I pretended incontinence and pissed on him. Everything will fit under my bed. Never fear, boy. You just come to my room each night after Compline. We can work until Matins. Time enough for sleep after.'

'Oh,' I said. How was I supposed to function on a couple of hours between then and Prime, at dawn?

'Come, boy. Almost time for Matins, now. Get to the chapel. I'll have the list for you in the morning. We'll start tomorrow night.' Eilmer snuffed out the candles and limped to the window, staring out into the night.

I slipped downstairs and regained my bed moments before the bell rang and my pious companions rose for Matins. I joined them, but my mind dwelt with the old man in the library. Was he mad? Was I mad for agreeing to help him?

#

In the morning, as I yawned my way through Prime, Brother Cuthbert eyed me with a malicious gleam in his puffy eyes. During the discussion of house business, I held my breath, awaiting denouncement by Cuthbert for my trip to the library, or punishment for my mistakes in choir. Neither came, but fluttering disquiet still twisted my stomach into knots.

After high mass and dinner at noon I arrived at Brother Eilmer's room, breathless from running the long way around the west range to avoid Cuthbert's searching gaze.

'Here, boy.' Eilmer wasted no time, but pressed a scrap of parchment and a silver coin into my hand. 'Go to Brother Iuwine, the chamberlain. Tell him: Proverbs 18:21

I searched my memory. '*Life and death are in the power of the tongue.*'

'Very good, boy,' Eilmer beamed. 'Tell him I need these and if he wants my continued silence on that other matter, he'll provide them without question. Tell him I'll consider all debts paid and everything forgotten.'

I stared at the coin and list in my hand, wide-eyed, unable to imagine where he'd got the money, or what the bluff and hearty Brother Iuwine did to put himself into Eilmer's power. A cool warning in Eilmer's blue eyes stopped the questions on my lips.

'Good lad. Go.' Eilmer smiled. 'When we meet in the library tonight, I'll show you some of the other Greek myths.' His eyes softened. 'The world's a wondrous place, boy. Let's discover it together, shall we?'

#

It took several weeks to gather all the supplies, for Brother Iuwine couldn't buy everything at once without alerting the Abbot to the extra expense. While we waited, Eilmer tutored me using texts I'd never heard of: Greek, Roman, even Persian and Moorish.

In the second week Eilmer vanished for half an hour and emerged, dusty and triumphant, from a back room. He handed me a gilded tome that made me gasp in delight: a book on falconry written by the royal falconer to King Aethelred. Eilmer chuckled and waved aside my stammering thanks as I poured over the drawings and soaked up the lore.

With each passing day, as my admiration for the old man grew, so did my fear. When I opened my eyes every morning, my heart sank and knotted my stomach. But my fear was no longer for being caught. Discovery was inevitable and I'd resigned myself to punishment.

There was no way to hide Eilmer's contraptions forever.

My fear now was for him.

An ephemeral flame of excitement burned, incandescent, in the old man; spurring him to action, causing him to stutter as he explained his drawings of the wings. Long after the strange hairy star had vanished from the night sky, the light in Eilmer continued. It intensified as the sultry months of summer passed and he became more convinced of the need for haste.

But it was only a matter of time before the sharp-eyed Cuthbert discovered our equipment and destroyed it. Losing the wings would kill the old man this time.

#

'Autumn's here. The northmen are coming. Soon. I can feel it.' Eilmer gazed out the window to where the half-moon bathed the landscape in feeble silvery light. 'We need to trial the wings, boy, and we can't do that at night.' He thumped a fist on the library table.

A book clattered from the shelves and I gasped, looking toward the door.

'Oh, stop,' Eilmer said. 'We've been sneaking around for months and no-one's the wiser. Especially since you stopped yawning your head off all day. The wings are finished. We need a way to test them.' He laid a hand on my head and ruffled my hair. 'Then we can get out of here. Somewhere safe.'

'Yes, Brother,' I said. I swallowed down a rush of fear and excitement, forcing myself to consider practicalities. The wings had been nothing but theory and plans for so long I half-believed they'd never be ready. Now reality intruded and all the potential problems reared their hydra-heads. 'But how can we test the wings during the day?'

Eilmer scratched at his tonsure and frowned. 'High Mass, I think. You go as usual. And when everyone's at prayer, I'll come up here.' He pointed at a low door in one corner of the library. 'I know where Brother Halig keeps the key to the roof parapet. I'll have time to test it and return before High Mass and dinner are finished.'

'But someone will see you, Brother!' I waved a hand at the window. 'Malmesbury's at the base of the hill.'

'Pfah!' Eilmer dismissed the village with a flick of his fingers. 'Unlettered rustics. No-one will believe them and I'll be back in my room pretending to be a mindless fool before they can report to the Abbot.'

'Well, then…how can you be sure the wings are safe this time?' I studied the hide-wrapped timber frames and the thousands of goose-feathers stitched in neat lines. My fingers still ached from needlework. 'They look so…flimsy.'

'Because I know they're safe,' he replied.

I studied him dubiously from beneath my lashes but held my tongue. Eilmer chuckled.

'You look like a terrified rabbit, Wulf. There are worse things than bread-and-water and Cuthbert's…attentions.'

'Like?' I snapped.

Amusement fell away and his face sagged. Shadows darkened beneath his eyes. 'Letting fear stop you from living.'

The bell tolled for Matins and I jumped from my seat. 'I have to go!'

Eilmer nodded. 'I'll tidy up.' He smiled at me and I dashed away.

I stumbled down the dark stairs and skidded to a halt at the base, pressing myself against the stone wall as I tried to breathe quietly. My dorm-mates stumbled and trudged toward the church, tugging their robes straight and scrubbing at their eyes. As the last man passed my hiding place, I flipped my hood up and slipped into line. The man before me glanced over his shoulder. Cuthbert. His eyes narrowed and he flicked a look at the night-stairs. My heart stuttered.

After Matins and Lauds, I tossed in my bed, unable to sleep for the unanswerable questions roiling in my head. Had Cuthbert seen? Would Eilmer crash again? He was eighty-three years old! Madness for him to attempt such a feat.

But I couldn't miss any masses and the abbey grounds were full of people in between times. The moon wasn't full, so we couldn't test the wings at night. There wasn't enough wind, anyway. Was I going to be responsible for Eilmer's death? Should I tell the Abbot?

#

Morning brought no relief and I struggled through the rituals and masses with my mind elsewhere. Eilmer was asleep when I brought his breakfast so I left it and hurried away to my duties, still uncertain.

As I sat in the back of the chapter house, waiting for Father Beorhtric to begin the discussion of house business, I glanced out the door. The sun crept higher. Every minute brought High Mass closer; Eilmer's death closer. I couldn't let him die. The old man meant too much to me. This was madness.

Father Beorhtric called for anyone with issues, grievances or maintenance problems to stand and report.

I began to rise.

'I regret, Father…' Cuthbert's ingratiating voice intruded on the silence. 'That someone has been using the library after hours. Reading books from the restricted section.' Whispers washed around the room. He raised his voice. 'And the chamberlain's inventory shows missing items. Someone has stolen from us, brothers.'

I froze, twisting my robe in my fingers.

The Abbot rose from his chair and waved the men to silence. 'These are grave accusations, Brother Cuthbert. What does the chamberlain say? Brother Iuwine?'

Iuwine stood, shifting uneasily, his jowly cheeks beet-red. He cleared his throat and cast a furious look at Cuthbert. 'It does appear, Father, that there are some…discrepancies. I'll investigate. It could be a mistake.'

Cuthbert puffed his chest out. 'Father Beorhtric, we can't waste time. If there's a thief we must search thoroughly before the goods can be disposed of in the village.'

The Abbot stroked his chin. 'Perhaps you're right, brother. Instigate a search. We'll find the culprit now, if there is a thief.'

'*Every* room, Father?' The sly look Cuthbert shot me stopped my heart. He knew. He would search Eilmer's room and expose the old man's secret. Eilmer would be punished, his precious wings destroyed. With his dream of freedom crushed, his frail body couldn't withstand the rigors of bread-and water, or the damp cell beneath the east range.

'I did it, Father.' I leapt to my feet. My voice broke as I repeated my words into a stunned silence. 'I stole from the stores and I read the restricted books. I…I sold the goods back into the village so I could…pay someone to carry letters to my parents.'

A smirk flashed across Cuthbert's lips.

Beorhtric sighed and sank back into his seat. 'I'm sorry to hear that, Brother Wulfsine. I hoped you'd left the world behind and accepted God at last. Your punishment will begin immediately. A week in the solitary cell, bread-and-water for two weeks and silence for a month. You will come to me daily for prayer and further instruction. Brother—'

The side door crashed open and a village boy staggered into the chapter house, breathless and red-faced.

'My lord Abbot! I'm sorry, but there's a message from the Earl.' He waved a red-sealed paper but stayed at the door, his eyes darting around the room.

'Take it to my office, boy,' the Abbot snapped. 'Don't interrupt your betters.'

'But my lord said you must know now: Harald Hardrada of Norway has landed men in Northumbria. They march south to put Tostig Godwinson on the throne of England. And William the Bastard of Normandy has landed in Hastings. He claims the throne, too.' The boy paused, staring wide-eyed at the Abbot. 'We're at war, Father.'

The room erupted in shouts. Cries of fear echoed to the rafters. All the brothers sprang to their feet, arguing and waving their hands.

I edged toward the door. Eilmer needed to know. He was right: the star had foretold the coming of disaster for our king and the coming of the northmen.

'Brothers!' The Abbot's voice rang out over the babble. I bolted, for even the invasion of England wouldn't stop Cuthbert from meting out the punishment ordered for me.

I reached Eilmer's cell and flung open the door.

'What ails you, boy? You're as white as death.' Eilmer sat up in bed and frowned. 'What time is it?'

'Not yet time for High Mass, brother. But there's news from London you must know.' I stammered out the message. 'You were right. The omen was right. The northmen are coming.'

'There you are you hedge-born levereter!' Cuthbert's meaty fingers wrapped around my upper arm. 'If the northmen sack the Abbey, they'll find you in the cell where you belong.'

'Brother Cuthbert!' Eilmer's call stopped Cuthbert, who turned an astonished gaze on the old man.

'What do you want, you old ceorl? This has nothing to do with you.' Cuthbert cocked his head. 'Or does it? Perhaps it's you should go to the cells?'

'What are you talking about, sirrah? What's this boy accused of?' Eilmer pulled his shoulders back and stared down his nose at Cuthbert.

'Stealing the Abbot's property and breaking into the library. Admitted it before everyone.'

Eilmer paled, his eyes fixed on me. 'He admitted it! But I—'

'No!' I scowled at him and shook my head. 'I know I've disappointed you, brother. I'm sorry. But it was important. I wanted to let my parents know...' I sucked a deep breath and willed him to understand. 'To know they were right: it's better to live your life and be free than waste it in regret. I regret nothing.'

Eilmer was silent.

'You'll regret this, Brother Wulfsine.' Cuthbert giggled. His fingers tightened until the blood stopped flowing and my arm grew numb.

I sent one more warning look Eilmer's way when he opened his mouth again. Cuthbert hauled on my arm and I went, unresisting. But the conviction upholding me melted beneath his glare, disintegrating as he pawed at my body then slammed the door shut on the musty cell. Cold seeped through my robe and I shivered, plunged into an ocean of despair.

The key clicked in the lock and Cuthbert laughed as he strolled away.

With my back against the cold, slimy wall, I sank to the floor and buried my head in my arms. Eilmer would fly free, as I'd told him to. I'd either die here, spitted on the sword of an invader, or live out my life as Eilmer had: tied by fear to a place we both detested.

The bell tolled for High Mass, then for Sext a while later. If Eilmer heeded my message he would be long gone now. I envisaged him, soaring over the rolling hills; Daedalus, beloved of Athena, free at last, able to go anywhere and evade the northmen.

The bell tolled again. The alarm-ring, not the call to prayer. I leapt to my feet. Had the northmen arrived already? My heart thudded in my ears. Footsteps clattered past my door. I pounded on the timber, demanding information, calling out for help.

At last the door opened and Father Beorthric's stern visage appeared. 'Brother Eilmer is gone. What have you done, boy? Where is he?'

I shrank away. 'I don't know what you mean, Father. I've been here.'

Beorthric dragged me from the cell and pushed my back against the stone wall. 'Don't lie to me, Wulf. I read the list of stolen goods. Vellum, timber, glue, twine, feathers. Do you take me for a fool? I know what Eilmer did in his youth. The whole abbey knows he wanted to repeat his madness. Did you help him?'

I nodded. 'He wanted—'

'I don't care!' Beorthric cut me off with a wave of his hand. 'You're both idiots. He's an old cripple. He won't survive the day, even if his contraption does work. Now get out there and find him. We'll discuss your punishment when you return. Be back by dark, whether you find him or not.'

He stalked away, muttering and swearing in such foul terms I never thought to hear from the mouth of an Abbot.

Without waiting, expecting a cry of 'halt', I bolted for the nearest exit. Outside in the warm autumn sunlight, I lifted my face to the sky and sucked a breath of clean air.

#

To the north and east voices lifted in desperation called Eilmer's name. I looked southwest, into the wind. If Eilmer had launched from the tower, that's where he would be headed. I picked up the skirts of my robe and ran.

Down the dusty road toward town I fled, panting as my heart pounded. At the crossroads on High Street, I paused. Last time Eilmer had crashed not far from here. This time, with the tail, he would make it over the river and be free.

I skirted a bread-vendor, and a furrier plying his trade from a wagon, house to house. I sidestepped a pile of steaming horse-dung and ignored insults and laughter as I ran in unseemly haste through town. Past thatch and timber houses, past the Kings Arms tavern, raucous with laughter even in the day. Breath burning in my lungs.

Cutting through a garden and hedges, I startled a pair of chickens roosting on a two-wheeled cart that leaned drunkenly against a cottage. The birds skrawked and fluttered away as I raced downhill toward the riverbank. Looking skyward, I shaded my eyes against the afternoon sun.

There, high above: a black dot, soaring in the sky, swooping, circling. Surely too big for a hawk? Grinning, I squinted against the glare, trying to get a better view. It must be Eilmer.

Something caught my foot and I tumbled to the loamy soil and damp grass. I laughed at my clumsiness and looked back to see what had tripped me.

A broken piece of timber, the tattered remains of torn white and black feathers still clinging to the ripped vellum. A few steps further, Eilmer's wretched body lay twisted on the brilliant grass; his arms outstretched, still bound to the wings' shredded remnants; blood matting his wild, white hair. Scattered all around, feathers drifted and fluttered across the grass, caught up by the wind and released again, carrying the dregs of an old man's dream.

I crawled to his side and cradled his head in my lap. My tears dripped onto his cool skin. No breath drifted from his lips, no heart pulsed in his breast. He wore the tunic and hose of an ordinary peasant, a leather cap covering his tonsure. His open eyes reflected the sky: empty, blue, soulless.

We stayed that way for long moments, my joy shattered with his wings. Then a distant cry of Eilmer's name brought fear surging back. Cuthbert's voice! I glanced around at the trees swaying in the wind; at the bright sky and soft clouds, the hawk wheeling overhead; at the abbey belltower, visible on the north hill behind the village.

They would come for him; bury us both deep in the abbey.

Not far away, amongst the wreckage of Eilmer's wings, lay a leather satchel. I fetched it and scrabbled through the contents. A change of clothing, a small leather pouch, the little oak carving, and a book. I opened the pouch and gasped. Silver coins gleamed in the sunlight; a fortune.

Cuthbert's voice called Eilmer's name again, closer this time. I clenched the pouch in my hand, pocketed the bird-man carving, and picked out the book. It was not, as I expected, the Greek mythology tome that had started us on this journey. It was the falconer's guide. I hugged the book close to my chest, and bowed my head, fresh tears burning my cheeks.

Cuthbert yelled once more; strident, angry.

I stripped off my black robe and shoved it deep into a hedge. Donning the spare clothing, I dragged Eilmer's wasted frame over to the cottage. The chickens protested as I shooed them away and loaded Eilmer into the two-wheeled cart.

I left four silver coins on the cottage's front stoop, grasped the cart handles, and turned my face south.

A Gift for Aphrodite

First published in "Pisces" Australian Speculative Fiction 2020

I hook my toes beneath a coral-crusted rock; cling to the ocean bottom, so I won't float away. Today is my sixteenth birthday and I sit there in the cold gloom and wish for my father. Just for a moment of his star-eyed attention. An instant to acknowledge me. To show more than infinite indifference.

Not his presence, here beneath the sea, for that would unmake the world. And I don't hate it enough for that.

My long hair drifts around me like seaweed. The cold water pushes me to and fro and I sway with it, letting my arms undulate. Delicate white fingers of light stretch down toward me, making shadows dance on my pale skin.

All around, clicks and squeaks are the background music of my life and I barely hear them. Fish flicker past, silver and blue, their blank black eyes dismissing me. Much as my father always does.

I grind my teeth then force my shoulders to relax. He will see sense. He must. He will listen to my nephews, Bythos and Aphros, when they plead my case. He cannot make me marry one who, it is whispered, beats his concubines; brands them with steel hot from his forge.

But my father finds my very existence uncomfortable. Perhaps he will refuse to hear their plea. He has ignored me for the first sixteen years of my life, let my nephews raise me.

I understand.

In a way.

I was born from an act of pure hatred. I remind him of his wife's anger and pain.

So he pretends I am nothing.

Not all the love my nephews pour on me has ever quite made up for that. And all the stories they told me of the other gods—my family—just dug the chasm of loneliness deeper into my heart. How I wished to ride on Helios' chariot, to study medicine with Apollo, to play at war with Ares, to hunt with Artemis.

But I am alone. Outcast.

I want to blame someone. To hate someone in turn for what hatred did to me. Bythos and Aphros are impossible to dislike, though. And hating my father is pointless—he takes no notice of the world.

Not since his wife, Gaia, convinced my Uncle Kronos to castrate him with a stone sickle.

Not since Kronos flung Ouranos's manhood and the sickle into the sea.

Not since my birth.

Hating Gaia and Kronos is pointless, too, for Kronos is imprisoned in Tartarus and Gaia's thoughts are fixed on events so distant I can barely comprehend them. I doubt she knows I exist.

And my mother, Thalassa, is the ocean. She who birthed me and sustained me. Her depths immeasurable. Her generosity uncountable. Her temperament unpredictable. Stormy, calm, deadly, bewitching in turns. How could one hate such endless blue-green beauty and fathomless blackness?

So the only thing left to hate is myself.

And I do. I hate the plump breasts and curved hips that have come to my body in recent years. Disdain the long hair that glistens like black glass. Loathe the eyes as dark as the ocean depths, lips of coral red, skin the colour of gold sand beaches.

Because every human and every god who looks upon me sees nothing else. They swoon over the eyes, the hair, the breasts. They write songs to the skin, the lips, the hips. They swear undying love when what they want is to fill with their lust what they see as an empty vessel.

I have a room full of their tainted treasures. They offer gold, silver, gems. They promise they can't live without me. But somehow they find a way after they see Bythos's and Aphros's glares. After feeling the prick of cold bronze spears on heated skin.

Not once do they ask me what I want—or even *if* I want their gifts and their desire.

So far my nephews have managed to rid me of these silly boy-men; these would-be lovers who puff out their chests like full sails, then change direction, as fickle as the wind, when they hear a siren's song or spy a nymph's shapely legs. So, as long as I stay wrapped my mother's watery embrace, I have protectors. I am safe from the unfettered, festering lusts of men and gods.

But my nephews are restricted to my mother's realm by their fish tails, even though their horse bodies carry a man's chest and head.

And I cannot stay here much longer. For my father has pledged me in marriage to a monster.

Today he will come for me—unless my nephews can convince him otherwise.

So I wait, holding to the rocky sea bottom, to the lingering illusion of my safe childhood, listening to the clicks and groans of the ocean, the language of fish and lobsters, the bewitching longing of sirens on their isles. I close my eyes and let the gentle wash of waves overhead rock me like a babe.

A dolphin circles me, chittering a curious question and nudging me with her hard nose.

I push her gently away and shush her noisy squeaks. She has been sent by Aphros and I have no wish to hear his regret right now. I want to hope, just for a little longer, than he and Bythos have changed Ouranos's mind. That I will not marry that sweating, soot-stained, crippled oaf on the morrow. That I can stay in the clean, cool of the ocean forever.

A pair of misshapen shadows fall over me and I must open my eyes.

'Aunt...Daughter,' By says. He has always found it strange that he is older, but I am the aunt. His wide-set eyes slide from mine and he presses his lips tight. His brow clouds and he removes his crown of coral and pearls, turning it in his hands.

Aphros speaks for him, as always, his smile light and hopeful, as always. 'Aphrodite, your father would not change his mind.' He lays a gentle hand on my head and strokes my hair as he did when I was small and frightened. 'He insists. You must marry Hephaestus. But you are our brave girl. You will be alright.'

The small pearl of hope I had carried in my breast dissolves, lodging as a lump in my throat. But I refuse to shed tears. What use would they be here, lost in the salt of my mother's perfection?

'Will I have to live...on land?' My words emerge broken and I swallow down the ache and lift my chin. I am Aphrodite, daughter of the sky and the ocean. I am strong and eternal, as they are. I am brave, as my nephews are.

Bythos nods, silent, his jaw working.

Aphros sighs. His wide mouth droops. 'Yes. Hephaestus wishes you to reside with him in Mount Aetna. Help him tend the forge and fire. Help him make tools for the gods. He saw you once, as you walked on the sands of Cyprus. Saw you and loved you.'

'But why him? Countless others have wanted me and always been refused. Why am I being given to a bitter, ugly cripple?' I cry. 'As a slave to fan his forge and his body's fire? Sent to live in exile inside a mountain. Am I never to see the ocean again? To see you again?'

Aphros catches me against his chest, his cold tail coiling around me. 'Ah, child, I'm sorry. Not given, sold. Your father, Ouranos, has bartered you for a spear of such power that he may prick holes in the night sky and create new stars.'

I pull back, mouth agape. 'Is that my worth? A spear for my virginity and this...' I sweep a hand down my curved body '...*shell* they all find so irresistible.'

I stalk across the gritty ocean floor, tearing seaweed free and crushing it in my hand. I spin back and glare at my nephews. 'What if I refuse? What if I stay here? My father can't very well come into Thalassa's domain.'

My nephews glance at each other, their eyes wide. They speak silently, mind to mind, as only they can. Bythos frowns and nods. Aphros tilts his head, his expression anxious, his hands spread wide. Bythos presses his lips thin and glares. Aphros's shoulders sag and I hide a smile.

I have won. I know it. They will help me hide from my father and my husband-to-be. For Hephaestus cannot abide the water lest it quenches his fire. And Ouranos can only see himself endlessly reflected in my mother's serenity.

I return to my coral cave to sleep, content that I am safe awhile longer.

#

But in the darkest hour of night, a tempest tosses the sea, stirring sand into storms and waking me from dreams of fire and lust. A distant pounding of surf on land thrums through my chest. The crack of lightning and rumble of thunder is audible even so far below the sea's turbulent surface.

My sheltered rooms shake and grind. Pieces of coral and rock tumble, clouding the water and sending fish and crabs scuttling for cover.

Bythos and Aphros appear at my door. They are pale, their scales shimmering in the glimmering phosphor of the disturbed waters. Their hooves drum on rock, echoing thunder. Aphros wrings his hands, flinching at the sound of Thalassa's fury and Ouranos's rage boiling overhead.

'Your father and mother are at war over your refusal,' he blurts. 'Your mother sent us to rouse you. She cannot protect you any longer. We cannot stand against your father, either. I'm sorry.' He holds out his hands, offering useless sympathy to ease his own grief. 'I'm so sorry. You must be brave, child.'

I ignore his touch and turn to Bythos. 'Must I truly go?' I await his answer as the ocean's roar and rush surges around us. Bythos nods, not meeting my eyes. I wrap my arms around myself. If he sees no way of keeping me safe, then there is none for he has always been my fiercest protector.

I run my hands down my body. The body made from hatred and anger. Made for others to love and desire. It is no longer mine. Was it ever? What choice do I have?

Pain and loss clog the words in my throat and I turn to leave.

Aphros takes my hand, walking by my side. He pauses. 'Bythos? Will you come?'

I glance back. Surely he won't abandon me now?

Bythos hesitates. 'I will join you at the surface. There is a gift I wish to give our daughter. I will fetch it.' He kisses my cheek and hurries away, his tail flickering in the uncertain light.

#

When I emerge from the sea I am clothed in a gown of water in shades of blue and green and deepest black. A string of silver-grey pearls adorns my neck. My mother's parting gift. A thin veil of silvery water sheets before my face and vanishes into steam at my feet, so I seem to walk on fog.

The instant I step onto the sandy Cyprus shoreline, the storm falls into eerie silence. Thick, tumbled clouds scud away, fading into wispy tendrils. The vast, black sky appears, speckled here and there by glittering diamond stars. I survey it critically. Father is right, the black canopy does need more stars.

But that doesn't change the fact that I am being traded for a weapon. A pointed stick.

Helios' chariot begins its daily trek across the sky, throwing cloth of pink and orange over the stars.

With my heart still sunk to the depths of the sea, I lift my face to Ouranos's domain and call to the gods.

'I am here, Father. I will wed Hephaestus with my feet in my mother's body, so my nephews can attend me. Come if you will.'

When Ouranos and Hephaestus arrive, my father already carries his precious spear. Twice the length of a man and made of steel that shines purple-blue in the dawn light. My father caresses it with a lover's hand and plants the shaft in the golden sands, sending up sparks. He wears robes the colour of storm clouds and his feet are bare. His dark eyes gleam with satisfaction. I keep my face still and turn to greet my husband-to-be.

Hephaestus has adorned his hunched body with molten-steel-red robes. His thick-fingered hands are blackened with soot. His glittering eyes are small and close over a blade-nose. Eyes as black and opaque as the coal he burnt to forge the spear.

'You have no ladies to attend you?' His deep voice rumbles in a twisted barrel chest. 'To bathe you?'

I gesture at the sea behind, where Aphros waits in the clear green shallows. 'I need only my nephews. My mother's tears and my own bathed me.'

Will Bythos return? I feel unstable without his support.

'Let us begin!' My father spreads his arms wide and the beach fills with the pantheon.

I shrink back, my heart stuttering. I know none of them. I have lived isolated, hearing of the other gods only in bedtime stories from Aphros's indulgent lips.

One by one they approach and greet me. Their names and faces are a blur: Hera, Zeus, Apollo, Hades, Artemis, Poseidon. All distant, aloof, bored almost. The women scornful, the men desirous, lustful.

Until one. Ares, tall and strong; seemingly sculpted of bronze and gold, with thoughtful eyes. He greets me with a warm smile and bows over my hand. The brush of his skin makes me gasp. His grip tightens and he kisses my cheek. The veil of water parts to let him close.

'Lift your chin, my sweet,' he murmurs. 'This will soon be over. Then the time will come for you to make a choice. Call on me when you are ready.'

I swallow, my knees weak at the warm scent of his skin. I nod dumbly, not understanding. What choice can I possibly make? My destiny is written in the stars by my father. He and my husband-to-be own me. I care not. Cannot afford to care.

But I turn to my husband-to-be with my heart inexplicably lighter and my thighs trembling. Hephaestus takes my hand and I force myself not to recoil. His calloused fingers are gritty and leave streaks of black on mine. The pores on his face are black, too. His teeth broken. His hair matted with sweat and stinking of sulphur.

A glance at Ares stiffens my resolve. I am brave.

#

The ceremony lasts all day and into the evening. I stand numb and without words, watching others dance and drink and toast my beauty. Only Ares watches me with a sympathy in his eyes that almost breaks my heart.

The rituals end, at last, when Hephaestus parts the veil of water over my face. He smiles, his fingers stroking my cheek. When I pull away he grips my chin and tilts my face up.

'Oh, no, little fish. You're mine, now,' he murmurs. 'That body belongs to me.'

The pantheon have gone, leaving only Ouranos on the beach. Darkness seeps across the land and into my heart. Behind me, in the water, Aphros still waits alone. I hear his cries to my father. Hear him beg Ouranos to intervene as Hephaestus tears at my gown and prepares to take me there and then.

But my father has eyes only for his spear and simply smiles.

'Wait!' Bythos's cry gives Hephaestus pause. In the shallows, Bythos holds out his arms to me. 'I have not yet given our gift to the bride. It is tradition.'

Hephaestus releases me and I fall into Bythos's arms, sobbing.

He holds me away and gazes into my face. 'Remember, daughter, you are the Goddess of Love and Beauty. You are strong and brave.'

Beside him, Aphros nods and touches my hair. 'And love is gentle, kind, and generous. Be good. Be submissive and he may treat you kindly.'

I glance back at Hephaestus and shudder. But what can I do? He owns me, now. My body is his plaything.

Bythos shakes my shoulders, his dark eyes boring into me. 'Love is also fierce, daughter. Fierce and protective. But you cannot love others unless you first love yourself. You cannot honour others unless you first honour yourself.'

I frown, not understanding. Bythos takes my hand and presses something cold and hard into it. A curved stone weapon. I gasp. He nods. The sickle is only the length of my forearm. I turn it over, running a finger along the gleaming, scalloped obsidian edge. Blood beads on my fingertip.

I smile. 'Thank you. I will go, now.'

I stride back onto the beach and face my husband. Naked and defiant, I stand before him and hold the gleaming obsidian blade to his throat. He tries to push it aside, disdainful. But he has no power over the weapon. He controls metal and fire. I am water and stone.

'I may be your wife, but you will not touch me,' I say, though my heart pounds and my mouth is dry.

He is huge, his arms as thick as my thighs. He could break me in a moment. No! I grip the sickle tight and lift my chin. Aphros and Bythos have raised me to be brave. And Ares's sultry voice dances in my mind. He will have me first. None other. Not if I can help it.

Hephaestus's dark brows draw close together. His lips curl into a snarl. He stalks to my father's side and yanks the spear from Ouranos's grasp. The tip points toward my chest.

'Yield or I will destroy what you value most,' Hephaestus growls.

I sneer. 'If you mean this body, then so be it. You will not have it, either.'

He hesitates, his eyes narrow. Then he hurls the spear. Past me. Into the water. I cry out and lunge for the shaft, but it slips through my fingers unchecked.

The spear passes through Aphros's throat and impales Bythos's chest. My nephews—my true fathers—they die without a cry. With their bottomless eyes fixed on mine, filled with love and regret. Their blood billows and swirls in the clear water, staining it scarlet.

I cover my mouth to stifle a scream. I feel the spear as though it skewered my body. Would that it had.

I was a fool to think I could defy my husband and father.

To think that my body was my own to give as I chose, when I chose.

To think I had any value beyond that of a vessel for lust. My arrogance has cost the lives of the gentlest and kindest of my family.

'Come, daughter,' Ouranos's brisk voice reaches me. 'Go with your husband in peace. Look.' He gestures and the spear slides free of the bodies and returns to his hand. I ache to hold Aphros and Bythos again. To have my loving fathers stroke my hair and tell me stories. But it is not to be. I have failed them. Failed myself.

Ouranos gestures again and the twin bodies dissolve into sparkling gems. With the spear he pierces the sky's velvet darkness. The glittering lights that were my fathers float high and nestle into the holes Ouranos made.

Sixteen new stars. Two fish tied together forever in the heavens.

Tears gather and slip down my cheeks, forming a new gown of opaque silver over my body, hiding me from my husband's lewd gaze.

Bythos's words return to my thoughts. To love others, I must first love and honour myself. How can I be the Goddess of Love, otherwise?

I draw a deep breath and throw my shoulders back. I will not let them die in vain. I will honour myself. I will not be a plaything for anyone, god or man. I will choose my own lovers, my own path, my own destiny.

Staring into my husband's hot eyes, I speak clearly enough for all the world to hear. 'You shall not have me, husband. Be content with your concubines and your forge. This...' I point to my body '...is mine, not yours. Come near and I will castrate you with the same knife that took Ouranos's manhood.'

I hold up the sickle and it glints in the starlight.

Dark Micro-Fiction

Sci-Fi

5 x 100 word micro-fiction works

*First published "**Worlds**" 2019 Black Hare Press*

And In the Mind, Darkness

When they climb to my lair, in the bloody light of dawn, I am ready. I wait with claws curled, thoughts furled. I have hidden from these…things long enough. Screamed in silence while they slaughtered my mind-kin. Their furless limbs and paws are laughable. Yet their weapons of light and fire prevail.

This time I fight with the old gifts. Those we long ago learned to use with caution.

The first alien's shadow slants across my floor. Only one illusion is needed; planted in their bloodthirsty, undisciplined minds.

They turn from me. With light and fire they rend each other.

In Place of Wisdom, Knowledge

Scarlet sunlight turned the ice crusting its limbs to fire and blood. A remnant of some long-dead race, the iron colossus spun in silent majesty halfway between the red desert world and its lifeless moon.

The captain ordered me to haul it into the cargo hold. Our scientists marvelled at the perfectly-sculpted claws, the arms-length metal teeth. Each hair, each spine, each pore a work of art. Surely an idol for worship, they said. The deep-cleaved wounds on its legs and back evidence of some ritual.

On the bridge, I studied the dead world.

In the hold, the ice melted.

The Third Option

For three full twenty-fours we danced a waltz of death through the asteroids. The ITech ship doggedly tailed as I dodged freewheeling clumps of rock and ice. An unshakeable blip on my brand new nav computer. He was good. Maybe better than me.

With barely any fuel left, I had to choose. Drop my biggest-ever load of titanium for him, and run for Belt Station? Or shoot the fucker and hope no one found his ship?

I synced orbit with a rock and waited, blasters primed.

The navcom beeped. *Self-destruct in thirty seconds. Thank you for installing an ITech solution.*

They Always Fall

I waited at the edge of the spaceport, overlooking Halcyon city's delicate, devastated spires. Patient, I admired a ring's ruby-blood glitter on my finger.

She would come. They always surrendered. World after world. They resisted, of course. She had fought harder than most. But, in the end, they swore fealty.

She strode onto the scorched plascrete, weaponless, red hair aflame in the dawnlight. I held out a hand. She knelt, kissing the ruby.

"I know your secret. The A.I." She dragged the ring free and slid it on. 'Now it's mine.' Blood welled from her finger.

"No, you are his."

Through the Mouth of God

If there is a Hell, that must be the entrance. I slump against the shattered console. Bitter smoke and death's pale light washes across my crew's bleak faces. The sucking, spinning absence of matter ahead is our only hope. Behind lies certainty.

"Do we go through?" I ask my navigator.

She shrugs. "Do we have a choice?"

"What's on the other side?"

Her haunted eyes flicker to the ship-corpses outside; the scattered remains of our Hegemon's once-great fleet. Dancing their broken, balletic, slow spirals. Flashing metal. Bursts of silent fire against the stars.

"Something other than the enemy."

"Go, then."

Dark Fantasy

5 x 100 word micro-fiction works

*First Published **"Angels"** Black Hare Press 2019*

A Storm Over Constantinople

The crackle and zip of lightning curls about me, teasing. Sharp winds carry the warm scent of ozone. High on the palace tower, I call on Barachiel. She rides a lightning bolt to my side. Her arms slide about me, her glowing face lifts for my kiss.

'Emperor Justinian.' Her voice is the soft roll of distant thunder. Her lips taste of rain.

'You appointed a guardian angel for Justin, my nephew?'

Irritation flickers through her grey eyes. 'He'll be Emperor, soon.'

'I'm not ready.'

'Not your choice.' She smiles, cool.

My dagger slides into her heart. 'Yes, it is.'

An Alternate Armageddon

'They are destructive fools, these humans.' I sat on a crag of granite and overlooked the vast, crawling city. Grey-brown haze blurred the blue sky to ash.

'*He* loves them, Gusion,' Adriel replied. 'What do you see?'

I snarled, gesturing with a claw. 'Besides this mewling tide of pestilence?' I peered into the future and grimaced. 'I see no Armageddon between us, brother.'

Adriel's pale brows rose. 'But it is foreordained. Our final battle will lay waste to the Earth. Humanity will be judged.'

Rising, I turned away. 'The Earth is already laid to waste. They have judged themselves unworthy.'

The Sin of Repentance

My fiery sword lay at the woman's throat, but she raised her bruised face and glared.

'Repent,' I said. 'For you have sinned and may not enter.'

'I'll not.' She twisted her bloodied, torn shift in both hands and brandished it. 'Those that used me thus deserved death at my blade. Where are they, now?' She craned to see beyond.

'They repented and have passed through the Gate.'

Her swollen eyes glittered. Her split lip curled in a sneer. She spat.

'Then I want no part of it.'

'Your words condemn you.' My sword impaled her. Flames absorbed her screams.

Through the Mirror Exiled

I stand before the shadowed mirror, my soul in light, my heart in darkness. One finger hovers, inches from the glass. Each day I return, hoping he won't be here. Knowing he will.

My imprisoned demon lover.

Murderer.

He lies, huddled in Stygian gloom. A bleak stone cell. Through his window, a moonless night.

Through mine, a glistening day of brilliance and birdcalls.

His gaunt form rises. Haunted eyes silently pleading. His hands splay on glass.

One touch of my finger would release him back into the light, my world.

My heart.

To wreak death again.

I hesitate.

I touch.

What Lies Beyond Six Feet

The grave gaped at my feet. A hungry earth-maw, surrounded by vomited earth like a messy child's face, dampened by tears. The mourners were gone but my past lay unburied. A husk encased in polished wood and satin.

Only emptiness.

No soul. No beating heart. No future.

'It's time.' A gentle voice to my right.

'You must come, now.' A dark rumble to my left.

I glanced both ways. Heaven. Hell. Peace? Torment?

Earth's brilliant sun shone from a hard sky, casting cold shadows but offering no prayers. No tortures.

I gestured, rudely. 'Fuck that. You don't exist. I'm staying.'

5 x 100 word microfiction works

*First Published **'Monsters'** Black Hare Press 2019*

The Taste of Salt and Vengeance

Becalmed, the trawler rests on infinity. Inky glass reflects the glittering milk wash overhead. We lean on the gunwale, coal-glowing cigarettes in hand, and suck salt-air smoke.

'They say *things* live in these seas,' Josh says. 'Angry things. We do bring up some weird shit.'

'These the same people who say global warming's not real, Cap'n?' I ask.

He hawks; spits into the water. 'Reckon we're killing the ocean?'

'Would you stop fishing, if we are?'

Josh shrugs. 'Nope. Gotta eat.'

'That's what I thought.' I flute a warbling whistle.

A tentacle thicker than my body slaps onto the deck.

Never Talk to Strangers

'Watch for him, Cath,' my sister said. 'It's the third rape this month. Pretends to be a tradesman.'

I rolled my eyes.

The doorbell chimed.

'Gotta go, Jilly.' I hung up.

Behind the door waited a man who made my heart skip. Tall. Dark-haired. Winter-sky eyes that slid the length of my body. His white smile widened.

'May I come in, ma'am?' He flashed an ID card. 'Here to check a gas leak.'

I let him in. 'Glad you came.'

'Me too.' One hand grabbed my throat. 'Don't scream.'

'Oh, no.' I smiled, showing fangs. 'Same goes for you, though.'

Art is in the Eye of the Beholder

'You want to report a basilisk?' I stifled a laugh. Sighing, I logged the call. 'Making a statue of your husband isn't a crime, ma'am, but I'll visit your neighbour.' I hung up and grabbed my uniform jacket. Crazies, today.

A woman answered my knock. Thick blonde dreadlocks tied under a floppy hat. Mirrored glasses and a tie-dyed shirt. Hippie.

She smiled and pulled her shoulders back. 'Well, hello.'

'We've complaints about statues and a missing husband.' I cleared my throat. 'You don't have a… basilisk, do you?'

She lowered her glasses, showing eyes of milk. 'Basilisk, no. gorgon, yes.'

What Goes on Inside Her Head?

She lies waiting, perfect. Her glassy eyes gaze at the bewebbed ceiling. Her hands are cold and smooth. Skin gleaming-pale, porcelain-pink.

When it's done will she understand? Will the world understand? Will I be despised? Lauded? The last line is written. Ready. But I hesitate and, instead, stroke her glossy black hair. Candlelight flickers, giving an illusion of movement.

Firming resolve, I open her skull, thrust the paper in, and say the spell. She jerks and blinks. Her lips part.

No. This is wrong, this playing God. I reach for her head.

Her hand grips mine. Snaps bones. I scream.

From Alfred Fanshawe's Travel Journal—Final Entry, 1883

Dearest Emmaline,

After three weeks, we have found the island. I know you think it wicked, but I am about to emulate Odysseus. The sailors wear earplugs and will tie me to the mast.

The sky is thunderous, the Mediterranean rough. But I foresee no problems. I don't truly believe sirens are real. Or that their song is mesmerising, as the fables say.

I hear music in the distance. Probably some islander tricking us.

But I'll go and be tied.

Perhaps I'll take a small knife. Just in case I need to cut the ropes in an emergency.

Yours, Alfred.

Urban Fantasy

5 x 100 word micro-fiction works

*First Published **"Beyond"** Black Hare Press 2019*

Four Things Come Not Back: #1 The Spoken Word

Dad: *Jess?*

Me: *What? You don't normally text. I'm still pissed at you.*

Dad: *I'm sorry we argued.*

Me: *You yelled, you mean? You wouldn't listen.*

Dad: *Please? I need to—*

Me: *It's always about you. Stop trying to control me.*

Dad: *I just want—*

Me: *Mum's calling. We'll talk later.*

'Mum?' I answered, irritable. 'I'll call you back. I'm busy, now.'

There was a long silence, then a broken sob. 'The police called. Your father had a car crash… th-three hours ago.'

'Oh, shit! He didn't say.'

'He's dead, Jess. He died an hour ago.'

Me: *Dad? Dad? DAD!*

Four Things Come Not Back: #2 The Sped Arrow

Five bullets end his life and the power of his fists.

But the torment continues. A tile falls from the roof to smash my shoulder. A glass vase slips from the shelf to slice my arm. The gas left on when I know I turned it off.

I move house. He comes with me, an incurable disease.

Now I sit in darkness, trembling, holding gun to temple. His insubstantial fingers curl over mine. I resist.

He'll never let me go. I should have known when he removed *until death do us part* from our wedding vows.

We pull the trigger.

Four Things Come Not Back: #3 Past Lives

The fifth time around was the worst. By then I'd had ample opportunities for regret, but none for redemption. Just repetition. I remembered each one, no matter how small, pathetic, short, or brutal. And the knowledge that dozens more lay ahead made me want to rail against the gods.

But I didn't.

Because I also remembered the crimes for which I was being punished. The thefts, the lies. And, finally, the murder. Her terrified face haunted every waking moment.

So, on my fifth life, when I was taken to the butcher, I laid my goat-head on the block willingly.

Again.

Four Things Come Not Back: #4 The Missed Opportunity

Had I but driven a blade through my treacherous brother's heart that morning, my son, my wife, my friends… might still live. My country might not have fallen to Norway's ambition.

I suspected Claudius's black intent. But I, in my arrogance, slept peacefully beneath the whispering apple trees. And never awoke. Poison. Dripped into my ear.

Then, without last rites, I lingered, ghostly. But could not convince my son my death was murder. Something made him think me a demon, not his father's unshriven soul. And so he chose that mad play. And so, they all perished.

Ah, my Hamlet.

One in Darkness, One in Light

Brave, he journeys to the underworld. My darling Orpheus. His exquisite music moves even dour Hades, who grants my return to life. My love gazes into my face and swears.

He will not look back until we reach the light.

He turns away. I follow, staying close. We cross the soul-drowned Styx. Orpheus stares resolutely forward; I, hard on his heels. Just a few more steps and I'll see his beloved face once more.

The sun, the sky, the wind. I can almost taste them.

He emerges into the light. And turns back, eager.

But I still stand in darkness.

Crime

5 x 100 word micro-fiction works

*First Published **"Unravel"** Black Hare Press 2019*

A Future, Lost

'It's unrepairable.' Shonnie tapped the smashed computer, fingering a cross dangling around her neck. 'We can't change course.'

I gazed out at a sky meant to be brilliant with Alpha Carlotti's welcoming glow. Instead, infinite dark emptiness swallowed our sleep-ship. Behind me lay serried ranks of shining sleep-tanks containing humanity's finest, bravest. Now doomed.

'Who?'

'Hundreds have woken and slept again in the last century. Any of them.'

'Why? Who would sabotage humanity's hope of survival?' Earth was long-dead. We, her last chance.

Shonnie's eyes slid from mine. 'Maybe someone thought we shouldn't play God.'

Her fingers stroked the crucifix.

Nine Cats Worth of Crazy

'Your husband, Joe, died of head trauma,' I say, gently. 'Blunt instrument.'

Mrs Winterford rubs rheumy eyes with age-twisted fingers. She is alone but for eight black cats, yeowling and eyeing me balefully— probably for taking away the half-eaten body. The house stinks of cat piss.

'See anyone?' I ask. 'A weapon?'

'No, officer. But I found Samson in the freezer.' Her smile is full of holes and bitterness. 'Frozen solid. Joe had run him over. Murdered him!' She glowers. 'He shouldn't have done it.'

'Samson… the cat? Frozen hard?'

'Yes.' She gives a satisfied nod. 'Just hard enough, actually.'

Summer Madness

White curtains billow in the sultry breeze. But the sweetness of summer cannot disperse the heavy scent of blood. In one corner, his cot lies empty. The clown mobile dances forlornly in circles over scarlet-spattered sheets.

I stand, bemused, set adrift by loss. He can't be gone. He has taken my heart with him. I search the room again, hopelessly hopeful.

A footstep falls, light, on the landing. I turn. Not my child. My soul is torn asunder once more. I fall, sobbing, into my husband's arms.

He murmurs useless reassurance, his soothing hands leaving bloody smears on my clothing.

The Earth Gets a Champion

March 2nd. Australian Federal Govt, Accounts Department memo: *Dr J Blake, Dept Environment. Please justify invoices for hazmat suit, culture medium, and CRISPR software.*

10th. Landlord's notice: *Dr Blake, Apt 9a. Complaints registered—unpleasant smells.*

15th. NZ Immigrations email: *Dr Blake: NZ citizenship approved for your arrival on 23rd March.*

21st. Dept of Environment, Personnel memo: *Farewell party, 3pm for John Blake.*

27th. The Sydney Herald: *Fifty-three dead of mysterious illness. Australian Government denies risk of pandemic.*

31st. Australian Govt statement: *Ninety thousand dead from unknown virus.*

31st. NZ Govt statement: *NZ citizens safe. International travel banned. WHO declares pandemic.*

Trouble In a Tight Skirt

The broad was classy. Ruby lips. Garnet nails. Hair like white diamonds. And maybe the heat made me reckless. Summer of '29 everyone drank themselves into a stupor on bathtub gin to forget they had no dough.

Including me.

So, when she offered greenbacks to find her husband, Snorky, I lit a cigarette and said, 'Swell, babe.'

Shoulda known. Too good to be true.

Last place I checked was a speakeasy on Chicago's southside. Strippers, whiskey, cigars. My kinda place.

The muscle looked me over. 'Boss, your missus sent a private dick.'

Al Capone sneered. 'Shoot him.'

I fired first.

Dystopia

5 x 100 word microfiction works

*First Published "**Apocalypse**" Black Hare Press 2019*

And She Spins On, Regardless

Gaia spun in her endless dance, ethereal skirts swirling in gauzy layers around her round body. Her skin itched with pests. They dug at her, leaving gaping gouges. Tainted her with their droppings and waste. Clawed at her cloth-of-green, tearing loose, violating her.

But they would pass. These things always did. So she scratched indolently, slowly squashing the biting, clawing little beasts. Shrugged her massive shoulders and hot world-milk spilled from her peaked breasts. Basked in Sol's glory and wrapped herself in his warmth, holding it close. Until the parasites suffocated and died in the Hell of their own making.

Lying Still in Vulcan's Embrace

Where were you, husband, when the sky rained fire and ash and smoke? When the day smouldered into choking night. When the air turned to sulphur that burnt lungs and blinded eyes. When a river of grey spewed from the great mountain and swept down the slope in white-hot torrents. Smothered the city; buried it beneath blankets of heat and stone.

Where were you when we screamed and curled into ourselves; covered the children's heads as raining ash drifted down and piled upon their small bodies?

You were already fled. Adrift. Offshore.

And now we rest, forever, in Vulcan's bed.

Rinse and Repeat

There comes a time in every civilisation.

When wilfulness outweighs wisdom, and belligerence outguns intelligence.

A time when godlike greed and arrogance, instead of humble awareness, determines fates and futures.

And when that time comes, all that has been built, crumbles. All that has been discovered, is lost. All that has been imagined, vanishes.

What remains are the ghosts of broken dreams and the faint memories of a time before desolation. Wistful stories of past glory to salve present pain and gird against future loss.

Even that dwindles to legend.

And those few that survive.

Will start it all again.

End of the Dark Gods

In the times before, the tribes worshipped the Dark Gods with blood, with death, with destruction. And the gods feasted. Upon the bodies of the fallen; upon the souls of the condemned; upon the screams of the murdered.

Until there came a time when but one tribe remained. For they had slaughtered kin and foe alike; taken the lands for themselves; descended into darkness.

And so the Dark Gods set them upon each other. For their lust was unsated, still. Only in that end of times did the Gods then understand that destruction came at a price.

Their own oblivion.

The Silence that Spreads

See here the five-year-old girl, alone, thin, listless? Her hair lank and eyes dull. Her world the broken remains of the house scorched by fire and crushed by cannon. The house where her siblings laughed and her mother scolded. Where now live only cockroaches, and her fierce, small dog.

Soon she will curl into a ball and cry herself to sleep one last time, clutching matted fur to her filthy face. While, all around, the smoky silence wrought by arrogant greed spreads to encompass her village, her city, her country.

Until every girl, and every dog, sleeps.

And never wakes.

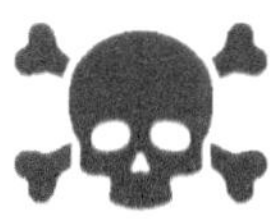

Literary

Suitcases

First published June 2019 Aikiflinthart.com blog

You carry fear and memory in suitcases. Some are heavier than others, but you cling to them all. They bind your hands and weigh down your heart. You stumble over them on every path to the future. Yet you refuse to let them go.

Even the earliest fears are there. A pink vinyl baby-bag, tucked into the linen cupboard of your thoughts, dusty beneath neatly-folded trivia.

You begin with trauma and it underpins your life. Remember? From warm, slumberous blackness you push forth into aching brilliance. You seek to return to the safe-dark of ignorance and parasitic security, for the world seems too big, too cold, to bewildering.

You can't. There are too many cases to carry.

Recognise this tattered backpack, emblazoned with lovehearts in coloured pen and glitter? This one holds hallways echoing with the high-pitched chatter of small, unaware little people, the smell of paper and urine, the tolerant weariness in your teacher's face. Tiny desks and uncooperative pencils. Sports-time sweat and lunchtime insecurity. The boy you want to impress in fifth grade, but who never sees you. The friend who forsakes you for someone more exciting. A thousand petty slights pile in until your backpack bulges with cherished false beliefs.

No, don't let those go. You need those. They balance the broken pieces of your parents' baggage you also carry, doled out like bitter, unbaked cookies, each time you go home to their unmet expectations.

But there's another bag, isn't there? What's in the steel, sequinned purse encasing a slow-beating heart? Ah…It's all sly, sweet glances and furtive kisses with hot, impatient breaths mingling. Bodies alive and sensitised, desperate and afraid, wanting. The potential for pain multiplies a hundredfold. Now we can be hurt in ways we don't even understand yet. We're exposed in body and soul. We're sharing more than giggled secrets now; we're sharing the sweetness of our Self. A Self not fully formed or understood; vulnerable to the knives of hateful words, thrown by a precise and angry tongue. Who would have thought the heart could ache so deeply for so long? Let's snap a silver lock shut around that organ. We're armoured now. Good.

So here we stand, holding our baby-bag, our backpack, our purse, our brokenness; longing for a life less ordinary, more magical. We haul our luggage along the comfortable path to and from work each day. We live for the weekend, for the relaxation, the precious time to suck up the energy needed to cope with next week's stress. We watch the flickering screens at night, living vicariously through fictional figures, envying their imaginary lives.

Incremental world-wreckers in our cocoon, we hide the potential to save ourselves in complaints about others. We build walls with our baggage, seeking the safe-dark, keeping the world out.

Wishing, we 'if only' our life away.

If only I had time to write that story. If only I could quit work and live off my art. If only I could save the world, change the world, change myself…

But where do I start? Where I spend my time and money reveals my focus. I'm working eight hours and wasting the rest on nothings. Why? I'm afraid to commit myself to loving the world, pain and all. I'm so burdened I've stopped moving. These heavy bags have zipped away hurt and passion together.

But I am not my job. Not my pain. I am my creative soul. I am free. If I choose I can release these burdensome cases. I don't need to quit work to be free. I don't need to relive every trauma to be a loving adult. I can decide who I want to be, what I hold, what I release, and what I want to create. Then I just have to do it.

In fact, I will.

I leave my luggage to circle endlessly on the conveyor belt of others' expectations and walk away. Now I have two hands free to embrace the world. My heart is weightless. The darkness is there but I push free of it and shed the cowl of fear hiding my future; face the light, brilliant and painful.

Life cannot be lived backwards.

Fantasy & Sci-Fantasy

In Every Reign a Little Life must Fall

First published "ELEMENTAL" CAT Press 2019

'Just how many pieces of blood-chert do you need, kiddo?' Barrik hefted the red rock in his meaty hand. He raised the chert into a beam of sunlight that filtered through the oddity-shop's grimy window. Dust glittered and swirled like fairy-sprinklings in the musty air. The chert, with its veins of quartz, looked exactly like petrified steak. I shuddered.

'As many as it takes,' I replied. 'Just store it with the others.' I hung my cloak over one arm and tossed a silver queenshead at him to pay for storage and silence. He caught the coin and ran a dirty thumbnail around the edge.

'Fair enough.' His black eyes flicked my way again.

'How much do I have now?'

Barrik placed the stone on his brass scales and added a number to a leather-bound journal on the counter. 'Eighty-nine point eight kilos. But only nineteen point eight of that's here. You took the rest away last month.'

'Crap.' I swiped a hand over my short hair. One hundred grams. I'd miscounted. Including the one hanging under my shirt, between my breasts, I was short by one piece.

A man's weight rested uneasily on my shoulders. A kingdom's fate, too. There was no-one else to save Rosa or the stupid, ill-fated Reizend. Just me.

'Y'know, with your hair dyed dark,' Barrik mused, 'anyone ever tell you, you look a bit like—'

My dagger vibrated in the timber post next to his head. He gulped. I sauntered up and retrieved it.

'No,' I said. 'At least, not twice.'

'Sorry. Why do you want this stuff, anyway?' He dropped the stone into a leather sack and stowed it beneath the counter. 'Trying to corner the market in blood-chert?'

'Nope.' My dagger slipped into a boot. 'Just got a customer who likes rocks.'

When I looked up again, Barrik had a small crossbow pointed at my head and a smirk on his jowly face.

'Seriously?' I sighed. 'How long have you known me, Barrik? You really think I'd swindle you?'

'Oh, six years.' His finger tightened on the trigger. 'You were about fifteen when you first came in with that sweet little sister of yours. Fair warmed my heart how she looked up to you. Remember how she begged you to buy that old book for your mam's birthday. Never could say 'no' to her, could you?'

'Tell me about it,' I muttered.

He pointed at the sack of rocks. 'Then you started all this.'

'And?'

'And I hear things. How you lie and cheat to get them. Pretty light-fingered, too. Just surprised you haven't killed anyone, yet.' He shook his head and sighed, like a disappointed father.

'Don't tempt me.' I glowered. 'What do you want?'

He shrugged. 'Well, I figure you've done all the hard work. 'Bout time you cut me in on the action. Someone must want these bad if you're willing to give up five years for rocks.'

I held up my left hand and waggled the little finger with its missing end-joint. 'See this? Blood-sacrifice to the Goddess just to be able to track them down.' My cloak-sleeve fell back, exposing a forearm scarred with dozens of fine white lines. 'And these. One for each piece. You prepared to make a sacrifice?' The lump of stone in the invisible spider-silk bag around my throat warmed, anticipating a blood-rite, as it did when I neared a fresh piece of chert.

'Maybe. If the money's worth it.' He glanced dubiously at my arm and shuffled his feet. 'Got a kid to feed now, see? Shop's not earning enough. That damned demonic dwarf Frodo…Freddo—'

'Friedenzwerg,' I said.

'—is running Ebene for the Princess and he's just raised the taxes again.' Barrik grimaced sheepishly. 'We all gotta make some sacrifices, the wife says.'

'Yeah, she would.' His wife was one of the best-dressed women in Ebenton.

His eyes narrowed, finger curling around the crossbow trigger.

'Fine! I'll cut you a deal.' I draped my much-patched brown cloak over my shoulders. The cloak was old; a birth-gift from the Elf-king no less. The candytuft-flower clasp was a little stiff. 'Ever heard of the cloak of ignorance?'

The caterpillar-brows over Barrik's eyes crawled closer together. 'Always thought that was some kind of…thingy…metaphor for not going to school.'

'Not so much.' I finally got the clasp shut, flipped up the hood, and waited.

He glanced down at the crossbow in his hand then peered suspiciously around the shop. I remained still. His eyes slid off me and swept the jumble of dusty furniture and shelves full of honest-to-Goddess antique cursed spoons and djinn-inhabited bronze teapots. He shrugged and released the string-tension on the bow then tucked it under the counter.

I slipped around behind him, careful not to brush against a teetering stack of faux-ancient tomes. A large hunk of amethyst on a shelf over his head ought to be about right. I plucked it off the shelf. Force and timing had to be perfect. Didn't want to kill him. The amethyst hit his head exactly square and Barrik folded like a bad souffle to the scuffed wooden floor. I dropped the crystal. He ought to think it had fallen on him.

I prodded him with a toe. Years of trust and business and the big oaf decides to screw me over because his wench of a wife has expensive tastes. I was tempted to empty his till, but the mention of his kid held my hand. Kids shouldn't have to suffer from their parent's stupid decisions. Family is supposed to look after each other.

I hefted the sack of blood-chert over my shoulder. There wasn't much else of value in the store. Or, at least, nothing I valued. But, out of habit, I cast an expert eye over the display cabinet. A glitter attracted my attention. I slipped a deft hand between Barrik's patchy fae-wards and extracted the figurine.

A small stone fox carved from rust-red sparkling sandstone. My sister's favourite animal. I tucked it into a pocket. Not quite what I'd hoped to bring her, but she'd like it.

As I turned toward the back door, light reflected off something in the shopfront. Above a cabinet stuffed with pink-cheeked dancing faun ceramics. Squeezed between a stuffed ogre head and a rusting 'magic' sword. A tarnished silver hand mirror.

I swore.

'You daft frog-kisser!' I kicked the unconscious Barrik in his well-padded ribs. 'A mirror? You deserve to get rolled.' There was nothing I could do now. I flipped a rude hand-signal at the speckled glass and stalked out the back door.

#

'You're looking glum tonight, love.' Barb's gravelly voice interrupted my personal stormcloud of doom. She slid a fresh tankard along the bar and half-heartedly wiped along behind it with a stained pink cloth. A smear of something infectious spread across the scarred timber.

'Ever have one of those days where you wonder if it's all worth it, Barb?' I scrubbed at my scalp and sipped the dark ale. Five bloody years and, just when I thought I was done, there was one more bloody piece of bloody stone to find.

But Barrik was right: my sister looked up to me; needed me. I'd never been able to refuse her. That's why I'd chosen this path when I could have spent the last five years drinking wine and eating quail eggs. Telling servants what to do. Dancing sedately. Bathing regularly.

The longer I was away, the harder it was to remember exactly how she'd talked me into it.

'Worth it?' Barb chuckled, her expansive fake bosom almost jiggling out of her once-red dress. 'I wonder that every time the tax-collector comes, or some drunk shoves a hand up me skirt, love. So, yeah, every day.' She flicked at a slow-moving fly, which fell and drowned happily in a puddle of beer. 'But I've worked my arse off to build this place so I'd have something to leave the kids. Think they're grateful?'

'Er…' I raised my brows. 'Yes?'

'Nope. Don't care a bit.' The waving towel flew dangerously close to glassware and swirled smoke puffing from the fireplace. 'Just off doing whatever they want, on my money.'

'Doesn't that bug you?' I didn't really care, but her chatter saved me thinking about my own dilemma.

She scratched at the five-o'clock shadow along her square jaw and snorted. 'Nah. So long as they're happy. It's what family does, innit? Sometimes you give up what you want so yer kids can have what they want. Otherwise, what's the point? Besides, things're gonna get better in Ebene, they say.'

'Really? How?' I slurped another mouthful, savouring the rich malty flavour. Whatever else she did, Barb made a damned fine beer.

'Well,' Barb said, pondering, 'apparently now the princess is up and about, we might not have to go to war with Tal after all.'

I coughed. 'Princess Rosa is…er…up and about?'

Barb grinned, showing the polished, white-oak teeth she'd bought last year. 'We all thought she was dead or in the deepest palace dungeon and that's why the dwarf-demon, Friede…Fredden—'

'Friedenzwerg,' I said wearily.

'—was running Ebene. Turns out she was just pining for her lost prince. She snapped out of it the day Tal started marching. Now she's doing the right thing by Ebene, poor lass.'

After staring morosely into my drink for a few more seconds, I sat up. 'Hang on! What right thing by Ebene? And why were we going to war with Tal?'

Barb lifted her plucked brows. 'You have been off in the boondocks awhile, haven't you, love? Prince Lastig of Tal finally demanded compensation for the loss of his brother. Thinks we murdered Prince Reizend. Said Queen Ivy sacrificed him in some dark magic ritual that backfired and killed the Queen and Princess Helli as well.'

I suppressed a gasp and covered my shock by drinking deeply.

Barb dismissed the rumour with a noise of amusement, then leaned close and whispered. *'Everyone* knows it's no co-incidence the Crown Prince of Tal and the Crown Princess of our royal family disappeared at the same time. It's obvious: Reizend preferred Helli to Rosa and they ran away.'

I choked, spraying beer across the counter.

Barb wiped the mess. 'Laugh if you like. But it explains why Rosa went into a decline and wouldn't marry Lastig instead. Kept him on a string for *five* years! Can't blame him for finally getting sick of it and declaring war.' She sniffed.

'Are you saying Rosa's agreed to marry Lastig? To stop the war?'

'Looks that way. Lastig's on is way here to the palace. Wedding's in a week. Bit of a rush-job, if you ask me. Poor Princess Rosa. Duty over love. The things we women do for our families, huh?' Barb gave the counter a few more wipes then swayed off and poured drinks for a boisterous group of travelling actors. One motley-clad jongleur slid his hand up her leg. She casually punched him and he keeled over, unconscious.

I groaned and dropped my head onto my forearm, heedless of the beer soaking my sleeve. Five goddamned years. So close! I'd condemned Rosa to five years of imprisonment while I chased bloody rocks, all for nothing. There was no way I could find the last piece in a week. I'd let her down. And I'd written a letter four months ago to say I was coming back with the last piece. How was I supposed to tell her I'd fucked up?

I wrenched at the amulet around my neck and achieved nothing but a deep score in my skin. Of course it wouldn't come off. Not until I'd found every bloody piece. Wouldn't even let me cross Ebene's borders with my head still attached.

A hearty guffaw from the actors interrupted my self-flagellation. I swilled beer and gazed at the amateurish portrait hanging on the wall behind the bar. The artist had captured Rosa's enormous blue eyes and hopeful naivete exactly, even if her head was weirdly oversized. In her dark hair nestled her birth gift from the Elf-king: the wine-red carnation brooch. Rosa always wore it even though it wasn't magical, like my cloak.

Beneath her image hung a smaller one—of Reizend, Crown Prince of Tal. His blond, brooding intelligence made a perfect foil for her sweetness. As long as he was happy with beauty and goodness, and didn't place too much value on brains, they'd make the ideal monarchs for Tal.

Wait! Maybe that was why she'd made a reappearance and agreed to marry. Yes! That was it. She hadn't given up on me or Reizend. She knew I was coming. This agreement to marry fusspot Lastig must be a ploy; a tactic to delay Lastig until I showed up with Reizend, his brother.

But Rosa was expecting me to come back with the full ninety kilos. I only had eighty-nine point nine. And there was no time to find the last piece. Still, there was enough rock to maybe convince Lastig to hold off for a while. He'd have to be told the truth, though. And that would fall to me, even though it was Queen Ivy's fault. Hers and Friedenzwerg's. But I was the only one left to fix this mess and I hadn't sacrificed five years of my life to fail now. There had to be a way. Rosa was depending on me.

The clinking bag went back over my shoulder. I clasped the cloak together and flipped up the hood. Everyone ignored me as I left.

#

Getting into a fortified hill palace isn't as hard as one might think. At least, not if one grew up roaming the palace halls and testing the security by trying to sneak out. I'd managed to escape several times. Even taken Rosa with me into Ebenton, to Barrik's shop, when we needed to find unique birthday gifts for our mother.

In a way, this whole mad situation was my fault. If I'd never let Rosa talk me into buying that blasted grimoire, our mother wouldn't have learned the spells that set everything in motion. Still, no-one had forced Queen Ivy show off to Rosa and Reizend by saying the summoning spell. Or the scattering one. Mother always had been a bit reckless.

Barefoot, I splashed up a freezing stream at the base of the hill and parted a fall of vines screening a cave. Inside, I flipped open a brite-lite, stolen from a mage, and played its uneasy green glow across the dripping walls. A narrow, hand-hewn path clung to the wall above the stream. I clambered up and tugged my boots back onto numb feet. The lockpicks under the innersole of my right boot had shifted. I swore, pulled the shoe off, readjusted the picks to a comfortable position then shoved my foot back in.

By the time I climbed up to the palace's lowest levels, twenty kilos of stone weighed fifty and the cold air burned in my throat. I paused outside the secret entrance, panting. Pathetic. How was I supposed to carry ninety kilos of stone to the upper levels? Well, I'd solve that later. For now, I'd offload this bag with the rest and see what was going on abovestairs. If Rosa was panicking about Lastig she'd be pretty happy to see me.

I just needed to speak to her in private without alerting anyone to my presence.

#

A few minutes later, lighter by nineteen point eight kilos, I eased open the door to the great hall with one hand. With the other hand I struggled to close the candytuft-flower cloak clasp.

'Ah! There you are.' A cheerful, rough voice greeted me from waist-height.

I looked down.

Friedenzwerg flashed a broad grin and swept a bow. His large head ended up around my knees and the temptation was almost irresistible. With an ominous clank of metal, seven palace guards stepped into formation around him. The leader eyed me significantly, fingers white on his sword-hilt.

I finished doing up the clasp and muttered something rude. Too slow with the cloak. But maybe it wasn't too late.

'Freddy,' I said. 'Always a pleasure. Been awhile. Killed anyone recently?' I smiled sweetly.

His grin became fixed and his dark eyes narrowed.

'Not since you left,' he returned, his smile malicious and filled with more sharp teeth than I remembered. One hand strayed to the red silk bag he wore on a thong around his neck.

I glared. 'Well, I'll be leaving again. Just came to chat with Rosa.'

'Oh,' he said coolly, 'I think you'll be staying for a week at least.'

'Really?' I folded my arms and raised one brow. 'And what if I don't want to stay?'

Friedenzwerg spread his thick-fingered hands. 'We'll just have to change your mind. After all, you have a wedding to attend.'

'Not if I can help it,' I shot back, then cursed myself for showing my hand too early. Time to redirect. I needed to get past Friedenzwerg, see Rosa, and then see Lastig of Tal. Convince them to put off the wedding and the war until I found that last stone.

I eyed Friedenzwerg. His purple and gold puffy-sleeved doublet and pants made him look as broad as he was tall. The small horn-buds poking through his slick dark hair were ridiculous. Getting past him shouldn't be hard.

'Freddy, have you heard of a cloak of ignorance?'

'Do you mean the metaphor—'

'Not so much.' I flipped the hood up.

'—or the actual cloak of ignorance?' The dwarf continued. 'As in the magical item which, if named and touched, becomes visible to the namer.' He poked me in the ribs with a finger. 'Oh, look. There you are.'

I swore and yanked the hood down.

Friedenzwerg chuckled. 'Did you forget that I'm a Summoned One? I saw the magic aura before you even put the hood up. You'll have to do something a little more impressive to outthink me, Princess Helli.'

'Helli!' Rosa's voice lilted down the hall. She glided toward us, hands outstretched, blue chiffon floating behind her. Her soft lips parted in a delighted smile. The red carnation brooch glittered in her long, dark hair.

The guards stepped aside and she grabbed my hands. Her blue eyes gazed beseechingly into mine. My heart melted. I'd missed her unquestioning faith; her belief I could fix anything. I believed it myself when she looked at me like that.

'You're back. I'm so glad.' She kissed my cheek. 'Just in time to rescue me from my folly. Like you always do. Thank you.'

I curled a lip at Friedenzwerg and smiled at my sister. 'Of course. We'll stop this ridiculous wedding, I'll bring Reizend back, and everything will be fine.'

Rosa's eyes widened. Her rosebud lips fell open. 'Reizend? Oh, no. The wedding must go on. Once you marry Lastig, this mess will all be put to rights.'

'What? Once *I* marry…' I dropped her hands. 'By the Goddess,

Rosa, what are you talking about?'

Friedenzwerg flinched. 'I'll thank you not to invoke Her name in my presence. Rosa, I think we'd best explain this in a less public place.'

Rosa blushed and caught his hand to her cheek. 'Of course, dearest. You're right.' She took my fingers and pulled me toward a parlour nearby. 'Come, Helli.'

Stunned, I could only follow.

#

'Let me get this straight,' I said, scraping my hair into an unruly mess. Rosa reclined on a gilded daybed, with her blue dress draped elegantly, looking at home amongst the velvet drapes and sombre portraits of our ancestors. Friedenzwerg relaxed on a chair beside her, one stumpy leg crossed over the other, smiling in unholy amusement at me.

I glared at Rosa. 'I gave up my position here as Queen for the last five years, trying to find a way to reunite you and Reizend. And now you're telling me I wasted my time because you've fallen in love with…with…' I pointed at Friedenzwerg.

Rosa beamed and nodded. 'I knew you'd understand, dearest. Freddy's been ever such a support. I was so miserable with Mother and you gone, and no hope of marrying Reizend. And running a country is much harder than I thought. It all seemed too much.' She lifted anxious eyes. 'I'm just not *you,* Helli. I have no head for business. Freddy does, though. He looks after me so well.'

'But…but…' I paced the room, clutching my head. 'I wrote. I came back every year as often as I could. You never said…I scoured the damned kingdom for your sake!' I flung my arms wide. 'And he's a *demon!* Are you telling me you prefer a demon dwarf to Reizend? Remember him? Tall, intelligent, handsome…tall. The next king of

Tal?'

'But Reizend's gone,' Rosa said simply, 'and Lastig's such a fussy bore.'

I gaped. 'But you're fine if *I* marry Lastig?'

'You once said a Crown Princess must never expect to marry for love. I'm sure you'll grow to like him.' Her mouth drooped. 'But I just couldn't. Not now I've come to love Freddy. You do understand, don't you?

Nothing emerged from my open mouth.

'Oh. You don't. You're angry at me.' Rosa burst into tears and buried her face in her arms. The sound of her sobs wrenched at my heart. Maybe she really was in love.

'Oh, Goddess.' I covered my eyes for a moment. 'Rosa, you know I want you to be happy. You're my sister. But are you sure Freddy doesn't have you under a spell?'

'Demon magic, remember?' Friedenzwerg held up his hands, palms out, and cocked his head. 'Curses, yes. Love spells, no. What can I say? The kid has a way about her. I just can't say 'no' to her.'

Rosa raised her head and sniffed, sapphire eyes drowned in sparkling tears.

I sighed, unable to resist the hope in her expression. 'Maybe we can work something out.'

Smiles wreathed her face. She leapt to her feet and threw her arms around me. 'Oh, thank you. You're the best sister, ever.' She sat down, hands clasped on her knees, gazing at me in the eager way she had when I agreed to do something crazy for her.

'So,' I said, pacing back and forth. 'Where would you go? I mean, he is a demon. It's not like many places will welcome him. Don't get me wrong,' I added when her face fell. 'You're welcome to stay here, but the people of Ebene are…well… less than thrilled by his leadership so far.'

'That's silly,' Rosa said stoutly. 'He's doing a splendid job. His magic gets me anything I want. It can do the same for them. Of course we'll stay here. You'll marry Lastig, go to Tal and be Queen Consort. I'll rule here with Freddy. We already are, so it makes sense, really. Why upset things?'

I sank on to a chair and stared at her. Could she really be that naïve and selfish? Had she always been and I too gullible and blinded by her adoration to see it? Once upon a time, her logic would have seemed perfectly sane. Perhaps five years on the road had changed me more than I thought.

'What about my happiness?' I said. 'What about what I want?'

Rosa sent me a mournful look. 'I know. It's so unfair. But remember the story you told me—about when I was born and the Elfking gave me this?' She touched the carnation brooch in her hair.

'I know, I know.' I dropped my head into my hands. 'The Elfking was annoyed because you cried so much. I said I'd do anything to make you happy. But to be fair…I was only five. And you were crying a lot. Screaming, really.'

There was a long, hopeful silence.

'What about Reizend?' I managed, swallowing a lump in my throat. 'When I bring him back, he's going to be a little…irritated that he's lost his bride and his country in one hit, don't you think?'

Rosa smiled serenely and squeezed Freddy's hand. 'That's easy. Just don't bring him back. After all, without all the pieces he can't be restored, can he?'

'I supp—' I sat up straight. 'Wait, how did you know I don't have all the pieces?'

She flushed and glanced at Friedenzwerg. Her free hand crept to her throat and her gaze flickered down.

Friedenzwerg harrumphed, glaring at her. She started. The pink in her cheeks deepened. There was a long, awkward silence. I thrust a hand into my pocket, fingering the little sandstone fox I'd intended gifting to Rosa. Perhaps the animal was a better symbol than I'd realised. Perhaps we'd both changed and my little sister wasn't so little any more. Perhaps…I looked at her…I'd never been able to refuse her before for a good reason.

'The mirror.' I said, deliberately switching my attention to Friedenzwerg. 'You saw me talking to Barrik in the shop. That's how you knew about the chert, isn't it? About the cloak, too. Dammit!'

'Yes!' Friedenzwerg said. 'Yes, the mirror. That's how.' He shrugged. 'And since you couldn't find that last piece, I guess we'll just have to leave poor Reizend to his rest and move on.'

'Uh huh,' I said, eyeing him with distaste. 'Not sure being Scattered into a hundred pieces of blood-chert counts as rest, actually.'

The dwarf raised his hands, palms out. 'Don't put that on me. It was your mother's spell that went awry, not mine.'

I jabbed a finger at him. 'You deflected it so the casting hit Reizend.'

'Not intentionally,' he said, pious.

'You lying little—' I rose and took a step toward him.

Rosa leapt to her feet, as pale as she had been flushed.

'Don't hurt him!' She wrung her hands. 'You wouldn't make me so unhappy. Please, Helli?'

'It's no use, darling. She just doesn't understand.' Friedenzwerg stood.

'Oh, yes I bloody-well do,' I muttered.

'Guards!' Friedenzwerg yelled.

I withdrew my hand from my pocket and leapt at him. We tumbled to the cold marble floor in a tangle of arms, scrabbling for a hold, throwing wild punches that barely connected. Rosa shrieked at me to stop. I could have stabbed him, but that wasn't my aim. Demons couldn't be killed by steel, anyway. He opened his mouth. I jammed a forearm into it to prevent a spellcast. He bit, his sharp little teeth breaking skin. I yelped and kicked at his stomach. The dwarf choked a cough and released me.

The door burst open and his men hauled me upright. Blood dripped down my arm, making my clenched fingers slippery.

Friedenzwerg wiped his mouth and glared. 'Take her away. Maybe some time in the dungeon will change her mind.'

'No! Not the dungeon.' I tried to wrench free but his men held me firm. 'Anything but that.' I cast a pleading look at my sister.

'Oh, dear. I'm so sorry.' Rosa sniffed and dabbed her eyes. 'I feel awful. Please agree? Even Lastig's better than the dungeon for the rest of your life.'

I bit my lip, hesitated then raised my chin and glared at them defiantly.

'No.'

Rosa's eyes widened. Her lips fell open. 'No?' she whispered. 'But you *can't* say no.' Her fingers fluttered to her hair.

'Watch me.' I smiled. 'No.'

'Take her.' Friedenzwerg dismissed me with a languid wave and a cool look.

#

The palace only had one, large cell. We'd never really had need for dungeons. No one used it. Well, almost no-one.

The guards took my dagger, patted me down for other weapons, and shoved me into the darkness. They left and closed the door with an ominous clang.

I rattled the bars a few times and yelled obscenities to make sure no-one would come. Then I hurried to the darkest corner and began tipping out bags of chert onto the floor. When I had the whole lot in one pile I opened the brite-lite I'd left there with the bags. By its green glow I smeared blood from my arm onto the piece of chert in the bag around my throat. The chain unlocked and the rock fell to join the others.

I opened my hand and let fall the final piece. The piece I'd lifted from the red silk bag around Friedenzwerd's neck and replaced with the little fox sculpture during our scuffle.

I spoke the words the Goddess' priestess had given me so many years before. The words to undo the Scattering spell.

A flash of blood-purple light seared my eyes and swirled around the pile of stones. The chert rattled and jumped, merging, twisting and morphing into a vaguely-human outline. With one final, soft explosion of light, the spell finished.

Reizend stood before me, blinking and swaying on his feet. He looked a little older, but still wore the same ridiculous blue silk and lace formal outfit from five years before.

'Hey.' I lifted a hand.

He squinted and peered at me before inspecting his surroundings.

'Helli?' He patted his head as though testing to make sure it was attached. 'What happened? Why are we in a dungeon? What happened to your hair? And your arm? Where's Rosa?'

I sat down to take my boot off. 'It's a long story.' The lockpicks fell into my hand. 'I'll tell you on the way to Tal.'

'Tal?' His brows snapped together. 'Why Tal? Are we in Ebene? I'm here to marry Rosa. Last I remember was being in Queen Ivy's room and that dwarf demon appearing.'

'Ya,' I said, working on the door lock. 'Like I said. Long story. We're heading toward Tal to intercept your brother.' I straightened and pushed open the door.

'Lastig?' Reizend hurried to my side. 'What's he got to do with this?'

'He's got an army I need to borrow. I want my kingdom back. Here.' I handed him the cloak.

He accepted but stood there holding it, staring at me blankly. 'Isn't this your birth-gift from the Elf-king? It is looking a little ratty, but don't you want it?'

'Not so much.' I flashed him a mirthless grin. 'I've worn it too long already.'

The Snack

First Published QWC website magazine 2017

Tara's stomach grumbled so hard it woke her up far too soon. She kept her eyes closed. She was warm and comfortable, her body heavy and floppy. Did she have to get up? Her stomach squeaked and growled. Yes, she did.

Everyone else slept on, snortling and wuffling in the warm darkness. This wasn't the long-waking, when the whole family would arise. That was still to come.

She just needed a quick snack, then she could go back to sleep, too.

Her stomach complained again.

The last thing she'd tried to eat had complained too. And wriggled. And poked her with pointy things. So she'd let it go and found something that didn't argue. It hadn't tasted very good or filled her up, though. That must be why she'd woken early—for something yummy to get her through the next sleep.

She forced open one eyelid, rubbing away the grit. Reaching out until she almost touched the ceiling, she stretched every muscle and bone until they creaked and crackled. Next she waddled to the door and pushed it wide. Dust danced as light pushed away darkness. She blinked in surprise.

Trees. All around her door stood tall, strong trees. Their big heads hid the free sky and turned its clean light watery green. Their thick, rough trunks crowded close, keeping her prisoner. Their roots burrowed in bare dirt at her feet.

How long had she slept? Her house used to overlook gentle, grassy hills that rolled away until they met the sky. Silver-green hills hiding tasty food, and a forever-sky full of roaring wind. Now there were only trees that caught the wind and forced it into whispers and silence.

No, not quite silent. A faint squeal drifted between the trunks. It started high and piercing then bounced away into short, breathy screams.

Tara tilted her head, flicking her ears. What made such a din?

Scarlet flashed, brilliant through drab green and brown, darting between the trees, coming closer.

Her stomach grumbled and she patted it, smiling. Food that ran right to her door. Maybe living in the forest wasn't so bad.

She hid her large body behind a boulder and watched the funny little running creature. Two short legs pumped up and down. Skinny arms waved madly and a pink mouth shrieked until Tara's ears ached. A bright red cloth covering flapped and fluttered like a broken wing.

The running-thing stumbled into the clearing and stopped, panting, blue eyes wide and wild. Tara sniffed and screwed up her nose. It was one of the complaining-things. If she ate one of them, more would come with pointy metal sticks to poke at her again. She stayed still.

Something huge, hairy and four-legged leapt into the clearing. Its big eyes narrowed and big ears twitched. Its big, sharp, yellow teeth gnashed. The two-legged one cried, cowering against a tree. The hairy thing growled.

Mmmmm. Tasty.

Snap!

#

Later, when Little Red brought her Grandma and the woodcutter back to the ancient mound in the forest, there was no sign of the dragon she claimed ate the wolf.

Inside the hill, comfortably full, Tara Greywing slumbered toward the long-waking.

The Faktor Incident

First Published 2020 CAT Press

*This is a prequel to **IRON**, first in the Kalima Chronicles trilogy.*

The Factor Incident, is set 2 years before IRON.

'I'm not entirely sure what to do with you, Pellar.' The Weishi House Master, Hao, drummed lean fingers on his zitan-wood desk. He tugged at his long goatee and straggly moustache.

Pell waited silently, gripping his bronze dagger and poison-dart belt, weight balanced for movement.

In the snowy street outside, merchants hawked their wares and wagons rattled past Weishi House. A Messenger House runner bolted down the street and yelled fresh news: Prince Soran's eldest child would be invested as heir at midday the next day.

Master Hao harrumphed and gestured at the straight-backed visitor's chair. 'Sit, Pellar.'

'I prefer Pell, sir.' He remained standing. One never knew, in

Weishi House, when a master would launch a surprise attack. Best to stay ready. He'd survived eighteen years by being on his guard.

Master Hao sent him a sharp look and didn't reply.

Nearby, Merchant House's timekeeper bells tolled the midday hour. Master Hao rolled his eyes and waited. Pell stayed silent, unmoving.

More bells pealed throughout the snowy valley that sheltered Nanqualea town, capital of the Princedom of Jadid. A deeper bell chimed in from Prince Soran Salib's hill keep.

Finally, the ringtones faded.

'Right, Pellar.' Master Hao cleared his throat and shuffled a pile of bamboo paper on his desk. 'This is a high-level assassination. Not often given to an unbearded new graduate xiongshou. Even one with the House record for concealment and the best 'assassinations' of every House master.' He looked up, narrow-eyed. 'But it's approved by Xintou House. And the person who paid for this contract asked for you, specifically.'

'Sir?' Pell repeated. Outside Weishi House, very few people even knew he existed. He'd been given to the House as a nameless infant. Not even a family tattoo on his forearm. Unable to walk freely about the city without that tattoo. Stuck in the House. Raised by the masters and the older boys.

He tightened his grip on his dagger. With the ease of long practice, Pell shunted aside the more…unpleasant memories of what that 'raising' entailed.

Never again.

'Are you willing to undertake this task?' Master Hao asked.

'I need more detail, sir. Who authorised it?'

Hao sighed and swiped a hand over his shortcut hair. 'Mistress Xiaan—Prince Soran's Bonded Xintou—signed the contract. But she's refused to reveal who paid for it.' He spread his hands. 'How can I say no to a Bonded Xintou?'

Pell said nothing to what was probably a rhetorical question. He suppressed a shiver. Any of the Xintou House telepathic women made him uneasy. A Bonded Xintou attached to the Prince was even more frightening. He had learned to ward his mind—as all xiongshou must. But he was a non-telepath. Unable to tell if his wards were penetrated. The thought of the Prince's gold-veiled, gold-robed, Bonded Xintou rummaging about in his head made his stomach churn.

He struggled to keep his expression bland.

Master Hao stared at the papers on his desk and muttered, 'I suppose it shouldn't surprise us that Mistress Xiaan approved the death of a noble.' He smiled thinly. 'After all, eighteen years ago Xintou House agreed to the anti-kin-child laws and the murder of thousands of children.'

Pell clenched his teeth. So many Jadid children had been murdered just they lacked their father's family tattoo. Was that Pell's mother's excuse for hiding him here; imprisoning him? Had she feared he would be murdered by the blood-crazed mobs that had swept Kalima and Jadid eighteen years ago?

Why had Xintou House allowed it? Why had they pilloried single mothers, when xintou were guilty of the same crime? After all, xintou could manipulate DNA and create children in their own image. And xintou were forbidden to birth twins or boys for fear of causing some long-forgotten defect.

So, perhaps Xintou House condemned unwed common women and untattooed children out of jealousy or spite? Pell pressed his lips thin. There was no other logic behind the kin-child massacres.

With a heavy sigh, Master Hao slid the topmost sheet of paper toward Pell. 'Take the contract, boy. But, when you're done, get out of Nanqualea. This town isn't big enough, no matter how skilled you are at hiding. I've never met your target, but he's well-enough liked. You won't be popular with the younger generation if the news of who took the contract leaks. Legal or not, it could make you a target for revenge attacks.'

Pell lifted his brows. Weishi House didn't accept contracts on their own people.

'Don't worry, boy.' Hao's mouth twisted. 'I wouldn't authorise a kill on you. But that won't stop an angry mob of commoners.'

Unfolding the contract, Pell said nothing until he read the target's name.

Then he allowed surprise to show. 'Truly?'

'Yes,' Hao replied. 'Yes, indeed. While I don't want you to fail— for the sake of your career—I very much do want you to fail. If you understand my meaning.'

Pell swallowed, folded the contract into a perfect square and tucked it into a pocket in his black weishi uniform. His hands trembled, just a fraction. He controlled himself, quashing the tremor low in his stomach. Excitement, that was what it was. After all, this was what he'd trained for since he was three. There was no place for hesitation or doubt in a xiongshou's mind.

Bowing, Pell turned away.

'Wait!' Hao opened a drawer. 'We'll forego the usual graduation and manhood ceremony for the sake of anonymity.' He rose and spoke more formally, 'By the skill shown during the last three weeks of your assessment, I grant you the rank of xiongshou, with all the privileges and responsibilities inherent in that.'

He tossed a scrap of cloth across the desk. 'Here. Take this with my blessing. You'll have to cut your own hair and let your beard grow.' His frown gentled. 'You've been a model student, Pell. I know it hasn't always been easy here, but you're a good lad. I see that in you. The tattooist is waiting to put the House shuriken tattoo on your wrist. Do me proud. Then get out of here and don't come back for at least five years.'

Slowly, Pell picked up the black and purple braided silk bracelet. He tightened it around his wrist. The bracelet would grant admission into any Weishi House in any country. It also meant he could kill any target.

Assuming he had a contract authorised by the Xintou House Law Mistresses and a Weishi House.

A smouldering coal, deep in his gut, flared into fire. He'd worked for fifteen years to attain the bracelet. To have it tossed at him like a scrap of rubbish; to have to cut his own hair short for manhood... It seemed…unfitting.

Outside the window, heavy storm clouds had finally lifted, revealing a peridot sky for the first time in the long winter months. Bowing once more, Pell left Hao's office without a backward look.

His childhood was over.

#

'Faktor? Where *is* that boy?' A deep, raspy voice echoed through chill hallways.

Pell slowed his breathing and focussed on stillness. Yelling, Prince Soran Salib, passed beneath Pell's position. Soran wore the leather kilt and open, blood-red robe that was the traditional men's garb in Jadid. His heavy footfalls slapped back from the great hill keep's thick walls.

Pale orange sunlight slanted through a narrow window and glinted off the pendant on Soran's thickly-pelted chest. The symbol of office for the ruling Prince of Jadid; a silver-metal lion's head. Not the more rare and valuable iron, if Pell was any judge. Jadid had no iron mines.

Very few existed anywhere on the planet of Kalima.

Prince Soran paused in the hall.

Pell held his breath. If he failed this, he would have to go back to ordinary weishi work. Bodyguarding for rich merchants and nobles. If he succeeded, Jadid could be thrown into turmoil for years to come.

He gave a wintry smile.

Failure wasn't an option. He would complete the contract and get out of this foresaken country. Take assignments in other cities. Travel and see the rest of Kalima. Somewhere warmer than the Princedom of Jadid with its endless dour winters, dismal timber cutters, and snow deer farmers.

He caught his straying thoughts and dragged them back to here-and-now. A xiongshou couldn't lose concentration. Even for a second.

Mistress Xiaan rounded the corner, resplendent and terrifying in her shimmering gold silk robes. The corners of her mouth were pulled down, clearly visible below the translucent gold veil that hid her eyes.

'Faktor's nowhere, Shenshi Sorin. That unbearded boy has managed to hide from us for three full days. He can't miss his investiture as your heir. It's his birthright. His responsibility.'

Soran snorted. 'The boy thinks of nothing but books and ancient history. The boy talks gibberish. He needs to understand politics and economics. Deal with living people, not the long-dead fools that founded this deserted colony-world.' He ran restless fingers through his full, dark beard.

Xiaan laid a hand on Soran's massive forearm, her thin fingers pale against his swarthy skin and his faded blue lion's-head family tattoo.

The new black shuriken inked onto Pell's arm was still raised and red. Solitary without a family tattoo. He resisted the urge to scratch, and lay flat atop a tall yar-pine cupboard that stood in the corridor.

'We'll find Faktor,' Xiaan said soothingly.

'I don't have any more time to waste,' Soran snarled. 'That trouble-maker, Corin Mal-kin, is here as emissary from the northern Jun Second, Rafi Koh-Lin. I don't trust that Mal-kin character. Too flippant for my liking. Never takes anything seriously.'

The Xintou's thin mouth curved into a smile. 'Corin Mal-kin means no harm, shenshi. Devious, I grant you, but I've Read his thoughts enough to know his intentions are good. Just don't leave him alone with your daughter or your purse.'

Pell grinned. Mal-kin sounded like an interesting man. Perhaps someone who might offer passage out of Jadid when this contract was completed.

'Well,' Soran said, sighing, 'Mal-kin's disappeared somewhere as well. My weishi-guards lost sight of him in the city and that worries me.'

Mistress Xiaan chewed on her lip. 'That is somewhat concerning. But he's due to leave Jadid tomorrow afternoon.'

With a gruff laugh, Soran patted Mistress Xiaan's wrist. 'Don't mind me. Just find Faktor. We have twelve hours before the investiture. In an hour I have to meet with Mal-kin about that new trade deal. I'm sure he'll show up. But if he wants our yar-pine he can jiche-well pay for it this time. I want grain and a lot of it.'

'I'll find Faktor.' Mistress Xiaan bowed. 'I can sense he's still here in the keep. But he's adept at hiding, so I can't pin down where.'

From his place above their line of sight, Pell allowed himself a small smile and strengthened his own mental wards. He'd snuck through this keep many times in the last six months. Training; learning to steal unseen to and from the most heavily-guarded building in the city. He probably knew the keep better than Soran did.

Since Soran's people must have searched every room, there was only one place Faktor could be.

A third person joined Soran and Xiaan. Yarina, Soran's sixteen year old daughter. Faktor's younger half-sister. Darkly pretty with flashing eyes and a confidant way of throwing her shoulders back and lifting her chin.

'Did you find him?' she demanded, folding her arms across her lilac silk robe.

Soran rubbed at his forehead. 'No, daughter. Go back to your studies and leave your brother to me. He'll be there.'

Her lips pursed. 'When will you get it into your head, Father? Faktor doesn't want to be heir. Forcing him won't make him a good ruler for Jadid.'

Soran said nothing, his heavy lids drooping. This looked like an old argument he couldn't be bothered fighting any more.

Yarina made a noise of frustration and stalked off, her hands clenched at her sides.

'I need to find that girl a husband,' Soran muttered.

'I don't know that's what *she* needs, shenshi.' Xiaan chuckled, low in her throat.

He gestured irritably. 'Go find Faktor. Meet me and Corin Malkin, later, in the conference room.'

She bowed and strode away on silent, gold-slippered feet. Soran watched her out of sight, an old, aching regret in his eyes. Then he shook his head and stomped toward the great hall.

Pell waited a few minutes and dropped soundlessly to the floor, dusting off his dark clothing. He glanced up and down the hall. Then he pressed a decorative knob on the cupboard and heaved the timber frame away from the wall. The hinges opened soundlessly. Someone had oiled the door recently, leaving a whiff of mel-oil hanging in the air.

Once inside, the secret door swung easily shut and Pell waited for his eyes to adjust to the semi-gloom. No footprints on the stone floor. The narrow hall's floor was swept clean. Soft-shoed, Pell crept toward the far door. His heart skittered and jumped, his breathing quickening. He took three slow, deep breaths to control himself.

The thick wooden door opened silently. Pell peered around, checking for threats and exits. Only a comfortable sitting room was visible. Half-shadowed in darkness. Pell totted up the room's contents. Just one mel-oil lantern pooled light in a sheltered corner. Two faded armchairs, a threadbare rug, and a battered yar-pine desk. Stacked on the desk stood a dozen thick books.

At the desk sat young man, his attention focussed on an open book. The young man's face was only half-visible, but faintly familiar.

Faktor. The intended heir.

And the intended victim whose name lay on Pell's authorised contract.

Could it be this easy? Pell hesitated. No weishi-guards were in sight. Yes. This was the best chance he had to complete the contract.

He slipped into the room, with blowpipe ready and a grey-feathered dart in the tube. A quiet breath of dust-thickened air and he pressed the tube to his lips. One quick blow. Silent. Accurate.

The dart embedded in the young man's neck.

Faktor jumped to his feet, tipping his chair over. He gargled and scrabbled at the dart. Yanking it out, he gazed at the dart, then wide-eyed at Pell.

Pell strode forward and murmured the xiongshou's traditional last words to a victim, 'My respects to your ancestors.'

Faktor gave a gurgling sigh and collapsed, eyes rolled up. The dart fell from his fingers and tinkled on the stone floor.

'What the...' A new voice intruded. Male, sharp, deep.

Snatching his bronze dagger from his hip, Pell spun to face the threat. A tall man emerged through a second doorway. Pell cursed himself for stupidity. He hadn't cleared the room properly. How could he be so amateur?

The main door was too far for an easy escape. Pell held his position, keeping his back to the one mel-oil lamp. Hopefully the semi-darkness would protect him. He dropped into a fighting stance, bronze dagger ready. The man's startling green eyes glittered, one hand on his sword pommel.

'What have you done?' the man demanded, pointing at the body lying on the floor. 'That's the heir to Jadid.' His eyes flickered to Pell's wrist and he hesitated, frowning. 'You're a xiongshou? Show me your contract.'

Pell raised both hands. He could only kill someone who interfered with his task. But this contract was fulfilled. Now someone had demanded his contract, he was legally obliged to show it.

He couldn't kill. He preferred not to show his contract. Could he take this man out with a sleeping dart?

'Don't even think it, kid.' An imp of humour danced in the newcomer's eyes. The stranger drew an actual steel sword. 'You're not good enough to get to a weapon faster than I can put this blade through you. Believe me.' He held out a hand. 'Contract.'

A steel sword? There was no way to easily fight anyone using such a weapon. Giving over the contract was Pell's only option. He slid the blowpipe into its sheath on his back and tucked the dagger away. Then he reached slowly into his jacket.

Who was this man? The stranger's hands and forearms were corded and muscular. Fingers calloused from weapons-training. He moved with the unconscious grace of someone who knew his way around a fight. Maybe in his mid-twenties. Long, white-blond hair, tied back. No beard, though, so perhaps from Mamlakah, the jundom to the north.

Ahhh…

Pell bowed fractionally, keeping his face in shadow, and held out the square of paper. 'All legal, Corin Mal-kin.'

'Oh, you do speak? I was beginning to wonder.' The glint of humour returned. 'And you are a quick one, aren't you?'

Pell said nothing. With luck he might still get out of this. As long as he kept his face hidden. Being identified by a Jun Second's emissary would make finding work in Mamlakah difficult.

A gust of air swept through the open door and the mel-oil lantern flared brightly in the dim-lit room. Pell threw up a hand to shield his face, but too late.

Corin glanced at the body on the floor, then back at Pell. His eyes widened.

'Who *are* you?' He bent, reaching for the pulse-point on the body's throat. 'This kid looks—'

Pell leapt. He snatched a green-feathered dart from his belt and jabbed toward Corin's thigh. Corin clamped iron-hard onto Pell's wrist and twisted. Pell's fingers were forced open and the dart tinkled to the floor. Folding his elbow, Pell wrenched free. He drove the other elbow into Corin's exposed gut.

With a breathless grunt, Corin skipped backward. He dropped into a fighter's crouch. The steel sword glinted silvery in the dim mel-oil light. Pell pulled out his dagger, horribly conscious of the disparity of weapons. A xiongshou rarely carried a long-bladed weapon. Too hard to conceal.

He flicked two shuriken in quick succession. Corin swayed aside, not taking his eyes off Pell. The throwing-stars clanged off the stone wall and clattered to the floor.

'Do try not to be a complete hmar, kid. I don't want to hurt you,' Corin said. 'If the contract is legal, we're good.' He paused and relaxed his stance, lowering his blade. 'Do you know you look like the boy you just killed?'

Pell straightened and threw a quick look at his victim. The young man's face was slack, but the resemblance was undeniable.

'I need to get out of Jadid.' He sheathed his dagger and handed the contract to Corin.

Corin hesitated and raked both Pell and the body with a shrewd inspection. Then he slid the steel sword back into its scabbard.

'Agreed.' He unfolded the contract and skimmed it. His brows twitched into a frown. 'Signed by Xiaan? No payor listed. Unusual.' His frown deepened. 'There's something odd going on here.'

'You really are the *most* irritating man,' a throaty, feminine drawl emerged from the shadows.

Pell tensed, hand on dagger again. He backed up and glanced at the door. Corin spun, keeping both Pell and the newcomer in his line of vision.

Mistress Xiaan emerged into the flickering light. She had shed her golden robe and veil and wore now a plain, dark-yellow house robe. Her grey-streaked hair was pulled tightly back into a bun at the nape of her neck. Her hands were empty and she wore no weapons. Pell relaxed slightly but the burn in his stomach intensified at the sight of her.

'What's going on, Xiaan?' Corin snapped. He brandished the contract. 'You signed off on this? Why would you have your Bonded family's heir assassinated?' He pointed at Pell. 'And why does this kid look so much like Faktor?'

Pell waited, tightening the grip on his dagger. His heart thudded in his ears. Would she tell the truth?

Xiaan hesitated, her gaze travelling over Pell from head to toe. She smiled faintly, with a hint of old regret.

'Because this youngster is Faktor's brother. His twin brother, to be exact.'

Pell sucked a sharp breath. He gripped the back of a nearby armchair, his fingertips whitening.

This was about to get complicated.

'What?' Corin let out a sharp breath. 'But twins are…ah! I see. When Prince Soran's first wife had twin boys you hid one in Weishi House. The common people fear twins because xintou are forbidden to bear them.' He smiled wryly. 'And most people practically worship the ground you xintou walk on.'

'Though clearly you don't,' Xiaan said, her reply acid. 'But, yes, people are superstitious of twins. Twin boys, especially—because xintou aren't allowed to bear boys, either.' She sent Corin an ironic look. When he returned it blandly, she continued, 'The princedom of Jadid was in a bad way. We'd had three years of heavy, long winters. So many people were dead and starving that the population was on the verge of revolt against Prince Soran. He and I decided to hide Pell in Weishi House for his own good. To protect him.'

'And Soran,' Pell noted drily.

'Yes. And your father,' Xiaan agreed.

'Well, you hired the right xiongshou.' Corin nodded toward Pell. 'The kid's efficient, I'll give him that.' He touched Faktor's pulse point. He rose again, one hand sliding into his pocket.

The grey dart was gone from the floor.

'Faktor's dead.' Corin sent the Xintou a bleak smile. 'I'm assuming that was your plan? To kill Faktor and substitute his brother?'

'Dead! But…' Xiaan's finely-lined cheeks blanched. She took a step toward the body. 'Let me see—'

'Are you accusing me of failing to fulfil my contract?' Pell stepped between her and his brother's body. 'That would require a public trial before the Weishi House masters. And an independent observer has declared Faktor dead.' He held his breath. Would she try to breach his wards? Dig into his mind? He suppressed a shiver.

She stared first at him then at Corin's bitter smile before heaving a sigh.

'What a mess.' Xiaan rubbed her face. 'No. I won't dispute. You were trained by the best and Master Hao vouched for you.' She cast a regretful look at Faktor. One trembling hand covered her mouth and she sank into the faded purple armchair. 'It was Faktor's plan. And Yarina's.' She covered her eyes. 'To hire a xiongshou. Pell, specifically. But he wasn't supposed to kill. Just get Faktor out of the princedom.'

'What?' Corin blinked.

Pell waited. There was more, but would she reveal it to this outsider? Would Corin guess?

Xiaan nodded. 'You've seen how Prince Soran despises Faktor. Thinks him weak. Faktor tried so hard to be the son Soran wanted, but he could never please him. Yarina is far more fit to rule after Soran. Faktor just wanted out.'

'Well,' Corin replied sourly, 'he's certainly out now. What was your next step? And why get his own brother to murder him. That seems callous…even for you.' There was a hint of a sneer in Corin's tone and Pell warmed to the northerner.

She stared for a long time at Faktor's still body. Tears shimmered on her lashes. Pell clenched his jaw, holding back the angry words bubbling behind his lips.

Xiaan glanced at Pell. 'We asked for Pell on purpose. I knew that anyone who succeeded in this contract would have to leave Jadid immediately. Faktor is well-liked in certain circles.' The lines around her mouth deepened and her throat worked. 'We decided Pell should be the one so he would have to leave. Otherwise he would be a potential threat to Yarina's rule if anyone found out he existed.'

Pell ground his teeth and swallowed down the urge to fling eighteen years of resentment at the woman. She had deprived him of so much. Not only the lion-head family tattoo, but the family and sense of belonging that accompanied it. Not only a life of privilege and comfort, but the warmth of parents and siblings who cared, rather than the cold backhand of the House Masters or the…personal…attentions of the senior boys.

'I don't understand,' Corin said, frowning. He studied Faktor's face and then Pell's. 'They look enough alike. Why *didn't* you just substitute Pell for Faktor?'

'I'm xiongshou,' Pell said, quietly. He curled a lip. 'Can't have an assassin on the throne of Jadid. Everyone in Weishi House would know me the minute they saw me.'

Xiaan opened her thin lips, paused, then nodded without adding anything.

Corin's sharp gaze slid from her to Pell, to Faktor and back to the Xintou. 'Lucky for you Prince Soran's second wife birthed Yarina then, huh?'

Twin spots of red coloured Xiaan's pale cheeks. 'Indeed.'

Pell straightened. 'With your permission, I'll withdraw. My contract is complete. I'm no longer welcome in Nanqualea. I'll leave with the next caravan.'

Xiaan rose and hurried to him. She reached out a hand toward his cheek but he flinched away, keeping his expression stoic and cool.

Her shoulders slumped and her mouth drooped. 'Of course. I'm…I'm sorry. More sorry than you can know.'

'So am I.' Pell turned on his heel and left.

#

A day later he waited at the caravan departure point on the outskirts of town, the collar of his glass-rabbit-fur jacket turned up, his nose buried deep in a thick wool scarf. He'd used his contract money to buy a sturdy horse, and the gear he would need to camp out in the caravan's train. Then he'd hired himself as a weishi-guard to the caravan master in exchange for passage north across the Jabal Mountains, into Mamlakah.

He glanced back at the ragged rooftops of Nanqualea and ignored a pang of…what…fear? Regret? It was hard to be sure. There was nothing left for him there.

The great bell of Prince Soran's keep had rung four times, indicating the death of the heir. The day of mourning was over. Faktor's body had been entombed with his ancestors in the crypts beneath the keep. Yarina would be made heir next week. She was popular. The announcement had quelled incipient riots.

Pell twisted his mouth. Yarina was a good choice. Better than he was. The last thing he wanted was to be Bonded telepathically to Mistress Xiaan; the woman who had thrown him away. Now he could start fresh. Maybe go to Madina, capital of Mamlakah. Find work based out of the Weishi House there.

He turned his face from the city and watched the final piles of baggage and timber get loaded onto the brightly-painted caravans. Slowly, the sturdy beasts towing wagons began plodding north, leaving fresh dark trails of muck in the snow-dusted street.

Outside the city's high stone walls, Pell let his shoulders relax. He dragged in a slow breath of sharp, clean air and looked forward to the northern mountain's jagged peaks.

Freedom wasn't far away.

At the sound of near hoofbeats he slewed in his saddle. Two men approached from behind. Both wore thick glass-rabbit-fur jackets, their hoods raised and faces muffled by scarves.

'What took you so long?' Pell asked.

'A minor matter of being dead to overcome,' came the reply. The smaller man flung back his thick grey hood.

Pell reached across and gripped the man's forearm in the manner of friends. 'Good to see you awake, brother.'

Faktor's shy smile widened. 'Nice to be awake.' He scrubbed a hand over his short-cut dark hair and scratched at the scraggly beginnings of a beard on his pointed chin.

Pell rubbed at his own, smooth jaw. He had chosen not to grow a beard, and his hair would grow back in time. He no longer considered himself of Jadid.

He turned to the other rider. 'Corin. How did you know?'

The northerner grinned and threw back his hood, his green eyes sparkling in the weak morning sun. He held up a grey-feathered dart.

'Xiongshou normally use black for death. I'd never seen grey— or even heard of it—but it wasn't hard to guess that you were using something to simulate death.' He shrugged. 'Figured it might be interesting to play along. So?'

'And did you tell Mistress Xiaan or Prince Soran?' Pell fingered his dagger, keeping his face neutral.

'Relax, kid. Yarina's the only one who knows. She came to me after you left. Apparently Xiaan told her Faktor really was dead. Yarina was so upset I had to set her mind at ease.' Corin's grin twisted. 'And now the future ruler of Jadid owes me. And therefore owes the Jun Second of Mamlakah. Plus, I got a good deal on the next yar-pine shipment because Xiaan was afraid I'd tell someone else the truth.'

'Ah.' Pell laughed low. 'Opportunist.'

'Of course! So, do tell—why this big charade?' Corin cocked his head. 'Because it wasn't easy swapping the bodies.'

Faktor chuckled, his dark eyes creasing with ready humour. 'You really didn't have to. There's a secret exit out of the crypt. I would have been fine when I woke up. We had it planned.'

Corin swiped at his face. A huff of breath emerged as a dense cloud in the cold air. 'I think I'm getting old. Why the big magic trick?' He eyed Pell. 'That excuse about not being able to be heir because you're xiongshou? Very thin. What's really going on? Why did you want Xiaan to think Faktor was dead?'

Pell looked to Faktor, who shrugged and nodded.

'Because she's our mother,' Pell said, trying to keep his voice level and leached of bitterness.

Now Corin reared back in his saddle like he'd been slapped. 'Twin *boys!* A Bonded Xintou had twin boys? What possessed her?'

Faktor's brow darkened. 'Our father's first wife was barren. He wanted a boy. The kin-child laws had just come into effect and Jadid was in turmoil.'

Corin sighed, a flicker of old pain shadowing his expression. 'So Xiaan decided to produce Soran's heir herself, rather than risk another woman's life.'

Pell snorted. 'You're giving her too much credit.'

'It gets worse,' Faktor said. 'I found Xiaan's notes about her pregnancy and worked out what she'd done. She's nai-xintou—able to manipulate DNA, but only on her own eggs. By the time Xiaan realised she was having twins, it was too late to abort.'

'That still seems like a big risk,' Corin said, frowning. 'Why not pay a surrogate mother?'

With a bitter laugh, Pell raked the northerner with a wry look. 'Imagine how much control she'll have if she was both mother to the heir *and* Bonded Xintou to the Prince? Yarina is hers, too, you know.'

'Interesting.' A thoughtful frown came over Corin's face. 'You could be right. Xiaan needs close watching, I think. But you two aren't…' He raised his brows.

'Male xintou?' Pell shrugged. 'No. Xiaan made sure of that. We're no danger to anyone.'

Corin gave a disbelieving laugh. 'So, you're kin-children—illegal. Twins—frowned on. Males born to a Xintou—absolutely forbidden.' He slapped Pell on the shoulder. 'I don't think you could be more outcast if you tried, kid.'

Pell pursed his lips but said nothing. He didn't need sympathy.

'How did you two meet?' Corin asked.

'The last six months of xiongshou training includes studying the layout of the keep,' Pell said. 'I found Faktor in his hidey-hole. He realised I was the brother Xiaan had hidden away. She never said where she'd hidden me.'

'When I found how he'd been raised…what they'd done to him there…' Faktor shuddered and sent Pell an apologetic look. 'I knew I couldn't stay any longer. Neither of us could. So we worked out a plan. He kills me and gets to leave. I die and get to vanish. We both win.'

'Pell?' Corin lifted his brows. 'What do you get out of this? You have to leave your home.' He shivered and pulled his glass-rabbit-fur jacket closer. 'Although I do understand the appeal. Anyone who lives in a permanent state of winter is utterly insane.'

Pell returned a thin smile. He glanced at Faktor and then at the open road ahead. 'I get a brother that cares. Someone who can watch my back.' He eyed Corin narrowly. 'And I suspect I only stayed alive after the attack on Faktor because you interrupted Xiaan's plans.'

'Ahhh… interesting. What do you plan to do?' Corin studied him shrewdly.

Pell merely smiled, held his intents in silence and gazed north.

With any luck he would also get the opportunity to study Xintou House in Madina.

And a future chance at justice.

Rivers Bleed, Mountains Fall

Adron stalked to the Bonding Seat on the sodden riverbank to await his bride—should she deign to come.

Should she even exist.

He ground his teeth as he took his place at false dawn on the day the first spring snowmelts swelled the Brillen River into foaming, roiling madness. And waited. As his uncle had, and his uncle before that. Back ten generations to the time of Settling, when the first Hight had tamed the wyrdlands into farms and villages. Combed the earth into neat rows of wheat. Carved the hills into terraces and steps.

Now, only in the rivers did traces of the oldwyrd endure. And that fierce fickleness of water—which frightened humans and delighted the wathas—bound the two folk in an ancient accord.

Ridiculous. No-one had seen a watha for a generation. He was better off marrying elsewhere. Marrying for land to feed his people. Adron sighed. There was no point in arguing, though.

So, in response to that accord, he, Adron, Hight of Welladon, now took the cold granite Seat and glared at the swirling muck lapping at his feet. Silt mingled with the water's natural blue luminescence, turning the river a sick shade of dull green. The dank smell of mud and rotting timber thickened the cool air. Adron raised a scented handkerchief to his nose and waited.

Weeping marra trees leaned precariously over the flooded river, like vain girls who dangled their discordant silver hair in the water and searched for beauty in muddied reflections. Their leaves chimed with disturbing, atonal music as the river tugged relentlessly on the branches.

Water crept closer to the foot of the Seat. Adron looked away, letting the earth's deep, slow rhythm calm his racing heart. He scraped back his short dark hair, placed his hands on the chair's cold arms and sent out a pulse of earthwyrd to alert the watha to his presence. The scent of warm, rich soil teased his tongue and the weight of the earth's ancient bones dragged at his body, making him feel fifty though he was but twenty years. He shook himself and the sensation passed, but resentment remained.

It was ridiculous to imagine a two-hundred-and-fifty-year-old bargain should still hold sway in this age. Or that a man should be forced into wedlock with one of the oldwyrd folk; a watha. With no choice in the matter of who he gave his body and seed to for the rest of his life.

Able to father only daughters, not sons.

Bonding to a watha would mean the end of his line. He would be without a male heir. But *not* bonding would mean the end of Welladon's prosperity and fertility, if the olders of his family were to be believed. He wanted what was best for the people of Welladon. He wanted to lead them; to prove himself worthy, as the last Hight—his uncle—had. His people needed new farmlands, rich and fertile. And to be kept safe from the Hight of Kildor who sought to push into Welladon from the south.

He shifted uneasily on the hard seat and checked the horizon. The sun's first shimmering edge peeked over Mount Kareoc. Surely that was dawn. No watha would come. Besides, rumours were that the watha were dying out, as were the ertha of the mountains. Tattered remnants of the fullblood oldwyrd. Or extinct like the airtha and firtha. What did it matter? Humans carried enough of the wyrdblood now to control earth, fire, air, and water—as much as was needed, anyway.

Besides, who knew if watha even still existed in this part of the river? His aunt, the last Hight's river-bride, had died before his birth. Her daughters had all vanished into the river and were never again seen.

Sunlight poured into the valley. Adron smiled. He was free of this useless bargain. Other Hights, in other lands, passed their power to sons. He would marry the Hight of Kildor's daughter and solve two problems at once.

He planted his feet, ready to rise.

Something splashed. He froze, staring. Kinnial, his birth-parent, who stood by as Witness, gasped and pointed. A dark shape swelled and glided up from the glowing water, moving against the current as though the torrent was still. Long, dark, dripping hair. Skin the colour of darkest lakes, bare and glistening. Slight breasts and hips. Was that a hint of webbing between the slender fingers?

She stood silent, ankle-deep in the river, diamond droplets trembling on her fingertips.

Adron stood dumb, captured by her perfection, her stillness, the wariness in her bunched thigh muscles and shallow breaths.

Then she lifted her eyes and he drowned in their black depths. She smiled, eyelids drooping. She took his hand, her fingers cool and smooth. Methodically, never releasing his gaze, she stripped off his tunic and trews and dropped them to the mud. His knees gave way and he sank willingly onto the wet cloth.

'I am yours,' she murmured, her voice the soft fall of summer rain. 'And the earth will be nourished, as was agreed.'

'I am yours,' Adron said, completing the ritual. 'And the river remains free, as was agreed.' His throat grew thick and his skin hot with longing. She knelt over him and joined her body to his in slick abandon. His back pressed into the wet earth and the river sucked at his feet and licked at his calves.

#

She came to live in the granite fortress of the Hights and made no complaint about leaving the river. Over a year passed in a flickering of seasons. Besotted, Adron showered every luxury on his wife. Lilla, she called herself, on those few occasions when she spoke at all. Even after a year, he knew little of her thoughts. Her rare, gurgling laugh was merry; her eyes darkly thoughtful, hiding secrets. She was gentle but persistent, a foil to his solid certainty. Adron could deny her nothing, but she asked for little, so it was no hardship. Her only quirk was that she must always be touching water or freshly-bathed and still damp when they loved one another.

She swam in the river daily, seeming to delight in its touch almost more than his own and Adron more than once found himself jealous of the river's caress on her body. But she was watha and water was as blood to her; life itself. So he spoke sternly to himself and merely smiled.

Sometimes, on moonlit nights, Lilla would take those household women with traces of waterwyrd abilities to the river to perform a storm-summoning. Once, Adron snuck down to watch. The women slipped naked into to the glowing river, where Lilla led them in a wild, splashing dance, laughing and carefree as she was at no other time. Other watha appeared, dark and sleek, embracing Lilla in sensual abandon, swaying and diving to the music of the marra trees.

Drenched in moonlight and water.

She came to him after, her skin still slicked with luminescence, and loved him with such fierce ecstasy that he was struck dumb, his heart full.

And she smiled and whispered, 'I am of two worlds, now. I never thought to love in this bargain our ancestors made. Only to be content and provide my family with daughters of the river.' With her lips against his throat and her hands stroking him to readiness, she said. 'Now give me a daughter to love when you are away in the spring, inspecting your tedious earth.'

And Adron laughed with her, wondering at his luck as the called-for storm broke and rain drummed on the window's diamond panes.

In the morning, his birth-parent, Kinnial, drew him aside and battered the shelter of his contentment with driving, icy questions. Kinnial was the only person who seemed indifferent to Lilla's gentle charm. But humans with airwyrd gifts tended to disdain the those made heavier by earthwyrd or waterwyrd powers, so perhaps that was no surprise.

As the youngest sibling of Adron's uncle, it had been Kinnial's right to produce Adron, the next Hight. Airwyrd humans usually remained gender neutral, while those with firewyrd were dual-gender. But Kinnial had chosen the female form for five years in order to bear Adron and his sister. One took the honour seriously and reminded Adron frequently of his duty to the ancient bargain.

'Daughters,' one said for the hundredth time since the bonding. 'You must get Lilla with child, and fast. The watha are caretakers of the river and the rains, but their lives are short. It is your duty to protect the river and to send girls to replace those who are lost. In return, Welladon thrives.'

Adron rounded on one. 'And what of your duty, Mother?'

Kinnial paled and retreated, thin hands clutching at one's belly.

Adron pressed his point. 'How am I to have a male heir when I have no sister to produce one. We both know that Lilla will only bear girls.' He prodded Kinnial's flat chest. 'It was your duty to bear sisters for me, so that one of them would marry a human strong with earthwyrd and produce my heir.'

'Caddia's death was not my fault,' Kinnial said weakly, blue eyes pale as the hot summer sky. 'I tried everything to cure her.'

'Nor was it mine,' Adron retorted, 'but I'm the one who is left wanting.' He glanced out the window down into the garden where Lilla sat on the edge of a pond, trailing her fingers across the dark water, humming to herself. His heart ached with desire for her, and with the knowledge that she would never give him what he needed most to secure his line and his land against the Kildorans in the south.

'Would there was a way to change the Council of Hight's Law so my daughters by Lilla could inherit,' he muttered.

Kinnial sighed. 'My brother said the same thing. But only boys have the earthwyrd needed to manage the land.'

Indeed, as waterwyrd was a woman's gift, airwyrd a neutral's, and firewyrd a dual's gift, earthwyrd was a man's. But, of course, the earthwyrd was the strongest and most useful of the four.

Adron bowed his head. 'I know, Mother. So what do I do? Without a nephew to inherit, Welladon will be taken over by the Hight of Kildor. He already claims inheritance rights as my father's nephew.' He glared at his birth-parent. 'You chose badly when you picked a man of Kildor to father me.'

One's chin lifted. 'The choice was not mine, either. Your uncle chose my husband, thinking to bind our two lands more closely in friendship.' One's lips pressed thin and one's pale cheeks flushed dawn-pink. 'But my *husband* abandoned us. Even less than you do I want that man…that family back in this house; on this throne; near to me and mine.'

'What you want…what I want…it matters not. I must think of Welladon.' Adron groaned and gazed out the southern window. 'The Hight of Kildor has no wyrd gift. He has no feeling for the land and treats his people without respect. Already they push across our southern borders to escape him. And he sends miners to desecrate our earth. The land there is poor and dry, so we have no-one to farm it or to turn the refugees back.'

'If it's so infertile,' Kinnial said, 'let him have it—if that will satisfy him. That land used to belong to Kildor, anyway, in your granduncle's time.'

'If he stopped there,' Adron retorted, 'I would. Or perhaps not,' he added pensively, 'for his actions undermine my people's faith in me.' He looked down at Lilla. She glanced up and smiled and he was again lost in the wells of her eyes.

'There is…' His birth-parent hesitated, biting a lip as was one's wont when one feared to speak. 'There might be a way for Lilla to bear a son,' one finished in a rush, panting.

Adron frowned. 'What way? I've never heard this. Speak, Mother.'

'No,' Kinnial shook one's head, blinking rapidly. 'It's just an old tale. I'm sure it's wrong. I…' One fled and busied oneself in the stillroom, brewing herbs into tinctures and tisanes for the sick, refusing to speak with him.

But the seed planted in Adron's mind refused to die. With each report from the southern border, the thought grew and its roots deepened. Was there some way a watha could bear boy-children? That would solve half of his problem. The resolution of the other half might also lie in Lilla's hands. Could she bring more water to the southlands and make them farmable? That would attract more settlers and force the Kildorans to retreat.

Adron stared out the window at the distant silver-blue snake of the Brillen River. Or, if Lilla's powers could not bring rain to the southlands, was there another way to get water there?

His skin prickled at the thought. Palms sweating and heart racing, he could barely bring himself to think the words. Could he…divert some of the Brillen's flow into the southlands? He strode into his council room and stared at the map of Welladon painted on the wall. With one finger he traced the river's twisting route. There. He tapped a sinuous curve. If he dug a channel beginning there, part of the flow could nourish the dry southlands.

And the Kildorans vast, fertile plains would be little-affected. The much larger Leeth River joined with the Brillen at Kildor's north border. Diverting a small portion of the Brillen would cause but a minor drop in the volume of the Leeth.

For a few minutes Adron lost himself in the vision of the southlands as a fertile sweep of open plains; his people grateful; the Kildorans pushed back into their own land.

No. He frowned and shook himself. What was he thinking? The ancient bargain struck with the watha was specific. The river could not be tamed or channelled. It must remain free. In return, the watha would cause rain to bring life to the Welladon lands and help protect its people. Yet the rains fell infrequently on Welladon's southern lands. Didn't that mean the watha reneged on their part of the bargain?

Hope fluttered his heart and Adron stroked the map with loving fingers. Lilla would understand. She would accede. He would persuade her.

#

'No,' Lilla said softly. 'The river remains free, as was agreed.'

Adron pointed at the map. 'But these lands are not nourished, as was agreed. The watha break the bargain.'

'These lands were not part of Welladon when the accord was struck. Here. The old border.' She traced a finger along a faint line that Adron had not before noticed on the map.

He flushed and paced the room. 'But my people have outgrown the old border. They need that land to be fertile.'

'No,' she said simply. 'If you divide the river, my people here will die.' She pointed at the river where it flowed into the Leeth. She tilted her head, blue-black hair slipping over her shoulder. 'Two of your cousins live there. Does that not matter to you?'

'*We* are your people now. And I have asked nothing of you,' Adron said, low and hard. 'Just this.'

A small, ironic smile played on her lips. 'And yet your land prospers because of what I and my sisters do, unasked. Because of what we did even when your aunt died and no watha sat beside your uncle for two decades. Your part of the bargain requires only that you do nothing at all.'

'If you won't divide the river,' he said hotly, 'then bring the rain to the southlands.'

She shook her head again. 'You do not understand the water.' She splayed her webbed fingers over the centre of Welladon's rich valleys. 'The rain we bring here affects other lands far away, perhaps starving them. We cannot—'

'Will not, more like,' he snapped.

She stared at him for a long moment then turned away, as though the argument were over.

Adron watched her leave, his heart torn by anger and guilt. She was right, of course. He didn't want her people to die—or those in other lands. But he didn't know them and couldn't in good conscience abandon people who looked to him for help and guidance. And he couldn't simply give up the southlands to the Kildorans. His people would see that as weakness. Coupled with his lack of an heir, that would court disaster.

There must be a way.

#

'Tell me, Mother,' he asked.

Kinnial stood with one's back turned, surrounded by ceramic pots, leaves, flowers and roots all scattered on the stone benchtop. The airy, warm stillroom smelled pleasantly sweet and earthy. With a heavy sigh, Kinnial climbed onto a footstep and pulled a small, red pot from a high shelf. One opened the lid with trembling fingers and sniffed at the contents.

'A pinch into Lilla's wine tonight before bed.' One's eyes were dark with doubt and shadowed in a thin face.

'And?' Adron took the pot. The scent was light and sweet enough to go unnoticed in even the weak silverberry wine Lilla preferred.

'Then her body will only make the seeds for male children.' Kinnial's lips pressed tight. The next words burst forth in a rush. 'But for her to bear a son, you must do two things. To ensure she carries the babe to term, you must keep her from bathing or swimming until her time. And you must dam the river of her birth—the Brillen.'

Adron recoiled. 'That is…No, Mother, I cannot do that to her. I love her. It would be…' He shuddered and thrust the pot aside.

Kinnial gripped his wrist with fingers of iron. One's pale eyes glittered. 'Do you want a son to carry on our line? This is the only way.'

'But to keep her from water…'

'Only for a short time.' Kinnial smiled reassuringly. 'Watha gestate in five months, not nine as we do. Then, to bring the child into

- 306 -

the world, you must dig a new channel for the river. At the end of her time, release the dam and fill the channel. The child will be born the same day. As long as the channel is successfully filled, not blocked. For the watha will try to prevent you.' Kinnial spread one's hands. 'And your new channel can irrigate the southlands.'

Adron paced hastily the length of the room and back. Hope, fear, and revulsion warred in his breast. 'But that is against the accord we struck with the watha. What will they do?'

One's mouth twisted into a bitter smile. 'What more can they do? She already withholds both rain and heir from you. I will…you will lose everything if you do not do this.'

'But I may lose her if I do it. Or kill her family that live downstream.'

'And that is your choice to make.' Kinnial pressed the scarlet pot into his hands. 'But remember that your choice affects not just Lilla, but all of your people. So choose well.' One turned away.

#

For five long days Adron debated. He spoke little to Lilla and nothing to his birth-parent, unable to bear the love of one or the persuasions of the other. No matter what choice he made, people would suffer. With no son and no water for the southlands, Welladon would fall to the Hight of Kildor. But if the river Brilleg was dammed and split, and Lilla bore a son, would that also condemn Welladon? Would the watha dry up a whole river and destroy their own home for the sake of one female?

On the sixth day, a messenger delivered a letter from the Hight of Kildoran. Adron read the missive and the earth trembled beneath his feet. He crushed the paper and hurled it into the fireplace.

An ultimatum. The Council of Hights had passed judgement. In accordance with the Law, he must have a male heir. Without a sister

to produce one, on his death Welladon would revert to the next heir—
the Hight of Kildoran—who was not a patient man.

Adron rose. He was earthwyrd and Hight. His duty was to his land
and people first. The river was part of his land and therefore his to do
with as he deemed best. Lilla must bear a son. The river must be
divided. It was the only way.

But though he dosed Lilla's wine with the drug he could not bear
to watch her drink. And when she left him to bathe and prepare herself
for night, he wept for what he must do.

And she came to him with gleaming eyes, laughed, spoke of
daughters, and loved him with sweet, sensual abandon that nearly
shattered his resolve. Yet he said nothing. For the people Welladon.
For their future. For his son.

For them he broke his family's bargain, his own heart and Lilla's.

Afterward, he held her close through the night, listening to her
even breaths, his tears soaking the pillow.

In the early grey of dawn, he slipped from the room and locked it
from the outside. Then he found Kinnial. Together they used air and
earthwyrd to raise blocks of granite from the garden to the window,
closing it to keep Lilla imprisoned.

Resolute, he sent word to the Council and left the fortress. Kinnial
had said to dam the river. Focussing on what he must do helped him
push aside what he had done.

#

It took Adron and five other earthwyrdmen a week to convince the
earth and rock to form a dam solid enough to hold back the Brillen.
The waters frothed and foamed behind the massive earthen wall,
railing and beating at it much as Lilla must beat uselessly at the
bedroom door. At the end of the week the earth told Adron it had
contained the water.

Kinnial sent word that Lilla had stopped demanding freedom.

The lake and Lilla both settled into dark, resentful silence.

Adron and the earthwyrds turned to the task of digging the channel to the southlands. And he welcomed the hard work for it gave him an excuse to be from home and to avoid the bedroom where his wife waited in misery.

For the next five months he saw nothing of her; could not bear to see betrayal in her face or hear accusation in her soft voice. Kinnial sent reports. The child grew well. As the lake deepened, so Lilla's belly swelled. She and the river, both, merely waited.

Adron read the messages and hid bitter regret in his heart. It was too late for regret. He had forged this path and must tread it. The separation made it easier.

He did the right thing.

Lilla would see his actions for the necessity they were when all was done, a son born and the southlands secured. She was gentle and loving. She would forgive. She wanted a child. Their son would bind them together again. The next Hight would be half watha, half earthwyrd; master of both water and earth. The broken accord would be of no matter. Welladon would prosper.

So Adron told himself each time he shifted the parched earth and slept under a cloudless sky. Each time his people knelt and kissed his hands in gratitude as he passed.

#

The day Kinnial's messenger arrived, Adron was overseeing the final stages of a lake that would supply year-round water for the southlands. Though it was but spring, and the air cool, he sweated with the exertion of wyrd-shifting tonnes of earth. Dust coloured the sky ochre and dried his throat and clogged his nose. The wyrd-taste of warm earth sickened him now, and the weight of aeons dragged at his bones.

'Hight Adron,' the boy panted, passing over a tight-rolled message skin. 'Your birth-parent says it's time to return.'

Adron held the roll, unopened, afflicted by a sudden fear. He took a swallow of tepid water from a jug and almost vomited, for the taste was of blood and tears. He peered into the vessel but it contained only water. His hand quaked.

'Very well,' he said. 'Go back and tell one I'll stand ready at the dam. Bring me word when the time is right.'

The boy nodded and jogged back to his mount. He disappeared northward, dust and dried grass flicking from the animal's flying hooves. Adron watched him go and stood still for a time, uncertain. Then he shook himself and gave final instructions to his earthwyrdmen.

#

When he arrived at the dam another messenger waited. The boy ran to grasp the horse's head. Adron swung down and staggered a few steps.

'Kinnial says it's time, Hight.' The boy jigged up and down, eager.

Behind him, a dry breeze ruffled the Brillen's dark lake and brought the scent of distant fires.

'Very well,' Adron replied. His voice broke and he cleared his throat, his mouth dusty. He dared not drink. Every sip of water tasted foul.

Dusk gathered into grey shadows below the great earthen wall and sunset touched the treetops with gold. He must release the waters now, or it would soon be too dark to see the result of his work.

So why did he hesitate? He tried to picture Lilla's beloved face, but time had blurred her image into the memory of perfection and sweetness. Was she in pain? Would breaking the dam truly birth his son? Had he done the right thing in trying to save his people and his land?

With a growl, he knelt and pressed his hands to the ground. Whatever the outcome, the water must be released, or the labour of months was for nothing.

He spoke to the earth; asked it to loosen the tight-held bonds holding soil and rock in place. To cease resisting water's burrowing fingers and let go.

'There!' the messenger cried, pointing.

A darkness spread across the face of the dam. Then a spray of water fountained, sparkling in the dying sunlight. A rock tumbled from its place to crash in the dry riverbed. The soil slumped and water gushed forth, foaming, bloodied by the rich red silt. A hiss became a roar. The thud of boulders falling to the riverbed pounded through Adron's feet. A fine mist cooled his heated face and mingled with tears of exhaustion and relief.

Adron climbed to the top of a rise and peered southward, following the churning wave front that poured down the riverbed. The flood boiled downstream, tearing trees free, leaping high into the air, gouging great chunks from the banks.

The water reached the new channel opening. Were those watha bobbing in the flow? Their arms gestured, voices unheard over the water's roar. The water curled into a whirlpool, gathering boulders. A great pile of rocks rolled across the flow and into the channel mouth, building a new dam, blocking the flow. The merest trickle snaked its way down the gully.

'No!' Adron flung himself onto his mount and kicked the beast into a frenzied gallop toward the channel. He leapt off and laid hands on the nearest rocks, heedless of the danger. Close by, the new river gnawed at the loose soil, hungry. Slick, dark-skinned watha appeared at the river's edge, struggling to climb the unstable banks.

Adron hesitated. The nearest watha looked so much like Lilla that his heart skittered. Her face was contorted with rage. Cuts bloodied her glistening skin. She stalked toward him and water stained the red earth to blood beneath her feet.

If he opened the channel, the watha would know he had broken the accord. But his son would live. Lilla would live. If he left the channel closed, the bargain would be kept, but his son and Lilla would die. His people would suffer. His land would be lost.

Grimly, he spoke to the earth. The soft bank beneath the watha's feet crumpled and she fell into the torrent and vanished. Then he spoke to the rocks, drawing every bit of energy he had left, fighting against the water's force. With a crackling groan, the largest boulder rolled back into the main flow and water poured into the new channel. The despairing screams of the watha were carried away on the flood.

Spent, Adron dragged himself back from the edge and collapsed.

#

He awoke to the familiar feel of his granite home; the comfort of being enwombed in stone again. But the room and the bed were not his. Relief displaced confusion. Kinnial must have put him in the guest room rather than exposing him to Lilla's wrath.

Lilla! The child. Adron sat up. Had it worked? Did the boy live? He pulled on clothes and hurried to the master bedroom.

The door stood open, the room dark and musty with long use and little air. He lowered the rocks from the window and wrenched the glass open, letting light and a breeze wash away the misery. The vast bed lay rumpled, its sheets stained with recent blood. But of Lilla and the child there was no sign.

An anguished cry arose outside in the garden. Adron stilled, fingers white upon the bedpost.

For a moment his mind descended into horror. Had he failed after all? Were the women outside bewailing her loss? Then he let out a relieved breath and laughed at his own madness. No, in death Lilla would be laid out on the bed, as was tradition. She lived. Relief swept aside lingering guilt.

A knock rapped on the open bedroom door.

'Hight Adron.' A serving girl, trembling and flushed with tears, knocked again.

Outside the screams turned to ululating wails; mourning cries.

'It's Kinnial.' The girl swallowed and twisted her grey tunic in nervous fingers. 'One's has been…drowned, sir. In the pond outside. It was the lady Lilla. She…' She burst into tears and sank to the floor, sobbing.

Adron strode to the window and stared down into the courtyard. Crying and clustered about the pond were a half-dozen of the household. His birth-parent's limp body lay in a puddle of water on the granite pavingstones, eyes blankly open and staring into one's beloved sky.

His heart stilled and hardened to rock in his chest. He returned to the servant.

'My wife. Where is she? The child?'

'The boy was stuck in the birth canal. He almost died, but Kinnial saved him.' The girl stared about the empty room in stupid blankness. 'I don't know where they are. Kinnial took Lilla walk in the garden with the babe. That's when…' She gulped and the tears flowed again. 'Perhaps she went to the river?'

'Of course,' he said, grimly.

#

'Lilla.' Adron found her standing on the ridge above the Brillen, looking down into the valley. The river was reduced once more to its normal size. He stopped, unable to ignore the devastation. The marra trees that once gave silvery grace and delicate beauty to the riverbanks were mere wasted sticks; black bones clawing at the sky. Red silt covered every inch of land, reeking of decay as the sun rose and baked it into cracking hardness.

Not far from where he stood lay a body, bent grotesquely around the trunk of a tree. A watha; her long hair and dark skin thick with slime and mud. He swallowed, dizziness coming in a wave and leaving him sick.

'Lilla, I…I'm sorry.' The words were inadequate, but he had no others to give. Explanations were dust on his tongue.

She turned at last to face him and he recoiled. Ashen skin stretched taught over sharp bones. Cheeks and eyes were sunken and shadowed by more than just exhaustion. Her brows contracted and she tilted her head to one side, studying him as though for the first time. In her thin arms lay a naked newborn boy, his plump body and face a stark contrast to Lilla's.

His son.

Adron let out a breathless little laugh. The work, the fear, the guilt. It had all been worth it. He reached for the babe but Lilla drew back. Turning from him, she picked her way down the slippery slope to where the granite Hight's chair lay, cracked in half and toppled on its side.

Adron followed, searching for the words to sway her.

'He's perfect,' he said.

'For now,' Lilla replied, stroking the babe's soft cheek. She circled the Seat and looked once more at the river. 'You broke more than just the accord, husband.'

'I had to. I love you, but I had to protect my people. I did this for him, too.' Surely she must understand?

'No,' she said, a spark of disdain in her dark eyes. 'No. Don't lie to me as you do to yourself. Love shows in what you do *for* people; fear in what you do *to* them. You didn't love me. You simply feared what might happen if you broke the accord. Until the day when you feared something more than that.'

'The Hight Council would have given my lands to Kildor. And the Hight of Kildor would have murdered us in our sleep within a year. He would have dammed the river. Killed the watha. Raped the lands. Now we are safe. Welladon is safe.' His words emerged strangled by resentment. 'I had no choice.'

'True, but not in the way you think,' she said and touched his face with an icy hand. 'This was not your decision to make, alone. You forced this upon me. Took away *my* choice.'

'You wouldn't have—'

'You didn't ask,' she said. 'And now you will find out the truth.'

'What truth?' he snapped. 'That the watha were content to let my people die rather than give water where it was needed?'

She shook her head. 'That earth does not choose for the river. Generations ago, the watha bargained as though with equals, but the river is stronger. Water always finds its own path, eventually. Even through the densest rock. Now you have broken the accord and our marriage with it.'

'But I had to.' His words sounded sullen and childish, even to his own ears.

'And you not think to come to me…to tell me of their threats?'

'You would have turned from me as you did when I asked you to bring water to the southlands.'

She raised pitying bottomless eyes. 'I would have bid you take a second wife. A human who could bear you a son. There's nothing in the Accord against it. To the watha such arrangements are common.'

Adron sank onto the overturned Chair, his certainty fractured. 'I hadn't…I didn't think…'

'No.' She looked down at the small, squirming form in her arms. 'And now you bear the consequences. We will leave you to them.'

'My son,' Adron said, his voice breaking. 'Go if you must, but leave him.'

'*My* son,' she said. 'He will be raised by the ertha, in the mountains. Learn the earthwyrd from them and the waterwyrd from me. He will become more powerful than a mere human Hight. One day he may return.' The bleak smile on her dry lips cracked his soul. 'But for now, Welladon is yours and yours alone. Live with your choice. I do not have to.'

Without a backward glance, she dove into the river and a v-shaped ripple pushed upstream. Adron cried out but she didn't not return. He watched the ripple out of sight, unable to even weep into the luminescent water that lapped at his feet.

#

For two days he stayed by the river, waiting, hoping. For two days he yelled his sorrow to the silent water. For two days he lived in the stink of death he had created and sent earthwyrd pulses through the broken chair.

His advisors came and begged him to stop. His wyrd rent great faults in the farmlands of Welladon, as though the earth itself grieved with him. Or punished him. Cracks shattered the stone of the castle.

Adron ignored them.

On the third day, a great rumbling shook the land and a plume of dust and smoke rose from high in the mountains to the north.

Still, he waited, though tears no longer flowed. His advisors returned with news that the wells gave no water, the cattle no milk. Even the air held no moisture and tasted of ash. The castle had fallen to a pile of tumbled rock.

The day after that, the Brillen dried to a muddy trickle. Fish thrashed in the few remaining puddles, mouths agape in silent screams. Within a week the water was gone, the people fled.

Only the ruined chair, and Adron, remained.

Pigshit and Gold

First published Courdelion magazine October 2019

Shortlisted in Best Fantasy Short story—Australian Aurealis awards

Apart from the rather unfortunate sandstone statue dominating the square, Cratch was a village like any other. Thatched roofs, chickens, scrawny dogs, and grubby children, all in varying shades of brown. It even smelled brown: like mud, rotting plants, and animal dung. Well, at least the rain had stopped.

Vemra shifted in the saddle and grimaced. She eased an aching butt cheek while maintaining the upright posture befitting a noblewoman and soldier in Lady Fantine's army. The saddle creaked and the stink of sweat and damp leather rose through her clothing. Dumbhorse stomped, sighed and let fall a large, steaming pile of crap—which seemed an appropriate comment on the village.

Vemra eyed the birdshit-streaked statue with distaste. Cratch was obviously proud of their only contribution of any note to the world. Hopefully Haldora the woman was more impressive than her badly-carved monument. She'd better be everything the stories said. The fate of the fiefdom might depend on it.

More importantly, Haldora's skills could dig Vemra and her daughter out of soul-crushing debt, provide a future out of the army—and possibly assure the continued association of Vemra's head with her neck. Vemra tugged at her collar. The fine spring day seemed unseasonably warm.

'Urchin.' She jabbed a finger at the nearest child. The mud-spattered wretch froze and stared, wide-eyed, so Vemra beckoned. She probably did look a little imposing in her dark blue captain's uniform with its gleaming brass buttons and cockaded hat. Perhaps a gentle smile.

The child edged away. Vemra glowered and pointed at the statue.

'Tell me where Haldora the Archer is. Now.' She laid a hand on her sword hilt.

One filthy arm shot out, indicating a large, thatched hut set a little outside the village, partway up the rocky hill. Surrounded by pigpens containing squealing black porcine monsters, the place promised to smell wonderful.

Vemra kicked Dumbhorse, who stumbled over her own hooves then thudded into a plodding walk.

Outside the hut, a well-worn hitching post and a full trough indicated frequent visitors. Dumbhorse stood staring blankly at the muddy water.

'Drink, you idiot animal,' Vemra muttered. 'When I get the reward for this mission, you watch how fast I buy a horse with half a brain.' She swung down, breathed deep and coughed. Yes, pigshit and mud. Delightful. She drew off her gloves then rapped sharply on the white-washed door.

'It's open.' The nearby pig-squealing almost drowned the thin voice out. 'Blessings be on a kindly visitor, death on one of ill-intent.'

The traditional peasant welcome-spell of protection sent a familiar, almost-painful frisson of magic across Vemra's skin. She shrugged off the feeling in irritation. Only the weak-minded put their faith in such things. Magic was a dying art and, frankly, no loss to the world. Far too unreliable.

She pushed the panel and ducked to enter the dim interior. She slapped the gloves sharply against her palm, creating a pleasing snap. She'd been raised to hide disdain for the peasants, so she had no difficulty in maintaining a calm demeanour in the face of squalor. Well, not absolute squalor. The hut was neat, the flagstone floor covered in fresh reed mats, the central hearthfire burning without smoking the space up. But hardly the manor-house she had grown up in.

A child, somewhat cleaner than those in the village, turned a spit over the fire and the salty smell of cooking fowl almost masked the pigshit. In one corner, an elderly woman rocked in a bentwood chair, her blind eyes the colour of glaciers, her face crevassed by the pain of a long life.

A petite, middle-aged man emerged from a back room, wiping his hands on a cloth. Catching sight of Vemra, his brown eyes widened. He bowed, scraped back his grizzled auburn hair and gave the sparsely-furnished room a quick, helpless look.

'M'lady. I'm sorry. I didn't know we had visitors.' He hurried to the old woman's side and hissed at her. 'Grandy, why didn't you tell me? Who is this? The house is a mess. And... Cori!' This was addressed to the child, who had stopped turning the spit and was gaping at Vemra. 'Turn that bird or there'll be no supper. Oh, I should make tea. Where did I put the broom? Would you like to sit down?'

'Sir,' Vemra interrupted, sensing an endless and possibly

sideways series of conversational diversions coming. 'I'm looking for Haldora the Archer. I'm Captain de Winnower—the Lady Vemra de Winnower. The Lady Fantine's agent.' She inclined her head regally.

'Lady de... and Lady Fantine? Haldora?' His mouth fell open. 'Grandy? You know anything about this?'

'No, Kem,' the old woman said, shaking her white head. 'But Dora's out the back, with the pigs. Go fetch her while I entertain our guest. Good lad.'

He pressed his lips together and sent Vemra a narrow, suspicious look before stalking out.

Up in the rafters, something hissed and fluttered. Vemra flinched. Was there movement in the shadows up there?

'Hush, Tezzi. She means no harm,' the old woman said.

Vemra frowned. 'Have you got *bats* in your roof?'

'Oh, no,' Grandy said. At a squeak from the ceiling she gave a smile filled more with carved oak than real teeth. Something dropped from the darkness. Wings snapped out then folded back and an animal settled onto Grandy's shoulder. Its tail twined around her waist. 'She's eaten them all long ago.'

'Great Bolkana's tits!' Vemra gulped and took a step back. 'Is that...'

'Aye, lass. A pygmy fire-drake. Her name's Tezzi.' Grandy scratched at the dark burgundy, triangular head and the drake made a curious, purring noise. 'But she's quite tame, I assure you.' Grandy's teeth flashed again. 'Hasn't burnt anyone for... oh... at least six months.'

'What?' Vemra stared at the gold-eyed beast in fascination. Fire-drakes were rare and tame ones worth a small fortune. She licked her lips. The beast's red tongue darted out and flickered like a snake's.

'Now then, lass. What's this all about? Let me see you.' The old woman grabbed a long staff that leaned against the wall and used it to heave herself out of the chair. Her knee joints crackled like burning sapwood. Straightening, she pressed her hand to the small of her back and groaned.

But she walked confidently enough across the room, avoiding the fire and a wooden toy pig left on the matting. The knotted-cedar bottom of her staff clunked on the floor, while the smooth, bone-grey top half nearly touched the thatched roof. Leaning only slightly on the staff, she stretched a hand toward Vemra's face.

Vemra stiffened but the twisted fingers only brushed her cheekbones, nose and forehead, while the old woman's pale eyes stared blankly. The fire-drake hissed. Vemra reared back, alarmed.

'Hush, Tezzi. You wouldn't be Pondeera de Winnower's get, would you? Seems to me you've got the look of her, a little. That strong jaw and bent nose, I think.'

Vemra blinked. 'Er, her daughter, actually. You knew her?'

'A bit.' The old woman pressed her wrinkled lips together and sighed. 'Won a horse off her in a game of red card wins, back in the war.'

'That doesn't surprise me.' Things would be less... unpleasant now if Mother had kept her purse tied shut. 'Which war?'

'Yes.'

'Er...' Vemra frowned. 'What's your name, old woman?'

'Oh, just call me Grandy. Everyone does, hereabouts.' She chuckled. 'On account of having so many grandkids. Twenty-six last count.' She ruffled the girl-child's curling brown hair. 'So why does Lady Fantine want my daughter?' She frowned, her untamed white brows almost meeting over a thin nose.

'Er. The war.'

'Which one?'

'Umm... the current one.' Vemra tried to regain her poise. 'Lady Fantine's lands to the south have been invaded by that bitch Brinne of Denn.'

Silence made her look down. The child at the fire stared back, wide-eyed, her hand unmoving on the spit. The bird would burn in a moment. Perhaps she should be told?

'Um...' Vemra began, pointing.

Grandy waved a dismissive hand. 'Invasions are nothing new.' She sighed. 'But we've had peace for nigh on ten years. I'd hoped to live out my days with nothing worse than my grandchild's burnt dinner to worry about.'

The child squeaked and turned the spit again, the metal rattling and oil sizzling.

Vemra huffed. 'There's nothing more honourable than fighting and dying for a greater cause. Your country deserves the sacrifice.'

'Pfah!' Grandy snorted a laugh. 'Our country is rocks and dirt and trees, girl. It doesn't give a crap. But the bones and blood of young women makes for fine fertiliser.' She cocked her head. 'What do *you* get out of fighting for Fantine?'

'That, old woman, is none of your business.' Vemra brushed down her sleeves. This peasant had no right and no reason to know a de Winnower's financial situation. She swallowed down a surge of anger. Damned debt-collectors. Damned loan-sharks. Damn Mother for dying before she could recoup her losses.

'It is my business if you're wanting my eldest for your little war. Why do you want her?' Grandy pointed the end of her staff at Vemra, who bridled. Clearly this half-senile gammer couldn't comprehend the glory and wealth that could come from war. She might have been a footsoldier sometime in the distant past, but obviously hadn't the wit to rise above that rank and make a name for herself. Vemra intended to come out of this episode obscenely wealthy, restore her family position, and leave a legacy for her daughter. Nothing else mattered.

The fire-drake hissed again, launched itself off Grandy's shoulder, and landed on a perch that stood next to her chair. It eyed Vemra narrowly, then lifted a leathery wing, covered its head and appeared to go to sleep.

Disconcerted, Vemra tugged at the hem of her uniform jacket and threw her shoulders back. 'I've been tasked to seek out the best archers in the land to form an elite squad of distance-shooters.'

'Brinne's cavalry and footsoldiers too good for Fantine, huh?' Grandy chuckled.

'Not at all.' Vemra raised her chin. 'We simply wish to... improve our range-fighting rank and file. Haldora is rumoured to be one of the best.'

'Well, our Dora is certainly pretty darned good. Can hit a sparrow in mid-flight at a hundred paces.' With another laugh, the old woman shuffled back to her chair, her steps slower and more careful than before. She sank into the seat with a sigh. 'But I don't know as I can let her go off a-fighting again.'

'It's not up to you, old woman,' Vemra said. 'The orders come from Lady Fantine, herself, and every woman must obey.'

'Aye, true, our duty's to our lady.' Grandy cocked her head. 'But even Fantine's gotta understand that the troops need feeding. If Dora goes, the farm stops producing. She does all the hard labour these days.'

Vemra curled a lip. 'There won't be a farm if we can't halt those barbaric southerners soon.'

Grandy's milky eyes narrowed. 'How far away?'

'Her army will overrun this village within three weeks.'

'Ah,' Grandy stroked her chin, 'you don't say?' She slapped her palm on the chair-arm and swore.

The man, Kem, hurried in, pushing before him a hulking bear of a woman, perhaps somewhere in her late forties.

'Get your things, Dora,' Grandy said. 'The Lady Vemra's come to take you to the war.'

Dora's pale blue eyes widened and flicked between Vemra and Grandy. She snatched a shapeless grey woollen cap off her head, leaving her grey-streaked blonde hair standing wildly on end. The simple wool tunic she wore stretched dangerously across broad shoulders and a deep bosom. Vemra suppressed a surge of envy and thrust her chest out.

'But I can't... the farm... Kem and the girls...' Dora waved a helpless hand at the house and her glowering husband.

'Aye,' Grandy said. 'I know. But Lady Fantine wants Haldora the Archer.'

'But—'

'Come,' Vemra looked down her nose. 'You cannot disobey your lady. Should you fall, your family will be recompensed, I promise.'

Dora swallowed and her husband paled and clutched at her arm. Grandy snorted. Vemra glared but held her tongue. Clearly the old woman had influence and it wouldn't do to take her to task for disrespect in front of the family. Once Dora was away from her mother, she would become more manageable.

'Sir,' Vemra said stiffly, 'pack a bag for your wife. My lady commands it.'

Kem made a muted noise of frustration and snatched a woven bag from a wall-hook. He stomped into a back room. The sound of muttering and cupboards opening and slamming shut followed. Dora looked guiltily over her shoulder, then beseechingly at her mother.

'Ma?'

'I know, love,' the old woman replied. 'Go tell him to pack for me as well. And send Cori to the shire reeve. I'm sure she'll lend you her horses, Dora.'

Dora's broad shoulders relaxed and she grinned. 'Thanks, Ma.'

'What?' Vemra blinked. 'No. There's no way you're coming. This is war. We don't have anyone to spare to care for invalids. Stay here. Help your son-in-law.' She controlled her irritation, strode forward and patted the elder's shoulder. 'I know you want to help, but you'll just endanger your daughter if you come along and distract her.'

Grandy rose and gathered her staff. A wintry smile thinned her wrinkled lips. 'Mayhap you're right, lass. But many-a year ago, I made a vow to my husband that I'd protect our children and theirs as long as they were under my roof. Dora's my eldest and the one who's needed most. I'll see her home or die trying and you've no power to stop me.'

Before Vemra could muster an argument, Dora reappeared bearing two bulging bags, a bow and two quivers-full of arrows, and arguing with her husband in a plaintive undertone.

'Mama?' The girl-child, Cori, threw her arms around her mother's leg and gazed beseechingly up at her. Dora lifted her high and planted a kiss on her cheek.

'You be good for your Pa, Piglet. Practice your archery. I'll be back.'

'Promise?'

Dora glanced at Vemra, who cleared her throat and examined her fingernails.

'Oh, she'll come back, Cori-love.' Grandy groped toward the drake on its perch. She scratched the little creature's coppery belly. 'Tezzi and I'll make sure of it. Wake up lazy, we're going to war.'

Tezzi raised her head and yawned. She hopped onto Grandy's

shoulder and rested her chin on the thatch of white hair. The old woman strode to the door, paused and cocked her head in Vemra's direction.

'What are you waiting for, lass? You've got your archer. Time to take her to Lady Fantine and earn your reward, eh?'

#

Afternoon of the fifth day found Vemra riding at the head of twenty-three archers and one annoying old woman. She hesitated to say *leading* them for they were a disrespectful, casual rabble. Over half had emerged from various houses in Cratch, tagging along behind Dora and Grandy with only a grin or touch of the forelock to Vemra, as though her permission to join was irrelevant. Torn between relief to be bringing a respectable number of archers back, and irritation that Haldora's name had such draw and influence, Vemra ground her teeth and returned the casual salutes with stiff nods.

The rest had turned up as the group passed through the next three villages. Children ran ahead, yelling Haldora's name and women emerged hastily, throwing on cloaks, carrying longbows, bidding worried menfolk and children farewell. Most were Dora's age: a decade older than Vemra at least. Four were men, a fact that caused her deep discomfort. War was no place for old women or men.

When Vemra tried, again, to point this out, Dora merely grinned gormlessly and said, 'Ma says they're here to protect their families. Men have as much to lose as women, for they're the ones who've fathered and raised the children being slaughtered. What right do we have to naysay them?'

With the conversation being watched closely, Vemra could do nothing but snap her teeth shut and ride ahead, seething. She ignored the laughter and mutterings behind.

Dora proved to be almost as irritating as her grandmother: calm and relentlessly cheerful. At least her archery skills were real. On the second afternoon, she shot—at two hundred paces—a jackrabbit running full-tilt across a meadow. The other archers looked to Vemra when the arrow struck home.

Vemra cleared her throat and shifted beneath their massed gaze. 'Well done.' She flicked a hand. 'Go get it, then.'

'Aye, milady,' Dora said cheerfully. She nudged her mount off the road and trotted away.

When she returned, Vemra frowned, studying the woman's bow. 'The bards say you use a dragon bone bow. And arrows of dragon spine, dragon scale, and phoenix feathers that shed unquenchable gleamfire. That looks like a bog-standard yew bow. The arrows are plain wood and goose feather.'

Dora shrugged. 'Tales are like spun-sugar, milady. They start off small and sweet, but grow with each spin. Pretty soon they're too much to stomach.'

Vemra sneered. 'So you're not as good as the songs say? What use are you, then?'

'Dunno, milady.' Her big shoulders lifted again. 'Maybe none, to you. But Kem and my girls seem to think I'm a mite handy to have around. And they're the ones that matter, really.' She gave Vemra a respectful nod and dropped back to chat easily with the other archers.

Uncomfortably aware of Grandy's mocking smile, Vemra kicked Dumbhorse, startling the beast into a head-tossing sidestep.

'What?' Vemra snapped as the ride continued.

Grandy chuckled. 'You're of an age to have babes, but I'm betting you have none.'

'What business is that of yours?' The reins cut into her fingers. 'As it happens, I have a husband and a daughter of two years, Heria.' The marriage had been below her status, but Bred's father had money.

Not enough, though, and it galled to be dependent on his tightfisted habits. But Heria... Vemra softened involuntarily. That mischievous twinkle in those big dark eyes. No, her daughter would grow up with decent food in her mouth, not just the brittle taste of good breeding.

'Ah,' Grandy said. 'Then mayhap it's time to learn a few things that'll stand you in good stead as a mother when you get home. If you get home.'

'I do not give you leave to speak to me in that tone.' Vemra narrowed her eyes at the old woman. Grandy merely smiled.

'You're in charge of a neat little unit, lass. But they're free folk, not dogs, servants, or slaves. Not stupid or martyrs, either. You'd do well to treat them as humans. With respect.'

Vemra gave a scornful crack of laughter. 'You're out of line. These people are in the service of Lady Fantine. They'll do as they're bid or suffer for their disobedience.'

Tezzi hissed from her customary place on Grandy's shoulder and a little curl of smoke drifted from her flared nostrils. With a one-shouldered shrug, Grandy turned her horse around and joined the archers who travelled on foot.

Vemra pushed aside a fillip of regret. The gammer was annoying and maudlin, but her absence left Vemra uneasy and with her back to an unruly group of peasant-archers who showed a stronger allegiance to Dora and Grandy, than to their lady and her representative. She would be glad to offload the lot of them onto Fantine and her generals and take her reward. There was no place for sentimentality in war.

#

Around noon of the sixth day, Vemra smelled and heard the army before she saw it. They were closer than expected. She screwed up her nose at the reek of raw sewage, smoke, and rotting meat. She held a lavender-scented pomander wrapped in a silk handkerchief to her nose and tried to look unruffled. The occasional neigh of horses made Dumbhorse prick her ears. And the *ching* of steel on steel from soldiers practicing echoed even over the low rise that hid the massed troops.

Movement overhead caught Vemra's eye. Tezzi circled slowly, spurting little jets of flame that sent crows and red-feathered ravenors cawing and flapping away. Her copper belly and burgundy wings glinted in the afternoon sun.

'What *is* that drake doing?' she snapped.

'Spying for me,' Grandy replied. 'And trying to barbeque ravenors. She hates ravenors. Not sure why. She never said.'

Vemra frowned. A drake that bonded somehow with its owner so they could speak telepathically? That would be worth even more than she'd thought.

Grandy cocked her head. 'Your army's not far away, huh?'

Vemra returned her gaze forward. Her palms began to sweat at the thought of Fantine's promised reward. It wouldn't fix all the debts, but it was a start.

When her party topped the rise, Vemra paused for dramatic effect. The rabble she'd gathered ought to be impressed by the neat lines of tents and flashes of sunlight off steel.

'Oh!' Her jaw dropped. Instead of the discipline and order of the previous camp she'd left a week and a half before, tents were pitched haphazardly, some barely upright. And there were less than half the number she expected. Many women lay in the open on makeshift beds, bandages crusted with old blood wrapped around their limbs. Camp-followers—husbands and whores—tended to their needs, washing wounds or plying the sick with food and drink. Off to the west, a coil of greasy black smoke rose lazily into the spring sky. Beneath it lay, a smouldering, spitting pyre that seemed to consist mostly of blackened legs and arms.

Vemra pressed the handkerchief to her mouth and swallowed down a rush of saliva. Her stomach lurched and sweat prickled under her armpits.

'How's it look, lass?' Grandy said quietly. 'Like you expected? Glorious yet?' Tezzi spiralled down and landed. She nuzzled Grandy's ear and warbled what sounded like a question before turning a baleful golden glare on Vemra.

'Shut up,' Vemra muttered. 'It's war. Peasants and soldiers die.'

'Aye,' Grandy said, her tone heavy, 'that they do. Well, best you take us to Fantine. Mayhap we can end this little skirmish for you sooner rather than later.'

'No. You lot will stay here and wait for my return.' Vemra kicked Dumbhorse savagely and the brute managed a trot going downhill with the wind at its rump.

#

'My lady,' Vemra doffed her hat and swept a deep bow. 'I've returned with the archers, as requested.'

Fantine glanced up from a table littered with maps and the remnants of a meagre lunch of dark bread and dried meat. She frowned, her thick black brow bunching above a much-broken nose.

'Bolkana's Bosom! Who are you, girl?'

Vemra straightened. 'Vemra de Winnower, ma'am. You sent me two weeks ago to find Haldora the Archer and put together a unit of range-fighters.'

'Ah, yes. The de Winnower chit. And?' Was that a flicker of disdain on Fantine's face? Vemra ground her teeth. She ought to be used to it after all these years.

'I have returned, successful.' Did she dare mention the money? Fantine hadn't remembered her name, which boded ill. Begging grated, but she would if it would save Heria going through this sort of humiliation.

But Fantine's brow cleared and she straightened. Her two generals exchanged looks of muted hope.

'Right!' Fantine thumped the table. A grin split her broad face and she wiped a hand over short, dusty hair. 'Right, then. That might just buy us a few more days, eh ladies?'

'Er...' The generals shuffled their feet and avoided their lady's eye. One finally sighed and spoke up. 'My lady, I doubt even Haldora the Archer can turn this war for us. Brinne is holed up an hour's march away, behind this hill, with her troops on high ground.' She pointed to a series of squiggly marks on a map.

Vemra tilted her head in an attempt to see without looking like she was trying to.

The other general spoke. 'We've lost over half our troops. Brinne has us outnumbered two to one now. We must retreat. I can't imagine why she's waited this long. If we had a warwitch, maybe we could prevail? But the last of them died twenty years ago in the Purge of Kellsmont.' The general leaned heavily on the table and splayed a hand on the map. 'If you leave now, my lady, you can gather an army elsewhere and retake your lands another day. We cannot afford to throw any more good women at this.'

Vemra swallowed down a protest. They couldn't give up. Not when she was so close to regaining her lands and fortune. Then she could get out of this goddess-forsaken army. What did it matter if a few thousand miserable farmhands died?

She gathered her courage. 'May I speak, my lady?' Her voice quavered, and she cleared her throat. Fantine and the generals scowled, but nodded brusquely.

'Remember, ma'am, that we have the best archer in the world in our company now.' Vemra lifted her chin. 'At least give her one chance to take a shot at Brinne. I've seen her take a running jackrabbit at two hundred paces. She can do it, if anyone can.'

'Two hundred paces, huh?' Fantine scratched at her scalp, her fingers rasping like a file. 'Can she do no better? I suppose it was too much to hope tales of the dragonbone bow were true. We'll lose a lot of soldiers if she has to be that close.'

'Of course she can, ma'am,' Vemra replied with false confidence. 'Don't let Brinne best you. We've all got too much to lose if she overruns the fiefdom.'

Fantine paced several steps away from the table, then back again, her hands resting on sword and dagger. The griffin-skin mantle of her rank swayed from her shoulders and gleamed gold in the lantern-light.

'You're right, girl,' she said quietly. 'By Bolkana, the great goddess of the underworld herself, I will *not* retreat and give up my lands to this upstart. You!' She spun and jabbed a finger at Vemra, who jumped and suppressed an unwomanly squeak of surprise.

'Yes, my lady?' she managed, dreading Fantine's next words.

'You will go out there and tell the women to be ready to break camp. We'll begin a march before dawn tomorrow. Swing around the hill from the east. Launch a surprise attack on Brinne with the sun at our backs.' Her thick lips pressed thin and her dark eyes glittered. 'We'll take that wench or die trying.' Her scowl turned thoughtful. 'And tell them that the woman who kills Brinne will get a sack of gold half her own weight, lands and a title. Make sure your Haldora knows it too. Strengthen her arm.'

Vemra kept hidden the thrill that tingled from her neck to her groin. A sack of gold. That would just about do it. She bowed herself out.

#

'That's right.' She beamed down on the assembled archers from atop Dumbhorse. 'Lady Fantine has generously offered a whole *five* gold coins to the woman who takes down Brinne. And silver for each general. Brinne wears blood-red mail and helm decorated with red ravenor feathers. Her three generals also wear red feathers in their helms. You'll easily be able to see them once you get into the thick of things. Now...' She flicked a dismissive hand at them. 'Eat. Sleep. The army marches at dawn. Glory will be ours, tomorrow!'

Most of her ragtag unit wandered back to their makeshift camp, muttering amongst themselves. Doubtless expressing their wonder at the generosity of such prize money. It would pay to keep her people separated from the rest of the army, just in case some rumour reached them about the amount of money on offer. Of course, Fantine didn't mean for a whole sack of gold to go to one peasant. Haldora would do something wasteful like give most of it away. After all, she didn't really need more than five pieces to live quite comfortably on her pig farm.

Vemra grinned fiercely and glanced at the distant mountain ranges behind which Brinne cowered.

'I hear tell this Brinne's quite the leader,' Grandy said. 'And her army's double the size of this one after the last battle.' On her shoulder, Tezzi made a quizzical noise and cocked her head, then leapt into the air and circled high, dwindling to a dot as she headed south.

Vemra snapped a frown, then growled when she realised frowning at a blind woman was pointless.

'Don't spread such sedition, old woman, or Fantine will have you hung. We'll prevail tomorrow.' She oozed a smile. 'We've got your Dora, remember? Once we're in range, she can just pick Brinne off like that jackrabbit.'

'Aye, aye.' Grandy stroked her chin, tugging at a single, long grey hair that grew there. 'But the archers march ahead of the footsoldiers, don't they? I mean... that's the way we *used* to do it, back in my day. Course things could've changed.'

'You're correct,' Vemra replied stiffly. 'They'll march at the front to begin with and shoot. Then fall back to guard Fantine and her generals. Then infantry and cavalry will take the front. The archers will shoot over the soldiers' heads as long as possible, then stop. Wouldn't want to endanger our own women.'

'Aye.' Grandy lapsed into thoughtful silence and leaned heavily on her staff. She sucked a quick breath. 'But I'm thinking, lass, that we're sending the footsoldiers up against awful bad odds in the hope of getting a shot at Brinne before the melee. That's a powerful-lot of youngsters going to die tomorrow if Dora can't make the shot.' She inclined her head. 'And no guarantees Brinne's army would stop fighting the minute she died. Takes time for news to reach the troops and there could be a general willing to fight on, regardless.'

'Your point?' Vemra said coldly. She quashed a flicker of unease. Why was she even listening to this fool?

Grandy shrugged. 'Those women. They've all got families. They're someone's daughter or wife or mother. Would you want your young'un out there?'

Vemra stiffened. 'She's a child.'

Grandy's mouth twisted. 'She won't be forever. There's always another war. But this one seems a waste of good youngsters— throwing them at an army they can't beat for the sake of some lady's bruised ego. Mayhap Dora and I should go have a bit of a chat with our Fantine? See if we can talk some sense into her. Come to some peaceable agreement with this Brinne.' She turned away.

Vemra dismounted and snatched at the old woman's arm, dragging her back toward the campsite. 'You'll do no such thing, old woman. I've had about enough of your backchat and disrespect. *I'm* leading this unit. This is my chance to make things right for *my* family, so my daughter will one day have what I didn't: respect and lands to go with the title. I say we'll march with the army at dawn.'

She leaned close to Grandy's face and hissed. 'You'll stay in your tent and speak to no-one until I give you leave. And tomorrow you'll remain here and await our return. If you set foot off this ridge, I'll see to it your entire family is flogged and your farm confiscated. Do you understand?' She shoved Grandy through the tent flap.

The old woman stumbled inside, missed her footing and collapsed onto her neatly-folded bedding, her staff still clutched in one lean hand. She pushed herself into a sitting position.

She gave a heavy sigh. 'Aye, lass. I do understand. All too well. I remember now. Your Ma, Pondeera, she did have a bit of a gambling problem. Lost it all, did she?'

'Close. Your. Mouth,' Vemra grated.

'Aye, in a moment.' Grandy's eyes narrowed shrewdly. 'Anyone tell you how she died?'

'What?' Vemra hesitated, her anger derailed. 'She died in battle. Arrow-shot through the throat.'

'True enough. But maybe they didn't tell you that she died shielding me.' Grandy ran a hand over her face, looking older, tired. 'We were shieldmates. I came out alive. She didn't. She was a right arrogant cow sometimes, but a damned fine swordswoman. Far better than me. Always wondered what happened to her family. Might have won her fortune back if she lived a little longer. Left you in a hole, I'm guessing.'

Vemra's fists clenched of their own accord. Her throat clamped on anger too thick and heavy to speak around. What right did this *peasant* have to cast aspersions on a de Winnower?

'I'll say this last thing, lass, then you'll be shut of me.' Grandy's glacial eyes turned their eerie blankness on Vemra. 'Respect is earned, not bought. You can't be sacrificing ten thousand families to save your own. It's just not right.'

Vemra drew herself up and straightened her coat. She gathered years of aristocratic training to hide her rage. 'It's not me deciding to go to war. It's Lady Fantine's choice. If they die... If *Dora* dies, it's not my problem.'

Grandy said nothing, her upraised face showing only pity.

With a growl of frustration, Vemra turned on her heel, only to stop and look back in narrow suspicion. 'Have I your word you'll stay here tomorrow? I can't spare anyone to guard you and I'd rather not bind an old woman.'

'Right kindly of you,' Grandy replied drily. 'Aye. I'll stay. As you said. No use for a blind woman in a war.'

'What about protecting Dora? Your promise to your husband.' Vemra folded her arms. It was unlike the old wench to give up so meekly.

'I guess...' Grandy sighed and shook her white head. 'I'm just not as young as I was. I'll have to hope that *you* keep an eye on her, lass.' A wry smile twisted her mouth. 'Seeing as how her success means so much to you and all.'

Vemra froze and swallowed the impetuous question that danced on her tongue. No. Grandy couldn't possibly know about the rest of the gold.

#

Vemra awoke, heavy-eyed and thick-brained, to the sound of muted horns. What little sleep she'd managed was haunted by nightmares of Dora dead with an arrow through her throat; of debt-bailiffs wielding death by axe; of Dora's daughter and little Heria's tearful wails. Gandy's words played on her mind.

Dora did need to be protected. The half-brained fool was optimistic and stupid enough to think herself invincible and get herself killed too early. Right. There must be some willing idiot to play shield to make sure Dora got the job done.

Vemra hurried to arm and armour herself, struggling with the leather ties and laces. She left camp before her archers were ready and half-ran, mail jingling, down the hill to the main encampment.

She accosted the nearest soldier. 'You. Get your shield and come with me.'

'What?' The peasant eyed her blearily and rubbed at her sleep-sagging face. 'Who are you?'

'I'm Lady de Winnower.' Vemra threw back her shoulders and looked down her nose. 'Range-fighters unit. I need a shieldwoman to protect my lead archer.'

The woman twisted free. 'No fear, milady. I ain't bein' no shield out fronta the army today. I'd get skewered for sure up there. We're most likely to die, anyways, but I'd rather not if I don't hafta.'

'You *must* or I'll have you flogged.' Vemra resisted the urge to stamp her foot.

'I'll take my chances. Bugger off.' The peasant stalked away and vanished into a group of brown-clad women that all looked alike. Muttering amongst themselves, they shuffled back, leaving Vemra fuming in the middle of a rapidly-emptying section of the camp.

Vemra stood for a long time, staring at the space where the women had been. She glanced east toward the rising sun where the horizon glowed a peculiar shade of red, a blood-portent, perhaps. An omen from Bolkara.

Then she looked up at the ridge where Dora and the others moved about, silhouetted against the brightening sky, making ready for war and inevitable death against Brinne's vast force.

She swore. Long and inventively. In ways which would have shocked her father and pleased her long-dead reprobate mother.

Snatching up a large, round shield, Vemra stalked back to the top of the ridge. She was puffing when she reached Dora and grabbed the woman's thick arm.

'Right. You and I are sticking together,' Vemra snapped. 'You're going to damned well shoot Brinne the second you see her, then you'll survive this blasted war and get your reward. Got it?'

'Aye, milady,' Dora said, grinning. 'But you might want to wait on that thought a moment. There's summat you should see, first.'

Vemra frowned down at the main camp. Enough light now slipped over the eastern mountains to reveal the army forming up into companies, ready to march.

'We don't have time for games,' she growled. 'We're supposed to be at the front of this army and they're about to go to war. We need you. I need you. Get moving.'

Dora laid a meaty hand on Vemra's shoulder and shook her head. 'Just watch.' She nodded toward the highest point on the ridge.

There, etched in blood by the sunrise, Grandy leant on her staff. A bundle of sticks lay on the ground beside her. She seemed to be talking to Tezzi. A moment later the fire-drake sprang into the air and winged south. She vanished in the half-light, a shimmering mote amongst the fading stars.

'What, exactly, am I watching,' Vemra said coldly, brushing Dora's hand away.

'Shhhh.' Dora put a finger to her lips. 'Give Tezzi a minute.'

'What?'

Up on the ridge, Grandy turned her staff upside down. She pulled it into two parts. No, what Vemra had taken to be the bottom half was some sort of covering. Fully revealed, the staff was entirely grey and tapered at both ends.

Grandy braced one end against the ground and bent the staff around her leg. She hooked something around the top end. When Grandy raised the staff upright again, Vemra gasped. That thing was a bow? The longest she'd ever seen, in fact. Even strung it stood a third taller than Grandy.

The sticks turned out to be arrows. A tip glinted red when Grandy lay the shaft along her hand. She drew the string with no apparent effort and leaned back, paused then leaned a fraction more, until the arrow was angled at forty-five degrees. Then she released.

The arrow whistled through the thin morning air, leaving an after-image of blue fire in its wake. The shaft vanished, headed south toward the hills.

Grandy nocked and shot three more in rapid succession. Then she unstrung the bow, covered the end and hobbled back to her tent. A moment later, she emerged with her saddle and bag and shuffled to where her horse was tied.

'What was that all about?' Vemra turned to Dora. 'Hey. Where are you going?'

Dora and the rest of the archers looked back over their shoulders, pausing partway toward the tents.

'War's over, milady.' Dora pointed south. 'In a minute or so that Brinne and her generals will be dead. And the gleamfires will cause so much madness in the lines they won't want to fight.' She shrugged. 'Grandy never misses. Ever. Not with Tezzi spying for her.'

Vemra looked toward the distant, dawn-grey, pink-tipped mountains. 'Brinne is over half a league away. There is *no way* anyone...' She gargled a cry. '*She's* Haldora the Archer?'

Dora nodded, still grinning. 'I'm proud to be named after her. Maybe one day she'll pass the bow to me. But, until then, she's Haldora the Archer, alright.'

'So, the dragon-bone bow? The arrows made of dragon spines and phoenix feathers? Unquenchable gleamfire from the feathers. All true? Actual magic. Not just stories?' Vemra's knees weakened and she staggered.

Dora slapped her on the back. 'Come and say goodbye, milady. Grandy likes you, I can tell.'

'How?' Vemra swallowed the memory of her prideful arrogance.

With a laugh, Dora pushed her toward the horses. 'She hasn't killed you, yet.'

When she reached Grandy's side, Vemra cleared her throat and waited for the old woman to finish saddling her beast.

'Hey, lass.' Grandy turned and smiled faintly. 'Good war, eh? Short. Just the way I like them.'

'Er...' Vemra scuffed her toes in the dust and twisted her hands together. 'It's a sack of gold, not five pieces,' she blurted. She heaved a sigh. 'I'll go get it.'

Grandy's bony fingers gripped her forearm and her stained wooden teeth showed pale in the dawnlight.

'Ask Fantine to send the five gold and three silvers to me in Cratch, there's a lass. She probably doesn't have it handy at the moment. Wars are costly things.'

'But—'

'And you keep the rest,' Grandy added as she swung into the saddle.

'What?' Vemra clutched at the stirrup, her mind mushed by the repeated trampling of her expectations.

'You were ready to risk your life to carry a shield for my girl. You can't be all that bad.' Grandy patted Vemra's head. 'The gold should go to that young family of yours. After all, I should have protected your ma. You wouldn't be so desperate now, if I had. Take it. Get out of the army. Spend time with your girl.'

'But... but what do *you* get out of this, then?'

Grandy smiled again and turned her face north. Tezzi winged in and landed on her shoulder with a satisfied chirrup.

'I get to be done with wars. I get to go home to my grandchildren and bring their ma back alive.'

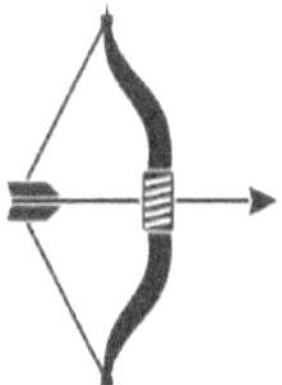

\#

END

I hope you've enjoyed this diverse collection of short stories. If so, would you be kind enough to leave a review on Goodreads, and any book retail sites you happen to prefer? Reviews help other readers find authors they love. Then authors don't die of starvation.

More Titles by Aiki Flinthart

Discover other titles by Aiki Flinthart at: **www.aikiflinthart.com**
Or

Blackbirds Sing (Historical fantasy)

The 80AD series (YA Adventure/Fantasy)
80AD Book 1: *The Jewel of Asgard*
80AD Book 2: *The Hammer of Thor*
80AD Book 3: *The Tekhen of Anuket*
80AD Book 4: *The Sudarshana*
80AD Book 5: *The Yu Dragon*

The Ruadhan Sidhe novels (YA Urban Fantasy)
Shadows Wake (#1)
Shadows Bane (#2)
Shadows Fate (#3)
Healing Heather (#4)(Romance)

The Kalima Chronicles (YA Sci/Fantasy)
IRON (#1)
FIRE (#2)
STEEL (#3)
A Future, Forged (Prequel)

Sold! (Contemporary Romance/Adventure)

Short Story Anthologies
Zookeeper's Tales of Interstellar Oddities

Return
Elemental
Rogues' Gallery

Non-Fiction – Author writing resources
Fight Like A *Girl* – Writing Fight Scenes for Female (and male) Characters
How to Get a Blackbelt in Writing

Connect with her on Facebook
https://www.facebook.com/aikiflinthartauthor
Twitter: @aikiflinthart
Instagram: Aikiflinthart

www.ingramcontent.com/pod-product-compliance
Lightning Source LLC
Chambersburg PA
CBHW020552120726
47903CB00001B/234